Remember to love me

BECKY BYFORD

*Suzanne
all my love
Becky xx*

Remember to love me Copyright © 2008 by Becky Byford

Remember to love me first published in Great Britain in 2008 by ABC

The right of Becky Byford to be identified as the Author of the Work has been asserted by her in accordance with the Copyright, Designs and Patents Act 1988.

An ABC Paperback

All rights reserved. No part of the publication may be reproduced, stored in a retrieval system, or transmitted, in any form or by any means without the prior written permission of the Publisher, nor be otherwise circulated in any form of binding or cover other than that in which it is published and without a similar condition being imposed on the subsequent purchaser.

All characters in this publication are fictitious and any resemblance to real persons, living or dead, is purely coincidental.

A CIP catalogue record for this title is available from the British Library.

ISBN 978 0 9560588 0 5

Printed and bound in Great Britain by
ABC
21 Vision Centre
5 Eastern Way
Bury St Edmunds
Suffolk IP32 7AB

To my kith and kin, as one chapter closes another opens…

Remember to love me

Ending

She stood in silence, her slender figure casting its long afternoon shadow. The early September heat penetrated the fine silk of her dress, as the rays of the intense sun emblazoned the words before her. Wearily, her head sank into her palms.

'It was not meant to be like this. How can I go on?' Her despairing words shattered the afternoon calm, but of course, there was no reply.

She slid her fingers down her salty tear-stained cheeks and her arms wilted beside her. A hand gently slipped into hers; it was soft, tender and it bore familiar warmth. She closed her eyes, savouring the silent moment, though she made no movement - how could she respond?

Her heavy heart lay spellbound, as slowly, time played out the ethereal experience.

'I love you,' she whispered.

She fell to her knees. The grass was warm and soft beneath the fine cloth of her petticoats, and her eyes, aching, wept streams of silent tears.

Gentle footsteps approached her quiet spot, but she did not turn to glance. From inside her ribcage, in the deep dark recesses of her pounding heart, she wished for peace.

Oh, how her heart ached.

'You alright there?' The young male voice was calm and reassuring.

'I'm well...' Wearily she took a handkerchief from her pocket and mopped her face. 'Thank you, Albert...yes.'

She did not look at him, as the disappointment that seeped from her very core kept her eyes boring their way through the stone, her mind preoccupied with tracing each carved letter of the name.

'I'm very sorry to disturb you.'

'No, that's...I mean you didn't disturb me, I was just...' She hesitated; somehow, he brought peace with his visit. 'Please don't go,' she urged, surprised by her own response to the visitor.

His footsteps moved with ease, emanating waves of assurance and serenity that washed over her being with a veil of comfort. The young man knelt on the downy grass, his tweed covered knees close to her hands. Her fingers idly played, fiddled with the grass, each long thriving lush blade brushed over her smooth fingertips. In the long silence, she coiled and entwined the green ribbons into intricate ringlets.

'I've watched you...from the beach,' his soft voice sang the words to her ears. 'I've watched you, I saw you both.'

'You watched us?' she enquired.

Ordinarily, the notion, the idea of being watched, observed, even by Albert, would have startled her, but her thoughts were of curiosity.

'I mean, I had no idea,' she added.

Discreetly, her eyes followed up his legs until they reached his face. She knew him; she knew his features and his voice. He was young, the same as her, early twenties; however his craving for nature, his work on the land, his years fishing, had begun to betray him. Tanned skin around his eyes had thinned with fine lines of his contented smile, his cheeks bronzed and dappled with freckles. The wildness of his hair, although neatly cropped, flowed in sandy waves over his freckled brow. However, as he spoke his words of condolence, just as so many others had done, she saw it, new light, a truer light.

His long blond lashes surrounding his bright blue eyes caught her stare and he smiled.

'Perhaps you should go home; there is nothing here for you now. You belong at home,' Albert nodded

Finally turning, she faced him straight on; his gaze was intense on hers. The soft afternoon sun flushed her cheeks and she squinted with its glare. She could feel herself slipping, almost hypnotised by the deep blue watery pools. A strange tranquillity and a restful peace adorned his face, his hand tenderly reached over to hers.

'You cannot find what you have lost, for what you have lost is still with you.'

Her male visitor rose to his feet, gently squeezing her shoulder.

She remained kneeling on the warm ground as her ears listened to his departure, the muffled tread of his soft leather boots on the lush grass, the crunch on the dusty gravel, and the light tap of the horseshoes on the cobbles.

Then it came, hush, stillness once more; left only with her forlorn thoughts and regrets, and the view of the headstone. With her forefinger, she gradually traced the words: *This lovely bud, so young, so fair, called hence by early doom, just came to show how sweet a flower in paradise would bloom.*

With no conscious thought for where she was headed, her feet wandered, leaving her lost loved one behind. Silently, she passed the cottages in a blur of memories, those sweet memories that carried her off on their melodic voyage of love and laughter. Moments slipped through her hands as the grains of sand under foot. High above the village she stood upon the dunes staring at the sea. Intense and rich, the purple dusky sky reached down to meet the horizon, where the sea undulated at the line of her eye. She yearned to fly and soar on the wings of the gulls; her body numb with pain and defeat, she wished to escape. How could she return to a life of routine and constancy, when life had become something very different? From up here the rest of the world appeared vast and majestic, the

Becky Byford

all-powerful elements, relentless in their custom for change. However, she was a mere mortal, a young woman with a great fear of the future, the changes that had been, and those she had yet to face.

Remember to love me

April

Filth and grease streaked puddles with iridescent rainbows of oil edged the roads, drenching the curbs as the wheels channelled through.

'I hate winter,' she spoke quietly under her breath; the words lightly steamed the window, 'Bloody weather!'

Mid November was cold and gloomy, projecting almost a melancholy feel to its captives. Strange effect it had, no longer the colourful era of autumn, the footpaths strewn with its golden debris; and yet, not quite the enchantment of the festive season with its joy and goodwill.

'Not long now, April.' Her father's words portrayed his natural cheerful disposition. 'We'll be home in, oh, about ten minutes.'

'Home?' she snapped.

'Oh, come on, it's home now. You had better get used to the idea!' The reply was her mother's; it came with a resonance of agitation. 'We really do understand the upheaval, but change isn't always bad. I think you'll be pleasantly surprised at how easy it'll be to settle - you've got to give it a chance, April.'

The car slowed at a set of temporary traffic lights, a team of men donning a uniform of bright yellow jackets, scrambled around a convoy of work trucks. The pitched sign with its interchanging date, stating work to be finished on the 20th of the month, seemed somewhat over optimistic, with the great span of raw road surface that stretched before them. Potent wafts of murky steam oozed from the heaps of hot gravel tarmac, as the tipper truck dumped it. April watched the swarm of yellow jackets shovel and sweep the mix into place. She pressed her cheek on the cold glass, the moist condensation dribbled down her face. Closing her eyes, her mind drifted to warm summer days, the soft lapping of waves on the beach, the maddening, yet familiar din of seagulls. The car swiftly jerked into motion, as did reality, and her eyes opened to the sight of the dismal winter afternoon.

The rest of the journey was relatively swift, soon arriving at their destination, their home. Home: the thought once again resounded in April's mind.

The house was cold and secreted a kind of sadness, an unloved sensation of loneliness and neglect.

'Just needs the heating on and with all our bits and pieces in, it'll feel like home before you know it.' Julia's face beamed. 'Besides, not long till the Christmas decs go up, hey?'

April simply nodded, no other action being possible, as she mustered up the remains of her energy to climb the staircase.

Afternoon soon became evening and the inevitable night; April took to her bed, tired from the burden of her sorrowful self-pity.

The grime-stained window blurred April's view of the street below, where a steady flow of pedestrians were strolling the footpath, periodically pausing at shop windows. April perched on the edge of a large tea chest with her chin cupped in her palms, her elbows resting on the windowsill. Old crumbling paint flaked off, clinging to the fibres of her sweater sleeves.

Straightening her posture upon the wooden chest, her eyes roamed the room. It seemed apparent that it had only been used for storage. The walls were uninspiring, decorated with grey-tinged woodchip wallpaper, probably having never been painted, as surely no one would choose to adorn a room with such a dispiriting colour. The floor wore a covering of old blue carpet, not much longer for this world. It was frayed and worn thin at the threshold; frequent movement of the door ruffled its threadbare edges, and wedged it half open.

Nevertheless, it was her new room.

Was it going to be surprisingly easy to settle in? The thought battered at her brain, whilst the image of her old room crept into her mind's eye, distorting her ability to think clearly.

Adapting to change had never come easy to her.

April was likeable, with a sweet nature, but could come across as quite unapproachable, never letting people too near. Nonetheless, that was how she liked it, never really minding what others thought. Strange, quirky, even abnormal: well, that's how she imagined others saw her, and they mostly did. Her needs, desires and passions were very different to her friends.

School had been quite hard; she had kept herself to herself, with only a tight knit circle of two friends. However, even with those, she never enjoyed activities outside school. April spent her time reading and studying, whilst they did the usual socialising. Although University had been different, the simple fact of being surrounded by like-minded people was easier, no need for a façade: no pretending.

Cambridge - April had found the whole city charming, bustling, but generally quaint. With her love for architecture, it suited her for the three years she was there. Most of her fellow students carried out their detailed examinations of the local bars and hot spots, the nightlife becoming a huge part of "Uni life".

April would listen to their discussions over cappuccinos and lattes, sat in their favourite coffee shop in a small back street. Never quite feeling part of the debates of whether Amy should have been wearing those skinny jeans "with an ass that huge", or how on earth Stephanie managed to pull that guy last night, "you know the one, the guy that particular group of undergrads were drooling over."

No, this was not her idea of the university life; her evenings were consumed by her studies, lengthy bouts of cloistered research in the magnificent library, table upon table of the same natured creatures, her species.

She had gone to study Art History at Cambridge University, standing out beyond any other for her, the whole aspect, the academic status, the degree qualification; these were important, of course, but not everything.

During the University open day, with each establishment exhibiting their own particular qualities, their outstanding reasons for attending, the prestigious status and famous past students, April found each much of a muchness. As long as she could study the history of art, the past masters, their techniques, their passions and reasons for creating, she would be happy.

It was during one of these thoughts that she'd met the eyes of a well-presented gentleman in a moss green blazer and tortoiseshell glasses.

'Can I help you young lady, what is your chosen subject? You seem a little bemused, if I may say so.' She hadn't needed to answer him, tilting his head to one side, he added, 'Art.' With that he simply added, 'Have you ever been to Cambridge, the view is wonderful for those who look up and not at their feet. So many wander in the present, there is an entire lifetime of history above eye level.'

She knew from that moment, she would be happy there, for a while anyway.

Her dwelling was a small one bedroom flat above a bookshop. It was ideal for her needs, off campus, and despite the two-hour journey home, which she made each weekend, it was only ten minutes' walk from her Uni. Between lectures and sessions of study, she would scan the shop shelves. Novels, autobiographies, local history, but her heart always led her to the back where a large blue armchair sat on a shabby Chinese rug; floor to ceiling, the old and second hand books sat.

There was something wholesome and real about holding one of these in her hand. A classic literature with the smell of time within the pages and the flecks of age on the leather bound, like liver spots on an old man's hand.

To read the words another has read, from the same pages another has held. These books were art. Not the brush strokes of Renoir or Chagall, or the precise anatomy of Michelangelo's David.

No, this was the written word, a material available to everyone, used by all, while mastered by some. She envied the eloquent, the articulate artists, those who could fashion inspired masterpieces from those same letters and words we are taught as infants. Her near reclusive existence in her vulnerable years of learning, had stunted her ability to communicate in such a verbal manner.

April's world began to exist in colour, consistency, and the sweep of a brush, inviting her into a world of visual passion, of optical enchantment, from the fine to the obscure.

'Damn place!' With that, she kicked a pile of tatty cardboard boxes.

April's trainer-covered feet hiked through the assault course of cardboard boxes, screwed up newspaper and piles of books that still covered the most part of her bedroom floor. She continued through her wedged door, along the hallway and down the narrow staircase.

'Lunch, sweetheart?' Her mother's tone was familiarly warm and loving, although April knew very well that the constant sight of unpacked boxes, piles of crockery and pans had just about got the better of her organised mother who was quite house proud; by nature neat and tidy, and very particular.

The resemblance between mother and daughter was undeniably obvious; long auburn hair and sparkling green eyes complemented their pretty features. At fifty-nine years, Julia was a little older than the mothers of April's friends were. She had a naturally sophisticated beauty, blessed with a perfect complexion and hardly a sign of ageing wrinkles, as if she owned her own special potion for youth.

'Lunch, sweetheart?' she repeated.

'No, not hungry, I'll get something later.' April moved a heap of boxes from a dining chair and placed them tentatively on the table as she sat down. 'Where's Dad?' she asked and glanced at the kitchen door, as if it was about to open of its own volition.

'He's still at your Nan's. He'll be home soon.' Julia simultaneously poured two tins of baked beans into an oversized stainless steel saucepan. Her meticulously manicured fingers placed four slices of white bread into a large, brand spanking new toaster.

'Think I'll go and see her in a while, if that's OK with you?' April asked peevishly.

'April,' Julia glared, 'you know you can go and see her. We only meant give her a day or two as she was feeling poorly.'

'She's the only reason I'm here.' April spoke the words quickly and under her breath.

'April, I think it's high time you stopped acting like a spoilt child; you're not a kid anymore. I really don't know where this has come from - get a grip. Look...things change, we needed to come home.'

'You needed to come home! I was quite happy where I was, thank you very much, that was home to me. I know you love it here, but I was happy there. I could see myself there.'

'Well...you're nearly twenty-one. When you've decided what you're going to do with the rest of your life, well...you can go back.' Julia took a deep sigh, and regained her composure, 'Sweetheart, I really don't like it when we argue. Things will be fine, it's a lovely place.'

'Yeah...I know.' April sat, her hands cupping her cheeks, the edge of the table digging into her elbows. 'I understand your need to come home Mum...you know...to be closer to Nan. I've missed her too, and it'll be good being able to see her every day rather than just having her on the end of the phone.'

'But?' retorted her mother.

'But, I'm not sure I fit here.' April looked at her mother with awkwardness, a fear of hurting her mother's feelings anymore than she'd done already.

'Not sure you know where you fit? Seriously, you need to give it a chance. We all have to accept change and get on with it; I don't like the thought of it, anymore than you do, no one does. You have your Nan; I think you'll feel better, when you see her, don't you? April...make the most of it, make the most of her.'

'I'll go when Dad gets back.'

Almost as if April had conjured up her father, the kitchen door opened and in he strode. Michael was a tall, rather handsome man, not of too great a build, in fact rather lean of stature. Now sixty in years, distinguished silvery white hair had found its way to his temples.

April imagined that to a stranger her father might seem a little outlandish, maybe even slightly eccentric. His dress sense and his intrinsic style ability somehow stemmed from an earlier decade, even an earlier century. It was not his immaculately tailored suits, so much as the way he wore them, expertly harmonized with brightly woven or intricately embroidered waistcoats, always with a matching tie, or when the mood took him, a lavish cravat.

Today, it seemed, was one of those; the vivid scarlet silk framed his still strong jaw line.

'How's Nan?'

'Not too bad. Good...considering.'

April barely heard his reply; she still bore the sickly emotion of self-pity. This wasn't her, not the real April. Well, she thought, who is the real April? Twenty she may be, but things were changing. Yes, she knew that it was an upheaval for them all, but her parents had always planned this, eventually coming home.

But where was her home, where did she belong? This town was lovely, quaint, and peaceful, pretty even. But hadn't she had that there, at home in Norfolk? Then, there was Nan. She longed to see her - why was she waiting ... and waiting for what: permission to see her own grandmother. She couldn't understand. Nevertheless, they'd said give it a day or so and that's what she did. Now the pain of it all; the move, the loss of home, the longing to see Nan, was eating at her, continually nibbling away at her insides.

Had she really become such a spoilt child? She was an adult, a mature young woman knowing where she was going in life, or did she? Mum was right; she had to stop this self-destructive behaviour. What would Nan say? That was just it; she knew exactly what she'd say.

Her mother spoke. 'Michael, did you ask her? Did you? You didn't forget, did you? What did she say? Well, I can imagine what she had to say!' Julia fussed over the position of her white apron, as she retied the ribbons around her small waist, and smoothed flat the front pocket. 'I don't know,' she mumbled.

'Julia, your mother amazes me at times, infuriates me at others. Now she insists she'll never slow down, despite her being eighty and well…especially now.' Michael turned, facing the kitchen door as it shut. 'All I'm saying is, it's just as well we're here now,' he muttered.

'You know what she's like. She's always been in charge and won't let anyone else interfere; you know that.' Julia stood with her hand on her hips in her standard schoolmistress manner, 'Although saying that…what did she say?' Julia's face changed, exhibiting a painful squirm in anticipation of the answer.

'Well, as you can imagine, she wasn't very impressed with the idea. Said it's her job, her place to do it. Always has been, always will!' retorted Michael.

'I just thought, well…I really hoped it wasn't going to cause such a problem.'

'I know you didn't, but your mother certainly didn't see it like that! I can definitely see where you get your stubbornness. She just wasn't having any of it. *"I have been looking forward to it; I am absolutely fine and dandy!"* Michael stated in a slightly sarcastic impression of his mother-in-law.

Julia continued stirring the beans with a large wooden spoon, as she stared at the heap of unpacked boxes by the kitchen door, her pretty face contorted with torment.

'I told her, "Sarah," I said, "you've got to start letting us help"…after all…especially now…' He stopped abruptly; his words were left unfinished. He fumbled with his coat buttons and slipped his paisley scarf from under his coat collar, taking a sideways glance at Julia; she sharply shook her head, wide eyed.

April sat up, her eyes on her father. 'What's all the fuss about?' she insisted, looking mystified. 'Dad?' April watched as her father continued to fidget with his coat and scarf. 'Dad!' she repeated.

'Well…your Mum just thought, well…we both thought, that it'd be better for your Nan if we took care of Christmas dinner this year, you know, give her a bit of a rest.'

'You told Nan you were going to do Christmas dinner? Can't believe you thought you were going to get away with that one!' April looked at her father with astonishment. 'What made you think she was going to let you do that? No wonder she lost it, she's been looking forward to this for weeks. It means everything to her, you know that, to have everyone at the house for Christmas.'

'Now…April, your Nan's getting old and…well…now we're here it just makes more sense that we take care of her.'

Michael stared at Julia as she stood tutting over the mess of cardboard boxes. He wasn't one to make much of a fuss, but he could see that lack of progress on the unpacking front had now become too much.

Perhaps it was sympathy or the anguish he saw on his wife's face. 'What's for lunch?' he announced, swiftly changing the subject, whilst rubbing his hands together.

'Beans…On…Toast,' mouthed April, in a silent voice.

'Mmm…beans on toast, again…my favourite,' sarcasm slipped from his lips.

'Well, if you help me clear this mess away, I'd have time to go shopping and cook a proper dinner! Besides, I can't find any other cooking pans. This is the only one I can find!'

An extremely agitated Julia abandoned the wooden spoon to the depths of the steaming beans. The pile of boxes toppled off the end of the table, sprawling their contents all over the kitchen floor. Tea towels, plastic bowls and beakers; the sort that were used on picnic outings, all rolled across the newly tiled kitchen floor and came to rest at Michael's feet.

'See, that's my lot! We're going to get this place tidied up right now!' Julia's voice echoed through the kitchen. 'I can't live in such a devastating mess!' Julia raised her voice as her hands flew into the air, and then covered her face, as if the mess was going to disappear like a magic trick.

'Ok, April, why don't you go see your Nan and we'll get finished up in here?' Michael asked in a get-out-of-your-mum's-way-while-you-can voice.

April made a sharp exit, passing her father and kicking a plastic bowl as she did so. Hastily, she headed out of the kitchen and down the stairs, through the back door of their new shop-fronted home.

The historical Suffolk market town of Bury St Edmunds was steeped in history and offered a rare rural beauty. Every nook and cranny, every street and alleyway, every building triggering a medley of memories of Julia's wonderful childhood.

Events and encounters of years passed, had embedded themselves in the very fabric of the brick and flint stonewalls. Personalities of those who had lived and passed through the aged yet charming town, were still apparent in the air.

It was not too dissimilar from her Norfolk seaside upbringing, but the simple reality of adjusting and finding her feet April felt hard to fathom. Change is all she seemed to have endured of late, leaving university, and now the upheaval of moving.

At least there was her grandmother, the one constant stability. She was the one person who truly empathized with her thoughts, desires and passions, and now she was close.

Remember to love me

April's grandmother resided in a large, period terraced townhouse, on an adjoining street from their new home; the rooftop was almost visible from her bedroom window.

As April wandered down the street, she studied the impressive panorama, the remains of the Suffolk town's medieval abbey, the cathedral, its newly erected tower soaring to the clouds, dominating the skyline. Tiny metal flags rose regimentally from the towers, the four corners reflected the wintry sunlight; and its massive stained glass windows with their recently cleaned appearance and sheer majestic proportions held a monumental beauty.

Further along the street, to the right, beyond the numerous period houses stood another sacred building. The equally large stone church stood wholly at the top corner of the road. Its large clock with chiming bell announced half past the hour.

April hadn't visited Bury since the Millennium, eight years ago. She had spent three weeks with Nan then. Somehow, life had been so uncomplicated, she had simply existed in a perfect bubble, but then she was only thirteen. Leaving Winterton-on-Sea for three weeks back then had been an adventure and Christmas was her favourite time.

Bury had taken on a magical feel for April back then. So many of the shops and the buildings were imposing and more majestic than home…there, it was the sea and the elements that she worshiped, the natural glory of the horizon, where sea and sky merged in a haze.

New Year's Eve they had sat snuggled in thick blankets on padded garden chairs, where they hugged mugs of hot chocolate with cream and chocolate flakes. April had lost herself then, utterly consumed by the magic, as the pitch sky was alight with celebration fireworks, great explosions of vivid colour that crackled and hissed.

As April headed past the cathedral towards the graveyard behind Nan's house, she couldn't help but wonder where that magic of those times had gone.

It was still here, she looked up, the beauty, the glory of the ancient but it wasn't inside her heart.

Becky Byford

The grass was hard beneath her feet as she walked between the gravestones, resting places of passed on souls, their lives engraved in stone for all to view. A footpath lined with tall trees led through the ancient resting place. Regularly positioned wooden benches situated on either side made it an eerie, but strangely pleasant, place to rest, and entwined branches formed a canopy over the walkway and its visitors.

She glided her hand over the tops of the stones, then sat upon a bench. It was cold under her jeans, numbing her bones as she sat and gazed at the back of the buildings. There was her grandmother's house.

If anywhere, the magic would be there.

Remember to love me

Regrets

The glossy black front door was small in comparison to the rest of the building. A large brass letterbox was worn by the unimaginable amount of letters that had passed through it in over a hundred years. Above that was an oversized brass lion headed doorknocker, though a century of meticulous polishing had almost erased its regal features.

Down to the right of the door, set in the old red brickwork was the original wrought iron boot scraper; it was worn to a smooth edge after the many years and many visitors, who had relieved their footwear of dirt before entering. The large sash window to the right was extremely clean, considering its close vicinity to the road; an elaborate lace curtain to deter passers-by viewing from the immediate footpath, obscured the front room window.

Grasping the brass knocker, April lifted it as the door opened anticipating her move; she pushed on the glossy black paintwork to reveal her grandmother.

'I knew it was my Little One. Come in, come in,' she spoke softly as she stepped aside to let her granddaughter through.

'I didn't even get a chance to knock. How'd you know it was me, Nan?'

Becky Byford

'It's been two days. I knew you couldn't wait much longer,' Sarah replied, as she closed the now seemingly larger front door behind them.

April entered the front room, down the three small steps to which they led. The room, although set in its own time warp and very old fashioned, was still as perfect as the day it was lovingly furnished more than a century before. Spotlessly clean, everything in immaculate condition, with nothing possessing a modern feel, April glanced down at her trainers and jeans and thought how totally out of place she looked.

'I knew you were feeling under the weather, Nan, so I thought I'd leave it a couple of days.'

'It was only a momentary ailment, and I am perfectly fine and dandy now, as well you can see. And don't worry; I know that your Dad told you not to bother me while I was under the weather…you needn't look so guilty! You know full well that there's nothing I enjoy more than spending time with my favourite granddaughter.'

'I'm your only Granddaughter!' announced April with her usual surprise and jest; this was a common exchange of words, many times rehearsed over the years since she was very small.

'Cup of tea, and some cake I think, as it's a special occasion. It is so lovely to see you, Little One. I have missed you so.' The tiny and immaculate lady reached over and hugged her granddaughter.

April inhaled her grandmother's perfume; the familiar childhood scent of roses conjured up idyllic memories. April's grandfather had bought her a bottle of expensive French fragrance; from then on, she never wore any other.

As a small child, April would admire the elegant bottle as it stood on her dressing table in pride of place next to their wedding photograph, and when she could, April would sneak a spray of the rich rose scent.

April's grandmother, Sarah, had had only one child. Though April gathered that she had lost another baby before April's mother was born, this information had been pieced together from fragments of overheard conversations. This had never really been discussed, and at the risk of inducing painful memories, April had never really been keen to ask. However, being the only grandchild over the years had had its advantages. April felt blessed to have such an amazing woman all to herself, never having to share her special time with any other.

April's grandfather, Edward, had passed away many years before April was born, although his presence was strong, the Victorian house accommodating numerous framed memories of him. He had stood tall and proud with strong military authority: his time in the Royal Air Force and service during World War II giving him a dominating presence, but his kind and gentle nature had shone through under his thick silver hair and large silver moustache.

Wearing a long, dark purple velvet skirt, pastel pink blouse of silk fastened at the neck with diamond brooch and diamond earrings, Sarah looked as elegant and timelessly beautiful as April had ever seen her. Her long, silver hair, which despite her age seemed to be in abundance, was kept tied back with a long piece of velvet ribbon.

'It's good to see you, Nan. I've missed you too,' she remarked with joy, as renewed warmth spread through her body and calmness seeped into her heart. 'And some tea and cake sounds great. But what's the special occasion?' An appetite suddenly manifested in the depths of April's stomach; she could almost taste her grandmother's baking.

'Sit down, sit down,' Sarah replied, seemingly unaware of April's question, 'I'll go warm the pot.' She hurried off to the kitchen with an excited skip in her step.

Seated in her favourite place, April rubbed her hand over the dark red velvet upholstery of the settee under the window. It was an antique piece, with a deep-buttoned back and intricate wooden arms and legs. A matching one stood on the other side of the room near the large fireplace, where a roaring open fire crackled and hissed; it gave the room a magical warm amber glow.

Becky Byford

A carved legged table with a highly polished surface stood central in the room. Sarah soon arrived back carrying what seemed an enormous tea tray; it was colossal in comparison to her very small stature. Her arms outstretched to cater for its large proportions; she placed it perfectly central on the shiny coffee table. An ornate white china and gilt trimmed teapot, with its set of matching cups and saucers, sat waiting to be served. Several small brightly iced cakes were balanced neatly upon the hand painted cake stand. Sarah sat in her favourite place opposite: a high backed, winged chair with bright pinkish-red, deep pile upholstery.

'Shall I pour?' Sarah reached forward and poured into the two waiting teacups. It was done with such an air of dignity, as if she were entertaining royalty, and she replaced the incredibly heavy teapot back onto the tray with total ease and balance.

'Nan, this is lovely, the cakes look delicious as always, Mum's aren't quite the same.'

'No, well.' Sarah paused, cocking her head to one side. 'So, how's university?' She added.

'Finished, you remember the graduation, Nan.'

'Oh, yes of course, of course. So that's it now, you are a qualified historian then.'

'Well...' April paused. 'I have a degree in Art History...so in a way.'

'Not in a way, surely. But the question is, what are you going to do with all that knowledge that's stored in those brain cells of yours?' Sarah sipped her tea and stared intently at April.

'Not sure. Don't think I had a plan, Nan, just a passion,' she answered modestly. 'Which leads me to...thank you Nan, you know, for paying for everything.'

'You had a desire so it needed fulfilling,' she laughed. 'Your university fund had been there since you were born. There is no need to thank me again; you've thanked me already, look at you. Who could have ever asked for more than to see their granddaughter study their passion? I never had that delight, times were different then, our priorities were different,' she paused a moment and smiled. 'Ah, anyway, how's that charming little car of yours?'

April closed her eyes, gulped, and then began to apologise. 'I'm sorry Nan; it was running perfectly well before.'

'I'm only teasing you; it just makes me smile every time I think of it. There was a bright red one, parked on the hill a couple of weeks ago. It made me chuckle. The poor elderly woman must have thought I'd lost my marbles.'

'I'm glad you can laugh about it. But, she's gone now, I reluctantly gave her to a good home, for the princely sum of fifty quid.'

'And fluffy seat covers?'

'Yeah, thought I'd throw them in for free.' April cringed at the previous summer's incident.

Her car, as much as the term was quite generous, had been her pride of joy. The rather old, rusty and dented Fiat 500, in a distasteful shade of congealed blood, had served April well. Tammy was purchased for the purpose of her weekly commute from Cambridge to Winterton.

She had lasted the three years, with very little fuss, until April decided to take Nan for a drive through the picturesque Norfolk countryside.

A wonderful idea, and the previous evening's rainstorm hadn't given them any concern, except for the problem of a ford and Tammy's untimely breakdown in the middle. "It's not deep, we'll be fine." It hadn't been so much the depth of the water, but the lack of car, Tammy being on the petite side, had drove in up to the door seal.

After a half hour wait with Nan, in hysterical laughter, a stitch in her side, unable to move from the car due to the water. Michael arrived with a local farmer who towed the Fiat out. It was a couple of weeks before Tammy was back on the road, and even longer for April to live it down.

April smiled and took a bite out of her cake.

'It's been such a long time since we've been able to spend quality hours together. It's so wonderful to have you here, finally where you belong, where you've *always* belonged.'

'I've missed you, Nan. I wasn't particularly happy about moving here. I'm sorry,' she coyly smiled.

'This is your home. Things will be different now. The time is right, more so now than ever.'

'The time is right? Nan what d'you mean?' An astonished April leant forward on the soft upholstery. She swept back her long auburn hair and stared in deep concentration.

'Our fate, our destiny, it's mapped out in front of us. Sometimes in our lives, we stray off course, whether we can help it or not. Sometimes it just takes a while for us to find our path, but when we do…' Sarah sat back sipping her tea. 'When we do, we know. We just know.'

'We know? We know what?'

'We know why we're here…who we are. When I was a young girl, I always knew where I belonged, but something…something just wasn't right, as if, a piece of me was missing.'

'Nan, I really don't have a clue what you're on about. What was missing?' Confusion and dismay consumed April's face, her forehead frowned, and her lips pursed.

'Oh, I was about your age actually, the perfect age…I really wish I'd been younger though…still a child…before…'

Sarah took another sip of tea. 'That's a lovely cuppa.' Her voice was soft and sentimental, 'Regrets.'

'Nan, before what? What regrets?'

'There was something missing, when I realised, there were, well…regrets.'

'Missing?'

'Just me…never mind. How's your tea and cake? Pink; I know it's your favourite. You always loved pink icing. I remember when you were small; if I decorated them in white, you used to make such a fuss. A proper little girl, pink every time.'

'Yeah, I remember, thanks Nan. They look lovely, really lovely.'

April reached out and carefully raised her teacup, holding the saucer beneath to catch any stray drops. The smooth bone china and smell of tea filled her head with a sweet aroma and warm sensations. It induced memories of their special times, reading and studying family photographs.

'What happened, Nan? You wish you'd been younger, before what happened?'

'Before it was too late, Little One, before it was too late.'

'Before it was too late, Nan, but too late for what?'

'Too late to say sorry,' she sat nodding, her eyes staring out into the cold street beyond.

'Sorry to who? What had you done?'

'Nothing, that was just it, I hadn't done anything.'

April took the conversation no further; instead, she sat, watching her grandmother with her heart, at last, filling with a sense of joy. April sipped her tea and watched her grandmother, then sat back, comfortably enveloped in loving feelings, and she pondered on her grandmother's strange words with their peculiar sentiment.

BECKY BYFORD

Remember to love me

Vision of Loveliness

Low bright winter sunrays seeped through the newly painted window, illuminating April's bedroom. Fortunately for everyone, the house was now neat and tidy, except for a few stray boxes of old odds and ends that no one had the heart to throw away. They sat in the hallway and were still to be put in the cupboard under the stairs.

April's new cream wool carpet, luxuriously soft underfoot, was now perfectly in place and it gave her bedroom an instant lift. Along with a couple of coats of cream emulsion paint on the walls, the space had taken on a new persona. The woodchip wallpaper was now no longer such an eyesore; its texture had almost faded into insignificance. It was much more inviting, clean and orderly.

It now bore April's hallmark.

Along one wall next to a marvellous, glossy wooden wardrobe with massive proportions, was a tall bookshelf, housing her extensive library of books. A stunning, satinwood dressing table with an oval swivel mirror, now had pride of place on the opposite wall. It was adorned with all of her favourite photographs, treasured in gorgeous silver frames. A large art deco frame in silver, with black corners, sat in the middle of the collection. It stylishly presented a photograph of her grandmother and April when she was very small. It had been taken one summer's day in her grandmother's garden, where both sat upon a large checked picnic blanket under the tree that dominated the depths of the garden.

The large bed dressed in white linen encased April as she lazed, watching the icy sky desperately try to overcome the last few dreary clouds. Sunday morning, no work, she mused, as she stretched her arms and her lazy hands pushed on the polished mahogany of her headboard, sinking, pushing her deeper into the feather pillow.

Work was in her parents' antique shop, their dream and retirement fund, until she decided where her life's path was going to take her. Finding herself surrounded by old and sometimes curious objects had lifted her spirits and was indulging her passion for the past.

April heaved herself from her warm place of slumber. Dressed in a fluffy white sweater and dark jeans, she left her bedroom, heading for the kitchen.

'Morning, sweetheart, how'd you sleep?'

'Morning. Lovely, warm and cosy, didn't really wanna get up!' she replied, yawning deeply as she poured into three enormous mugs from the coffee pot that sat on its hot plate. The fantastic aroma of freshly ground coffee flooded the kitchen.

'Will you just call your Dad for breakfast? He's downstairs arranging a box of stuff he bought yesterday,' said her mother, reaching down for three breakfast plates from the cupboard beside the cooker. 'He's been down there for ages.'

'Dad's in the shop already? It's Sunday!'

'I know, but it was so busy yesterday, he didn't get time to do it. Thought it was better to spend half hour this morning, than trying again tomorrow with the constant stream of customers through the door. Although, I must say it has been an incredible response so early on. We didn't think we were going to be so busy so quickly! And with Christmas so soon we couldn't have wished for a better start.'

Remember to love me

    Julia served smoked bacon, brown and crispy, with double fried eggs on to each plate. A pile of toast, brown and white sat on a separate plate, hot and buttered.

    April descended the staircase, entering the antique shop from behind the old mahogany counter, which was extremely long and glass fronted. She fancied that it had been there since the shop was built. April imagined the assortment of goods that had been sold over its worn yet still polished surface, and what had been exhibited in its glassy enclosed display cabinet.

    She caught a glimpse of her father. He was standing in front of an exceptionally large pair of matching pine shelves near the shop door. By his feet sat a small undersized tea chest, full of what looked like old brown straw and shredded newspaper.

    'Morning, April...breakfast ready? I've nearly finished here. The last one…there you go. I'm pleased with them. They're all so beautiful!' Michael placed the last ornate brass candlestick neatly on the shelf next to another identical one. They were amongst an assortment of hand painted bone china candlesticks, displaying scenes of bouquets of flowers and elaborately feathered birds, which April imagined being pheasants, and an array of delightful hand engraved silver ones.

    The pair headed back towards the door, turned off the shop lights and both made their way up to the kitchen for breakfast. The odour of fresh coffee and home cooked English breakfast wafted down the stairs to meet them.

    Twelve noon. April sat pondering on the date of a silver punch bowl from its maker's marks, flicking through the pages of a book on 19th century silver as she examined the series of marks. The peal of the church bell rang through the house with twelve long chimes - so piercing, that it seemed almost pointless possessing such a large oak grandfather clock apart from, of course, its stately beauty. It sat centre stage, with its intricate brass dial, in their newly decorated living room. The clock stood most dignified over the hi-tech modern gadgets in the space. The room was a magnificent amalgamation of old and new, with strategically placed antiquities. A huge creamy leather sofa garnished with raw silk cushions in shades of caramel, coffee and chocolate, sat opposite the large plasma screen TV. Michael would claim that this was only on when the History Channel aired documentaries on Victorian Britain, Ancient Egypt or the like, although both April and her mum knew full well that he could never resist the odd game show or celebrity dancing programme. However, it was so far from his outward guise he would never admit it.

Sunday lunch with Nan, considered April, as she rose from the sofa; her heart warmed at the idea. Sunday lunch at her grandmother's house was very welcome indeed, after the busy few weeks they had had with the festivities looming.

Michael reached for the noble features of the lion doorknocker; so low was the door in comparison to his tall stature that the lion was at eye level with his own. Once again, as it had done so before, the door opened, so Michael found knocking was unnecessary.

Sarah stood at the bottom of the steps on the front room carpet. They entered the splendid early Victorian townhouse in turn. April closed the front door behind her, as she admired the rather dominating holly wreath.

The silk holly and ivy leaves glistened with droplets of moisture left by the morning frost, and the embellishment of red crystal berries glittered in the sunlight. It encased the brass knocker in a frame of greenery, as she closed the front door behind her and descended the steps into the room below.

Sarah's traditional festive charm had cast its annual magic on her dwelling. April roamed over to the huge Christmas tree that stood ceremoniously in the far corner. Bushy and full, it was totally out of proportion with its surroundings, the top branches sprawled across the ceiling.

It was adorned with heirloom decorations: brightly coloured glass baubles and ornate silver bells. With its aroma of fresh pine needles and the sight of antique loveliness, April's heart soared with a medley of festive memories of Christmases long passed.

Close to the tree stood the small upright piano, so close, in fact, that she imagined it almost impossible to sit and play without being prodded by stray branches of pine needles.

A white linen runner with colourful embroidery lay perfectly central across the top of the piano. April ran her fingers over its finely stitched Christmas garlands.

Unexpectedly and without warning, a peculiar sensation came upon her. A memory, a recollection, the sensation of singing Christmas carols around this very piano, many years before, danced into her mind's eye. Not quite able to remember when, she could feel herself standing beside the fireplace, near the piano, singing. A strong impression of warmth and the spicy taste of mulled wine and mince pies cloaked her body.

April closed her eyes, desperately trying to summon the memory in greater detail; instead, it weakened and faded, leaving her feeling dazed and heady.

Still slightly hazy, she made her way to the dining room. Through the hallway, she passed a half moon table, where a citrus bouquet attacked her senses. There, balanced within an etched glass bowl, was an array of oranges, satsumas and lemons. Next to the fruit neatly sat a festive ornament, a frosted glass Christmas Angel. She recalled playing with the trinket as a small girl, feeling very privileged to have been allowed to do so as she now noticed its glassy vulnerability.

She paced the hallway, passed the staircase, to where another hall table stood almost identical in its appearance, right down to the etched glass of another fruit vessel, this time accommodating apples and pears. Sat next to the festive fruit feast was a small but very clear pair of photographs, in a double frame of shiny silver, inlaid with shimmering mother of pearl. The frame was fashioned with ornate scrollwork rising to an intricate bow at the top between the two oval apertures. It sat securely upon two feet and a dark blue velvet stand. Both pictures were encircled by a row of tiny silver beads. It was truly the most impressive photo frame even with its tiny proportions.

Sarah's house was practically untouched by time. Almost every piece of furniture, book and painting April knew so well, having studied all very closely as a child, with her passion for the past and everything linked to it. However, not these: these photographs she had never seen before.

She stood for a moment delving into her memory where she must have examined them.

The two young women within the photographs were of such beauty, that April was adamant she would have remembered them.

Both women in turn had been perched upon a pale coloured, seemingly white, cane chair with a scrolled fan back, visible behind them. The younger one, around eighteen or nineteen in years, wore a dress very pale in colour in contrast to her darker locks. The other was slightly older with fairer hair.

Then she recalled somewhere in the depths of her psyche, filing through many photos she had studied – she had seen the fairer woman before but much older than she appeared here. April stood mesmerized by the small sepia photos.

Sarah appeared in the doorway of the dining room.

'We were wondering where you'd got to. Dinner is almost ready. Come, sit next to me.' She beckoned April into the room. For a moment, April was motionless, still perplexed.

Slowly coming to her senses, she followed her grandmother in for lunch.

Lunch was as tasty as anticipated: a banquet of roast lamb, mint sauce and vegetables, all followed by homemade apple pie and custard.

The whole family, very full from such large portions, sat in their favourite spots in the front room; Michael sat on the settee beside the fire very close to the Christmas tree, though being attacked by numerous pine needles, he moved to the other end nearer the crackling logs.

Julia sat on the matching settee, next to April under the window, the velvety fabric and warm glow of the open fire made her feel drowsy. Content from an amazing lunch, she puffed the large gold silk tasselled cushion behind her and settled into it, closing her eyes.

April giggled at her mother; Julia just opened one eye and smiled. April glanced at her father, who had almost instantly slipped into a snooze as soon as getting comfortable on a matching gold cushion.

April's eyes wandered to her grandmother, who also found the sight of them sleeping like bookends on matching cushions and settees, very humorous. April felt it was the perfect time to quiz her grandmother and took advantage of the quiet situation.

'Nan, the photos in the frame that sits on the hall table, the silver and mother of-pearl frame?' April shuffled her way to the very edge of the settee as she eagerly questioned her grandmother.

'Yes, I know the ones. They are beautiful aren't they?' Sarah replied very casually.

'I can't ever remember seeing it before. Where did it come from? Do you know who they are? Are they family or….' April spurted out the words, almost waking her parents. They stirred as her voice carried across the room. However, she was too excited and just turned to stare directly at her grandmother once more.

'One thing at a time,' responded Sarah. 'Come with me.' She rose from her sumptuous velvet winged chair gracefully. April, on the other hand, was already on her feet; she followed her grandmother out of the front room, leaving her snoozing parents behind.

Sarah headed for the hall table where the silver frame occupied its space. Gently picking it up, she walked to the foot of the staircase. April stood in the doorway watching with anticipation.

'There are some things I think you would like to see. I found them a few weeks ago.' Sarah said this with an air of almost dismay, in great contrast to her previous indifferent manner. '…I didn't know they were there,' she continued.

April followed her grandmother up the staircase. Climbing the richly patterned carpeted treads, they passed many panelled doors, stunning paintings and gilded mirrors on the lavishly papered walls, perfect and immaculate as the day the paper was hung. April stopped, something attracting her attention. A delicate gilt frame hung at the level of her eyes, as they scanned the painting it held. Soft but definite strokes of paint swept the canvas in a surging tint of blue, the sea and afternoon sky blushed with pink, made her heart ache and her eyes water. She felt the passion and fury of the seascape, the ancient command of the waves. Yet, in the foreground, the fresh newness of the grassy sand dunes so crisp, she felt her hand reach out to take a blade of grass. Her fingers hung in the air, their tips millimetres away from the canvas. She shook, first her hand, then the body trembled with a deep sadness. Something inside her, an inconceivable familiarity was tearing at her heart, and it ached. As her eyes closed tight to stop the tears, her fingers began to move, as if holding a brush; she swept it through the air, great sweeps of colour in her mind; muted blues, greys and flashes of white, then her mind was black: darker than night, dense and endless.

'April.'

With a start, she opened her eyes, the painting filling her view. Her grandmother stood with her hand on her shoulder, steadying April's shaking body.

'Come on.'

That painting; but the words never reached her lips, instead her feet followed

Sarah stopped at the foot of a very narrow staircase leading into where April imagined was the attic. They climbed these last few steps and went through a door, much smaller in comparison to the others they had passed. The space was quite large with tiny windows along the opposite wall, within the slope of the roof. Chests and clutter obscured one and the other was very measly on the light it gave to the area. This was the one place in the house April had never been, and she hadn't given it much thought, not knowing it held within it such an Aladdin's cave.

'Come, let's sit over there.' Sarah pointed to a somewhat opulent gold chaise-longue, the variety to have been found in a rather stunning French boudoir.

April sat down on its well-sprung upholstery. Sarah walked over to a large collection of battered tea chests in the far corner of the room. There was an old hat stand nearby, and a distasteful hollow, real, elephant foot. April hadn't ever seen them on show in the house, but remembered seeing a picture of her late grandfather standing in a dignified pose holding a walking cane, next to the elephant foot umbrella stand.

Sarah headed to the chaise longue and sat beside April. She passed her a collection of treasures.

The light from the small window being rather inadequate for such a glorious task, Sarah reached behind her and pulled a large tassel cord on a barley twist, dark wood standard lamp, topped with a pale pink pleated shade.

'I was up here having a tidy up and found these in one of the tea chests', declared Sarah, as she turned to her granddaughter.

'Were the photographs in here too?' asked April, already guessing the answer.

'Yes, the frame was in this case,' she answered.

'Who are the women in the photographs, Nan?'

'One of them is my grandmother, which would be your great-great-grandmother.'

'Nan, can I have a good look? I'll be careful,' requested April.

'Of course you can. Come down when you're ready. I'll go and put the kettle on. Time for a lovely pot of tea I think. I'll also wake those two up. I don't know, old age!' Sarah raised herself from the chaise and headed down the stairs, chuckling.

April sat beneath the warm pink hue of the silk shade and relished the treasures before her.

Becky Byford

There sat a small leather case, in rich tan, old and tatty. As she lifted the lid, inside the case, on the top of the pile was a white handkerchief with a lace edge and finely embroidered pink roses, and the initials ERW. It reminded her of the fine embroidery of the linen runner downstairs on the piano top. April gently folded the handkerchief and placed it on the gold satin upholstery beside her.

Then, neatly wrapped in a linen cloth, were three silver items, a large paddle hairbrush, an ivory-toothed comb and a large view hand mirror. All were extremely shiny and polished with a simple swirl of engraving.

Such a gorgeous dressing table set and it was intricately engraved with the same three initials, ERW. Loving care had kept these objects in the finest condition, so they looked almost newly purchased. April re-wrapped the set into their cover of linen and put them to one side.

At the bottom of the old case lay a stunning wooden box, a magnificent marquetry box inlaid with exotic woods and mother of pearl - not small; quite substantial considering its painstaking workmanship.

Placing the case on the floor, April held the shoebox-sized work of art in her lap. She gently tugged at the lid but to no avail. A very small fancy silver lock situated on its front face sat empty, devoid of a key. April rummaged around in the bottom of the leather case but no joy.

Where was the key?

With meticulousness, April placed the treasures one by one into the case. She gathered up the silver frame from the gold satin upholstery where her grandmother had sat. How beautiful these two young ladies were. April acknowledged the older, fairer lady, as being her great-great grandmother. She was extremely beautiful; it was obvious where her grandmother inherited her flawless features. However, who was the other beauty?

For some reason and unaware of why, April looked up and fixed her gaze upon the pile of tea chests in the corner of the room. She hadn't heard a noise and there certainly had been nothing of interest there before. But, nevertheless, she felt compelled and could not move her eyes from the spot.

The small amount of light that passed through the window, cast a glow across the room a few feet in front of the chests. They sat behind the hazy light in shadow. April was transfixed, glued to her seat.

A sudden coldness travelled her feet. The icy chill slowly crept through the air, touching every part of her body. Encasing her, it encircled her physique as she sat upon the gold chaise. The large lamp behind her, which was giving its subtle pink glow, hissed and crackled, flickered rapidly and then its light was no more.

The attic felt almost pitch black as April's eyes adjusted to the darkness; the dusky light was falling on the December afternoon. The light that the window cast was now fainter than before. Not even the artificial light from the street lamp had any hope of shedding an illumination on the subject.

Her heart beat erratically.

Faster and faster it pounded, as if to burst from her ribcage.

Her breathing grew heavier and heavier.

Her warm breath became a cloud, visible before her face in the chilling air. A heavy feeling in the pit of her stomach leapt to her chest. She tried desperately not to panic as this inexplicable feeling pumped through her veins.

April's eyes wandered the room, looking for a logical explanation for the situation. Her gaze fell upon the direction of the tea chests once again. As she shook, her eyes fixed to that spot, intent on making sense of what she could see.

The air in the room was incredibly frosty. Her body shuddered and her skin tingled with a swathe of goose bumps. April took a deep breath. Something curious caught her awareness.

Her nostrils grasped at the arctic air. An odour travelled the space piercing the coldness, a sweet fragrance, a delicate floral perfume.

She sat bewildered.

Where was it coming from?

BECKY BYFORD

In the mounting darkness of the attic, April could see a light, a small blue flickering light. For what seemed several minutes it danced and darted around the bitter air, becoming brighter and bluer, as it flitted through the freezing atmosphere.

Then, as quickly as it had appeared, it was gone.

The attic room stood still with an unearthly silence, as if for a moment, time paused.

Gradually, a grey mist appeared at the site of the tea chest. Twisting and coiling, slowly at first then more speedily, it swirled across the frosty setting.

A numb sensation, induced by the stabbing coldness of the air, filled April's body. Totally paralysed from any movement she watched as the figure slowly but surely took shape.

Before her stood a ghostly apparition.

April stared hard at the apparition, amazed and stunned, but strangely no longer afraid.

Still holding the silver and mother of pearl frame, she gasped in disbelief.

The most beautiful young women stood before her, she was clad in a long pale dress, her red hair bore a translucent gleam. The woman did not move or gesture.

April stared deep into her eyes; the young beauty simply smiled a soft, serene smile.

April pulled all her senses together, closed her eyes and shook her head, thinking she was losing her mind.

The air was still filled with a coldness she had never known before, not like winter coldness, but an eerie chill that had penetrated her whole being.

Still clutching the frame, April felt herself drifting, her vision became blurred, her mind dizzy. Light-headedness filled her brain and all judgment vanished.

She clenched her eyes shut hoping it would pass.

With a sudden impulsive deep breath, warm air filled her lungs as if for the first time.

Her face felt the heat of the summer sun; the light it gave shone through April's tightly shut eyelids.

A moment passed.

Then slowly, tentatively she opened her eyes.

Remember to love me

Gathering her bearings, she saw a garden. Her grandmother's garden; but not at all how she knew it.

Standing atop the steps that led down into the garden below, with its wonderfully scented flora, embraced by lusciously green and deep grassy lawns, April entertained, with both dismay and wonderment, the fleeting thought of having died and gone to heaven.

On the vista before her the garden was in full bloom; borders of rose bushes in shades of pink and white edged its boundaries, and magnificent flourishing lavender shrubs paved the way down the steps which led deep into the grounds of the Victorian house.

The floral aroma travelled and captured April's senses; the mid summer sun drenched her body with warmth. The far corner of the garden housed a charming shaded area; a large tree spread its boughs across the grassy walled enclosure, casting a vast shadow, under which settled a scrolled fan backed cane chair, most *definitely* white.

April's ears became aware of whistling coming from the depths of the garden. Anxiously, she watched her feet, as she passed down each step. Not sure whether she could move at all.

A gentleman, bald, middle aged, short, and very stout, entered into view. He carried a large brown leather handled case. April stood transfixed on the second step. Unable to move, she watched in astonishment, as the man assembled his photographic equipment.

April stood in silent contemplation for a moment. What was happening? She didn't understand. She knew where *she believed* she was, but everything was strange and somehow wrong. Lavender and roses? It was December, almost Christmas: why was the sun as warm as a midsummer day?

'Oh, do come along, the gentleman is ready for you.' A man's voice boomed through the warm air. A fainter, female reply came from deep inside the house.

'Please wait, Father. I shall return momentarily!'

April heard a loud, quite harsh male voice come from behind her. She swung round sharply.

Becky Byford

A very tall gentleman, middle-aged, rather attractive, with white hair and an equally white beard, was dressed in his finest. A light coloured suit, perfect for the summer weather, and a grand gold pocket watch that hung from his waistcoat by a thick chain. April stood glued to the spot, as the man passed her and descended gracefully down the garden steps. To her absolute amazement, the gentleman passed utterly oblivious of her presence.

'Ah, Captain Warner, everything is ready when the young ladies are, Sir,' announced the photographer loudly, as the tall gentleman reached the grassy depths.

'Ah, yes, Mr Brown, so I see. My daughters shall be ready in just a few moments.'

'Well, it surely is a wonderful day for it, Captain Sir.'

The photographer rummaged around in the bottom of his brown leather bag once more before standing upright. Next to Captain Warner, he took a deep breath, inflating his waist-coated chest, in the hope of giving himself some air of authority.

April turned on her heels to gaze back into the house through the open glass doors. Heavy, lacy curtains swung gently in the soft summer breeze, through which she caught sight of a female figure. The figure was robed in a white lace gown, not heavy like the curtains, but delicate and dainty. The dress was high at the neck and rather demure, perfect for a modern bride desperate to capture a period feel. Her long auburn hair was elegantly piled up into a sophisticated style of the day.

'I could not have the photograph taken without this,' exclaimed the young lady, whilst holding a gloriously detailed cameo brooch. The tall gentleman was now deep in the garden, conversing in depth with the photographer, over the weather and such like. He seemed unaware of the young lady's comment; he simply gestured up towards the doorway, to quicken her descent into the garden. April budged as far to the edge of the step as she dared, pushing her way into the lavender, trying to vanish from view. As the young woman gracefully passed through, she eased aside the drapes. She too made no acknowledgement of April's presence. As she moved, a sweet scent of perfume lingered under April's nose, that same sweet floral fragrance.

April's breathing became erratic. Her heart once again drummed in her chest. She swayed on the spot, giddy and woozy. She clenched her eyes shut. Her ears were numb to any sound, silent. Her face was frozen once again, her hands paralysed from her tight grip; she was still clutching the silver and mother of pearl frame.

'April, wake up.' She opened her eyes slowly to see her mother, 'You OK?'

April simply nodded; her head threatening to fall and roll off her shoulders.

'You must have fallen asleep, sweetheart. Do you fancy a nice cup of tea now?'

April sat up, debating this for a moment as she looked over at the tea chests. The room was practically black; the lamp was still out and the only light was that which was glowing from the hallway down the narrow staircase. The figure was gone.

'Cup of tea sounds great,' she replied, rising to her feet, steadying herself on her mother's arm as she did so.

'Are you feeling alright?' Julia enquired in a concerned voice.

'I'll be fine when I've had a drink Mum, don't worry!' she replied, reassuring her.

The two of them headed down the staircase and into the front room, where Michael and Sarah were both sitting, sipping their tea. April took her usual seat under the window.

No one spoke for a few moments; all simply delighting in the teatime treat. She watched, digesting their faces and expressions. How could they be so calm? However, the truth was they didn't know; sublime ignorance, she thought. April turned and looked at the tea laid out on the table, thankful for the afternoon tradition.

There was a large Victoria sponge cake with strawberry jam and butter-cream filling. The cake was mounted on an embossed frosted glass-footed cake stand; beside the stand was a white bone china cream jug on its own small china plate. Once the tea and cake were all consumed, Sarah rose from her comfortable chair and lifted the tea tray from the carved legged table where it had been residing.

'Nan, let me do that!' April stood up, taking the tray from her grandmother before she could argue.

'OK, you can help me wash up.'

They left the room, and headed into the kitchen. April ran a sink for the washing up and her grandmother cleared the tray.

'Nan?'

'Yes?'

'I'm not sure what happened earlier. I felt a little strange as I looked through the case.' What April really wanted to say was that she believed she'd seen a ghost. April stood by the kitchen sink carefully washing the fine bone china teacups, trying to find a way to make such an alarming statement.

'When you say you felt a little strange? What do you mean?'

'Strange, Nan, something really odd happened. I don't know how to explain it.'

'Well…I have also felt very odd feelings over the past few weeks since I found the leather case.'

'How strange, what sort of things, Nan?'

'Nothing I can be certain of. It may be my imagination.'

April had begun to question her sanity, but her grandmother's answers were such that she wondered if she could read her mind.

'Have you seen? Err…what I mean is do you…' April couldn't finish her sentence; she felt too ridiculous thinking it, let alone saying it.

'The beautiful marquetry box, yes, it is lovely, and before you ask, no, I don't know where the key is!' replied Sarah.

The marquetry box - she had forgotten about the beautiful heirlooms; her thoughts had solely been on the apparition of the young woman.

'Yes, the box, it is gorgeous. So, you don't know where the key is, Nan?'

'No, as I said, I only found the case a few weeks ago. I'd never seen it before then. I've never seen photographs of my grandmother that young before either. Wasn't she lovely?'

This conversation wasn't going anywhere. The only thing April could do was to have another look at the treasure.

'Nan, any chance that I can take the case home with me to take a closer look? I will be extremely careful. You do know that?'

Sarah paused for a second, and then replied as her usual cheery self. 'Do you know? I think that's a splendid idea.' She smiled at April with a very calm and clear expression. 'Shall I go and get it for you? Or shall we go together? Come on.'

April followed her once again up the flights to the attic door; it was already open.

'I left the lamp on Nan. Sorry I didn't think it….' April stood, looking for an explanation and hoping that her grandmother had one.

'Never mind, there's no harm done.' Cautiously, April followed her grandmother over to the gold satin chaise-longue. The old leather case with all its contents sat on the floor. The silver and mother of pearl frame lay on the gold upholstery. Sarah lifted the frame and neatly placed it next to the box at the bottom of the case, then reached across and pulled the cord on the lamp. The attic room was dark once more.

'It's quite heavy, Nan, let me carry it down for you.'

April tentatively took the case, unsure of what effect it would have.

For a second, she stood glued to the spot.

Nothing! She analysed for a moment, then headed back down the stairs followed by her grandmother, closing the door behind them.

Kissing her grandmother goodnight, she trailed behind her parents as they walked the two-minute journey home. Unaware of her own movements, her every thought was occupied by the strange events of the day.

Wishing them both goodnight, she climbed the staircase to her bedroom. Hurriedly, she closed the door behind her and placed the old tan leather case on the floor beside her bed. April drew the curtains on the outside world. She undressed, continually watching the case, as if it was about to jump into life. She climbed into her soft bed and pulled the luxurious feather duvet around her; cocooned.

The beautiful young woman April had seen occupied her thoughts once again.

She reached down into the case, taking hold of the silver and mother of pearl frame. Staring deep into the photographs, studying and absorbing their content.

There, worn on the high-necked dress, was the cameo brooch.

April had seen it in her vision, the young woman had been adamant about not having her photograph taken without it.

It had been an exhausting day; April snuggled down into her cocoon, still clutching the frame in her hand. Her eyes gradually closed, not able to stay awake any longer, she drifted off to sleep.

* * *

June 1900.

The smooth black ink flowed, etching the date onto the back of the two photographs that lay before him. Carefully, he pressed the rolling blotter onto both dates to seal the ink. Meticulously, in turn, he inserted the photographs into position. After a few moments, he stood the frame on the writing desk, to view his masterpiece. The stunning silver photograph frame with its intricate inlay of shimmering mother of pearl and tiny silver beads encircled the sepia photographs; it stood majestically.

The very proud middle-aged gentleman arose from his leather-seated chair, and with military precision carefully positioned his pen onto its rest and replaced the brass lid onto the cut glass inkwell. The desk and chair had an adorable aspect of the garden. The study was airy and flooded with light, which spilled in through the large sash window.

High shelves of oak reached to the ceiling. On them a library of books; a multitude of leather bound volumes, books on art, poetry, literature and history. Positioned between them, acting as bookends and stations, were a menagerie of framed memories; photographs of seaside trips, wedding celebrations and portraits capturing the family's life.

The richly patterned carpet complemented the dark red velvet of the matching settees with carved arms and legs. They sat either side of the window, with the contemplation of a perfect position to settle and study one of the glorious books. From the high ceiling hung the most magnificent light with five glass-globed shades, each suspended by a brass arm.

He strode through the panelled door, from the study across into the hallway. He reached a neat half moon side table, elegant with sweeping legs and a small drawer for keys and the like. An abundance of fresh pink roses sat on its polished surface.

Smelling, inhaling the delicate fragrance of the roses as he went by, he passed the stairs to the end of the hall.

Like a mirror image, on the other side of the staircase resided an identical side table. Approaching it, he raised the silver and mother of pearl frame, once again admiring the beauties he had entrusted to it. Captain Charles Warner lovingly positioned the frame onto the polished surface, pride of place to be admired.

* * *

April awoke to the chime of the church bell. Her eyes roamed across her bed; there on her pillow lay the photograph frame. She held it close to her cheek as she remembered her dream. The quiet seconds drifted to minutes, with her mind wandering through the rooms of her dream, her grandmother's rooms, so alike and so familiar, but still so different with the thick atmosphere of another era.

The church bell chimed once again. Opening her lazy eyes, she abandoned the frame and heaved herself up.

April arose and opened her bedroom curtains, allowing the morning sun to seek every part of the room behind her. The day was bright but bitterly cold; frost clung in natural forms of sunburst flakes, decorating the glass windowpane with its Christmas gift.

She got dressed and neatened her bed linen. Lovingly, she took hold of the photographs and headed for the window.

Almost hypnotised by her beauty, she looked deeply at her great-great grandmother. How exquisite she was, how wonderful it would have been to sit and converse on their family history; hear stories of her childhood, her life.

Then something caught her eye; around her great-great grandmothers wrist was a bracelet, a charm bracelet.

She hadn't noticed it before.

Her eyes then travelled to the other sepia memory; once again, she admired the ornate cameo brooch worn on the high neckline.

April was aware that her grandmother had many family heirlooms, which she kept in a huge jewellery case of creamy leather. As a small child, only on special occasions, her grandmother would let her admire them, under the watchful eye of the mother. Had she ever seen the cameo brooch or the charm bracelet?

April's eyes penetrated deeply into the portraits. Her whole body consumed by their image. She leant against the window frame, clutching her stomach. An upsetting sensation of emptiness spread her body, a feeling of cold, loneliness and despair.

Remember to love me

Past Impressions

Christmas approached.
The streets were bustling with busy shoppers, all looking for something a little different.

The Antique Shop had had a remarkable start to business; they had worked flat out to cater for the stampede. April hadn't had much time to consider her strange encounter in any more depth than she had already done so. They had been so busy; there hadn't been time to think of anything else.

However, today was Christmas Eve, and she had the day off to do her last minute shopping.

Best of all, it was Christmas shopping with her Grandmother.

April strode down the frosty street and crossed the busy road, with its hordes of frantic, festive shoppers, jams of cars, all busy with one thing in mind. April lifted the lion doorknocker, as the door opened.

'There you are. I've been looking forward to this for days,' squealed Sarah with excitement, shutting the door behind her.

Both were wrapped in long wool coats and scarves. April noticed her grandmother's emerald brooch upon the lapel of her dark green coat. It reminded her.

Becky Byford

'Nan, when I was little, I remember playing with your jewellery, the jewellery in the large cream leather case...do you remember?'

'Of course I remember,' she beamed. 'You used to sit on your Mum's lap in front of the mirror trying on all the pieces. You were so sweet, you could never just try one piece at a time, you'd have everything on all at the same time.'

'Can I have a look again later, when we've finished shopping? I don't have to go back to work; we've got the whole day together, it's going to be lovely.'

The warmth of shared memories eased the chill of the December weather. Both looked at each other, there was no need for words to be spoken, the excitement shone in their faces; both knowing what the other was thinking.

The bitter Christmas Eve air chilled the faces of the bustling Yuletide shoppers. Arm in arm, grandmother and granddaughter headed along the busy streets of the market town.

Festive lights illuminated the view; garlands of twinkling bulbs in a multitude of colours, suspended from the rooftops, reached from one side of the street to the other, creating a canopy of light over the roads below.

An extremely impressive Christmas tree stood in the centre of the paved hill. Its path led to the magnificent stone arched gateway of the ancient ruins of the Abbey, once the heart of this old town.

The splendid tree glistened with a mass of sparkly lights, and small children gazed in wonder at the enchanting sight, full of wonderment that there was only one more sleep until Christmas morning.

The angelic voices of a choir carried through the frosty air; the festive carol brought smiles to the faces, as many gathered to join in the merriment and joyful singing, rejoicing in the occasion.

April and her grandmother headed through the bustle into the depths of the crowd. The annual festive market was in full swing, at the heart of the busy town centre. Stall holders, selling their fresh produce of fruit and vegetables were ready for the Christmas feasts ahead.

Traders competed with their mountains of satsumas and Christmas nuts. Stacked boxes of dates and hand tied bunches of mistletoe adorned the displays to entice the passing shoppers. Holly wreaths encrusted with ripe berries hung from the heights of the market stall frames. Sights and smells induced recollections of past Yuletides. The aroma of hot roasted chestnuts wafted through the town, evoking memories for the crowds.

There were stall holders selling beautiful handbags and purses, mobbed by impatient bargain hunters squabbling over one off pieces.

Shop windows displayed Christmas trees decorated with their products, perfect for festive gifts. Boutique windows exhibited their most beautiful seasonal party gowns; bright jewelled colours in velvets and satins, embellished with a multitude of faceted beads and iridescent sequins, perfect for any Hollywood starlet, along with fur stoles, beaded handbags, and the most elegant evening shoes. Customers emerged through store doorways, laden with bags and boxes, barely able to pass through the crowds.

April and Sarah ambled the streets, dodging the clusters of shoppers gathered around shop windows and huddled at the market stalls.

'What can I get Mum? That's the last present I have left to get,' asked April, at her wit's end. They had visited many shops and stalls that sold lovely gifts, the usual, perfume, handbags, and scarves.

'I always think that she's the hardest to buy for. If I ask her what she wants, she just says, 'Nothing, just a hug.'

'I'm not quite sure. What do you get someone who doesn't need anything? Anyway, I must admit, when she asks me what I'd like, I say the same thing, just a hug. It must be a mum thing.'

'Oh, so it's you that started it, was it? Well, when I have kids, I'll give them a list, so they don't have the same dilemma every year,' April beamed. 'But that doesn't solve the problem today, so what do I get her?'

Becky Byford

'Maybe, something really special, something she wouldn't normally buy herself. Something she would adore, but never indulge in.'

'Like what? I know - jewellery,' she replied with a beaming smile, as though by some divine inspiration. 'Something really special, perhaps; something that she would think was too extravagant.'

'I know the perfect shop, follow me. They had some beautiful earrings in the window earlier. I couldn't help but have a little peep as we walked by. You can never have too much jewellery; you should always surround yourself with beauty,' Sarah stated with excitement, rubbing her hands together.

April clutched her grandmother's arm in hers as they strolled.

The Abbey Gate was visible from the top of the street; it stood majestically against the icy blue sky. The serene chorus of the festive carol travelled the air as they approached. How perfect, April thought, more perfect than she could have imagined; her heart felt warm and settled, the perfect day, the smell of delicious hot roast chestnuts, the sound of carols and the largest twinkling Christmas tree known to man.

Half way down the street, they reached the jewellers.

April glanced up at the clock; it was mounted proudly on the outside of the shop. The clock reached twelve noon.

As April studied it, she held on to the varnished woodwork of the shop doorway. She viewed the clock up high on its ornate wrought iron bracket.

The winter sky transformed from its dull icy grey to a bright cobalt blue, setting a stage backdrop to a gleaming new clock. The sun glared into April's face making her squint.

Through barely opened eyes, she observed a young man wearing a flat cap; his straw blonde hair was short but visible from beneath it. He stood at the top of a tall wooden ladder, polishing the digits of the new clock face. The hands sat at twelve, as he frantically rubbed the last of the roman numerals. He pushed his polishing cloth in the back pocket of his dark trousers, held up by a pair of brown leather braces. His lean but muscular torso was evident through a thin cotton shirt. April watched as the young man carefully descended the numerous struts of the wooden ladder.

'There you go, Sir, perfect!' The young man spoke in a soft polite voice to a portly gentleman with a large moustache, who stood within the doorway of the jewellers. The young man took an old, large silver, rather battered and worn pocket watch from his trouser pocket. He flicked opened the engraved case to reveal the jewelled timepiece within.

'Perfect time as well, Sir, two minutes past the hour, precisely.'

'That's a wonderful job young man. Yes, wonderful job,' the portly gentlemen replied with a very jovial beam.

The jeweller strolled from the doorway and stood on the cobbled road in the centre of the street. Fists clenched on his hips, his paunchy stomach thrust out, inspecting his new clock with admiration. He reached into his waistcoat, pulling a shiny gold watch from a small pocket. With a quick flick of his thumb; he opened the watch to examine the time.

'Yes. Wonderful, wonderful,' repeated the rotund man, beaming at the young man once more.

April looked back up at the clock. The sky was again, wintry and icy. The clock had aged somewhat, but had gloriously withstood the ravages of time. Everything was as it should be once again.

April, slightly stunned and confused, examined the jewellery shop's enchanting premises. The newly sanded and varnished woodwork was in keeping with its old world charm. The windows were very stylishly decorated with classy glass baubles, enhancing the classic pieces of gold and platinum that resided behind the frosty glass.

A young couple stood at the window, contemplating, their heads almost resting upon the icy panes. The young woman's eyes gleamed at the array of stunning diamond rings which made such an impressive display; the interior shop lights beamed, giving the gems a blinding sparkle.

Becky Byford

The young man held his lady's hand tight, as she stared in bewilderment, trying to choose between the many beautiful engagement rings; the young lovers headed for the jeweller's door. As they entered the shop, April and Sarah took up the place where the couple had stood.

Further along the highly varnished window frame, a show of gem set earrings and necklaces adorned the display stands.

'There! What a magnificent pair of earrings,' exclaimed Sarah, pointing to a pair of long drop gold earrings, with a cascade of graduated amethysts of the brightest purple. April gasped in delight, they were perfect, her mother's favourite gemstone.

'Nan, they are lovely, well...do you think Mum'll like them?' giggled April, 'I'd love to borrow them.'

'I think they are perfect. It's much better to buy one beautiful gift, than lots of things that no one really wants,' Sarah answered.

'Shall we go inside and have a closer look at them?' April pushed open the glazed door.

The shop was full of elated customers, all gasping with delight at their chosen purchases. The young couple that had been pondering over the engagement rings were conversing with a rather tall, debonair gentleman. He had taken the tray of diamond rings from the window, and was helping the now very excited young lady try them on.

Her young man stood with his hip leant against the counter, looking admiringly at his fiancée as she sat on a luxuriously upholstered chair. His appreciation was clearly at her beauty, not that of the diamond on her finger, to which he gave hardly any acknowledgement. The young lady glanced up at the tall gentleman, who instinctively smiled and reached for a leather ring box.

The couple gazed at one another, completely oblivious to the presence of the other eight people in the shop. The jeweller returned the ring tray to the window, and boxed the chosen diamond ring, before the couple had even said a word.

April and Sarah wandered over to the far end of the shop. A glass case of watches on one wall was being heavily scrutinised by a pair of elderly ladies. One was describing a watch she had once owned when she was young; she wondered how much it would have been worth if she had still possessed it. The other elderly lady seemed unaware of her companion's reminiscing, and examined the detail on a pocket watch in the far corner of the cabinet. She was muttering to herself, something regarding how her father owned a much finer one, and wondering where it had gone to and why she hadn't inherited it when he died.

The tall gentleman coughed quite forcefully. Clearly not to relieve his throat, but to make himself noticed. The two elderly ladies just looked at one another, huffed loudly, and walked out of the shop.

Within a few short minutes, all the customers had dispersed, leaving only Sarah and her granddaughter.

'Good afternoon to you both, can I help you at all? Searching for something special as a Christmas gift?' the tall gentleman enquired, smiling with a warm polite expression.

'We would love to take a closer look at the amethyst earrings in the window, please,' Sarah requested as she loosened the silk scarf from around her neck.

'The long gold drop...' added April, but before she could finish her sentence, the gentleman returned with that precise pair of earrings.

'They are rather stunning. Such a beautiful colour, 24 carat gold with three faceted oval Brazilian amethysts in each earring.' stated the jeweller, as he placed the earrings on the velvety jewellery tray.

'April, what do you think? They are so perfect for your mother; I think she will absolutely adore them. Does she still have that lovely purple satin blouse? That would look stunning, don't you think so?'

April was unaware of her grandmother's questions; she had the strangest sensation.

Clutching the edge of the display cabinet to steady herself, she stared down into the glass. Beneath her reflection, the contents of silver hipflasks, letter openers and engraved fountain pens, hazed in and out of view. Her grandmother's voice seemed a million miles away, despite her actual close vicinity.

April's heart beat erratically.

Her ears felt utterly numb to all but the pounding of her own heartbeat, which echoed through her skull. She clenched her eyes tightly in the hope it would pass.

Time seemed to stand still.

Slowly, the dizziness eased and she opened her eyes, her head still bowed over the glass display cabinet. The silver items that had graced the glass shelves had been replaced with ornate brooches, adorning dark green velvet trays. April stared down in dismay at the sight, her fingers still tightly gripping the edge of the counter, her legs heavy like lead weights. She clenched her eyes tightly shut once again. Desperately, April counted slowly in her head; one, two, three, four….

'Yes. I must agree, that one is delightful, Sir. A good choice if I may say so.'

April slowly opened her eyes.

The portly gentleman with the large moustache stood behind the jewellery counter, in huge contrast to the tall debonair jeweller, with whom April had just conversed. His near balding head shone under the bright summer sunshine flowing through the windows. His rather round stature made it nigh on impossible for him to get close enough to the counter: his waist-coated stomach touched the mahogany of the display case. He reached down, presenting a dark green velvet covered tray upon which laid a multitude of brooches.

April examined the view before her. She had never seen such a spectacular display of antique jewellery. These were far superior to the collection of Victorian jewellery she had arranged in her parents' antique shop.

Several large gem set brooches glistened in the light. A large faceted emerald, brilliantly cut, claw-set in a round frame of silver marcasite, caught April's eye. Blue flashes glowed deep magnificently, within the dark green gem. The gentleman gracefully removed one particular brooch from the bottom row of the deep pile velvet; it was an extraordinary work of art, not just a piece of jewellery.

'This one is sterling silver and set with a glorious Wedgwood blue Jasperware cameo. It is extremely individual as you can see, perfect for a special birthday gift, Sir.' The jeweller offered the brooch in his outstretched plump hand.

April stood in amazement as she turned to her left. Where her grandmother had stood, was now a young, tall, extremely handsome man, impeccably dressed in his finest beige summer suit; his hair, dark in contrast to his pale attire, was neat, glossy and well groomed. His features were strong with high cheekbones, a square jaw line and chiselled chin, with a perfect complexion and bright green eyes. An unexplained familiarity lay within the alluring features of his face. He smiled as he reached out and took the brooch from the stout gentleman.

'Oh, I must agree, this is beautiful; I have never seen such an incredible design, perfect in fact. The Wedgwood blue Jasperware is wonderful.' The handsome figure studied the silver design of the brooch, whilst checking the security of the clasp. The jeweller stood with his hands in fists on his hips as, with a somewhat elated expression, he watched the gentleman inspect the detail.

'Such a lovely design, I think the shade of blue will complement her colouring beautifully. Don't you agree, darling? Would you like to take a closer look?'

The elegant man turned to look in April's direction, offering the Wedgwood brooch in his long slender fingers.

April gasped in disbelief. The gentleman, seemingly unaware of her response, smiled, his striking features glowed attractively, under the gentle sunlight that bathed the jewellery shop.

April's legs crumpled beneath her. Closing her eyes, she gripped the counter so tightly her fingertips became white and numb under the pressure of her weight. Slowly steadying herself, she daringly opened her eyes. The array of antique brooches gradually transformed into the modern silver articles.

Becky Byford

The aged atmosphere, the soft summer sunlight of the richly Victorian shop, transformed into the brightly lit contemporary interior once more.

'April, are you OK?'

Her grandmother's words seemed faint, fading in and out of earshot. April tried to gather her bearings, slowly steadying herself.

'April! April!'

Her grandmother's voice now ringing through her head, April finally came round to find herself sitting on a decorative gilt chair in the corner of the shop.

'April, how are you feeling now? Here, drink this glass of water. You'll feel better.'

April sipped the water. She scanned the shop around her. How could she explain this to her grandmother?

'I'm feeling a lot better now. Thank you, just a little faint.' April smiled at the jeweller and turned to her grandmother.

'Shall we head home?' Sarah asked with a concerned expression.

'I think I'm OK now, Nan. Please don't worry.' April really didn't want to alarm her, she rose from the chair slowly, so as not to sway and cause concern.

'Thank you very much for your help.' April smiled at the jeweller, handing him back the empty glass. 'Now, those earrings, can I take another look?'

'Of course,' the jeweller replied, handing her the earrings. April stood at the counter, inspecting the beauty of the gems in a rather nonchalant manner, desperately trying to dismiss the previous incident.

Both Sarah and the jeweller stared at April, nonplussed...

'Well, what do you think? They are so lovely and perfect,' announced Sarah, adopting the same unperturbed tone.

'Yes, Nan, I agree they are perfect for Mum. I think she will adore them,' April declared with an unnaturally calm voice.

April paid for the beautiful amethyst earrings, and the jeweller carefully boxed and wrapped them. Thanking the gentleman once again, they departed through the shop door. The cool Christmas air enlivened April's senses, clearing her of the drowsiness.

'I really am feeling a lot better now, Nan - just got a bit hot inside the shop.'

'Well, as long as you are sure?' Sarah still looked quite concerned.

April tentatively looked up at the clock. The icy blue Christmas sky was viewable through the bracket's black wrought iron. The frosty air seemed almost refreshing now.

'April, are you ready to go home now? I think we've finished. Time for a nice cuppa and some cake, then we'd better wrap these last few presents before your mum and dad shut the shop. We don't want your mum seeing these gorgeous earrings before tomorrow, do we?'

April took her grandmother's arm, and they both headed back down the hill, through the merriment and festivities.

They passed the magnificent Christmas tree on the hill, where the carol singers were now standing. A mammoth crowd had gathered; all were singing euphorically. Sarah kept a tight grip on her granddaughter's arm. Neither spoke a word.

April could not remove the image of the tall, charming man from her mind.

They reached the small black door of the Victorian house, the stately lion doorknocker proudly festive with its frame of holly, shone with a polished gleam in the winter sunlight. Sarah turned the key in the brass lock as April leant against the large sash window frame, her fingertip moving over the brickwork, her eyes idly tracing the mortar between each brick surrounding the window.

Her mind empty, drained of thought and exhausted from her experience in the jewellers.

They entered the front room down the steps onto the inviting carpet below. April sensed a wonderful feeling of security, a safe homely sensation stronger than ever before and remarkably familiar. April put her shopping bags down onto the floor next to her favourite seat. She unbuttoned her long coat and un-wrapped the scarf from around her neck, abandoning them on the arm of the settee; they fell to the floor covering her bags with a blanket of black wool. The toasted warmth from the open fire and the soft twinkle of the Christmas tree lights almost captivated and relaxed April's mind.

'I'll go and warm the pot,' announced Sarah as she draped her dark green coat and scarf neatly over the high back of a winged chair, and then headed towards the kitchen.

April said nothing.

Wordless, paralysed, and unable to conjure up any expression she slumped onto the velvet upholstery. The gold silk cushion comforted her head, cradling it, as she lay spellbound by the glimmer of the tree lights and the soft amber glow from the fire. Sweet, festive reflections battled to soothe and settle her mind, her troubled and confused mind.

What had just happened?

What were those things, those tricks her mind had played? As she had stood in that shop, it was as if it wasn't for the first time, not that she could recall the memory, the incident, but it felt familiar.

The gentleman, she felt, well, she couldn't possibly put into words how she felt. She couldn't decide if he seemed familiar, or maybe it was simply his alluring presence, that had completely seduced her entire being for those few short moments. Nevertheless, she couldn't help wondering, what had just happened?

These occurrences were not the norm, was she experiencing some kind of hallucination?

Oh my God! She thought, maybe it was some sort of mental condition or brain tumour. No, don't be so ridiculous, so melodramatic. But, whatever was going on, somewhere in her twisted mind, she certainly had no control over the situation. First the clock and the men - their clothes - they had seemed slightly odd and out of date, as if - well, as if they were from another era…no surely not. It must be her subconscious mind playing tricks, aided by the book she had just read on the town history. Yes, that was it; she must have seen a photo, an old picture that triggered it. That was it, of course, that was it, surely, the most obvious and rational explanation to all of it, unless of course she was going mad...

The distant crackle of the large logs on the fire began slowly relaxing her. The repetitive tick of the gilt mantle clock created a hypnotic chant deep inside her consciousness. With heavy eyelids, it became increasingly impossible to keep them open, gently drifting into a deep slumber, soft and comfortable on her red velvet settee.

* * *

'Darling, do come outside, it is such a glorious day. Some fresh air will do you good. The sunshine will brighten your cheeks - you have been sat in this room all afternoon,' softly requested the gentleman from the doorway. The young lady raised her head from the book, which lay in her lap.

'Maybe, in a while I feel comfortable and at ease in here please...let me finish this book and then I shall join you all in the garden. You must not worry so. I am perfectly fine and well.' The lady replied in a sweet but resolute tone, and smiled in her usual enchanting way. The tall, handsome gentleman nodded and smiled in return. Not saying another word, he turned on his heels and silently closed the door behind him.

The beautiful lady sat upon her most favoured red velvet settee in her most preferred room. The study overlooked the charming garden, in full bloom with roses and lavender. The light penetrated the space with an illumination perfect for the task of reading. The soft, lacy drapes billowed fluidly under the influence of the breeze, as the gentle murmur of distant voices crept through the open sash of the bay window. Summer warmth cocooned her as she reclined upon the warm upholstery, captivated by the words within the leather binding of her book.

Becky Byford

'Annabelle, Annabelle.' The words carried on the air into the room. The sweet female voice came from the depths of the garden. 'Annabelle.'

The young lady softly closed the book, as if not to disturb those who lived within the pages. Gracefully, she rose from her secure place of rest and replaced the book with care upon a high oak shelf. She tenderly gazed at the contents of the photographs, which sat stationed between the leather bound novels. She glided over towards the open window; her glossy blonde hair softly caressed her fair complexion. She brushed her locks from her face with her long fingers; the warm sunrays enlightened her exquisite features, her glorious hazel brown eyes and perfect pale skin.

The usual tranquil view of the garden was today bustling with her family enjoying the summer sunshine. The garden had seen many happy summer days with family fun and games.

'Annabelle, are you coming to join us? Please do. It is such a wonderful day.'

'Emily, patience is a virtue,' she softly called down into the garden. 'I am on my way.'

The sweet voice came from the bottom of the stone steps which led down into the grassy grounds. A young woman stood smiling up at the study window. Her auburn locks blew gracefully in the afternoon wind. She wore a pale blue dress, long to the floor in soft wispy layers with a lacy high neckline and long fitted lacy sleeves. It was nipped in at the waist and hung gracefully over her slender hips enhancing her petite figure. High on her lacy neckline sat a stunning silver and Wedgwood blue Jasperware cameo brooch.

Annabelle moved from view and headed towards the study door. Gently closing the door behind her, she passed through the hallway entering the dining room, a most luxurious space. High walls decoratively papered in rich golden brocade, a glorious backdrop for many antique oil paintings. An impressive polished table, six matching chairs and two carvers upholstered in rose pink damask complemented the red radiance of the mahogany. A large grandfather clock courtly resided against the far wall; it would strike hourly with its melodious chime. A set of full-length glass doors dominated the long wall; a pair of oversized ceramic potted plants enhanced their surroundings with large green foliage, standing regimentally either side.

   She glided toward the doors. The drapes undulated under the direction of the breeze. Passing the lacy drapes, she was confronted by the warmth of the summer climate. Annabelle descended the wide stone steps lined with lavender shrubs and stepped onto the grassy-carpeted garden. Her long gown swayed, the delicate layers swishing under her movement. The low square cut neckline revealed the soft pale skin of her décolletage, elegant puffed sleeves trimmed with a frill of cream lace to her elbows. The pale lemon fabric enhanced her sleek tresses with a soft, golden lustre.

   'Annabelle. There you are! Do come and join us. Mary has made some lemonade and I am beating Richard at chess!' Emily's words sung through the fragrant atmosphere.

   Annabelle gracefully strolled over to the shaded area under the large leafy tree.

   'You are so impatient, my darling sister,' Annabelle stated with a sweet smile.

   She seated herself on one of the reclining wooden garden chairs. A jug of homemade lemonade with matching glasses sat on the garden table. Emily and Richard sat opposite each other, a small folding table between them with the old family chess set; its slightly discoloured ivory pieces mid-game. Both of them deliberated their next move. Richard's serious face was devoured by concentration. Emily scanned the chessboard, and then looked over at Annabelle with a suppressed giggle.

   'Your husband is becoming increasingly frustrated with me, Annabelle. He was expecting to beat me as usual.' Emily's elated features made Annabelle smile.

Becky Byford

'My dear sister, I always knew you had it in you to beat him. You just had to realise it yourself.' Annabelle reclined back into the chair on which she sat. Her eyelids closed, the warm heat soaked them as she lay under the great tree. The soft chorus of bird song travelled on the summer breeze.

'Annabelle dear, how are you feeling this afternoon?'

Her father descended into the garden down the stone steps. The Captain's tall physique was garbed in his Sunday best. His neat moustache and white hair gave him an elegant air.

He placed himself on a chair next to Annabelle, then reached out and took her hand in his.

'My daughter, I know Dr Hickson said you must rest, but I am glad to see you outside. The fresh air will do you good. Please, don't lock yourself away.' Annabelle could hear the concern in his voice, although she knew he was desperately trying to hide it.

'I'm fine. I wish you wouldn't worry so. I have been resting; I do understand how important it is.' Annabelle squeezed her father's hand in reassurance.

'Both you and your sister have always been the most precious things in my life. I don't want you putting yourself at any unnecessary risk.' A very serious look came over his face, an expression Annabelle had seen before. She knew how lost and helpless her father had felt with the passing of her mother.

Annabelle was a small child of four years when Rose, her mother, was expecting Annabelle's sister, Emily. Rose was a petite, young woman. She had managed to carry the baby almost full term, despite many recurring, life-threatening difficulties suffered through the pregnancy. Then, in early June, three weeks before the baby was due, labour started. After many long, painful and stressful hours, the baby was born, but Rose had lost so much blood she became extremely ill and passed away a few short hours after the birth. Captain Warner had raised both a young Annabelle and baby Emily on his own, with the help of Mary the family housekeeper, whom under her own steam had taken on the roll of nanny.

Mary had been with them since Charles and Rose married and moved into their beautiful town house. A prominent female figure in the young girls' lives, she had been regarded as a member of the family since their mother's death, a time when Charles had appreciated Mary's ability to take a great deal of the burden of single parenthood off his shoulders.

On reaching the age of eleven, both girls had followed their mother's example and attended Miss Amelia Hitchins' Selected Establishment for Young Ladies. It was a very reputable, well-ordered school, and taught all the necessary and expected requirements, essential to nurture respectable young ladies.

Charles had a sister who had never married, so, having no children of her own; she would relish the time she spent with the girls. Aunt Anna lived in a small coastal village a few miles away from the market town, in the next county.

Annabelle and Emily spent many wonderful hours playing on the sandy beach, which was visible from the garden. Their father had given them the perfect upbringing and neither had felt deprived. Annabelle and Emily were extremely close, closer than average sisters. The absence of a mother made them rely on each other more for female companionship.

Charles restated his concern for his daughter as he squeezed her hand very tightly.

'Father, I am completely fine and everything is going to be wonderful. When the baby is born, Richard and I shall be a complete family and nothing is going to take that dream away.'

Annabelle lay back on her chair, still holding her father's hand tightly.

Emily squealed with absolute delight. The afternoon air filled with her glorious rapture as she jumped to her feet, her face beaming.

'Well I never. Your dear sister has finally beaten me. Well Emily, I did think you could have won before now.' Richard's voice had an air of both sarcasm and disgrace.

'You are just annoyed that you lost, dear brother-in-law.' Emily danced from around the small table at which she had sat. She gracefully glided over to the spare chair next to Annabelle.

'My dearest sister, how are you feeling this afternoon? You gave us such a fright yesterday.' Emily's tone was serious after her dancing display.

'Emily, both the baby and I are perfectly fine. The doctor instructed me to rest and rest I shall do.'

'He also said you should get lots of fresh air and not lock yourself away in the study. Would you like me to get your book for you, so you can read out here? Or I can read to you, as you did for me when I was small?' Emily clasped Annabelle's hand, the other still tightly held by their father.

'No, I'm fine. I'm happy enough just sitting here with you all.' Annabelle glanced over to where Richard was resetting the chess pieces.

'Belle, how about a game of chess?' Richard got to his feet, carefully picking up the folding table complete with chess set.

'I am not sure I am a worthy opponent for you, Richard. Perhaps you would rather a re-match with Emily to regain your title of reigning champion?'

'I see your condition has not affected your sense of humour.' Richard lowered the table onto the grass near the seated area. He carefully knelt before Annabelle. Both Emily and her father released their hold on Annabelle hands. Richard took her pale hands in his strong but elegant ones.

'My dear Belle, is there anything I can get you, perhaps a chilled glass of lemonade, or a nice cup of afternoon tea?' Richard took one of his hands and gently placed it on her stomach.

'Well, I shall go and see Mary and we shall have a nice pot of tea.' Emily jumped to her feet and strolled up towards the house; her father gracefully followed in her steps. Richard got to his feet and took up residence on the chair, which Emily had vacated.

'We shall be a complete family when the baby is born.' Richard whispered as he gently rubbed her stomach. 'To think that I shall be a father.'

'You will be a wonderful father. I just know it.'

'And you, a delightful mother. I'm sure that you were born to be a mother,' he paused and smoothed his large hand over her gilded hair. 'You are a mother to Emily…you always have been.'

'I suppose you are right. Even when she was so small, and I myself no more than a child, I knew it…deep down inside of me, why I was here, my purpose if you will.'

'Belle, you have far more purpose in this world, in your life, than just to be a mother.' Richard paused.

'You don't understand, do you? To me it means so much, a worthy vocation for my life.' His wife was stern.

'My Belle, please forgive me, all I meant was…'

'It's me, who should apologise,' she shook her head, 'It's in my heart Richard; that is what I am.'

'You need to rest, Belle.'

'I shall make sure I do not do anything to put our baby at risk.' She closed her eyes, her pale face to the sun, absorbing, recharging with its energy.

With a sudden wail, Annabelle abruptly clasped Richard's hand with hers, clutching at her lower abdomen. Richard gazed deeply into Annabelle's despairing eyes. She looked away, still tightly gripping Richard's hand; as she bent doubled over with pain. Her blonde strands of hair draped across his arm and onto her lap.

'Belle! Annabelle! Please, my love, what is it?' Richard's voice, full of dread, echoed in the warm atmosphere. Annabelle pulled herself upright, her pain stricken face obvious. Annabelle's features were illustrated with distress and agony. Richard slowly took his hand from her belly and rose to his feet.

'Richard, please! Please don't leave me!'

'We must get the doctor quickly! The doctor, get the doctor!' Richard shouted up into the house as he dashed across the grass. Within seconds, Emily came rushing down the garden steps and was at Annabelle's side.

'Father is getting the doctor. Everything is going to be fine, I promise my dear sister.' Emily's voice was strained and high pitched with the effort to keep calm.

Richard returned with a large cream blanket from the house. He wrapped Annabelle in the blanket as he whisked her up in his strong arms. He carried her quickly up the stone steps into the house.

Annabelle closed her eyes tightly, too much to bear, her pain threshold stretched to its limits. Everything and everyone around her became immaterial and insignificant. With the misery of the immense consuming agony and the desperation of the situation, Annabelle lay on the bed in Richard's arms. All her surroundings became distant; she was aware of nothing but anguish, sorrow and loss.

The doctor reached the bottom step, with a grave expression overshadowing his otherwise calm but ageing face.

'How is she, Doctor?' Richard sat on the plush dining chair, desperately not wanting to hear the inevitable reply.

'I am so sorry, Richard. There was nothing I could do, the baby just wasn't meant to be. Annabelle will be fine, but. I am not sure at this point what the implications will be for future pregnancies.' He paused, seeing the plea in Richard's eyes. 'I will know more in a few days. Annabelle needs total bed rest for the next week. Richard...I think it is best if you both stay here with Charles and Emily for a while. You will both need the support. I shall check on her again in the morning. I have given her something for the pain; it will let her sleep.' Dr Hickson stood with his hand on Richard's shoulder.

He was a rather lean elderly gentleman of not too great a height, maybe only five and a half feet. His hair was thinning and pure white with a large matching moustache that almost covered his face, thin and weathered by the years, but still very kind and gentle.

Emily stood cradled inside her father's arms, both speechless and motionless, only her faint sobs muffled by her father's shoulder.

'She had rested just as you had instructed. Why did she lose the baby? We have been trying desperately for months. It was only a few weeks in!' The despairing words flew from Richard's mouth.

'The Lord only knows why these things happen. It was better for Annabelle that it was at this very early stage. Believe me, Richard; it could have been far more detrimental to Annabelle's health if it had been later in her pregnancy. She will need you to be strong.' The doctor's face expressed past anguish and pain.

'Better? That's my baby you are referring to. Wasn't there something you could have done? You're the doctor! God damn it!' He paused, desperate to remain composed. 'Well the Lord can jolly well explain to my wife why she has lost the one thing that meant more to her than...well, even me.'

'Richard, now there was nothing I...'

'This was our baby, and that is my wife lying up there,' Richard shouted, as his anger grew to full velocity.

'Now, Richard, you must keep your voice down.'

'Does she know, does Annabelle know it's lost?'

'Yes she knows, she already knew, before I knew. She knew it was gone, and there was nothing to be done.'

'Will you stop referring to our baby as 'it'? Have you no decency at all?' he demanded. 'And I will not keep my voice down,' he stated, as he indeed lowered the volume of his outburst. He looked at the doctor with pleading eyes.

Dr Hickson had been the family's doctor before Annabelle and Emily were born, and therefore had been with Rose, the girls' mother, through both her pregnancies. The stress and memory of that loss as well, was very apparent on his ageing features. Dr Hickson turned to leave the room.

'I shall see myself out. I shall return early in the morning.'

The doctor left, leaving the grief stricken household behind him.

All was still in the house, the atmosphere thick with misery. The cool air of the late hour travelled as they sat silent at the dining table. The cold teapot stood on the tray before them, their cups full and untouched.

Nothing could be said. Nothing could be done.

Remember to love me

Richard

April awoke to the sound of clinking china. She opened her eyes to find her grandmother pouring two cups of tea. The large tray complete with bone china tea set sat on the table before her. Sarah perched on her large winged chair, leaning forward to serve the tea. She raised her head and their eyes met.

'All that shopping must have really exhausted you.'

'How long have I been asleep, Nan?' April sat upright as she leant forward to retrieve her teacup.

'Not long, maybe half an hour. I gave your Mum a call at the shop, just to let her know we were home.'

From her grandmother's voice, it was obvious that she had called to inform her of the incident in the jewellery shop.

'Oh...what...what did she say?' responded April with an uneasy tone.

'Well, she thinks you should take it easy. Perhaps you've over exerted yourself lately, or maybe you're coming down with something.'

'Nan, what do you think?' April wasn't sure how her grandmother was going to react. Did she know what had really happened in the jewellery shop, and what about in the attic the other day? Nothing was said for a few moments. Sarah continued to attend to the pot of tea, arranging the china items on the tray, searching for the right words. April sat back on the settee, the gold silk cushion once again cradling her head. She pondered on the strange dream, if that's what it was, the total sadness of its contents. She could still feel the desperation and agony in the pit of her stomach.

'Nan, I need to talk to you. About something...well, I just need to talk to you.' The words had spurted from April's mouth before she realised.

'A good idea, but maybe later. First, I have something I think you want to see.'

Sarah got to her feet and disappeared out of the front room door. April sat motionless; all energy had drained from her body. Tentatively, she closed her eyelids and her head relaxed. She recalled the bizarre events of the day.

Why?

Why was she having these strange visions, if that was what they were? Was it just her imagination, or did they mean something? April lay weak with fatigue, desperately trying not to fall asleep again, the last dream being so disturbing she didn't care for another.

Sarah soon returned, carrying a large, creamy leather jewellery case. April opened her eyes; they sat together on the red velvet upholstery.

'Nan, your jewellery, I'd completely forgotten about it.' Her eyes lit up, her expression as total contrast to her previous anxiety.

'Do you know, I haven't had this case out of the cupboard for years, probably since the last time you looked when you were very small.' A nostalgic smile appeared on Sarah's face. A tiny key hung from a red cord, tied to one of the brass handles, which were secured either side of the leather case. The case was almost square and slightly larger than a chocolate tin, the sort you have at Christmas full of toffee and caramel filled delights. The tiny key was inserted into the brass lock, the large lid opened to reveal an incredible array of glittering antiquities.

April was entranced by the glamour of the jewels. Long, hand-knotted strings of perfect cultured pearls, with their lustrous sheen, lay entwined with equally splendid lengths of glowing amber beads. Both were reminiscent of those worn by Flappers in the roaring twenties, swinging to and fro, as they danced the Charleston. One of the compartments accommodated an Art Deco bracelet; round brilliant cut rubies sat stationed between incredibly large baguette diamonds, all expertly set in what April imagined was platinum with its distinctive icy glamour. As she lifted it from the case, it glistened in the light reflected from the crackling fire and twinkling Christmas lights.

'This is amazing!'

'My mother wore that on her wedding day in…it must have been around 1924. Yes, she was just twenty-three. It was a wedding gift from her mother, my grandmother.'

'My great-great grandmother, the beautiful fair haired lady in the photograph?' announced April.

'Yes, Annabelle.'

'Annabelle was my great-great-grandmother!' April sat her eyes fixed to the ruby and diamond bracelet she held in her hand. The concept ran wild in April's mind.

'Yes. You did know the young blonde lady was your great-great grandmother, didn't you?' Sarah reached into the case and pulled out a leather drawstring pouch.

'Yes, of course I knew we spoke about it, that day I saw the photo frame.' April just hadn't given it much thought that *Annabelle* was her great-great-grandmother. Was the vision correct and true? Was it history or a made up event from the depth of April's own imagination?

Sarah gently pulled the cords of the leather pouch and tipped out its contents into her other hand. A shiny gold watch and long heavy Albert chain lay in her palm.

'This pocket watch belonged to Captain Charles Warner, my great grandfather. He was an elegant and proud gentleman, very sophisticated.' Sarah's eyes surveyed the antique gold pocket watch.

'There, look on the back, his initials.' In fine scrolled engraving were the letters CW. April leaned over towards her grandmother to take a closer look.

'Captain Warner, Annabelle's father?'

'Yes, she was a Warner until she married my grandfather.' April knew what was coming next: she had already *met* Richard.

'Yes, my grandfather, Richard Hardwick. He was quite a catch in his day, extremely handsome and came from a very well to do family.' Sarah was still admiring the pocket watch. She held it up in the afternoon light from the long gold watch chain; it dangled gloriously like a clock pendulum, glistening as the light caught it, whilst it swayed from side to side.

'Nan, what sort of family did Richard come from?' April was intrigued. Sarah jumped as April spoke as if becoming hypnotised by the movement of the watch.

'Well, I don't know a great deal about that side of the family. They were landowners and had a large country house a few miles from here. It had been in the family for generations. I think Richard Hardwick was either an architect or a solicitor something like that. My mother never seemed to be able to give me much more than that. She never really spoke about him at all, come to think of it.'

'Nan, what about Captain Warner and his wife?' enquired April, desperate to retrieve as much information on her ancestors from her grandmother's knowledge as possible.

'Well, my great-grandfather had joined the army when he was very young. He came from a comfortable family - however, not at all rich. He retired from the army after about twenty years or so and found employment as an engineer in a local business ... and that's when he married my great grandmother, Rose. Now, I think she was quite well educated, having gone to a private girls' school. Her family were very well off. Her father had made a lot of money from the factory that he owned up north. He and his wife had moved here when Rose was a small child. It was Captain Charles Warner who bought this house when they got married in the 1870s.'

'Wow, Nan, are there any photos of Captain Warner and the family from around that time?' April was excited at the thought, and although she knew she had never seen any, she still hoped.

Remember to love me

'I'm not sure if there are any that early. I hadn't seen my grandmother looking so young until I found that photo a few weeks ago. I have an idea, tomorrow is Christmas, and as a special treat, you can sit all afternoon and look through the albums. Your mum and dad will probably fall asleep after dinner anyway; it's their age, you know.' Both chuckled at the idea of them sleeping like festive bookends.

'That would be wonderful. I haven't seen your photos for years. It will be a real treat. Thanks, Nan.' April leant towards her grandmother and kissed her cheek.

'Well, you are my favourite granddaughter.' Both giggled again.

They continued rummaging in the depths of the jewellery case.

'Nan, do you have any brooches?' April passed her eyes across the contents.

'Let me see, maybe under here.' Sarah placed the watch back into its pouch, then lifted a tray from the middle of the case to expose a ring tray with almost more rings than the jeweller's window: rubies, emeralds and diamonds glinted in the glow from the fire. As the tray was lifted out, it revealed another compartment. April reached inside to retrieve a black, velvet cushion. A dozen or so brooches and pins were fastened to the fabric. April scrutinized each one. A brooch caught her eye. A large silver dragonfly with marcasite wings, tail, and a huge faceted claw set garnet. The gem glimmered with a blood red blaze in contrast to the antique silvery finish of the marcasite that surrounded it.

'This one is lovely, but do you have any cameo brooches Nan?' April scanned the view of brooches and pins.

'No, I don't think I do. Not in here anyhow. I may have one upstairs amongst my jewellery. Yes, I think I do. It's black onyx with mother of pearl engraved flowers.' Sarah looked at April. 'Would you like me to get it for you?'

'No, Nan, that's OK. But do you have any Wedgwood jewellery?' enquired April. Sarah looked slightly mystified at her granddaughter.

'Wedgwood jewellery? No definitely not, I do have a collection of Wedgwood, but no jewellery. I do really love Wedgwood, I always have. I remember, as a child, dusting my mother's collection of Wedgwood Jasperware vases….' Sarah developed a misty, glazed expression.

April left her to her reminiscing and continued to study the marvellous treasures. After a while of rummaging through the trinkets, April realised that there was no sign of the Wedgwood brooch. April searched through the bracelets, rings, and beads, however, there was nothing that caught her eye, no cameo and no charm bracelet.

April pondered for a time, searching through the jewels. There was no way she could keep it to herself. She had to tell her, ask her. April took a deep breath and gulped.

'Nan, do you know who the younger lady is in the photo, the beautiful one with the dark hair?' April slowly lifted her gaze from the stunning diamond and pearl earrings she was holding, to her grandmother's face.

'I did wonder how long it was going to be before you asked me again.' Sarah's voice was calm and had a matter of fact tone.

'Well Nan, do you know who she is? Do you know her name?' April already knew these answers but somehow, hearing her Nan give her the information, she hoped would make it real and not in her imagination. April still doubted her own experiences, her own judgment. The past few weeks had been so bizarre that she felt her whole world had been tipped upside down.

'Well, I'm afraid I don't really know much about her at all. I think she was Annabelle's sister. Apart from that, I have no more idea than you do.'

'Do you know her name, Nan? Are there any other photos of her?' April's voice was impatient.

'I don't know her name. I'm only guessing she's Annabelle's sister by the age and resemblance between them. I've never seen a photo of her before. Well, certainly not to my knowledge.'

April hesitated for a second as she studied her grandmother's expression. 'Her name was Emily and she *was* Annabelle's younger sister. Her hair was auburn like mine, and Annabelle's was very blonde. They were both very beautiful.' April knew how ridiculous the words must have seemed. Transfixed onto her grandmother's features, April waited for a response.

'Ah, Emily,' responded Sarah.

'Yes, Nan, I think those things you found up in the attic were hers. I think she was ERW, Emily Warner I'm not sure what the R stands for though.' April's voice was certain; she spoke adamantly and with conviction. There was a short pause.

'Ah, maybe the R stands for Rose,' announced Sarah.

'Rose?' asked April.

'Yes. My mother was Rose and I imagine she may have been named after her Aunt. It was the sort of thing that happened in families, names would be passed on, generation after generation.'

'Well it certainly makes sense, because if she is Annabelle's sister then her mother's name was Rose, wasn't it? But…Nan, I know this is going to sound as if I've lost my marbles but…' April hesitated once again. Her grandmother's expression was normal and not at all surprised, as April assumed it would be.

'Nan, the thing is…'

Then Sarah interrupted, 'I know, you don't need to tell me. You've seen her, haven't you? You saw Emily, that afternoon you were in the attic looking through her belongings. You saw her then, didn't you? It's OK, you can tell me.' She clasped April's hand with reassurance.

April sat paralysed for a moment, it was not quite the response she had expected. Unable to move or react, April just sat for a minute of two, contemplating the situation.

'Nan, did you see her too?'

'Well, the day I was clearing out and having a general tidy up, I did see something. But it was getting dark and maybe my eyesight isn't what it used to be, you know?'

'Nan, you know as well as I do that there's nothing wrong with your eyesight. It's as good as mine! But did you see her?' April was getting almost impatient, with desperation in her words.

'As I say, it was getting dark and I just felt a little strange. It was over very quickly, but I felt so odd after that. Not frightened, mind, just a bit giddy and a headache that I couldn't shift.' April and her grandmother sat looking at each other for what seemed an age. Neither really knowing what else to say, April took a gulp.

'Nan, that's not all! Yes, I did see Emily in the attic, she was so beautiful, and she smiled at me. Was she a ghost? I mean, of course she was a ghost… I mean, oh, I don't know what I mean any more. Everything has been so strange lately. I haven't just seen Emily. Well, what I mean is… I haven't seen any more ghosts but I have seen…' April was getting more flustered with each word, and even more frustrated with herself, as she struggled to make any sense.

She took a deep breath and closed her eyes. The heat from her grandmother's hand still clutching hers, created warmth that spread through her whole body. The glint from the Christmas tree lights glowed through April's eyelids. The sound of the mantle clock ticked inside her head, creating its own rhythm. Slowly, she opened her eyes and looked straight at her grandmother with concentration.

'I've been having dreams, but not like normal dreams. They are as real as if I'm really there. I can feel the sun and smell the flowers; even the feelings are real. I don't really understand. I'm dreaming about a family that I don't know anything about. I'm not sure if it's all made up or what? Nan, I think... I think I'm going mad!' Tears were building in April's eyes. Desperately trying not to cry, she looked away and fixed her gaze upon the Christmas tree.

'Everything's going to be just fine and dandy. I don't know why you are having these dreams, but we need to keep a clear head. I'm sure there's a reason for all this. Perhaps it was meant to be. Perhaps…' Sarah hesitated for a few seconds then continued with a jovial tone. 'Well, I don't know…a haunted house! Well I never!' She smiled and winked at her granddaughter.

April knew full well that she wasn't making light of the subject and was just trying to ease its uncomforting mood. April had the most unusual thought cross her mind. Not sure whether to share it with her grandmother or not, a small smile crept up on her mouth.

'Nan, Richard Hardwick. He really was the most perfect man I've ever seen - really tall, dark and handsome. He had incredible green eyes and perfect skin. I had the oddest feeling when I saw him. Well, what I mean, y'know, in my dreams.' A beaming grin consumed April's features; the words had left her mouth before she'd time to think about what she was saying. Sarah said nothing; she just smiled. April had a sudden rush of reality run though her spine, wiping the grin from her face and replacing it with an expression of embarrassment. Sharply she stood, uneasily straightening her clothes, running her fingers through her hair.

'I think I'll go home and have a bath. I'll be back with Mum and Dad later ready for dinner.' April took the few short steps over to where her coat and bags lay and grabbed them, coyly smiling at her grandmother as she opened the front door. 'I love you Nan.'

April closed the glossy black door behind her.

* * *

The fragrant scent of bath salts and warm steamy air filled the bathroom. She lay submerged beneath the soapy foam; the warmth and softness of the water relaxed every muscle and bone in her body, cleansing away the uneasiness of the day's events.

April contemplated the conversation she'd had with her grandmother, soothed by the fact that she'd shared it with her, no longer needing to keep it to herself. Although her response had not been quite as April had expected, the fact that she didn't react with any shock to April having seen a ghost - or the dreams, that to April, were not so much dreams but recalled memories. Memories of a past that she knew nothing of, a family that she knew very little about, and this was her family.

Then, as suddenly and surprisingly as before, April's mind wandered in reflection of the tall physique, perfect skin, dark hair and elegant character of Richard Hardwick. His handsome image imposed itself onto her mind, inscribing each detail into her mind's eye. April's heart beat rapidly beneath her skin, a fluttering of butterfly wings in the depth of her stomach, she couldn't shift the sight of his features from her head.

She'd never had this feeling before; no one had ever come close to having such an effect of her, even though she was a young woman, soon to turn twenty-one, romance never ranked high on her list of importance. However, Richard, unlike any guy from Cambridge, was a man, a real man, tall and graceful. Was this how infatuation felt; was it a crush or something more? How could she know? Men had certainly caught her eye before, of course they had, but their appeal and attraction had only ever lasted a few days; her mind had always wandered off to more crucial concerns, study, her love of history and books.

There was no doubting the contrast of priorities between April and friends, they were obsessed by the very idea of boys, how good they looked, what car they drove, how much money they had, and of course, inevitably, sex. Some, she knew, were engaged or planning weddings. Well, the ideal to her was of romance and commitment, probably a result of her parents' idealistic views. Nevertheless, she stood by it. In her heart, she was saving herself for the one, the love of her life, her soul mate.

Was she so naive, young in her heart?

Was this now changing? If she was now becoming a woman, with needs and longings, surely the stunningly handsome Richard was the perfect one to awaken these urges.

April pondered on this, the thought of how good it would feel to have the softness of his lips on hers, the heat of his breath and smell of his skin, strong arms wrapped round her body, the tightness and the closeness. Richard, was he the one?

April sat bolt upright, shook her head, and took a deep breath.

What was she thinking?

Richard Hardwick was indeed a man, a gorgeously handsome, elegant gentle man, with all the essential qualities of a first love, even a lover, or more. However, he was gone; he was from another time, another era, a ghostly memory from the past…long gone. Most of all, he was April's great-great grandfather. The whole thing was completely bizarre!

Ludicrous and unthinkable!

On pulling the plug from the bath, she snuggled into her fluffy bathrobe and left the steamy environment that was now clouding her senses and judgement. She headed across the hall and opened her bedroom door.

Almost throwing herself onto her bed, she was still desperately trying to shift Richard's image from her brain. She reached for the silver and mother of pearl photo frame from a small chest of drawers nearby. Lying tightly wrapped within the softness of her robe, she clutched the sepia vision of her ancestors, Emily and Annabelle. The cosy bed beneath her was comfortable and inviting. April closed her eyes and quickly drifted off to sleep.

* * *

In Warner family Christmas Eve tradition, all gathered to watch as Captain Warner reached high, placing the heirloom festive angel on the top of the huge tree. Protruding pine needles prodded his chest as he stretched to reach the top branch.

'This is going to be the best Christmas, I do so love Christmas Eve, it is for sure my most favourite day of the year,' chanted Emily as she jumped on the spot with excitement. 'I love Christmas,' she sang.

Annabelle laughed. 'Not forgetting your wedding day. I do believe we shall have snow tomorrow, so even more magical, I feel. You shall have the most enchanting wedding day anyone could wish for.' Annabelle sweetly leant over towards Emily and squeezed her hand.

'Annabelle, I can't wait to marry James! He is the most...well...wonderful man,' whispered Emily; her voice was filled with delight and excitement as she squeezed her sister's hand in return.

Captain Warner turned to face his family with a joyful smile and festive sentiment.

'There, the angel is on the tree and all is complete. This will be a wonderful festive season with my beautiful daughter's wedding. I do believe I shall be gaining a son rather than losing a daughter.' He looked over at Emily and James with sheer pleasure in his eyes. 'And I'm sure the New Year will bring us hope and maybe a new addition to the family.' Switching his gaze to Annabelle and Richard, they both smiled in return. 'We shall say goodbye to the old and welcome in the arrival of the New Year. 1900 is sure to be a year of changes for us all. A toast, I think?'

The Captain raised his cut crystal glass of mulled wine; the family raised theirs in return. Settled on a polished side table, an oval serving plate, piled high with warm mince pies, oozing with soft plump fruit and dusted with icing sugar; the festive smell of pies and potent spicy mulled wine enhanced the merriment.

'Merry Christmas,' they sang in joyful chorus and sipped the warm spicy beverage, warming them to the core.

Emily eased herself closer to her fiancé James, as they stood near the enormous Christmas tree. Between the fragrant pine needles hung large colourful glass baubles, that glistened with the reflection of the fire.

Lance Corporal James Wright of the West Suffolk Regiment's Second Battalion, was a gentle soul of twenty-five years, the only son and heir of a local family. The Wrights owned a thriving bakery and grocery shop in the market town, founded by an ancestor in the latter part of the 18th century. The family were comfortable, which Emily's father regarded as apt and suitable. James was gracious, had a strong mind, and was of noble intentions. His attractive features were youthful, almost boyish; his complexion was fresh and fair, with a sprinkling of warm freckles, and eyes of bright blue and hair straw blond that held a slight wave. James was tall, carrying a height of over six feet, and muscular in build, which gave him a dominating presence.

The outbreak of War in South Africa earlier in the year had created a real threat. With this hanging over their heads, the wedding had been brought forward to the 27th of December. The whole family were keeping a continued optimistic view of the situation. The First Battalion had already been mobilised and sent to the Cape in early November, with growing fears of the inevitability that more troops would be needed.

'Emily, how about a Christmas carol? You do play so wonderfully,' requested her father. Emily headed over to the piano and gracefully seated herself. Her rich, dark blue dress hung demurely to the carpet, covering the legs of the piano stool. The piano had sat in position along the end wall for as long as the sisters could remember. Stories of how their mother had sat and played, the romance of their mother and father in happy times, filled their memories.

'What shall we sing?'

'As we know you sing so beautifully and your playing is so accomplished, I'm sure we would all love you to play what ever pleases you,' replied her father with full agreement from the rest of the room. Emily positioned herself ready, coughed sweetly, straightened her long cuffs, and stretched her fingers.

'Very well, Silent Night,' she declared, as she opened the piano lid and glided her fingers over the ivory keys. The sweet melody, the pure clarity of her voice travelled the festive room. Spirits high, all worries of war dispersed as the space overflowed with joy and optimism. Emily's clear and delicate tone evoked recollections of previous, wonderful Christmases, and inspired positive thoughts of the approaching new century.

Becky Byford

Annabelle and Richard clutched hands as they stood beside the large fireplace. The logs in the hearth crackled and hissed, casting a rich ambience to the front room. Richard turned and kissed her cheek, trailing his lips over her warm skin, and wrapping his arm around her waist his hand gently caressing her back. He gazed longingly into her hazel eyes.

'I do believe that this coming year will bring us bliss and contentment, my dearest Belle...You mean the world to me, you know that, don't you, everything to me.' His voice trembled as he took hold of her hand; Annabelle squeezed it with hers as she looked down at his palm.

'I do believe you are holding my heart right here.' She ran her thumb across his palm, her delicate fingers barely reaching round his large, masculine hand. She looked at his hand, remembering the first time she touched it, how it had stirred every emotion in her body, her soul exploding with a new sensation, a new awareness to her body, nothing she had ever felt before.

'Well then, my Belle, my Belle of the ball. This must mean that you are mine, to do with as I please,' Richard whispered the words lightly into her ear.

She blushed.

'I think you will find, that I have belonged to you since the first time you touched my hand.' Her face was burning from the heat of the fire and the emotions that bubbled inside her. 'How could any woman have resisted those green eyes?'

'No other woman has ever been offered them, never having the inclination to offer myself before I met you.'

He added, 'I have a very special Christmas gift I would like to give you, but in private,' his emerald eyes glinted as he winked.

Annabelle, taking a deep breath as her heart pounded with the memory of that first encounter answered, 'I shall delight in it I am sure. I would give you the world if you should wish for it, darling.'

'Belle, I shall only ever wish for you. You are my world.'

Remember to love me

Revelations

It was half past six before April awoke, still wrapped in the cosy warmth of her bathrobe.

'You ready for dinner, sweetheart?' called Julia from outside the door. April jumped, sat upright, and looked over at the brass carriage clock on her dressing table.

'Nearly! Give me about fifteen minutes, Mum?' she replied, flustered. She hadn't realised she had fallen asleep. Now, thoroughly dry from the soft snug comforts of her robe, she hunted through the contents of her wardrobe, searching for something suitable, something perfect to wear for dinner. Christmas Eve dinner was a traditional affair; dressing up was a must, a necessity!

From a very small child, she could always remember the importance of the correct attire, the perfect festive outfit. They would arrive at Nan's early Christmas Eve; lunch and evening dinner would both require a separate outfit, a long sparkling, glitzy dress of luxurious fabric for the latter. The following two days were no different, more resplendent if anything. She loved it, the dressing up, and the family indulged in this eccentricity.

In addition to dinner, tonight at eleven thirty, they were going to attend the Christmas service at the Cathedral. This was something April had always longed to do. To hear the angelic voices of the choir, the Christmas carols travelling and filling every part of the elaborate building. She was not what you would regard as religious, but did feel that at this time of year it held a sort of requirement, an instinctive need that she felt inside, not an effect of her upbringing so much as an inherited must.

Deep within her clothes at the back of the wardrobe, she found the perfect outfit. April pulled out a pair of black satin trousers; beautifully cut and embellished with sparkly crystals down the side of each leg.

Next to the trousers, hung a stunning black velvet top. It was long, with slits both sides, and long flowing sleeves. The tunic had contrasting metallic silver thread embroidered along the bottom edge. The deep 'V' neckline complemented her pale skin. She dressed in her black evening attire and finished off with a pair of new black suede boots, high heeled, pointed and elegant: an adult, more mature contrast to the satin party dresses she'd worn as a child, but still, she thought, as appropriate.

April reclaimed the silver and mother of pearl photo frame from her bed and returned it to the chest of drawers.

'Almost ready, April?' called Michael, from outside in the hallway.

'Nearly, I'll be ready in a moment, I promise,' she replied, straightening her bed linen.

April stood in front of her mirror, combed her hair, and brushed a little colour onto her cheeks and a dab of gloss to her lips.

A large silver jewellery chest sat central on her dressing table. Opening the lid, she retrieved a pair of shiny silver drop earrings; large onyx teardrops surrounded and suspended by sparkly marcasite. The earrings complemented her long red tresses, and shone beneath her locks in blinding flashes of light between the flowing auburn strands.

April closed the door behind her, and headed down to the lounge.

'Got everything, sweetheart? Are we ready to go?' I thought we'd take the presents over tonight and put them under your Nan's tree, ready. What do you think?' Julia asked April, as she pulled the long heavy cream curtains, shutting out the cold dark evening.

'That's a great idea Mum…oh, no!' April dashed for the door.

'What is it?'

'Nothing, I'll be back in a min. Nothing's wrong, I just forgot to wrap the last of the presents I got today, that's all.' Her words faded from earshot, she was already half way up the stairs before she finished her sentence. She ran through the door, grabbing her shopping bag on the way in. Quickly, but perfectly April wrapped her last minute gifts in metallic silver and gold swirl paper with small red bows.

The festivities were at their height. As they entered the Victorian house, Christmas carols enchanted the space with a spellbinding charm. At the far end of the front room, near the piano, sat a small mahogany cabinet, which secretly accommodated a stereo system: too modern in appearance to be on show, it resided within the traditional feature.

A sweet, potent aroma filled the room. On the polished table sat a tray. A huge silver tray only used during the festive season, engraved with garlands of holly and ivy around the edge. It was adorned with Yuletide treats: deep-filled mince pies, a small frosted bowl of dates, and a matching glass vessel of brazil nuts and walnuts.

Central on the tray was the large steamy bowl of sweet and spicy mulled wine, slices of orange floated on the surface, with four cut crystal glasses.

'Anyone fancy some mulled wine? Dinner is going to be ready at eight o'clock sharp, so we have time to sit and enjoy a treat first.' Sarah took her seat in her usual winged chair as she reached over to the crystal glasses. Julia and Michael sat on the settee between the Christmas tree and the crackling open fireplace. April positioned herself opposite her grandmother in her favourite spot.

'Mmm, mulled wine, it smells intoxicating, Sarah. You'll have us all thrown out of the church for being drunk and disorderly!' Michael chuckled as he reached for a date.

'Not too much wine! Just one bottle, some orange juice, and the traditional spices, it must be the splash of brandy I put in that you can smell!' she replied.

'A *splash* of brandy, Nan - are you sure it wasn't the whole drinks cabinet?' April took her glass from the tray and sipped it. Alcohol wafted from the wine to April's nose.

'My goodness Mum. Well, that's warmed me up although I'm not sure I should have too much or I will be utterly drunk and very disorderly!'

They all sat, sipping the mulled wine and listening to the beautiful, choir-sung Christmas carols. The perfect Christmas Eve. April sat back on the soft, velvety upholstery and watched her family, as the twinkling of the tree lights and the mesmerizing glow from the fire bewitched the room with their magic.

April scanned her eyes around the Christmas filled space, the large open fireplace and surround, that housed the old gilt mantle clock. She blinked in disbelief; there, for a moment, stood Richard Hardwick, close by the crackling fire, sipping his own spicy mulled wine, his long elegant fingers holding the cut crystal, as he lifted it to his full soft lips. His bright green eyes twinkled as he smiled in her direction; his dashing elegant looks enthralled her mind once again.

April stood up sharply, almost dropping her glass as she did so.

'What on earth's the matter?' gasped Julia, as she dashed over to retrieve the glass from her daughter's shaking hand.

'I'm so sorry, Nan. I nearly broke the glass. I'm fine Mum. It's OK, it was just… oh, nothing.' April felt extremely embarrassed at the thought. Her heart was still beating rapidly under her black velvet tunic. Butterflies were once again fluttering madly inside her stomach. She had goose bumps up her spine and tingled all over. With a swirling head and repeated flashes of his image, she fell back on the settee.

'It's all right, the glass is perfectly fine and there is no harm done. But are you OK?' Her grandmother had an almost knowing expression on her face. This didn't, however, make April feel any less embarrassed. Not only could she not stop thinking about Richard Hardwick, but she now imagined she was seeing him too.

The clock that resided on the mantle piece chimed the hour. Eight o'clock.

'There, I think dinner is ready. Come! Let's go into the dining room.' April followed her grandmother through the hallway and into the room, where the most delightful Christmas table was laid ready. Julia and Michael took their seats at opposite sides of the impressive mahogany table. April pulled out the chair near her mother; still slightly shaking, she sat down on the rose pink upholstery.

The view of the garden, visible by day through the glass doors, now reflected April like a mirror. It was almost impossible to see, outside the darkness was dense and thick, only the reflection of the dining room interior with its large chandelier brightly lit. April looked closer into the glass, past her reflection.

'Oh, it's snowing!' April left her seat and darted over to the glass doors. She unlocked and slowly opened one of the doors. She took a deep breath and the cool frosty air filled her lungs. Large, soft snowflakes drifted down to the ground.

The grey stone steps, which led down into the garden, were quickly transformed into a glistening white carpet, which had soon covered the whole garden. It brightened the entire view with its reflective finish: the sky, pale and full of snow clouds, the atmosphere thick with frosty flakes. It was the perfect finish to a most strange day and the perfect beginning to a wonderful Christmas.

Michael dimmed the bulbs on the chandelier with the brass switch on the wall. He returned to the table and, striking a long match, lit the new wicks. A display of five tall church candles, and an abundance of the greenest ivy and holly complete with red berries, in the centre of the mahogany dining table. The centrepiece twinkled in the dim light with Yuletide cheer.

'Come, April, dinner is served.' Sarah had adorned the table with a Christmas feast fit for royalty. April closed the glass door on the glorious snowy scene. She returned to the dining table and took her seat next to her mother, opposite her grandmother.

Dinner was indeed served. Each had a warmed plate graced with succulent, carved roast beef and two enormous Yorkshire puddings. Either side of the candle display were large pristine white china serving dishes, and large silver serving spoons, roast potatoes, steaming mashed swede, buttered sprouts and julienne carrots. A large gravy boat on its own china plate and a pair of antique silver salt and pepper servers sat next to a small dish of horseradish sauce.

'Well, I have never seen such an incredible feast, Sarah. You've excelled yourself, it all smells so amazing.' Michael took hold of a long handled serving spoon and started to dish everyone some roast potatoes.

'Come on, let's tuck in before it gets cold. There's plenty to go round. And don't forget the dessert.' Sarah stood up to reach the dish of swede. The table was so large and dominating, and impossible to reach from a seated position. She winked in approval as April also stood up and passed her the dish.

It was the most incredible dinner. After every sprout and Yorkshire pudding had been consumed, they all sat back in their rose pink upholstered chairs with total delight and satisfaction.

'The most delicious meal, Mum, thanks; it was wonderful. There really isn't anything quite like your cooking.'

'It was fantastic,' announced Michael.

'It was rather lovely, wasn't it? Now before we have dessert, I have a special Christmas gift for everyone.' Gracefully, Sarah rose from her chair and walked over to the large sideboard along the far wall of the dining room. She opened a long drawer and lifted out three small boxes, each beautifully wrapped in shiny metallic red paper tied with golden ribbon. As she sat back down at the table, she carefully moved her plate to one side and placed the boxes in front of her.

'Now, Michael, this one is for you. You are like a son to me and have always been there when I've needed you. I've always been extremely grateful, even if I haven't showed it; I understand I can be very stubborn. This is just a little something to say thank you and Merry Christmas.' She handed Michael a beautifully wrapped present. 'Please open it; these are to be opened tonight.'

'Thank you.' Michael looked stunned as he took the box. With care, he un-wrapped the red paper to reveal a small, dark green leather box. Slowly, he lifted the lid. Inside on the green velvet sat an antique gold watch fob. Ornate scrollwork embellished the large charm, an oval blood red garnet, faceted and claw set, stationed at the bottom of the fob.

'I do hope you like it; it belonged to my great-grandfather. It was handed down to me from my mother; I thought it should now go to you. You are as dear to me as any son could be.'

'Sarah, it is splendid. It will look particularly elegant on my pocket watch. Thank you.' Michael leant over and kissed his mother-in-law on the cheek. Sitting back on his seat, he looked admiringly at his special gift. The garnet reflected magnificent deep red hues in the candlelight as well as in his amazed eyes.

'Now, this one is for you, Julia. You are the most wonderful daughter any mother could ask for. You have always made me proud. I love you so much. It is so lovely to have you back here close to me. Merry Christmas.'

Julia reached over and took the gift from her mother. She unwrapped it revealing a small black velvet drawstring pouch. Gracefully, with her long painted fingernails, she pulled the strings to open the pouch and tipped the contents into her hand. There, in her palm lay a beautiful gold necklace, set with a large pear cut amethyst, surrounded by brilliant diamonds.

Becky Byford

'Mum, it's incredible. I don't know what to say.' Julia sat stunned by the sparkle and beauty of the gems.

'I've always known that you loved it. It was a gift from my mother on my twenty-first birthday. Now, I'm giving it to you. I know that you will treasure it, just as I have.'

'I shall always treasure it. It's simply stunning. Oh Merry Christmas, Mum, I love you so much.' Julia skipped round the table giving her mother the biggest hug, lavishing kisses on her cheek.

'Now, as you are my most favourite granddaughter, I have something very special for you.' Sarah reached across the mahogany table to her granddaughter, handing her a long wrapped present. April eased off the golden ribbon and pulled the shiny paper away from the box. There before her lay a red leather box, long with gold inlay around the edge. April moved her dinner plate and rested the box upon the table in front of her.

'Nan, I don't know what to say,' she said, shaking her head.

'Of course you don't know what to say, you haven't opened it yet,' replied Sarah, as she gestured to the long box. 'Well, open it, the suspense is killing your mum and dad.'

Her parents were both looking with impatience at April and the gift in front of her. She took hold of the box and lifted the lid, its long hinge squeaked slightly as it revealed its contents. April sat transfixed as she gazed in amazement at the treasure held within. She looked up and her eyes met her grandmother's.

'When I found it, I just knew it was yours! It's a special Christmas gift to celebrate you being back here where you belong - a sort of coming of age gift, if you like.' Sarah's face beamed with jovial delight, as she clasped her hands together and pressed them close to her lips, in waiting anticipation.

'But, Nan…' April didn't quite know what to say. Her heart leapt inside her ribcage and a stirring sensation began in the pit of her stomach, for what lay before her was the most beautiful thing she had ever seen. Something she had seen before, but this was the gift she never expected to be receiving. April reached inside the box and took hold of the silver piece.

The heavy silver artwork draped across her hand, the substantial links of the bracelet were adorned with numerous silver charms. An oval silver and mother of pearl charm, an onyx set cross, and an opal set heart were amongst the most incredible abundance of charms: shoes, keys, fans and musical instruments, every shape of charm she had ever seen. Truly, the most wondrous piece of jewellery, far more splendid than April could ever have imagined it to be.

'It was my grandmother's. It now belongs to you April. Merry Christmas.' Sarah looked at April; her eyes twinkled in the candle glow as she winked.

'Oh, Nan, I can't believe it. It's Annabelle's charm bracelet.' April's eyes filled, the emotion that had been churning in her depths exploded, and she burst into a flood of tears.

'No, it is your charm bracelet. It belongs to you,' answered Sarah; she too had a multitude of tears in her eyes.

April composed herself, wiping her face with her napkin. Numerous thoughts spread the expanse of her brain. She felt excited and confused; she was holding Annabelle's bracelet. Where had it been for all these years? Questions sprung from her lips.

'Where was it, I didn't know you had it? It wasn't in your jewellery case was it? I know I would have remembered seeing it.' April was still stunned and extremely emotional, the rambling words spat from her lips and tears from her eyes. She took a deep breath. She sat gazing upon her treasure.

'I found it in the leather case with the photo frame. I knew then that you must have it.' Sarah got to her feet and wandered around the table.

'Here, let me put it on you.' She took the piece of jewellery from April's palm and fastened the silver charm bracelet around April's wrist. The strangest feeling came upon her, a now familiar feeling. Her body trembled and her ears fell numb, as goose bumps crawled across her skin. With tear-covered cheeks, she laid her head back on her high backed chair and clenched her eyes tightly shut.

Snow had indeed fallen through the night. Christmas morning was crisp and glistened with a crystal carpet. The bright sky cast a blinding glow over all. The landscape was frosty and twinkled with a magical charm. Beyond the large garden wall, family tombs and gravestones each wore a white veil, and the trees that lined the graveyard bore heavy branches of snowflakes, where once were flourishing green leaves.

She stood close to the glass door, gazing upon the enchanting view; the outside chill penetrated the glass, making her shiver. The icy panes steamed periodically with the warmth of her breath. The lavish dark green moiré silk of her dress elegantly draped to the floor, the long sleeves and high neckline perfect for this bitter Christmas morning.

'Merry Christmas, my darling,' announced Richard, as he entered the dining room. She stood unmoving, seemingly unaware of his arrival, her sight fixed on the breathtaking landscape. Her long blonde hair cascaded, covering the most part of her silk covered back. He stood behind her.

'Close your eyes.' Richard spoke softly in her ear, folding his arms around hers, and holding a long red leather box detailed with gold inlay along the edge. She closed her eyes tight as instructed. He held the box in front of her, his strong muscular arm encased her whole body; his tall stature towered above her petite build.

'Merry Christmas, Belle, open your eyes.' Richard lifted the lid of the box in front of her.

'My dearest Richard, it is the most beautiful thing I have ever seen!' Her voice filled with exhilaration at the sight, the most dazzling vision.

'Nothing can match your beauty, but it is lovely.' He kissed her pale cheek. 'Here, let me put it on you.' He took the silver charm bracelet from its velvety bed and fastened it around her petite wrist.

April opened her eyes. The family sat around the table with concerned faces. She sat, motionless and transfixed on her grandmother's eyes for a few seconds, then she wiped the tears from her cheeks.

'I'm OK, just very overwhelmed; it is such a beautiful bracelet. Thank you, Nan.' April smiled at her grandmother who knew instinctively it was time to change the subject.

'Well now, who's ready for some dessert? There's raspberry pavlova, homemade of course, none of that shop bought stuff, or sherry trifle.' Sarah stood up and started to gather the empty plates and cutlery.

'I think I shall have the pavlova. Any more alcohol and I shall be unable to stand up, Mum.' Julia tentatively eased herself up from her chair to help clear the table.

'That sounds delicious; I think I shall have that too,' declared Michael. He collected the serving dishes and followed his wife and mother-in-law into the kitchen.

April remained, planted in her mahogany dining chair. The silver charm bracelet shone in the candlelight. She was amazed and astounded by her Christmas gift, and still very emotional; once again, she had seen the image of Richard Hardwick, his gracious character, his love, and devotion to Annabelle.

April closed her eyes, laid back on her chair, her head rested upon the polished mahogany. She longed for the picture of Richard to impress itself on her mind once again. Her heartbeat was pounding in her chest, her body tingled, her stomach fluttered, this new, but now familiar feeling, cocooned her being. She had no choice but to embrace it, she no longer had the strength or desire to resist these emotions.

The sensation and mood of the dining room had changed; she could no longer hear the clanking of pans and clinking of cutlery coming from the kitchen. The soft mellow choir-singing carols could no longer be heard from the stereo. A delicate sound of song was still coming from the front room, but it was not that of a choir, but a familiar female voice.

The lingering smell of roast beef and horseradish had also evaporated, replaced by the sweet aroma of a delicate perfume. April opened her eyes and rose from the dining table. She headed for the door. Passing through the room, she noticed it had also changed, but not knowing quite how. Somehow, the space was different, still festive but lighter, the view though the glass doors were still frosty, a blanket of snow, but it was brighter, as vivid as day.

She drifted into the front parlour; the familiar dulcet tone of Emily's voice filled the space and her ears.

'There you are, dearest Annabelle, isn't it wonderful? You were quite right, or course. The snow has such a magical feel.' Emily stood by the window, her back to the room as she fixed her eyes on the outside, onto the snow-covered footpath.

'Merry Christmas, dearest sister. Oh, your charm bracelet, isn't it beautiful? I helped Richard choose it; I knew how much you would love it. Although, I must say, he didn't really need my help; Richard knew exactly what to get you. Well dearest, do you love it?' Emily had turned to face her, and rushed over to grab her hands. Her excitement was apparent. 'Of course you do. I can't wait till after dinner! Are you coming outside with me? Let us go for a walk in the snow, under the trees and through the graveyard, as we did when we were very small. It has such an enchanting, magical feel.'

Emily jumped on the spot, her enthusiasm infectious.

'Of course, dear Emily, as when we were small.' April felt the words fall from her mouth before she could comprehend them.

'I love you so much, Merry Christmas.' Emily flung her arms around her in sheer happiness. April stood, motionless in amazement, not knowing what to do. Then, instinctively, her arms enfolded Emily in return; she squeezed her younger sister tightly. On closing her eyes, her lungs were engulfed with the sweet scent of her perfume. Time stood still, a wonderful, captivating moment, the epitome of love.

'Annabelle, what is it dearest, whatever is the matter?' Emily's eyes lingered on her sister's face. 'Oh darling, why are you crying? It's Christmas; there is absolutely nothing for you to be crying for. Whatever is it?' Emily took a white linen handkerchief from a concealed pocket in her long, red velvet dress. Gently, and with the utmost of tenderness, she brushed her sister's cheeks. The soft fabric of the finely embroidered handkerchief absorbed her tears.

'Emily darling, I love you.' The words sprung from her mouth, automatically. April felt that her whole body and soul were drenched in emotion; she had no control over the situation, or her actions. Once again, she tossed her arms around Emily and held her tight. 'I love you Emily, my darling.'

April stood central in the festive parlour, her arms tightly wrapped around her sister, her whole being utterly consumed by this intense, unbelievable and unexplainable feeling, her heart felt fit to burst.

'Oh my God!' April shouted, she opened her eyes and jumped out of her chair. 'No, this isn't happening, it can't be real, I really am losing it, and I've gone totally mad!' April paced the dining room, up and down the richly patterned carpet.

'What's wrong?' Sarah walked back into the room, holding a large serving plate with an enormous raspberry pavlova. April turned to look at her, ashen faced and panic-stricken.

'My goodness, you look like a ghost! What on earth's wrong?' April's grandmother quickly abandoned the dessert on the table and rushed to grab her. She took hold of April and held her arms tight, fixing her to the spot.

'Nan, I think I've gone totally mad! I have finally lost it!' April stepped back from her grandmother with the most palest of faces, and an expression of sheer confusion.

'I'm sure you've *not* lost it, and you're *not* going mad. Just sit down and tell me what the matter is.' Sarah guided her back towards a dining room chair. She sat with her head in her hands, her long auburn hair draped over her knees. Her voice was muffled as she tried to explain.

'April! Sit up and tell me properly.' Sarah lifted her head up straight, swept her hair from her very pale complexion. April's face was wet, tear stained and fearful. She took a deep breath, closed her eyes for a moment, took another breath, and looked directly into her grandmother's eyes.

'Nan, I've just seen Emily. But, this time she wasn't a ghost! This time I think I was the ghost!'

'Oh, my dear granddaughter, how can you be a ghost? I don't understand.' She wiped April's tears with a napkin from the table. 'Now, you say you saw Emily again. Was she in here with you?' She gazed around the room, as if trying to find some paranormal evidence of a ghostly manifestation.

'No, Nan, she was in the front room, she was singing a Christmas carol whilst watching the snowfall outside the window. I heard her singing, so I went in there and she saw me. Oh, Nan...she was so beautiful. I held her in my arms. I could smell her sweet perfume. It was so real.' Once again, tears fell from her eyes. 'She saw my bracelet... I mean Annabelle's bracelet! She told me how she had helped Richard choose it. What's happening? I'm not sure, if I'm here or if I'm really there. I've spent most of today in another century. Nan, what's happening to me?' April dropped her head back onto her lap, sobbing.

'Well I think it may be time for a nice pot of tea.'

Tears fell from her chin, resting on her legs. 'What is a cup of tea going to do? How is that going to help?'

'Well, I'm not sure if it will help. But it is easier to think things through over a nice cup of tea. Now, you'd better wipe your face because you don't want your mum and dad to see you like this,' her grandmother replied, passing her the already wet napkin.

April raised her head and wiped her face. She had forgotten about her mum and dad; they had no idea of all the strange visions she had experienced.

'Let me do that, Nan?' April anticipated her grandmother's move. She got to her feet and took hold of the tea tray. The large serving plate that had exhibited the dessert was now empty, except for a few broken pieces of meringue and the odd raspberry that sat amongst the icing sugar.

'I'll help you, April,' stated Julia, as she too stood up.

'No Julia, that's OK, you washed up earlier. I'll go and help in the kitchen.' April caught sight of her grandmother's face, as she tried desperately to look occupied by the dessert bowls; they both left for the kitchen. Julia and Michael headed to settle themselves in the front room, where the Christmas carols were no longer playing.

'Mind if I change the CD, Mum?' Julia called from the hallway, as she passed the kitchen door.

'Of course, the Christmas ones are in the cupboard with the stereo.' She pushed the kitchen door too and turned to April.

'So, April, whilst we're alone, tell me again. You saw Emily in the front room?'

'Yeah, but I was in the dining room still. Nan, I never left the room. I *was* in the front room with her but…well, I know this sounds totally ridiculous, but, I suppose I dreamt I went into the front room although I *really* was there. Do you understand? I know it sounds mad!' April's voice was strained and tired.

Sarah remained silent for what seemed an age, and then she replied. 'I suppose if you say you were in the front room with Emily, then you *really* were there.'

'What? That's what I've been saying but it doesn't make any sense. I can't be in two places at the same time.' April felt extremely frustrated with both herself and the odd conversation.

'What I mean is, perhaps you had been there before. You were just reliving or remembering a memory, just as you've been remembering all day. I saw the look on your face earlier, when you were drinking your mulled wine.'

April said nothing. She guessed her grandmother had seen it in her expression. However, Richard Hardwick hadn't really been there, he was only a figment of her imagination. How could she be having these feelings for him, she'd never met him; he'd lived over a century ago. She became increasingly perplexed with each second that passed.

'I think, if we look hard enough, look at all the facts and look at it with a clear mind, I think we shall find exactly what this all means!' Her grandmother's statement put April slightly on edge. What on earth was she thinking now?

April carried on washing the dessert bowls and the delicate serving plate. Things were different between them, April was different; she felt herself getting frustrated with her grandmother, something that had never happened before. However, everything was different now. Strange and inexplicable.

'I think we need to start at the beginning! Then, look at everything, step by step. What do you think?' Placing her tea towel down onto the draining board, Sarah looked directly at April's confused face.

'Well, I suppose so.' April took a deep breath. What did she have to lose? She needed to do something, or she was going to go mad, or had she already done so?

'Well, it started in your attic when I looked through the box of things.' April calmed herself, and attempted to take a rational perspective on the odd situation.

'Yes. Yes, I knew that something strange was going to happen when I found it,' replied Sarah.

'Nan, what exactly did happen? Where was the box? I can't believe that you never knew it was there, that you'd never seen it before.' April questioned her grandmother; they had both stopped what they were doing and looked straight at each other.

'I think we need to sit down,' she answered very calmly.

They both took a seat at the small table in the centre of the large kitchen floor. The table was old and no bigger than three foot square and looked lost in such a vast space. It was covered in a blue and white checked cloth; the two chairs were plain wood with no upholstery. April sat with her head in her hands, elbows on the checked cloth, and sighed.

'Nan, you saw Emily that day, didn't you, why didn't you say something?'

Her head still in her hands, her voice was tired, not only by the strain of the situation but also by the lateness of the hour. She looked up and caught sight of the pine kitchen clock that hung on the wall above the door. It was now ten o'clock. This extraordinary day had been so far-fetched, so unthinkable, she was exhausted.

'I'm still not quite sure what I saw that day, it was rather dark. Well, as you know the windows don't give you much light at all up there. It was the day you moved here. I thought I'd go into the attic and fish out the Christmas decorations ready. I know how much you love Christmas trees. I thought I'd use the heirloom baubles. I haven't since you were very little. You know, the lovely jewel coloured glass ones.'

She started to reminisce, and her eyes wandered as she gazed into mid air, obviously recalling their festive glamour.

'Nan, what about the wooden crate?' April's voice was louder than before, to recapture her attention.

'I was moving some old boxes and I found it in the bottom of an old tea chest. I can honestly say I had never seen it before that moment. I took the crate and sat on the chaise longue, just as we did. When I found the photo frame...well, I was amazed; I'd never seen my grandmother looking so young. She was so incredibly beautiful wasn't she? But what really amazed me was the other photo. I didn't know who she was. I'd never seen her before. As I sat there, just gazing into the photos, I felt something, something strange, I went cold, and there she was. It was over very quickly. But, I am sure that it was the young girl from the photo.'

She looked at April, and smiled with some confirmation that her granddaughter wasn't crazy.

April was calmer; the fact that someone else had seen Emily did reassure her. But what about the dreams?

'Emily. She was very lovely, wasn't she, Nan.' April spoke steadily. Her voice was softer now.

'Yes, very lovely! Well, I was in so much shock, I ran out of the attic and down the stairs. I was still holding the frame so I put it in the hallway on one of the tables. For the next couple of days I felt her with me. I wasn't frightened, mind...I went back up into the attic the day your father came round. I was up there when he knocked on the door; it took me a few moments to get down the stairs and of course he'd started to worry. I told him straight I was only tidying the attic! Well, you can imagine his reaction! He said I should be slowing down at my age and taking it easy. Really...anyone would think I was getting old!' Her eyes met April's and they both chuckled.

'Nan, when you went back up there, did you see her again?' April straightened herself on her chair and took a more serious tone. 'Have you seen her again since then?'

'No, I haven't, and do you know, I am sorry to say I haven't, but I suppose more than anything, I would love to know who she was and why I know nothing about her. There are no other photos of her in the house. After I found the frame I searched through the old albums, but she isn't there. In fact, I'm not sure there are any photos any older than when my mother was a child. But, I do think she's Annabelle's sister.'

'Nan, I've seen her many times, and Annabelle.' April fidgeted on her chair. 'I know it sounds odd!'

'Do you want to tell me? You don't have to, whenever you're ready.'

'No, I want to tell you. I think I need to... you know...get it off my chest.' April took a deep breath, holding it for a couple of seconds, before exhaling. 'I saw her in the attic, just as you did, when I held the frame. I don't think I've ever seen anyone so beautiful. Then the oddest thing happened. Mum said I must have fallen asleep...I don't know...but I saw Emily for real. What I mean is, she wasn't a ghost; she was in her own time. Her hair was long and auburn and...'

'Just like your hair,' interrupted her grandmother. April stared.

'Yes, just like mine.' April sat for a moment. Then she continued. 'It was the day the photo was taken. I was in the garden...your garden, Nan...but everything was different. It was warm and sunny, full of rose bushes and lavender. I saw the photographer and Captain Warner...that's Emily's dad.'

'You saw my great-grandfather?' Sarah beamed at April in delight.

'He was talking to the photographer. Emily was late for her photo; she was looking for her brooch. There was no way she was having it taken without it!' April said this with a matter of fact tone.

'Her brooch?'

'Yes, the brooch she's wearing in the photo. It was wonderful, blue Wedgwood. That's why I asked if you had any Wedgwood jewellery earlier.' April stared deep into her grandmother's eyes. 'Nan...Emily...she walked straight past me...so close I could smell her. Was I dreaming?'

'I don't know. I'm afraid I really don't know. But you saw her properly as you can see me now?'

'Nan, to be quite honest, after today I'm not sure what's real and what isn't.' April looked down at the table. The strong image of Richard Hardwick had pressed itself onto her mind and no matter what emotion filled her, Richard brought love and desire to her heart.

'What is it, April?' She reached across the table and took hold of her granddaughter's hand. 'Darling, please...what is it?'

'I've seen Richard Hardwick. Nan...he is the most charming man you could ever see. He's tall and striking, his hair is dark and always perfect and, oh, he has the most startling green eyes which twinkle every time I see him.'

The words had left her before she could stop them. However, she didn't care; she didn't feel embarrassed saying it this time.

'This is a completely new emotion for me. I know it sounds...well...mad I suppose. I'm not really feeling like me anymore...does that make any sense?'

The pair of them sat opposite each other holding hands. The charm bracelet chinked on the table as April rested her hands down. Both their faces consumed by smiles.

'Well, I'm not sure if these kinds of feelings ever really make any sense, but…well…you really like him don't you?' declared Sarah after a few seconds.

'Nan…I've never felt this way about anyone before. I do understand how totally and utterly ridiculous it sounds. But…' April hesitated and pondered. 'I feel as if I know him, his strong arms, his elegant hands, his smile…' she sighed.

'I'm not sure it does sound ridiculous; it just doesn't sound like you. Maybe that's what feels different.' There was a pause, 'April, what about Annabelle? Have you seen her?'

'I have, in my dreams, but…'

'But, what?' Sarah squeezed her granddaughter's hand.

'It's different with Annabelle; I've dreamt about her, it was awful…' April stopped. How could she go on, with the pain of losing a baby? April knew very well that her Nan had felt this feeling of loss for herself, the dream had been so terrible for April, and how could she tell her?

'Please, it's OK. What's the matter?'

'It's always different with Annabelle.' April tried to muster up enough to tell her. 'I had a dream about her. She was pregnant; they were both so happy…her and Richard. Dr Hickson had told her she had to rest, to be careful. They had lost her mother giving birth to Emily when Annabelle was four years old. But…Nan, Annabelle lost the baby. I saw her. I felt the pain and sadness, her pain. It was the most awful thing. I ache every time I think about it.'

April couldn't help herself, she could no longer hold it back; she broke down in tears, sobbing into her sleeve with the recollection of the terrible feeling, the total loss and fear of not knowing. Her grandmother stood up from her chair and walked around the table.

'Darling, it's OK, I understand.'

'Do you…do you understand? Because…I'm…not sure I do!'

'Well.' Sarah paused, looking at April, then continued in a very gentle voice. 'I think it is quite straightforward but maybe hard for you to take on board... obvious nevertheless.'

'What on earth are you on about, Nan? What's obvious?'

Sarah crouched down, looking April in the eyes and held April's tear-stained cheeks between her hands.

'April, you saw Emily earlier, didn't you?' April was too tired for words; she simply nodded. 'You held her in your arms and you smelt her perfume? She saw your bracelet?' Her words were strong and clear, but April could not respond. In April's head, her experiences were real and tangible, but spoken aloud the reality was that these things were impossible and absurd.

'Darling, your feelings *are* Annabelle's!' Her grandmother's words were adamant, direct and not to be misunderstood. 'Do you understand what I'm saying?' She gently kissed April's forehead.

'What?' April couldn't find any more words. Her mouth was dry, her head fuzzy, and she had a pain deep within her heart. She was desperately trying to erase the feelings of loss: the memory of Annabelle's miscarriage lingered inside her entire body.

'I know it's hard, but let's look at this logically,' Sarah began.

'LOGICALLY, there *is* no logic to any of this. I don't think anyone can look at this logically!' April stood up sharply. She'd not meant to raise her voice, but this was incredibly bizarre.

Sarah simply hugged her granddaughter and kissed her cheek trying to calm her.

'OK, perhaps 'logically' was the wrong word. Maybe, there is logic to all of this, darling, if you believe. This is about life, death, love and family. It is my belief that our souls come back time and time again; in new bodies, with new lives and new names...but our souls remain the same. Not everyone can remember past memories, past events and past loves...maybe we are connected to the same souls, life after life.'

She gently pushed April back onto her chair, perching herself on to the edge of the table and took hold of April's hand. The charm bracelet jingled, the silver charms glistened and twinkled beneath the kitchen light. April said nothing, lost for a reply. Her grandmother's words did have a strange reasoning, but this was mad, utterly mad - this meant she was feeling her own great-great grandmother's emotions!

'Nan,' April's voice was shaky. 'What about Emily? Why is she still here? She was a ghost, Nan, I saw her with my own eyes, and you saw her too!'

'I don't know why she's still here, and I don't know why her spirit hasn't moved on.'

She coughed slightly and then continued. 'You saw Emily tonight, and when she spoke to you she was speaking to Annabelle. Yes?' April just nodded. 'And you have seen Annabelle in your dreams. You felt her pain and sorrow. Am I right so far?' April nodded once again and closed her eyes.

'Now Richard, you keep seeing him too, don't you? You're sensing feelings for him, Annabelle's feelings, yet, feelings that you've never experienced.'

Both sat silent for a few moments, contemplating these revelations, as the mood of the room altered.

The kitchen now possessed a weird atmosphere. April and her grandmother looked at one another, but still said nothing. A cold sensation crept slowly through the air. In the silence, their breath became visible in front of their faces.

'Nan, what is it?' April's voice shook, she slowly stood.

'I'm not sure.' Sarah rose from the table's edge where she'd settled and grabbed onto April's hand.

The light flickered and then was gone. The two of them stood glued to the tiled floor. A splinter of light glimmered through from the hallway. The ray of light lit a small section of the room; a million dust particles danced in the beam.

April turned around and looked at the kitchen window. In the darkness of the room, she could just make out the window frame; tightly shut…not the reason for the unearthly still coldness.

The atmosphere became even rawer and the frosty air was overlaid with an aroma. The smell travelled the room, a sweet scent of perfume.

The delicate aroma caught April and her grandmother.

April recognised it at once as it filled the kitchen; it was strong but sweet, an exquisite, floral smell. A flickering light, small with a slightly blue hue, flashed and danced through the air. Then, just as gradually as before, a silver misty substance swirled through the atmosphere encircling the space in front of them.

Gently lit by the hall light, it slowly formed into a smoky apparition, gradually becoming a clear figure. There she stood, the most wondrous beauty, a tangible loveliness with a golden glow. Her long pale lacy dress adorned with a cameo brooch, her perfect complexion, and her glorious red hair piled high and elegant as in the sepia photograph.

Automatically, and without consideration for the strangeness of the circumstance, April took a step closer to the young woman, releasing her grandmother's grip on her hand.

'Emily.' April's voice was gentle and soft. 'Dearest'.

Sarah watched her granddaughter with a combination of fear and wonder. She had changed; not her appearance or her voice, but her manner, the words that left her lips. She turned her eyes from April and then to the image of the young woman. She was indeed incredibly beautiful. The figure held her arms outstretched and smiled peacefully.

'My dearest sister, Annabelle, how I have missed you, I have waited for you for so long.'

Becky Byford

Remember to love me

Until death...

'Have you two finished cleaning up in here? It's quarter to eleven. If we're going to the midnight service, we need to leave in about half an hour.' Michael spoke quite loudly as he entered the kitchen.

'Why have you got the light off in here?' He flicked the light switch on again. 'That's better. I think I'd better take a look at that light fitting for you, Sarah, looks like it's playing up. Don't be long you two!'

He turned and strode back out the door.

Neither April nor her grandmother spoke a syllable. Sarah simply stared, wide-eyed, at April, still in bewilderment. The room was normal once more; the scent had gone and the figure had evaporated simultaneously with the stark brightness of the kitchen light. Both stood rooted to the checked floor tiles. April quickly took hold of her grandmother's hand as she saw her start to sway.

'Nan, you OK?' April guided her back to the kitchen chair.

'Oh, I'm fine. Just a little stunned that's all; it's not every day you get to meet your great-aunt.' Sarah sat down quite heavily, overcome with immense emotion. There was an uneasy pause.

'April, you just saw...well, we both saw...well...' she paused again, perhaps looking for some answers.

'Well, Nan, do you know?' April stepped towards her grandmother and kissed her soft cheek. 'I love you.'

'April? Are you all right?' Her voice was slightly shaken. She had expected her to be astonished by their ghostly experience, as indeed, she was.

'Nan, I'm fine. Everything seems to make sense; I now understand why I have these feelings for Richard.'

'Darling, I am a little concerned. Do you really understand that these are Annabelle's feelings and not yours?'

'Nan, it was you that said it was straightforward and obvious.'

'Yes, I am aware of that. Nevertheless, we have just seen a...well, a ghost I suppose and...and I don't know about you, but I am a little shaken by the whole thing,' answered her grandmother, as she sat back against the hard wood of the kitchen chair.

'Nan, that wasn't a ghost...that was Emily!' Her tone was odd.

'April, sit down and listen to me for a minute.' She grabbed April's sleeve. 'It's one thing to embrace your past life...but it's a very different and dangerous thing to try and relive it,' continued Sarah.

April sat on the wooden chair, twiddling with her charm bracelet.

'Nan, honestly, it's OK. I do understand that we have just seen a ghost. But I'm not afraid; the ghost is Emily, Annabelle's sister. How can I be afraid of her? I know there's a lot ahead of me, but I finally understand. I can finally take on these feelings...finally put some reason and logic to all these...' April felt unsure whether she should continue.

'Go on, I am listening,' interrupted her grandmother, not meaning to sound impatient with her, but the whole conversation was as bizarre as it could be, and April wasn't acting her normal rational self.

'...Well, these feelings I have for Richard.'

'Darling, Richard, he was your great-great grandfather...and he is dead.' Her grandmother didn't want to sound cruel, but April seemed to be missing these most important facts. Sarah did understand April's feelings for Richard; after all, it was she who'd pointed out that they had, possibly, once been connected.

April sat and stared hard into her grandmother's eyes. Tears fell down her cheeks. She looked at her bracelet, as it sparkled and twinkled beneath the kitchen light once more.

'I know all that's true. But all these feelings are so real and strong. I know all the facts. I know he is dead. I know how odd all this sounds. But Nan, here, in my heart, all these feelings are alive. They have been getting stronger; I've been feeling different, strange, since we got here. Life seemed so normal back home, but, I've realised that maybe I belong here; this is why I've never felt as if I've belonged. After all...Nan...it was you who said maybe it was meant to be.'

'Yes, I did,' Sarah nodded.

April continued with her flow of self-revelation.

'I know I have only seen him today, but I can't shut out these feelings I have, not just for Richard but also for Emily. She was Annabelle's sister; they were so close. I can feel it deep inside me, in every bone and every beat of my heart.

'I need to know why there are no photos of her and why you knew nothing about her.' April's voice was calmer, her expression sweeter. 'But most of all, why Emily is here now!'

'OK, darling, let's take this one day at a time.' She reached out and clasped April's hands with hers. 'I am here for you. You do know that. We will get through this together, no matter what happens. I think we had better make a move or we won't be able to get a seat in the church. Go and wash your face and I'll get all our coats. Don't worry, it will be fine.'

April stood up and opened the kitchen door. Sarah remained seated for a few more moments, and then took a deep breath. April turned in the doorway to face her grandmother with her hand on the light switch. Taking another deep breath, Sarah, with her usual grace, rose from the wooden chair and left the room with April.

'Don't worry, Nan, maybe I belong here now.'

* * *

They entered through the large arched wooden doors. Festive crowds were gathering, some already seated on the long polished wooden pews, row after row of merry folk donned in their smartest winter coats with scarves and hats. The sheer magnificence and grandeur of this antiquated and holy piece of architecture, its highly decorated arched ceiling, and the enormous stained glass windows, blew all clouded thoughts from April's mind.

Long waterfall chandeliers, with dozens of glittering lights suspended from long chains, hung in regimental rows, illuminating the glorious structure. The floor of highly polished stone tiles, like mirrors, reflected the glowing multitude of lights. Rows of tall pillars of the smoothest stonework reached up to form high arches, stonework executed by talented craftsmen centuries before. They extended high to line the long aisle with a canopy of elaborately carved and intricate paintings.

The most impressive pair of Christmas trees, decked with festoons of broad twisted metallic ribbons, lavish decorations, and huge baubles in shades of festive reds and golds stood, identically majestic, on either side of the top of the endless aisle.

April and her family settled on a pew close to one of the enormous Christmas trees, a few rows from the front. The air was cool, and the scent of fragrant fresh pine subtly penetrated the atmosphere. April sat at the end closest to the aisle, with full view of the magnificent church organ. The pew was dark, polished and lovingly kept. All were wrapped up warmly on this snowy Christmas Eve; its late hour was cold and frosty. The church organ began and all became still, only this truly resplendent sound to be heard.

Remember to love me

April held the polished wood of the pew where she sat, her leather glove covered hands gripping the worn oak either side of her legs. The sound of the festive carol faded from her ears, leaving them familiarly numb. Her heart beat fast, as it had done before, pounding rhythmically inside her head. Nevertheless, she remained calm. She inhaled deeply, the cool air filling her lungs. Her skin tingled, and shivers travelled the length of her spine. Calmly, April steadied herself on the pew, and stretched each finger as she slowly opened her eyes.

Her clothes had transformed, no longer the black satin of her trousers and wool of her coat. Now, before her eyes, a long gathering of dark purple silk covered her legs. Daringly, she moved her sight to the person sitting next to her.

A tall graceful gentleman sat beside her, his long legs covered in dark tailoring and shiny black shoes. Slowly, she traced her eyes across his muscular torso, his dark, debonair suit fitted to perfection, his strong arms evident through his sleeves. She jumped as the gentleman slid his manly hand over to hers, folding long elegant fingers around her petite fair hand.

She sat rigid, her eyes fixed on his hand, his soft skin, warm and real on hers. With a rapid beat her heart pounded, confined to the tightness of her corset beneath the purple silk of her dress. She clutched his hand, her pale fingers entwined with his; unable to distinguish whose were whose. Her body began to tremble.

'What is it my darling? You are trembling. Are you warm enough?' He gradually took his hand from hers, brought it up, and touched her face. He brushed her blonde hair from her cheek. This was by far the closest she had been to Richard. She couldn't help herself. The sheer sound of his voice and touch of his hand stirred emotions deep inside her soul. Tears gathered; crystal pools slowly released in waterfalls down her fair complexion. She could not move her stare from his face; his close location exhibited his full radiance, his eyes glistened with the likeness of emeralds, his hair was the darkest brown with a

Becky Byford

lustrous sheen, and the soft smooth lips of his mouth were full and kissable. Her chest hammered beneath her dress.

'Oh darling, I knew you were going to cry, you get so emotional. You are not losing Emily. As your father said, we are gaining James.' Richard leant even closer and lovingly kissed her cheek, his lips warm and so real and tangible.

She gasped with the intensity of this unbelievable moment in time. It felt so real; she didn't want this to end. The emotions and feelings that had manifested in the deepest depths of her heart were now so strong and so overwhelming. How was she going to cope? She never wanted to leave his side, longing to forever feel the touch of his hands, the warmth of his skin; see the spark of life in his young eyes. This was real! The stirring in the depths of her stomach; the palpitations of her heart as its beat pounded in her throat.

The magnificent church organ began again, a familiar piece of music. Everyone around her stood up from the polished pews. She had been unaware of the congregation that surrounded them both - an abundance of gracefully clothed ladies and gentlemen, dressed in feathered hats of glorious shades and long gem coloured gowns, smart, distinguished suits and immaculate top hats. The joyous atmosphere consumed the great vastness of the sacred structure.

As she rose from her seat, holding the back of the pew in front she eased herself round to view behind her. There was the most enchanting vision. Emily glided the length of the church aisle, her bewitching beauty more apparent than ever before, dressed in a long satin gown of buttery cream, embellished with deep decorative lace. The neckline was high and modest; the sleeves were lacy and fitted to her wrists. Her bouquet trailed to her knees as she held her proud father's arm, his expression honoured by his fatherly duty, his face overrun with pride.

James stood, dashing and handsome in his Suffolk Regiment military dress uniform; his red jacket with gleaming gold buttons, the pristine black trousers and shoes that shone like mirrored glass. He gazed in wonder at his mesmerizing bride as she stood by his side. The Wedding March finished and silence fell, the whole congregation's attentions on the bride and groom.

Richard once again returned his gaze to his wife. He viewed her beauty with passion and enduring love. Leaning towards her, so close his smooth skin touched hers, he kissed her cheek and whispered softly in her ear.

'I love you, my dearest Belle.'

April sat silent and motionless for the rest of the Christmas service. Not singing, almost unaware of the loud church organ and the jubilant festive crowds. Sarah chose to leave her granddaughter to her memories and thoughts. Once again, the admirable personality of Richard Hardwick had cast its spell. She was captivated by his charm, enraptured by his glory. In love!

The family walked the short journey home. The late hour was bright and crisp. The cars and footpaths wore a blanket of fresh snow. April walked arm in arm with her grandmother. From time to time, Sarah glanced at April's face, her expression the same, just a peaceful smile.

Sarah inserted the brass key in the lock and they all descended the few steps into the front room. The house was warm and inviting compared to the raw night air.

'Well, that was wonderful, truly a festive treat of merriment and joy!' announced Michael with jubilation.

'I agree...lovely. The Christmas trees were beautiful and I think we should go every year!' replied Julia. 'How about you, Mum, did you enjoy yourself?'

'Oh yes, it was marvellous.' Sarah had settled herself in her favourite chair, and was gazing at April as she sat opposite on the red velvet settee.

'Well, it's late; I think we should be getting home. We'll be back nice and early in the morning. Don't forget, I'm cooking the turkey tomorrow. It's my turn to do dinner, and you could do with a rest, Mum. You look absolutely shattered.' Julia had noticed her mother's pale face, her features seeming older than usual.

'Yes I'm just a bit tired; it's been a long and busy day, what with all that shopping this morning as well. I'm going to have a nice mug of hot chocolate, and then I'm going to bed.'

'Come on then, April, let's go home and let your Nan get to bed,' requested Michael.

'Actually, Mum, do you mind if I stay here with Nan tonight?' April had arrived back in the land of the living.

'Well, I don't mind if your Nan doesn't,' replied Julia. She was quite relieved at the prospect of someone else being in the house with her mother for the night, her age seemed all too apparent tonight. For once, she looked every one of her eighty years.

Michael and Julia kissed Sarah and April, wished them sweet dreams, and turned to leave, closing the front door behind them.

'Nan, I'll go and put the pan on, and make that hot chocolate.' April rose from the settee, and headed through the hallway and into the kitchen. As she entered the room, her eyes roamed over the space; only a few hours before, she had seen Emily standing in this very room. April pondered on the day, it had not frightened her, and how she had loved seeing Emily standing there.

April poured the milk into the pan and switched on the hob; she leant with her chin in her hand and elbows on the work surface. Watching the milk, as it got hotter and boiled, and so unaware of the world around her, she hadn't noticed her grandmother had entered the room behind her. April filled the two large mugs with hot chocolate, and turned to see her sitting at the table. She saw at once how different her grandmother looked, how tonight she wasn't her usual youthful self, dynamic and full of vigour.

'Nan, is there anything I can get you?'

'No, I am fine and dandy. As I told your Mum, I am just tired after the busy day we've had.' Sarah hugged her warm mug. 'I just need a good night's sleep.'

'Ok, well we'll have this and head off to bed then. Nan, I do love you.' April had sat down on the other wooden kitchen chair. She lifted her mug to her lips and watched her grandmother as she sat opposite, her eyes shut, just holding her mug. This wasn't normal. Where was the vibrant lady that she knew, full of life and zest? Nevertheless, she was eighty, and maybe all this had been too much for her. It may have been April, who'd had the encounter and sensed these memories of the past, but her grandmother had been there as support, and she'd also observed the apparition.

Both finished their chocolate. April washed the mugs and placed them face down on the drainer. She followed her grandmother out of the kitchen and turned off the light.

'Nan, you head on upstairs and I'll lock up.'

'It's OK, I'll wait for you, and then I'll find you a spare nightdress to wear.' Sarah stood by the bottom stair, waiting. April walked through to the front room, tipped some coal on the fire for the night, and replaced the empty scuttle on the hearth beside her grandmother's chair.

'All ready! Nan, are you sure there isn't anything I can get you? You really aren't looking yourself.'

'Honestly, please don't worry so. I'll feel right as rain in the morning. We're going to have the best Christmas ever.'

April held her grandmother's arm as they ascended the staircase. They reached the top and both headed into her grandmother's bedroom. Sarah walked over to a large tallboy that stood along the outside wall close to the window. Slowly, she glided opened the large bottom drawer. Its silky rosewood veneer had a touchable quality, and April ran her fingers over the surface.

'There you go; I'm sure this one will be fine. I know it's not very young and trendy, but it'll do for tonight and it will keep you nice and cosy.' Her grandmother handed her a long white cotton nightgown, with long sleeves, and a small ribbon tie at the neck. The front yoke and cuffs were wonderfully embellished, with prettily embroidered pink roses.

'Nan, it's so sweet, it'll do perfectly.' April stepped closer to her, took the nightgown, and kissed her grandmother on the cheek, then hugged her tightly.

'What is it, April? Are you OK?'

'Nan, I really do love you. It is lovely to be so close to you now. It's going to be the best Christmas ever!' April held her once again.

'Now, off to bed with you. You can go and sleep in the room at the end of the hall. There's a spare toothbrush in the cupboard in the bathroom. Do you realise it's nearly one o'clock in the morning? It has been an exhausting day!' She hugged April back.

April closed the bedroom door behind her. The spare room was lovely, with matching curtains and bedspread, all pink and pretty. The nightgown was perfect. April stood in front of the long swivel mirror to observe her reflection. The silver charm bracelet still hung decoratively from her wrist. The charms sparkled and glittered with antique, heirloom lustre. The whole atmosphere of this room looked untouched by time, and now, wearing this nightgown, April looked and felt as if she belonged here. She knew she had come home.

Climbing into the large wooden bed, its headboard prettily carved, she lay warm, snug and peaceful. The garden and the aged graveyard beyond, with its newly laid snow, cast a bright glow through the large bay window, spreading a magical enchantment. There seemed to be nothing around her from her modern time. Both the inside décor and the timeless, glistening snow outside, gave everything the look of another era.

April studied the day's events with an equal measure of logic and wonder. No matter how she tried, no real logical explanation could be found for these events.

* * *

A dense blanket of fresh snow covered the whole aspect of the garden. Boughs of the large tree hung covered and heavy, over the crisp whiteness. It had been a glorious Christmas and it was New Year's Eve, the eve of a new century.

A large, cut crystal bowl full of punch, stood in the centre of the dining table, accompanied by its matching glasses. Mince pies and candied fruits resided on large serving plates.

Captain Warner strode into the parlour where the rest of the family were seated. He steadily carried a large silver tray with the crystal glasses brimming with punch. He handed one to each of them and took his place proudly beside the fireplace. The gilt mantle clock's intricate hands displayed two minutes to midnight. He raised his glass high in the warm air before him. Dancing flames reflected in the heavy engraving of the lead crystal.

'I would like to make a toast.' He cast a noble view across his treasured family, his heart full of love and adoration. They all rose to their feet and lifted their glasses high.

'To my beautiful daughter, Emily, and my new son-in-law, James, I wish you love and happiness. To my wonderful daughter, Annabelle, and to Richard, who is like a son to me, may this be a fruitful year for you both.'

'To the family!' The room filled with their voices in unison.

'Now, it is almost midnight and a new year is dawning, our hopes are that 1900 will bring us prosperity and peace, with a swift end to the War in South Africa, and the safe return of our local young men who are serving their country.' They lifted their glasses once again, as the mantle clock chimed midnight, and the family toasted the new century.

'Happy New Year!'

January was cold and frosty with renewed snow throughout the month. As it drew to a close, the approach of February brought yet more, relentless, snow. The forgotten green grass lay deeply hidden under its thick winter blanket. The sky was grim, bleak and grey.

Becky Byford

James stood in the dining room looking out onto the garden below. The room was quiet with just the repetitive snowflakes resting upon the glass panes. He stood in silent contemplation with no regard for the miserable weather; it simply dampened the day with empathy for James' misery. Richard entered the room and closed the door behind him. James made no movement or response to the loud creaking of the door's hinges. Richard glided across the carpeted floor, and he too stared at the disheartening view through the glass.

'James, have you told Emily yet?' Richard's voice was filled with anguish and worry, and concern for everyone's welfare.

'I have not seemed to be able to find the words. Emily has been full of song all morning. Every moment I think is the right one; she starts to sing so joyfully, I just don't have the heart to tell her.' James turned to look directly at Richard. Both stood with great height. Richard had such an elegant air of nobility in contrast to James who stood tall with his military honour.

'Come on, you really need to tell her. It will only make it harder the longer you leave it. It's inevitable. You should be making the most of your time together; she needs to know as soon as possible.' Richard placed his hand on James' shoulder. 'You know she will have Annabelle and me for support.'

'You are right.'

'You'll feel better once you have told her,' Richard sympathised.

'I said you're right,' James rubbed his hand over the back of his neck, desperately trying to ease his tension. 'I just can't find the words, you know.'

'If you keep leaving it, it will only make things worse, she needs to know now.'

'I shall go and find her.' James drew himself up and breathed deeply into his large muscular chest. He opened the dining room door and passed down the hallway to the parlour.

On entering the space, he heard Emily's sweet tone. She sat at the family piano singing quietly to herself as her fingers glided effortlessly across the ivory keys. Her long dark blue dress hung delicately to the floor, long leg-of-mutton sleeves covered her slender arms down to the pale skin of the talented fingers. She turned with a beaming smile on her sweet face.

'James, my darling, oh James, isn't it such a lovely day?' He thought Emily seemed unaware of the snow, and remarked as if it was a glorious summer's morning.

James closed the door carefully behind him, almost with no sound at all. He strode over to the piano at which his new bride sat. His head was low as he stared at the patterned carpet.

'James, whatever is it?' Emily stood up, her height so petite compared to his, that she looked straight up into his eyes as they gazed at the floor. James guided Emily to the winged chair near to the fireplace. He remained speechless, his eyes downcast. He thought better to say nothing than to break such sad tidings without preparing her first. She reluctantly sat. He knelt with one knee on the carpet in front of her. A large log crackled and hissed, and small burning red sparks flew in the fire. He sat, gazing upon the glowing embers, pondering, searching for the right words to say. His heart was beating with adrenaline, as his stomach reached his throat, choking him of oxygen.

'James, James, what is the matter? Please tell me what's wrong!' Emily's voice had become alarmed and harassed.

She took her tiny hands and placed them on his face, cradling his strong features inside her soft palms; his manly countenance became young, boyish, and as vulnerable.

'Emily, I do so love you. You mean the world to me, you do know that?' His voice was weak and he could not find the strength to look at her face.

'Of course, of course I know, I love you.'

'Emily, I don't know how...'

'James, whatever it is, we can get through it together. Darling, I am your wife.' Emily leant forward and tenderly kissed his soft lips.

'Darling, I have to leave next month.' James finally looked into his wife's features, his own eyes dewy as tears formed.

'Next month? You are leaving next month? James, I don't understand.'

'My battalion, Emily, we are being sent to South Africa. We leave on the eleventh of February.' James' words were full of dread and fear. Fear for Emily and fear for the future.

Emily sat silently for a moment, deep in thought, and a lonely tear fell from her eye. Numbly, she stared deeply into his eyes. She knew what this meant; he may never return; her life with James, that had only just begun, could be ending. After what seemed a lifetime, Emily pulled herself upright on the chair and took a silent breath, and then her expression altered.

'Don't worry, my dearest James. All will be well, and you shall return home to me and we shall live the rest of our lives together, gloriously happy. The ghastly war out there shall be over very soon, and you shall be returning before you have even left!'

James understood Emily's reaction; this was her way of dealing with the situation and its harsh reality. Both sat motionless, making no sound, just holding hands. Nothing more was said on the matter. The next couple of days were lived as if nothing had changed. All spoke of peace and of aspirations for the New Year. Annabelle periodically took Emily in her arms and hugged her, but not a word was uttered. Captain Warner kept morale high with long reminiscing tales of summer holidays by the seaside, of years long passed and of the girls' dear mother, Rose.

Emily perched at her dressing table, staring hypnotically into her oval swivel mirror, looking past her reflection, preoccupied by what life lay before them. Slowly she re-entered her conscious mind as a light rapping sound came at her bedroom door.

'Emily, can I come in?' Her sister's polite voice whispered through the door.

'Of course, darling.' Emily turned on her stool as she replied. Gently opening the bedroom door, Annabelle glided across the carpet, and took a seat on the end of the bed, a few feet away from her sister.

'How are you my dearest sister?' Annabelle's tone was warm.

'I am perfectly fine,' stated Emily, her voice determined not to show any emotion; instead, it shook under the pressure of her sadness.

'I know that there are some hard times ahead. But no matter what may lay before us, you will always have me here by your side.' Annabelle reached over and placed her hand on Emily's knee. 'You are my sister and I have always been here to look after you, it is no different now you are married to James. We shall always remain the same.' Both young women smiled.

'When are you heading back home?' Emily knew Annabelle had only planned to stay for Christmas, postponing her departure due to James' news.

'I shall stay as long as you need me here. Richard can cope without me for a while longer,' Annabelle replied with a smile.

'But it's not fair on him, having to come back here every weekend. I do appreciate you being here but your loyalties lay with Richard, at home with him, as his wife.' Emily squeezed Annabelle's hand.

'He has Martha there to cook and clean. Besides, he is extremely busy with his work. He understands my need to be here with you.' Leaning forward, she kissed her sister's cheek.

'Annabelle, you are so lucky to have such a wonderful husband.'

'And so are you dear Emily. James is wonderful too, and he loves you so very much.' She looked reassuringly into Emily's face. The young sister before her had grown into a woman, almost before her very eyes. Annabelle sat and continued to gaze at her.

BECKY BYFORD

'You look so much like Mother. It's like having her still here.' Annabelle gulped with the need to hold back the tears, which she could feel forming in her eyes.

'Do you miss her?' Emily sat, looking at her knees, her face consumed by her melancholy expression. She didn't want to look at her sister, as she felt sure they would both start to weep.

'Of course, she was very beautiful. I remember her still. She is so very clear in my thoughts, and I miss her dreadfully. But I have you to remind me, you look so much like her.' Annabelle stood up and wandered over to the large bay window, resting her hand on the back of the bedroom chair. The soft drapes of pretty pink floral fabric framed the white snowy scene like a stage setting.

'Annabelle, do tell me about her.' Emily silently moved across the floor and stood next to her sister, resting her head on Annabelle's shoulder.

'She had the most wonderful auburn hair like yours. It shone with the likeness of silk ribbons in ringlets down to her waist. She would sit at her dressing table brushing it for hours...I would sit and just watch her.' Annabelle's face became wistful with the recollection. 'The sunlight would shine through the bedroom window and light up her face. Her skin was as fair as porcelain, and her eyes the deepest brown. When she smiled, the room would light up; she was the most breathtaking beauty. I am sure she was the most elegant and exquisite woman there ever was.' Annabelle's voice quaked as she spoke.

'Go on.' Emily remained static, her head still resting upon her sister.

'As I approached the age of four, Mother became pregnant. We would lie on her bed and I would rest my head on her stomach. I could feel you moving and kicking, the most incredible thing, the notion that I had a brother or sister inside. Of course, I couldn't really comprehend it, but I took her word for it and that was how it was; a sister I hoped, someone to play with,' she smiled at Emily.

'She would stroke my hair and call me her Little One, promising me, that no matter what, I always would be.' Annabelle broke down and began to sob.

'I sometimes can imagine her in my mind; from all the stories you have told me over the years. How lovely she was and how much she loved us both, even if she never knew me...' Emily's face was pale and sad.

'She always loved you, from that very moment she knew you were growing inside her, she loved you.' Tears trailed Annabelle's face.

'I have always loved her, even though I never knew her, I suppose it's the same.'

Annabelle pulled herself together, producing a handkerchief from her pocket; she gracefully wiped her eyes, composing herself once again.

'We would sit for hours in the study. I would sit beside her on the velvet settee; the sun would fill the room. She would read to me, book after book. Sometimes she would create stories about long lost and far off places. And then…and then one day she was gone.' Annabelle stopped unable to continue, her voice paralysed. Emily stepped forward and pulled her closer, as she flung her arms around her. Both stood for a few moments, sheathed in their sorrow, the loss of their mother, the gaping hole it had left in Annabelle's young life; the desire to be a mother herself strong and true.

'But then…' Annabelle continued with a shaky voice. 'But then we had you to look after. Father did his best and I loved so you much. You were so small and perfect. Every time I looked at you, I saw Mother. As you grew up, the more like her you became. Oh Emily, I am here for you just as I have always been. No matter what life brings, we shall always have each other.'

The harsh reality of war and of James' imminent departure returned to Emily's thoughts.

'I shall remain strong for James' sake; I have to be strong for us both. He must know that I can cope; I don't want him worrying about me. It will be terrible enough for him over there.' announced Emily, her voice adamant and strong.

'Come on, let's go downstairs, dinner will soon be ready. You must make the most of the time you have left with James.' Annabelle took her sister's arm and both left the room.

'When you return, dear husband of mine, we shall go on a wonderful honeymoon and take in some lovely sea air.' Emily announced as she placed her silver knife and fork onto her empty dinner plate. 'That was a delightful meal, Mary. You are such a wonderfully capable cook.' She smiled at Mary as she began to collect the family's plates.

'Yes, it was a lovely dinner, Mary, thank you.' Captain Warner carefully folded his crisp napkin, resting it on the table as Mary took his plate.

Annabelle caught sight of James' face across the table. His eyes remained fixed upon the lonely potato that he was pushing around his plate. He made no attempt to answer Emily, by either words or facial expression; instead, his eyes bored their way through the china. Annabelle could see the pain on his face, his eyes dull and tired with the weight of the anxiety of leaving his wife behind. Annabelle just couldn't imagine how much the feeling must be destroying the pair of them. With one night left here with his wife, James was increasingly concerned for what lay ahead, both for him and for his new bride.

Dinner was over far too soon for James' liking, as the approach of morning drew ever closer. The cruel certainty of the situation dawned with the dark coldness of the frosty February morning. The hour was brutally early, the sky outside was a dull shade of light grey, the clouds hung abundant with snow. Emily drifted silently down the stairs, to be greeted by the sight of her husband in full army uniform. He stood, tall and honourable, with his regimental station. But his military presence was outshone, swamped by his young and boyish features; innocence that she could almost taste in the air, desperate for the warm embrace of his love.

As all that had gone before and all that were to follow, there he stood, yet another young man in his prime, ready to serve his country with no knowledge of when he would return home, or if indeed he would ever step back onto native soil.

Remember to love me

The callous weather was harsh; the blinding snowstorm began, the clouds exploding as the wild wind whipped cold faces and hands. The large crowd of hundreds of local people cheered, and the railway station wore a coat of uniforms. Another wave of British Military was to descend upon South African shores. A veil of melancholy and misery hung heavy beneath the cheering. The large steam train rested upon its rails, awaiting its departure. Heaps of chests and kitbags lined the platform's icy surface, as the snow continued to camouflage them in a guise of white.

Emily stood, overwhelmed and bewildered by their fate. She cast her eyes across the crowd and became aware that the same expression covered many other young women's faces, the prospect of becoming widowed at the hands of this ghastly war, so far overseas that it made no daily effect on normal life, except for the chance of utterly destroying it.

A piercing whistle blew, loud above the sound of the bustling crowds; the vast number of young men began to collect up their kitbags and board the stationary steam train. The blizzard and mass of uniforms made it nigh on impossible to distinguish man from man.

Emily flung her arms around James with lost composure, as her heart fell into an abyss of darkness. Her silent tears fell onto his strong uniformed chest. The smell and softness of his youthful skin penetrated Emily's senses, something to remain with her until her husband's return.

'It's all right, Emily, everything is going to be just fine. I shall be on my way home to you very soon. Please, my darling, you know that I love you more than the world, never forget that.' His soft words warmed her eyes as he whispered, and kissed her silky skin.

James carefully eased Emily's sobbing face away from his jacket; her wet tear stained cheeks pink and flushed with the thrashing elements. James reached down to retrieve his kitbag from the platform surface.

'I must go, I have to go now. Remember that I love you, Emily. Please never forget that, I love you with every beat of my heart, which right now is breaking.'

James took Emily's hand and placed a tiny, neatly folded piece of paper into it, Emily squeezed her fingers around it. The loud whistle blew for the second time, as the rest of the men stepped onto the waiting train. Steam billowed across the platform.

'I love you James. I will always love you and when…'

'No more words. If anything should happen, I want you to read the letter, but only then.'

'I love you, my darling, I love you so much, James.' Emily could hear herself having to shout over the din of whistles and the gradually moving steam train.

'Promise me, Emily,' he shouted.

'But…'

'No Emily, promise me. Only read it if anything happens to me and not before.'

'Yes, James, I promise, but you will come home won't you?'

'Of course, only God could keep me from you. No man on this earth is strong enough.'

James leant down and kissed his wife goodbye. Their lips softly touched, stopping time in its tracks for a brief moment, all was silent, nothing else mattered, and no one else existed.

James turned and jumped onto the train as it gradually gained speed. Steam consumed the air, as a multitude of uniformed arms waved frantically from the countless, open windows. An eerie silence began to fall upon the platform, the whole station, as steam fogged the atmosphere. The distant sound of the train evaporated, and the locomotive and its reluctant passengers were gone, leaving only the icy footprints of where they once stood.

Remember to love me

Love & War

Hours became days and days became weeks. The harsh reality of the heartbreaking circumstances did not alter during the days Emily locked herself away in her bedroom. She soon came to realise she had no choice but to continue. Things were as they were, and Emily knew she had to see it through to the end, whatever that would bring. James had promised to write when he had the chance, so hope of a letter arriving kept her spirits high.

The family did their greatest to keep life as routine as possible.

As the weeks moved on, the first signs of spring could be seen in the garden, the grass was a lush green and blossoms and buds were starting to emerge. The warmer days brought brighter mornings and lighter evenings. The dull grey winter, with its bare trees devoid of foliage had ceased.

Annabelle and Emily sat beneath the large tree at the end of the garden.

'So, Emily, my dear sister, as it's your birthday tomorrow I thought we should have a special treat.'

'What are we going to do?' Emily's voice was almost excited, something that had not been apparent in her tone for many months.

'Well, if I tell you it will not be much of a surprise, will it?' Annabelle clasped her sister's hand and squeezed it tightly with great joy at the normality of the conversation.

Annabelle had devoted as much of her time to her sister as possible over the past weeks. Some days were easier than others. The continued ritual of waiting for a letter had started to become Emily's unhealthy obsession. She would sit in the high backed chair beside the fire staring out of the window, just waiting.

The warmer days had moved her waiting to the garden, and although her frame of mind had not altered; at least the location was a change of scene. The letters from James, however, had not yet arrived; in fact, there had been no news at all. The not knowing was hard for all to endure. Annabelle was aware of how agonising this was for Emily, a new bride with no husband.

The early morning sunshine whispered through the floral curtains, and the bedroom was engulfed in a soft pink blush. Emily lounged - warm and cosy - in her lonely bed. As she lay in the quietness of her room, voices could be heard from down stairs, bright lively voices.

'Emily, are you coming down for some breakfast?' Her father's words bellowed up the staircase to her room.

'I shall be down in a moment,' Emily replied through her closed bedroom door.

As she descended the stairs, she could hear the continued excitement of the family, their voices chirpy. Following them into the dining room, Emily was greeted with a beautifully laid breakfast table, along with the family's best bone china and a pile of neatly wrapped gifts.

'Happy Birthday!' The room boomed in unison, as she stepped across the threshold. The sun glistened through the glass doors, flooding the room with a magical glow.

'Well, dear sister, sit down.' Annabelle gestured to a space with a perfect vision of the lush green garden below. Emily sat elegantly upon the dining chair looking at the view; the sweet lavender shrubs and rose bushes made it a remarkable sight. Captain Warner entered the room and sat on the chair beside his youngest daughter. Annabelle and Richard sat at the other side of the table, the picture of the garden still visible between them.

'Happy Birthday, dearest sister! Would you rather open your presents now or after breakfast?' Annabelle's excitement was apparent, and she beamed as brightly as the morning sunshine.

Emily looked at the pile of gifts between her and her father. They were all wrapped with precision in pink paper and tied with white ribbon. She took hold of the top one; it was quite small in comparison to the large one on which it rested. Emily pulled the delicate ribbon and the package unfastened gently in her hand. Beneath the pink paper laid a square box in deep blue leather. Emily lifted the lid to reveal an amazing, glorious work of art.

'Emily, do you like it? Both Richard and I thought it was so beautiful, we knew it was perfect.' Annabelle squealed with exhilaration.

Emily sat in astonishment as she lifted the brooch from the box. Its proportions were substantial as it lay within her delicate palm. The wonderful leafy tendrils and delicate floral frame of silver sparkled in the morning light. It entwined and encased the bisque finish of the blue Wedgwood Jasperware cameo.

'I love it, it's incredible,' announced Emily, trying unsuccessfully to hold back the tears.

'Open this one now.' Her father slid the large wrapped box towards her.

Emily opened the next as gracefully as the last, easing off the ribbon, and letting the paper fall away to reveal its secret. A large wooden box lay on the tablecloth in front of her, its great magnitude was remarkable considering its painstaking workmanship of marquetry and fantastic inlay of mother of pearl. A small silver key lay beside the box upon the pink paper, the key hung from a white cord tassel.

'Open it, there is more.' He retrieved the key, handing it to his daughter. Emily placed the small silver key into the equally small silver lock, both intricately carved. On turning the key, the box clicked and the lid rose slightly with release. Inside, lay three shiny silver items. She reached inside, removing them in turn.

'They are wonderful.' Tears still trickled from her cheeks down to her chin, as she inspected the silver dressing table set.

'They were your mother's. Both your sister and I thought it was time you had them, knowing you would treasure them dearly. I had them engraved with your initials; your mother would have wanted that.' Her father reached over and took hold of the large hairbrush. As he turned it, the bright sunlight beamed on the silver with a blinding glow. Indeed, in deep scrolled engraving ERW detailed the back of the brush and equally intricately on the hand mirror.

'I don't know what to say, they are so very lovely; all the gifts are so very lovely.' Emily's voice was overwhelmed with emotion.

Annabelle watched her sister as she placed the silver items back into the marquetry box. Tears still fell, but Annabelle knew that these were not of joy for the gifts, but those of sadness and sorrow for the absence of James. Annabelle looked at her father and gave him a knowing and encouraging nod.

Captain Warner silently placed something else in front of his daughter. Emily's heart leapt from her ribcage. Excitement glowed across her delicate features. The perfect birthday gift sat before her eyes, an envelope bearing her name in James' distinctive hand. The large swirl of the E and W made it unmistakable.

With contained exhilaration and not a word, Emily tenderly placed the unopened letter into the marquetry box along with her other gifts. She eased the box to one side and gazed at her family around the breakfast table.

'So very many wonderful and beautiful gifts, thank you.' Emily had regained her graceful poise and sat with a demure smile. 'Now, what is for breakfast this wonderful morning?' Emily gazed over at Mary who stood beside the dining table. 'I am so hungry this morning, Mary.' Emily's tear stained cheeks flushed as she beamed.

'Well, my lovely, you will be happy to know it's bacon, eggs and fresh baked bread and butter, and there is plenty to go round.' Mary stood rubbing her plump hands together and returned Emily's beaming smile.

'Wonderful,' announced the Captain. 'A good, hearty breakfast, just what is needed.'

After a splendid breakfast, Emily took her gifts and headed back up to her bedroom. Placing the glorious marquetry box on her dressing table, she eased open the lid to retrieve the letter. Emily tentatively took the envelope and simply stared at the handwriting. This was what she had waited for. For so many weeks, she had longed to receive some correspondence from her loved one. Now it was here, she couldn't bring herself to open it.

Perching on the pink velvet chair in the bay window of her bedroom, Emily eased open the envelope to reveal James' words as she began to read...

My Dearest Emily,

It is so very hard to sit here with the blistering sun, knowing that you are there without me. I promise you, my love; I will be home very soon. You are my life and being without you is no life at all, just an existence.

I'm not sure how long this letter will take to get to you. It is your birthday in a few weeks, and I hope it will be with you by then, so, Happy Birthday, my Emily. How is life there? I hope everyone is well, please give the family my regards. You must not worry about me, the war will soon be over, and I will be...

'You alright there, Jim, my boy,' the familiar gruff voice startled James. He put down his pencil and carefully folded the piece of paper. 'It's all right my lad. You go ahead, you write to your gal,' the gruff voice continued. 'We don't have much else, do we, than think of who we've left behind,' he paused with a sharp, crackling cough.

Becky Byford

'This damn dusty air, give me some good old, wretched English weather any day.'

James simply nodded with a half-hearted smile. 'Yes, Sir. Thank you, Sir.'

The dusk was falling, and the air was thick with the warmth from the day's blistering heat, corrupted by the stench of sweat and fresh blood; comrades lay bandaged and bleeding, muffled, suffering murmurs tainted the atmosphere.

His Sergeant's coughing travelled into the distance as James' thoughts once again revisited his love. His mind wandered to the vision of her long hair and big eyes, longing to touch her petite curves.

His loneliness was immense, mounting with each dawn. James knew that he was not alone, but his fellow comrades with their own tales of beauties back home, were no consolation to him.

Emily, his gloriously exquisite love, his wife, now alone, each with only their memories, as few as they were. James had envisioned their lives to be full of happiness and joy, never letting Emily out of his sight; and her absence was tearing a hole in his heart.

James imagined Emily's embrace; the sweetness of her breath on his face and the softness of her lips pressed against his.

With the tip of his forefinger, he eased the collar of his jacket around his neck, releasing the stench of stale sweat on his skin. The coarse material of his uniform, tinged with blood and ground in dirt, chafed his sun burned skin.

Unfolding the paper and licking the end of his dull pencil, he continued...

...with you very soon and our lives will be full of happiness. All the boys have been writing to their families. John, he's a really good chap, his wife's expecting a baby. He talks of nothing, but his lovely wife and how good it will be to go home. He comes from a small town by the sea; he tells stories of how good the place looks in the summer and how much he misses the sound of the sea. I like hearing him talk of home; I think life by the sea would

suit us. What do you think, a little cottage near the beach, and our children playing in the sand? It's thoughts like these that are keeping me going, and the thought of holding you in my arms, my dearest Emily.
I love you always
James

The room overflowed with the warmth of the May morning air. The curtains fluttered in the tranquil breeze. Her whole being was engulfed by a warm tender sensation as she glided her fingertips across the words of the letter. She consumed and absorbed each syllable of every word.

With her body drenched in sunlight and her heart and soul saturated by James' letter, this was indeed the only birthday gift she needed.

The morning ticked by. Emily, hypnotised by James' thoughts, wandered the house and garden, oblivious of time and space. The large clock in the dining room struck noon with twelve long chimes, as Annabelle walked through the open glass door and descended the stone steps. Emily sat beneath the tree in the sunshine wearing a lovely pale blue dress and a distant smile. She was unaware of her sister's approach.

'Darling, your brooch looks stunning with your dress. That is just what I had in mind when I chose it.' Annabelle stood in front of Emily casting her in shadow. 'Well, are you ready, Emily?'

'Yes, sorry... ready for what?' Emily came to, a little bemused, as she had absolutely forgotten her sister's birthday surprise.

'I hoped we could spend some time together, just you and I. We are going on a picnic. Mary has made us a wonderful feast. Cakes, fruit, everything you can imagine. Go and fetch your parasol, and I shall get the basket from the kitchen.' Annabelle reached down to take Emily by the hand.

As they strolled, the air was balmy, the sun beamed down. Birdsong could be heard high in the leafy foliage of the trees. There was nothing of worry or sorrow; the moment was of peace and happiness. The park was full of green, flourishing trees and a lush, thick carpet of grass. Annabelle led the way down towards the river.

The old Abbot's Bridge made its way across the stream; two stone arches bowed over the river's calm surface; its aged flint stonework dripping with the history of the monks that once passed over it, centuries before.

As they reached the bank, the trickling river with its soft chanting soothed and eased its surrounding. They saw overhanging boughs of the border trees, their image reflected upon its glassy glistening surface, tips of the branches paddled in the warm water creating gentle ripples.

Annabelle came to a stop close to the bridge, resting the picnic basket on the soft bank, as she shook the checked blanket. It billowed in the calm breeze, and gently came to rest on the grass, the sisters sat down.

The landscape was breathtaking, the remains of the old abbey, with its once magnificent sacred presence, the monks and friars that formerly trod the grounds, residue of their hymns and prayers, still evident in the flint fabric of the ruins.

They sat, shaded by their parasols, in awe of the surroundings. Annabelle opened the wicker basket, removed a small white linen cloth that she laid between them. The basket held a delicious feast. Emily reached in and took out some fresh baked bread that was still warm and some sliced ham and placed them on the cloth. Mary had baked some small cakes dusted with icing sugar and the girl's favourite sweet homemade fudge. There, at the bottom of the basket, wrapped in a checked cloth were two red shiny apples and two ripe, juicy pears.

'This is wonderful, thank you. It is just what we needed and Mary has been baking all morning by the looks of this,' stated Emily, as Annabelle poured them both a glass of Mary's homemade lemonade.

'Well, it isn't every day that you turn twenty. I think that Mary has a special dinner planned for later; she mentioned roast pork, I think.' Annabelle teased Emily, she knew it was her favourite and just couldn't keep it a surprise.

'Just don't tell her that I told you. You will have to look exceedingly surprised when she tells you,' warned Annabelle with a giggle.

'Of course I will, you know that. She is so very amusing when she is trying to keep a secret. I know that she went to the butcher's this morning because she made such a fuss when I walked into the kitchen after breakfast. I knew she was trying to hide it in the cold larder.'

Both of them giggled at the thought of Mary. She was a jolly lady in her fifties. She was plump and wore her long silver hair high in a bun to keep it neat and tidy; she constantly wore a starched white apron that tied in a large bow at the back. Mary was always pristine and kept the house that way too.

She was not of great height, only about five feet, but she was definitely not someone to mess with, as the grocer and butcher frequently found out if they sold her anything below her very high standard. She could be very hard and stubborn; she didn't care much for those who got under her feet, and thought they should be off doing something worthwhile.

Mary had never married, as she felt that her place was with the Captain and the girls when their mother had passed away. She had loved both the girls as if her own. Mary was warm and caring, and both the sisters loved her dearly.

'Annabelle, thank you so much for my brooch, it is wonderful. I have never seen anything so beautiful. In fact it is a beautiful day.' She lay back with a gentle sigh, resting her head upon the blanket under the shade.

'I am glad you love it. I am so glad you got a letter from James. Did it take long to get here?' Annabelle replied with caution. She wasn't sure if her sister had the desire to talk about it.

'Yes, he had written it many weeks ago. But he assures me that everything is looking good. He says he will be coming home to me very soon.' Emily paused with a dreamy expression.

'It is lovely to see you smile. It has been so long since we have had a day like this.' Annabelle turned to look at her sister and continued in a softer whisper. 'Darling, I have something to tell you.' She couldn't contain herself, and her fair features wore an immense beam.

'What is it? Do tell me.' Emily returned with a curious smile.

'Richard and I are expecting a baby. It is due to be born in December.'

'That is the most fantastic news! Oh, I am so pleased for you both.' Emily sat up, and leant over Annabelle, squeezing her in her arms. 'It is going to be wonderful, darling.'

'It is still very early and Dr Hickson said everything should be fine as long as I rest.'

'What does Richard think? I should imagine he is thrilled at the concept of having an heir. Have you told Father yet?' Emily's excitement at becoming an aunt was unmistakable and contagious.

'No, only Richard knows. I wanted to tell you today before we told anyone else, an extra birthday present for you. Darling, I think we shall tell Father this evening. I wanted you to know before anyone else. I shall feel complete; to be a mother is the most important thing to me.'

Annabelle laid herself back upon the homely checked blanket, closing her eyes.

'Oh Annabelle, how wonderful it will be, to be a mother and have a child of your own. I would love to be a mother one day…when James returns home, we shall live happily ever after.' Emily's tone aired a slight unease. Annabelle caught sight of her sister's concerned expression.

'Of course you will. I am sure that James will be home very soon, the war will be over, and you can make plans and start your own family. You will be a wonderful mother.' Annabelle clasped her hand in reassurance. 'Everything is going to be just fine. I promise.'

The dear sisters lay holding hands, basking in the warmth of the sunshine, their hearts elated.

* * *

'Glorious. What a glorious June morning,' announced Captain Warner, as he sat down at the breakfast table. The soft breeze billowed the lacy curtains, blowing them against the open glass doors. 'Thank you, Mary.'

He breathed deeply into his large chest, taking in the fresh but warm morning air. Mary poured them all a cup of morning tea from the large silver teapot, and the family sat in conversation as they consumed breakfast. Captain Warner sat at the head of the table with both his daughters in view.

'The photographer is arriving at eleven.' the Captain declared.

'Of course. May I enquire, will it be Mr Brown?' questioned Emily, in a falsely sweet voice, as she continued to push a pork sausage across her plate.

'Yes, it is.' He sat himself back on his dining chair, inhaling deeply with readiness for the imminent conversation, which was to follow.

'Father, how can you tolerate his manner? He is so infuriating!' Emily knew she was fighting a losing battle with her father, but she did so delight in the debate.

Captain Warner agreed with his daughter that Mr Brown was indeed a strange gentleman with peculiar mannerisms, but he stood by his judgement of him as a photographer. He was always prompt in his time keeping, reliable, and undoubtedly worked to the highest standard, even to the Captain's degree.

'Yes, I agree. The wedding photographs of James and I are wonderful. However, they would have taken half the time if the delightful Mr Brown had not insisted we continue to pose outside the church in the snow. The weather was indeed wonderful and gave an enchanting feel to the day, but for the wedding party to stand for an hour or so in the snow was ridiculous.

'My personal thought is that the family photographs taken in the warm and dry are equally desirable to those with the harsh snow; and all for the sacrifice of art.'

Emily sat back on her chair in conclusion after stating her case, her eyes showing her obstinate belief.

'Well, dearest sister, let us hope we do not have a freak snowstorm this morning.' Annabelle sympathised and related to Emily's opinion of Mr Brown; their encounters with him had always been somewhat memorable.

When they were the aged eight and four, Captain Warner had commissioned Mr Brown to take a collection of photographs of his daughters. Annabelle recalled the day to be warm but rather breezy.

Mr Brown had positioned a large, Indian silk parasol, to shade the girls from the sun and to add a touch of drama to the setting. Both small girls were dressed in lace dresses and sat upon a large garden seat beneath the parasol for many hours.

Annabelle recalled, the exasperating Mr Brown had positioned and repositioned them to create the correct picture. However, to Mr Brown's disapproval, he had no control over the weather, and he became increasingly distressed as the wind blew the long silk tassel trim of the parasol and the lacy frills of their dresses, and that just would not do for the photograph.

Both Annabelle and Emily had sat patiently for what seemed an age, when Emily announced that she required the ladies' room, as she had consumed a rather large amount of Mary's homemade lemonade that afternoon.

Mr Brown had been insistent that she continued to stay where she was because we have to make sacrifices for art and beauty. Mr Brown obviously had not made a very agreeable impression with Emily on that day. Since then, the mere mention of his name made her furious.

The morning sunshine was marvellous; the garden was in bloom, and the birds were chirping their summer chorus. The light glimmered through the study window. Annabelle sat upon her most favoured settee, admiring a photograph of her wedding day. The study exhibited a menagerie of framed memories, and she sat patiently

Remember to love me

awaiting the arrival of the photographer, and indeed, her sister, who was still dressing for the occasion.

Annabelle's pale lilac gown hung gently to the floor, with a softly fitted bodice and elbow length, puffed sleeves. Her square neckline was trimmed with deep lace in a harmonious shade, complementing Annabelle's fair skin, and radiant beauty. Blonde locks piled up elegantly, revealed her slender neck.

Around her delicate wrist was fastened the elaborate silver charm bracelet. The numerous gems sparkled and twinkled in the bright sunshine.

Captain Warner popped his head around the study door. 'The photographer is here Annabelle. Are you ready?'

'Yes, I am ready, I am on my way. Is Emily ready?'

'I have not seen her yet. Upstairs, dressing I presume. I shall give her another call.' Captain Warner walked over to the stairs. 'Oh, do come along! The gentleman is ready for you,' he bellowed loudly, as Emily appeared through the parlour doorway. 'There you are, Mr Brown is in the garden waiting,' he continued in a softer voice, as she headed back into the dining room, through the glass doors and gracefully descended the stone steps.

Quickly, Emily headed back up the staircase. 'Please wait, Father, I shall return in a moment!' She swiftly returned, holding her wonderful Wedgwood cameo.

Captain Warner was in the garden chatting with the photographer. Mr Brown had assembled his photographing equipment, and had placed one of the white scroll back garden chairs under the dominating tree at the far end of the sumptuous lawn.

He stood with his great height, all of five feet, and his plump build. His large, round belly was barely housed inside his brown waistcoat, his balding head shone in the sun as if it had been polished. This eccentric gentleman flattered and tittered as Captain Warner made small talk. Breathing deeply into his already over stretched chest, he desperately tried to match his stature to that of the Captain's obvious and natural air of authority. Emily arrived back at the glass doors, seemingly unnoticed by her father.

'I could not have the photograph taken without it,' she stated, as she walked through the open doors, past the lavender shrubs down the steps. Captain Warner gestured to Emily to be quick, his frustration with Mr Brown all too obvious on his face. Emily's *I told you so* expression was all too apparent on hers.

Despite Emily's considered opinion of Mr Brown, the sitting did go rather more smoothly than anticipated. With thanks to Mother Nature, there was no wind to contend with, the sun shone wonderfully, with not a rain cloud to be seen. Annabelle had the foresight to sit for her photograph first. Mr Brown had been quite accommodating, the frills and lace of her dress had behaved appropriately, so as not to bother him.

She sat, extremely dignified, upon the cane chair, her hands neatly clasped in her lap with her charm bracelet just catching the sunlight, which Mr Brown found delightful. After only a few minutes, it was Emily's turn.

Annabelle made her way back into the house, the sun had become too much for her to cope with. These past few days she had been easily tired.

Annabelle watched from the study window as her sister posed for her photograph. Emily sat perfectly still upon the chair, made no fuss and smiled sweetly. Annabelle could imagine her thoughts, but could see that she withheld from voicing them for her father's sake.

'Ah, that is just perfect, my dear. That's it, hold still…wonderful.' As Mr Brown leant over the tripod gazing at the image of Emily through the camera, his bald shiny head reflected the sun like a mirror, blinding Emily. Desperately trying not to move, she could not help herself, she could not contain it, and with a suppressed giggle, Emily squealed. Mr Brown shot up from his tripod with startled expression.

'Whatever is it?' he shrieked, his head still glinting reflectively.

'Oh, I am sorry, Mr Brown, I think there was a wasp, and it was buzzing around my head. I do apologise, I think it has gone now; please continue.' Emily's voice shook as she curbed her laughter. Nevertheless, she held herself together beautifully.

'Please don't worry my dear, we shall have another try. No sacrifice can be too great than that which we make of our art. Hmm...' He pondered for a moment, and then continued. 'Maybe, if you sit facing the other direction...yes, I think that would be better, and lift your chin my dear, let's show off that wondrous cameo shall we?' bellowed Mr Brown with his imitational grandeur. Annabelle stood at the study window in disbelief, as the photographer continued, oblivious of his humorous figure.

Regardless of Emily's slight waver, the sitting went well. Both girls retired to the study afterwards to observe their father and the photographer arrange the garden back to its usual refined setting.

'Oh Emily, I cannot believe that you could be so cruel.'

'Well, it was the reflection off his shiny balding head. I had to tell him it was a wasp. I could not really tell him he was blinding me now, could I?' As Emily gazed out of the window, both chuckled.

Annabelle sat upon her red velvet settee and opened her book. The dark green leather bound volume lay in her lap, as she reclined upon her restful seat, and her mind wandered from the words on the page. Suddenly, she felt a stabbing pain in her lower abdomen. Frantically trying not to alarm her sister, she steadily rose from her seat and stood, leaning with one hand on the desk beside her.

'Darling, whatever is it?' Guiding her back to the settee, Emily took her hand and looked into her face. 'Annabelle, tell me what is wrong. Is it the baby?' Emily's heart pounded beneath her dress, in fear and panic, not knowing what she should do for the best.

'Please, get Richard.' Annabelle's words were weak and few, she lay back on the upholstery and closed her eyes, and her body ached. Emily quickly dashed out of the room.

BECKY BYFORD

Richard was sitting in the dining room talking to Captain Warner, who had just wandered in from the garden.

'Richard, quick, it's Annabelle! I think it is the baby!' Emily rushed in and rushed out again, tearing back off into the study, closely followed by Richard and her father.

As they entered the study, Annabelle sat motionless on the settee, her head resting back on the velvet her hands clasped in front of her. She made no movement as Richard took her hand and sat beside her.

'Belle, darling.' His voice was soft as if not to disturb her. 'Darling, tell me what's wrong.' Richard placed his right hand on her flushed cheek and eased her round to face him.

Very slowly, she opened her eyes. 'I am fine now, really, it was just a little discomfort. But I am fine now.' Annabelle spoke softly in a whisper. 'I think I shall like to have a lie down; maybe too much sunshine. It was quite warm earlier having the photograph taken.' She affectionately took Richard's hand, with a reassuring plea in her eyes. 'Please, do not start to worry. I am fine, really.'

'I will fetch Dr Hickson.' Captain Warner left the room.

'Come along, darling, I shall help you upstairs, you need a rest.' Richard walked Annabelle to the bedroom, where she lay upon the bedspread, her head resting on the pillow as she stared out of the window. Mesmerised by the chanting birdsong, she lay cocooned, her eyelids becoming heavier and heavier, as she drifted off to sleep.

'Ah, Dr Hickson, thank you for coming so quickly.' Richard met the doctor at the staircase to the bedroom. Annabelle lay still and peaceful on the large bed.

'It is all right Richard, you can wait downstairs. I shall be down as soon as I have looked at her. I am sure everything is going to be fine.' Dr Hickson gracefully closed the bedroom door, as Richard descended the staircase. Annabelle slowly opened her eyes.

'Dr Hickson, I am fine really. Just a little discomfort, a small stabbing pain, it passed very quickly. I am just extremely tired.' Annabelle began to ease herself into a sitting position on the bed.

'It's fine, my dear, you lay still. Let me have a look at you.' Dr Hickson examined Annabelle, before leaving her to sleep. Annabelle changed into her nightgown and slipped into the smooth sheets.

The doctor entered the parlour, where Richard was watching passers-by out of the window. He turned upon hearing Dr Hickson's approach.

'Dr Hickson, how is she? Is the baby going to be all right?' Richard with his greater height loomed over the doctor. His hands shook as he held them behind his back.

'Richard, sit down. Annabelle will be just fine if she rests. I cannot express this enough, she must, for her own and the baby's sake. I have told her to stay in bed for the remainder of today. She should be all right to get up tomorrow afternoon.' The doctor headed for the front door. 'I shall call round again in a couple of days, just to check on her.' Richard closed the front door as Dr Hickson left.

The afternoon drifted into evening. Dusk fell upon the bedroom, as Annabelle lay sheathed in her cotton sheets, her bed warm and comforting. The room progressively darkened and her eyes gradually became heavy.

Becky Byford

Remember to love me

From heaven to hell

B right light glistened through the drapes, the warm honey glow wrapped the room, and she lay submerged in its warmth, cosy and safe.

With the smooth linen of the pillowslip against her cheek, she lay on her side, her arm about her head, her fingers entwining, wrapping her fair hair tightly, as if to stop all circulation.

It will all be fine, life will be perfect, she repeatedly drummed in her head. It'll be fine and dandy. She couldn't bear to think of what might be, yet her consciousness wouldn't let her think of anything but.

Turning over onto her back, she gazed at the window.

The long curtains billowed very slightly, almost a waltz as the warm breeze caused them to dance. She closed her eyes again; letting the magical amber penetrate her eyelids, soothe her soul. It will all be fine, perfect.

Annabelle eventually arose from her bed and dressed.

'Ah, my dear, are you feeling better today? How about a nice cup of tea?' Mary asked, as Annabelle approached the bottom step of the staircase. 'You're looking better for some rest,' she beamed.

'That would be lovely, thank you; I shall be in the study.'

BECKY BYFORD

Annabelle placed her hand on the cold brass knob of the study door. She eased it open to reveal her favourite space, pushing the door to behind her, encasing herself within the safety of its walls. For a moment she stood with her back to the door, resting her head back against the wood, her eyes tightly shut. She absorbed the warm calming atmosphere, soothing her soul. The door nudged her back, and she quickly stepped forward in time for Mary to enter, carrying a tea tray.

'There you go, my dear, and I thought you must be hungry, so I've cut you a slice of sponge cake.' Mary glided her way across the carpet, resting the tea tray upon the side table near the settee. 'It's very stuffy in here, let me open the window. You could do with some fresh air.' Mary reached over and pushed up the sash. The breeze lifted the soft lacy drapes as they waltzed in the light wind; the afternoon sunshine hit the depths of the garden. 'It's such a lovely day.'

'Thank you Mary, the cake looks delicious. What time is it? I didn't realise it was so late.' Annabelle reached over to her china teacup and saucer.

'Oh, it's about four o'clock, my dear. You obviously needed the rest. I told Emily she wasn't to wake you and that you needed your sleep.' Mary headed back to the door, giving her usual beaming smile as she returned to the kitchen.

Annabelle reached over to her book, *The Silent Yearning*, where she had left it yesterday. It sat on the mahogany desk, the book's green leather binding soft and hot to the touch, warmed by the bright sunlight in which it had sat all day. Enchanted by the words of the characters that resided in the pages of her novel, Annabelle sat snug and relaxed.

'Darling, do come outside, it is such a glorious day. Some fresh air will do you good.' Richard entered the room, his face alight with joy at seeing her.

'Maybe, in a while, I feel comfortable and at ease in here. Please, you must not worry so; I am perfectly fine and well.' Annabelle smiled at him and he knew to leave her be. There was nothing she enjoyed more than losing herself in the pages of her beloved books. Richard turned and left the room, gently easing the door to as he went.

'Annabelle, Annabelle,' Emily called from the garden, and the melody of her voice carried on the afternoon breeze. Annabelle returned her book to the safety of the oak shelf and strolled to the open sash. The summer wind whipped a golden strand of hair across her pale cheeks, as the view of her family was visible between the lacy curtains. She walked across the room, heading for the glassy doors of the dining room. The large grandfather clock displayed a quarter past the hour, as she passed through onto the stone steps of the garden.

'Annabelle, there you are, do come and join us, Mary has made some lemonade and I am managing to beat Richard!' Emily was playing a game of chess with Richard. They regularly amused themselves with it, although Richard always won and Emily would constantly accuse him of cheating. Richard thought she needed to pay better attention to her moves; her casual approach to the game made her easy to beat. Emily was the only member of the family willing to take him on; Annabelle, on the other hand, preferred to occupy herself with a good book.

The soft grass was deep and plush underfoot as she sat down on one of the reclining wooden garden chairs. Calming heat from the afternoon sun penetrated the leafy shelter of the tree. Captain Warner strode with military precision down the stone steps onto the grassy carpet. His daughter lay back in her chair absorbing the sunrays. He placed himself on a chair next to Annabelle and reached for her hand, which lay tiny in his dominating palm, a child's.

'Annabelle, please don't hide away.' Her father gripped her hand tightly, in painful memories of losing his beloved wife. Annabelle saw the pain in his eyes, a pain that she too shared, maybe now more so than ever. She longed to have her mother there, to hold and comfort her.

'I am fine; I do wish you would not worry so.' Annabelle reassured her father. There was no way she would risk her chance of motherhood, feeling the bond between her and her child.

'Both you and Emily, have always been the most precious things in my life.'

'I know, please don't worry.' Annabelle smiled in reassurance.

Emily squealed with absolute delight, filling the summer air with her glorious rapture, as she jumped to her feet, her face beaming.

'Your dear sister has finally beaten me.' Richard couldn't believe his eyes. For the first time in four years, Emily had triumphed. Emily's satisfaction at Richard's defeat was all too clearly evident on her features, as she skipped around the table to sit next to Annabelle.

Emily and her father sat either side of Annabelle. The peace and enchantment of the idyllic afternoon travelled the warm scented air, bright blue sky, and hazy rays of sunshine, slightly visible through the thick foliage of the tree. Annabelle lay, resting on her chair, happy and content. Richard reset the old family chess set on the small folding table on which it sat. Emily rose from her chair and headed to the kitchen up the stone steps, closely followed by the Captain, to fetch the afternoon tea.

Richard took up position next to his wife, placing his strong hand on her stomach. The fabric of her pale lemon dress was soft under his touch and Annabelle placed her hand on his in reassurance that soon life would be whole. Their dream of parenthood, their completeness as a family, it was very important to Richard that he had an heir, and what she longed for was to be a mother, more than anything.

Annabelle squeezed Richard's hand incredibly tightly, her fingers numb, her fingertips white with the pressure. She couldn't move. The pain inside her was too immense. Richard sat up and looked at her pale face. Despair and agony were expressed on her features and he felt helpless, sensing the pain and sorrow himself. She slumped forward, the stabbing, knifing pain penetrating her lower body, and her long golden tresses hung across his arm into her lap.

Remember to love me

    Richard ran across the garden and leapt up the steps. Within seconds, Emily came rushing to her sister's side with a calm voice of reassurance. Inside, Emily's heart was breaking; she shared her sister's desire for parenthood, her closeness to Annabelle made the pain unbearable, and her own body ached with the shared emotions of loss, agony, and desperation. Emily observed her sister, her soul mate, her Annabelle, being devoured by this most horrifying moment in time.
    Richard dashed back to Annabelle's side, and with a single movement, he encased her inside a large cream blanket, and carried her into the house in his strong, capable arms. Emily sat bewildered, under the shaded veil of leafy branches, lost and paralysed in the panic stricken moment.

    'How is Belle this morning, Dr Hickson?' asked Richard, as the elderly doctor descended the staircase. The morning sunshine filled the whole house, illuminating every object with its glorious warmth, but inside each and every heart was deep overwhelming darkness. Dr Hickson reached the bottom step and followed Richard into the bright dining room.
    'She will be fine, Richard. She will need lots of rest, I cannot stress that enough. She is very distraught and needs everyone's support and understanding.' The elderly gentleman looked at Richard, who stood in despair, staring at the large grandfather clock, studying its intricately carved face, willing it to turn back the time.
    'I just cannot understand why this happened? She had rested, I made sure. We all made sure.' Richard's tall stature seemed weak and helpless. 'What can I do? There are no words that I can say to make her better.' Richard took hold of a mahogany dining chair and sank onto it.
    'I understand your grief, Richard, and that you have also lost your baby. In a few days, why don't you both take a trip? Spend some time at the coast. The sea air will do her good, and the holiday will be good for you both.' Dr

Becky Byford

Hickson placed his thin seasoned hand on Richard's young shoulder.

* * *

Annabelle sat with her pale face close to the window, the bright morning sunshine illuminating her radiant features, the repetitive motion and regular rhythm of the train journey ensnaring her senses; the continuous sight of the trees and fields that passed Annabelle's dewy eyes made no effect, she was oblivious to all around her. Annabelle's heart ached with its hollow emptiness, as empty as Richard's hand that held hers. Annabelle's pale fragile hand lay lifeless and devoid of feeling. She was numb, a detached impersonator of her once affectionate self.

The train continued on its tracks, the minutes turned to hours, with no more change than the repeatedly flat fields of the Norfolk countryside, it felt as monotonous as the beat of her heart. Despite numerous attempts at polite conversation from her husband, Annabelle sat in silence for the entire journey. When the train, with its billows of hot steam, came to rest at the station, Richard stood up, grabbed the bags from the luggage rack, and Annabelle rose from her seat and took her husband's waiting hand. The sun beamed down as they dismounted from the train onto the platform, and the distinctive sea air filled her lungs; closing her eyes, she lifted her face to the sun, absorbing its rays. Her heartache eased slightly, with the recollections of her childhood; a time of simplicity and carefree days.

How could life ever be the same again? How could it ever be fine? No, it will never be fine and perfect. Only now, in the full bright light of this glorious summer day, could she feel, really sense the dark doom of reality, that life would never be the same. Never would she have the chance of her perfect life. Her life was over; she now had to live another's.

* * *

Remember to love me

Vivid orange wrapped the horizon, as the sunrise climbed to meet the morning. The early hour brought hope of peace and an end to her restless night. Annabelle sat beside her bedroom window, watching the gulls fly the dawn sky, swooping low upon the glistening surface of the sea then far beyond the gaze of her eyes.

The hour was no more than five.

With lightness of foot, she wandered the polished boards to dress. Removing her cotton nightgown, she stood at her mirror. Her reflection was another's, scarcely a resemblance of the woman she had hoped to be, the chance of which had faded. Her nakedness was not what she had wished for, her body was gaunt, and her limbs willowy as she folded her arms about her stomach. Skeletal hipbones protruded through her thin skin, her ribs rippled below her small breasts. No sign of motherhood remained; slight as it was, it had vanished.

The past few days had been cruel; Richard had left without a word. Not a single uttered phrase of reassurance or love. The bereavement she was suffering was more than the physical pain of miscarriage; it was losing the part of her soul that made her Annabelle. Never before had she felt a stranger inside her own skin. As she stared down at her hands, they were white and empty, as they had been on the train, despite the presence of Richard's. Alone was all she could be; how was she to fill the void that was a vast gaping chasm in her heart?

She covered her body, the sight of which turned her stomach, the strong nauseous sensation reaching her throat. Annabelle sank to her knees, weeping as she gripped the fabric of her simple gown. The sickness grew more forceful; her mind sank into her familiar abyss. She retched, but her body was empty, she hadn't been able to eat for three days, mere nibbles of bread being all she could muster. Although now, as the nausea consumed her, her heart swarmed with the tortured reminder of her pregnancy, the sickness she had felt each morning she awoke.

Becky Byford

She lay upon the floor; her cheek pressed against the bare wood, wishing it would end.

Remember to love me

Seascape

Sleep was something of the heavenly life that had long gone. Now, Annabelle's days and nights mingled into one long, continual misery. She had never felt so alone. Even with the death of her mother, recalling the confusion and not understanding why, was nothing to this. This loss brought comprehension, knowing, yet still she had no control.

A little past five, she crept from the cottage, and headed for the sand dunes. Under her arm, she clutched a canvas, in her hand an easel, in the other a large case with paints and brushes. The sun was already high; she felt her heart curse its bright abundance, lavishing the seascape with copious amounts of brilliance. She had adopted this part of the dunes, naming it her own. As the day awoke to the sunshine, she made her journey in her daily ritual.

Time was simple up here upon the lookout of life. She could exist with the elements, having to hold no regard for their feelings. The last two days had weakened her soul beyond what she thought could be healed. One simple phrase had crumbled the walls around her insular world. She would not listen to it any more.

Amongst the long spear-headed grass and bare patches of rough sand, Annabelle pitched her easel. Removing her shoes, kicking them in the grass, she stood barefoot on nature's carpet. Random clusters of dusky mauve heather and groups of small violet flowers, adorned the otherwise bland dunes. Holding her dress above her ankles, Annabelle strolled, watching her bare feet caress the grass and blooms, the sand seeping between her toes.

She unfolded a blanket, spreading it over the rough ground, and then unpacked her paints. She squeezed colour onto her palette, tones of blue and green, and amid them a daub of stark white. Eyes closed against the world, Annabelle swept her brush. A flood of intense azure blue masked the rough weave of canvas. This was her world, sedated and numb. She continued to paint, as the sun grew high above her. She could feel the hours pass as the shadow cast her art.

'How long have you been out here?' There came no reply. 'Belle, what time did you get up?' Anna trudged the sandy dune, her long gown skimming the grass. Annabelle didn't move, her brush simply gliding the paint along the shoreline, white foam lapping the sand in gentle strokes.

This was her place of solitude, and Anna was intruding.

'Come on Belle, come, have some breakfast.'

Annabelle glanced at Anna; she stood close, her shoulder touching hers. Still she said nothing; she couldn't bring herself to open her mouth, the words felt stifled and lost somewhere in her misery.

'You need to eat today.' Anna sighed. 'I know you think it is harsh of me, but you will get through this, Belle. Life must go on.'

Anna walked to the edge of the dune. The drop was steep, the sand below untouched. The long stretch of beach smooth, the sea settled on the horizon with only the slightest of movement along the shoreline. She turned back to Annabelle, who quickly glanced back at her painting.

'Your mother...she felt the same. I tried my hardest, we both did...your father and I. She locked herself in her room for days on end.'

Anna gazed back at the sea and up to the bright morning sky. 'At least you're out here; it is beautiful, glorious even. I do understand, Belle.'

Anna walked back to her niece and sat down on the blanket. She stretched her legs before her and neatened her petticoats over her ankles. She faced the sky, her eyes closed against the sun.

Annabelle watched. The absurdity of it! She knew what this was.

Whilst out here, high upon the dunes overlooking the glistening sea, Anna knew she had her attention. She wouldn't walk away from the conversation. Not that she felt it had been a conversation. Aunt Anna had expressed her views of the situation, but there had been no reply.

Just as now, as Annabelle stood there with the sand between her toes, she had no response to give. The emotions were hers, to be dealt with as she felt fit. What did Aunt Anna know of loss, of the emptiness left by an infant?

'Richard loves you,' she hesitated. 'You can try again. You can still have the family you desire. It needn't be lost.'

'Lost?' Annabelle spat. 'Lost, you say it needn't be lost. You really don't understand do you? All this time, I thought it was just condolence.' Her paint brush dropped on her palette, white paint splattering the front of her dress.

'But you can try again.'

'You speak as if I've lost a handkerchief and could go find another one.'

'Your mother felt the same. But you must remember that things do change.'

'My mother again; yet another loss of mine.' Annabelle's mouth stung, her mind bitter and hostile.

'Perhaps you should listen, and stop torturing yourself for things that are God's doing. Not yours and not Richard's.'

'Richard left me.'

'No Belle, he went home.'

Annabelle discarded her palette to the blanket. The painting finished, thriving, alive with emotion, whilst its artist was dead and lifeless. She headed a couple of yards to the edge of the dune, seating herself with her legs dangling.

'Your mother felt the same. Your poor father had no idea how to get through to her. It was months before she was her bright self again, although, there was always something missing from her smile.' Anna sat beside her niece, her arm about her shoulder. 'She thought I never understood, but I did.'

Slowly, her aunt's words began to seep through the cracks, her brain gradually absorbing their meaning. She couldn't take her eyes from the sea, but she spoke. For the first time in days, she spoke with note and regard.

'My mother, I'm not sure what you mean, Anna. What about my mother?'

'He would have been two years older than you, if he'd survived.'

'He?'

'Your brother. Thomas, she named him. He was born too early; the mite didn't stand a chance. Your mother, well, as you can imagine, she was devastated, no…more than just devastated, well you know…' Anna sighed and took a deep breath.

'You see, they had been here. The doctor had said the sea air would be good for her in the last few months of her pregnancy. She loved it, just as you do,' she stared back at the easel. 'She didn't have the talent you have. She wanted to be in the sea, have her feet soaked up to her hem. Your father would curse, but she didn't care.' Anna laughed. 'You see it was Rose's young nature and lust for life that grasped your father; as soon as they met she had captured him. He'd never known anyone like her, so vulnerable, yet at the same time, full of passion.'

'Emily.'

'Yes, just like Emily.'

'Thomas? How is it I never knew?'

'It was the saddest day I have ever known.' Anna removed her arm and lent over the dune to see the beach.

'She said she was going to the beach, walking across the sand, probably to wade up to her knees in the sea, no doubt, her usual evening journey. Your father was in the cottage, I was in the garden. I shall never forget that evening as long as I live.' Anna hesitated a moment, took Annabelle's hand in hers before she continued. 'It was never spoken of after, you know, after the initial weeks, and then life carried on. I'm not saying it got better, but life changed, eventually.'

'That night, Rose had been down on the beach longer than usual. Normally, she would have her wander, her wade in the sea, then head back to the garden. The evening was hotter than it had been; we were to have supper in the garden. Without knowing why, your father suddenly came into the garden white faced, as if all life had been sucked from his cheeks and that look on his face. It was as if he knew, like they had a kind of connection; do you know what I mean?' She stared at Annabelle.

Annabelle knew that connection. It was Richard and hers. Words had never been necessary, she knew his thoughts and the emotions held in his heart, how he loved her. But now, that had changed. She felt blind, his love seemed invisible to her eyes now. No matter how hard she tried, she couldn't hear his heart.

'So, your father came rushing outside. Well, I didn't know what was wrong. He didn't speak to me, just dashed past me to the dunes. I ran as quickly as I could.

'Rose, your mother; she hadn't made it as far as the beach. He found her on the sandy path to the beach. It wasn't that it was steep, as you know, it's quite a gentle slope, but…well, I don't exactly know what happened. Maybe she tripped or fell, but she lay there, bruised and bleeding. It was the bleeding that made me gasp. "The baby", she kept saying, "my baby".'

Annabelle gripped her hand. 'The baby, Thomas.'

'Your father grabbed her. I remember her dress, a beautiful shade of dusky rose, it was your father's favourite, well, now it was red and soaked with blood.' Anna took a long pause. They both watched a flock of seagulls soar across the sky, white darts piercing the cloudless blue.

'I had no idea. I can't believe this, I just can't take this in,' her words broke their silence, and Anna continued, her hand gripping her niece's.

'I can still remember the sound, the silence, all but your mother's tears. By the time the doctor came, she was in full labour. He had never known it to advance that quickly. She hadn't been on the beach for more than half an hour and the doctor took, well, maybe fifteen minutes. But as I say, it was nearly her time. It was bad!

'Rose had lost a lot of blood, I could see by the colour of her dress and the dune was drenched with red stains. Your father knew it too. He never looked at me at all that night. Too afraid that he may break down, I figured.'

'My father?'

'Yes Annabelle, you see a man now that has seen many things. You know him as your father, strong and maybe reserved. But it wasn't always like that. He was tender and gentle, and I knew that night, if he looked at me, then he would lose that composure.'

'He loved my mother, I know that. I remember when she died. I was tiny, just an infant myself, but I saw the pain in his eyes when he looked at me. That used to haunt my dreams.'

'I know, darling girl, I know. But he had Emily to care for. He did his best.'

'He always did his best when it came to Emily. It was different with me, it always was.'

'Belle, he loves you.'

'I understand that. He loves me, as a father loved a daughter, but there is a special connection between Emily and Father. I could see it in his eyes when she was a baby. He would watch her sleeping; I could see he loved her, because she reminded him of Mother.'

'There is no doubt that Emily has your mother's enthusiasm and bounce. But that doesn't mean he loves you any less, only differently.'

'Maybe.'

'Anyway, the doctor was with her for not more than another hour before it was time. This was supposed to be the most precious day of their lives. Instead, it was the beginning of the end. Rose regained her strength within a few days, but the baby, well…' she broke off as Annabelle began to shake. Anna could sense her tears and feel the spasm of her crying. She said nothing to her, and taking a deep breath, she continued.

'A boy, she named him Thomas after her father. He was very weak, and the tiniest thing I had ever seen. The doctor said, even without the fall, he was so weak that he would have been a sickly child. He lay in Rose's arms for no more than a few minutes before he passed. His tiny hands…' Anna broke into tears.

'For weeks, Rose never spoke. After the funeral, she locked herself in the bedroom and never came out, for days she was there. She never ate and I'm not sure if she ever slept either. Sometimes, at night, I would hear her pace the floor for hours on end. It's strange; sometimes I think I can still hear her. Then again, I know that you have done the same; I know you are not sleeping and not eating either.'

'I have no appetite, my insides feel dead.'

'I know, I understand. That is what I tried to tell her.'

'Anna, I know you want to help, but…'

'Belle, you need to hear me. It was very early one morning, so early not even the birds were awake. I could hear her treading the floor boards, her usual pacing. I quietly dressed and went down to the kitchen to make some warm milk. I thought if I could only get her to drink something.

'She sat on the chair by the window, she drank some of it, more than I thought she would, but she never said a word. She looked dead behind her eyes. Something I see in you, and believe me, I had seen it before. I talked, tried to make her hear. I couldn't quite tell if she could hear me at all, let alone listen. She had drifted off to another world, somewhere your father wasn't allowed. Do you understand what I'm saying Belle? Richard, don't shut him out. He loves you, just as your father loved your mother.'

'But...he left me Anna.'
'He didn't leave you, he had to go home. You are as lost as your mother was, but as stubborn as your father.'
'Did she listen to you, my mother, did she hear you?'
'Eventually, she started to. You see, I knew that pain. I knew all too well, the pain of loss, of losing a child. Although, I never had the chance to hold mine in my arms. The same pain as yours, Belle.'
'Anna?'
'I lost my baby, only a few short weeks into my pregnancy. It wasn't even noticeable; my clothes still fitted the same, my corset still as tight. But, I knew.'

Annabelle felt paralysed, as if she had grown roots beside the wild heather. This was incomprehensible, the single most startling revelation she could imagine. Aunt Anna sat beside her, with her fingers tightly gripping hers; she knew it to be true.

'I was young, far too young and far too naive.'
'The father, who was he? I can't get my thoughts around this. Does my father know?'

No, your father doesn't know and as for the father, well, he knew, but acted as if he didn't. And, even if he hadn't, it would have made no difference. It was never meant to be.' Anna sighed; almost a hint of laughter left her lips. 'I was a child, Belle. Nothing more than a child, there was no way I could bring a baby into this world.'

For a moment, a sudden stab of panic clenched Annabelle. She sat in silence, waiting for Anna to continue. She dared not speak, for the lump in her throat. Why had this family been doomed never to carry a child? What could her family have done that was so awful, to have God take a child from its mother's womb?

Anna continued in a soft voice. 'He was handsome, tall and blond. I had never known that a man could look so fair. His eye lashes were golden around his amber eyes. His cheeks would blush in the sun and were rich with freckles. I was so in love. Those who knew said it was ridiculous, not to be so naive and stupid. A silly young girl. But I knew that I loved him, there is no doubt even now. I have never felt that way since and, as the years pass, I never will again.'

'Who was he, Anna? Why was it so stupid?'

'He was my Master. I worked in his house, Maidwell Hall. Oh, I haven't spoken that name aloud for years.'

'Oh Anna.' Annabelle found no other words. Her mind was swirling with these new thoughts.

'My mother had got me the position, through an older cousin of hers. The house was a very respectable place, and they needed a scullery maid. I was a little over sixteen and full of ideals. They were a young couple with an infant son.

'I was happy there, I kept myself to myself. I was very conscientious, which made me favoured. The housekeeper was keen to take me under wing, so to speak. She treated me like a daughter. I loved it there.'

'Anna, how long were you there, before…'

'It was just before my seventeenth birthday, I was in the parlour, cleaning out the fireplace. It was the last one. The master came into the room, that wasn't unknown of in itself, apart from the fact he closed the door and I felt him stand behind me. I had wished for a moment like that for months. Don't misunderstand me; I never went looking for trouble. I knew my place and he was married and the Master of the house.

'But, as he stood in the same room as me, with no one else present, I felt my heart leap. This was what I had dreamed of, for months I had watched him. I wanted him and I loved him. I know you may find it impossible to comprehend. This was a man out of my reach in every way, but, at that moment, I realised he had done the same, watched and wanted.'

'I don't find it impossible at all, on the contrary I understand that feeling, you know I do. But Anna, it was in vain, surely.'

'I can't say it was easy or right. I knew every time I kissed him that he would never belong to me, but it didn't stop me. Belle, our hearts don't choose with any rational thought, anymore than love asks permission. I loved him and that was that. It continued for a few months, we would sneak around at night. I had a room to myself at the top of the house. During the few months following the birth of their youngest child, his wife had become introverted, and well, let's just say I was satisfying him in that way.'

Annabelle sat in utter shock at her aunt's matter of fact account of an illicit affair. She let Anna's hand slip from hers. Her silence spoke enough.

'I see you don't understand, do you? You have a very strong moral fibre running though your soul, inherited from your father. But Belle, I shall ask you one thing, if Richard belonged to another woman, would that stop you loving him? Would that love fade?' Anna rubbed her palms down her thighs. 'Well, perhaps we should go in for some breakfast or lunch, as the morning seems to have slipped away.'

'Anna, what about the baby?'

'It wasn't meant to be. I knew that from the very first moment, but it was mine, a small part of him that actually belonged to me.'

'You told him, didn't you? I mean, he just couldn't go around taking advantage like that.'

'He wasn't like that; none of it was as sordid as it may sound. He loved me, in his own way. We were both young, they were a young family. His wife was ill and he found solace with me.'

'But he didn't leave his wife for you, did he?'

'Of course not. Why would he? He was Samuel Maidwell of Maidwell Hall, a very respectable house; I knew that would never happen.'

'So, you told him then.'

'We were alone in the garden, it was late summer and the sun was just setting. The house had a glorious orchard; we would spend our time there. I can still remember the smell, the sweet aroma of the ripened apples. He kissed me, and then it was all over. I never saw him again. I left that night.'

'Why, what did he say? Did he make you go? Anna, what about the baby?'

Remember to love me

'The baby was mine, not really his. He had his own family, I knew that really. I knew I was fooling no one but myself. He never saw me again.' She stopped and stood up. The thin cotton of her gown had absorbed the now midday heat. Her feet trudged the grass until they reached the bare sandy patch where the easel was pitched.

Annabelle followed, enfolding her arms around her aunt. 'I'm sorry, Anna.'

'I left the house, but really I had nowhere to go. There was no way in this world your grandmother would have understood. I felt alone and betrayed. As the years have passed, I understand why; his commitments, not only to his wife, but to his position. The trouble was, I was a child and wanted my fairytale. And, the baby just wasn't meant to be. I went to stay with my mother's cousins. Without, I hasten to add, my mother knowing. But within a few days, it was gone. A mere memory.

Annabelle whispered softly. 'I understand how hard it was for you, you lost your love and your baby.'

'You see Belle, life changes.' She looked into Annabelle's eyes. 'Life always goes on, regardless. A new day breaks every morning, the only thing you can do is live it. Those we lose are not gone, just not within our reach. You will never forget your baby, just as I never forgot mine, and your mother, Thomas. You must remember to love the living. Your parents, at that moment, never thought life would continue. But it did, they had you then Emily. Your poor father lost Rose; she was the love of his life. You have Richard, Belle.'

She drifted over to Annabelle's easel. The sun had baked the oils dry. It was pure and innocent in its execution, but underlying the brushstrokes of paint was pain. The wildness and unpredictability of Mother Nature emanated from the canvas, expertly mingling with the delicate virtue of the seascape.

BECKY BYFORD

Remember to love me

Trinkets & Charms

Thick snow had settled during the night in a rich, dense blanket, and the landscape had the look of an idyllic Christmas card scene.

Bright daylight permeated the rosy floral drapes, casting a blushing tint over the bedroom as April stirred at the sound of clinking china, then a gentle tap on the bedroom door.

'Merry Christmas!' announced Sarah, as she gently eased open the door. She was carrying two identical bone china cups and saucers.

'Merry Christmas, Nan. How did you sleep?' April heaved herself into a sitting position and puffed the pillow behind her back. Taking her cup of tea, she watched as her grandmother wandered over to the window, and with one hand drew back the floral curtains. She then seated herself on the pink velvet bedroom chair nestled inside the bay window, the winter sunshine glistening through the frosted windowpanes, as she sank back into the deep springy upholstery.

'Your mum and dad shall be over in an hour or so. Your mum phoned to say she was bringing you a change of clothes. How did you sleep after such a busy day?' She didn't look at April as she spoke, but persistently stared out onto the bright white veiled graveyard beyond the boundaries of the garden.

'I'm fine, Nan. I had a good night's sleep, although I did dream a bit. But are you OK? You look a little pale.' April tried to gain her grandmother's attention, but to no avail. She continued to stare through the chilled glass.

'Nan, what is the matter?' April put her cup of tea down to rest on the bedside table, pulled back the blankets, and jumped out of bed. She quickly dashed across the room to where her grandmother was sitting.

'Nan?' April knelt down at her feet, the white cotton nightgown cushioning her knees. The concern in April's voice quickly turned to panic, as she saw her grandmother's pale vacant expression.

'Nan! Are you all right?'

For a few seconds she sat motionless, still gazing at the Christmassy view. Then, she turned to look at April, who by this point, had taken her grandmother's cup and saucer and placed them on the floor beside the chair. April stared into the face, on which old and tired features had appeared over night. The morning rays defined each line and flaw in her aged complexion. Her usual youthful characteristics were gone; an unrecognisable little elderly lady sat in front of April. An impostor garbed in her grandmother's pristine outfit.

'Oh Nan, whatever is it? Please, Nan, you are scaring me! Nan please!' April tightly held her grandmother's hand.

'Don't worry, I am fine and everything is going to be alright. I know it is. I think it's nearly my time. You are back here where you belong and my job here is done.' She smiled at April, a peaceful contented smile.

'Nan, don't say things like that. You're not going anywhere. It's Christmas Day and we are going to have the best ever. Perhaps you are just feeling a bit tired. Why don't you go back to bed for a while. Mum's cooking, and I can help her while you rest, Nan.' April's thoughts churned, attempting to convince her that her grandmother was just a little weary, after their previous day of even stranger occurrences. In truth, she had never known her to look so old and frail.

'I think I shall go and put some more logs on the fire; the coal is probably all burnt out by now. Make sure we are all warm and toasty.' The elderly lady gently rose from the chair, and headed out of the bedroom, with not another word said. April remained there, still kneeling beside the chair with only a cold cup of tea, and the harshness of reality seized her heart in the bright morning light.

Her grandmother had always seemed invincible, unaffected by the passing years. April had never really given consideration to life without her. She had always been such a major part of her life.

'Merry Christmas!' The greeting came in harmony as April opened the front door to her mother and father, and Julia and Michael stepped down into the warm and cosy space.

'Mum, can I have a word?' April grabbed Julia's arm, virtually dragging her to the furthest corner of the room.

'Whatever is it?' Julia took off her coat and laid it across her arm, then removed her gloves, and unravelled her scarf. Taking her mother's coat from her, hugging it to her chest in comfort, April replied. 'It's Nan.'

'Is she OK? How's she feeling this morning? I knew she wasn't right last night. I shouldn't have left her like that, she'd overdone it, I told her to take it easy, but she never listens to me.' She stood close to April, keeping her voice discreetly at a low volume.

'Mum, is there something I should know? She is OK, isn't she?' April had a sudden apprehension that her grandmother was not well, and more to the point, her mother had not told her. 'Mum, is she ill? Mum, will you please tell me?' April's voice rose above the sound of the Christmas carols coming from the stereo beside them. Michael popped his head round the door as April's voice carried into the hallway.

BECKY BYFORD

'Everything OK in here? Breakfast is ready in the dining room when you are. Julia, you both all right?' His face dropped at the sight of his wife's fraught expression.

'We are fine, darling. We'll be there in a moment.' Julia nodded; her tone peculiarly sweet and calm. Michael returned to the dining room without a sound.

'I think we should have this discussion after breakfast. You can help me in the kitchen with the washing up.' With an expression of, *not another word,* her mother turned and strode to the door, leaving April slightly bemused by the conversation, or rather lack of it. Julia stopped in the doorway and turned.

'Don't worry; everything is going to be fine. I promise. It's all part of life.' Her smile was peaceful, almost identical to her mother's smile of earlier.

April had no choice; she followed them into the dining room, where the aroma of eggs, bacon and warm buttery croissants met them.

'Sit down you two, don't let it get cold.' Michael ushered his daughter to the chair next to her grandmother. It was the same seat she had occupied the evening before, the same crystal covering of white concealed the view of the grass and the huge tree. The same beautiful dining room, the same beautifully laid table, the same festive atmosphere. However, this morning, things were not the same. April's heart was heavy and aching, a feeling of fear and dread swam in the pit of her stomach. The events of the past few weeks had been the most bizarre she had ever encountered, but the strain they had had on her was nothing to the anxiety and sheer panic she felt at this precise moment.

Breakfast passed almost unnoticed by April. She picked at her croissant, tearing off small pieces, nibbling them as the pastry flaked onto the plate. The dining room was so silent that the festive music from the front room boomed through the air in an assault on her ears. Michael gazed across the table at its occupants, placed his knife and fork neatly on his plate, and discreetly cleared his throat.

'Well, I must say, isn't it lovely to have snow? I can't really remember having snow on Christmas Day for years.'

Remember to love me

Michael looked across the table, eager to start some conversation. Coming out of her trance, April looked at her plate piled high with crumbs, and abandoned her half-eaten croissant on top. She brushed her fingers together over her plate, and then wiped them on the napkin which lay on her lap.

'Yes, it is beautiful today. It is just like a Victorian Christmas...' Her words stopped dead. Her thoughts turned to Annabelle. She had stood in front of those very glass doors, on a Christmas morning, much the same as this one, over a century before. The realisation of yesterday's events came to the foreground of her attention. For the first time during breakfast, April turned to look at her grandmother's face. She reached over, gently placing her palm upon Sarah's pale wrinkled hand. Her skin was soft and warm under her touch; she squeezed April's hand in reassurance. Sarah straightened on her dining chair, gracefully smoothed her long white hair down to the ribbon, which held it back. She spoke gently, her voice tender and reminiscing, but slightly unsteady.

'I remember when I was a small girl on Christmas morning. After breakfast, I would walk with my grandmother in the snow, whilst my mother prepared the turkey. She would bundle me up in my long red scarf...I only remember wearing that scarf on Christmas morning.' She paused for a second with a glazed expression, before continuing.

'We would wander through the graveyard, treading through the snow. I'd follow behind her and walk in her footprints, placing my feet in the imprint made by her boots. Back then, there were some wrought iron benches under the trees along the footpath, not like the wooden ones there now. She would clear the snow off with her glove and we would sit there for ages. My feet would dangle off the seat; I couldn't quite touch the ground. I'd swing my legs backwards and forwards, with my toes skimming the snow, until I had made a channel,' Sarah continued, recalling memories of her childhood Christmases, her voice soft and content. April sat mesmerised by her grandmother's accounts. April only had recollections of Annabelle, the young woman desperate for motherhood. But here were stories of her as a grandmother, her Nan's grandmother, an older and mature woman. April longed for more information.

She placed her elbow on the table and turned to face her, her head resting in her palm.

'Nan, what was Annabelle like?' April squeezed her hand; she had never heard her festive tales of walks in the snow.

'Annabelle? Well, she was in her fifties when I knew her. But she looked so beautiful and young. She had the longest golden hair that was always neatly tied up. It was only at night, when she would take it down and brush it, only then would you realise how lovely it was. If I was good, she would let me brush it with her lovely silver hairbrush. She would sit at the dressing table, and I would push the footstool over and stand behind her, looking into the mirror, my face next to hers.' She paused again and sat back on her chair, resting her weary head on the mahogany. She slowly closed her eyelids, recalling the image in greater detail. A sweet smile graced her aged face, a reminiscing smile, of recollected memories.

'Mum, you never told me any of this. Come to think of it, you have never really mentioned your grandmother much at all.' Julia placed her elbows on the dining table, leaning forward in intrigued concentration. April studied her grandmother's face, as she opened her eyes. A single tear fell down her cheek, tracing the lines.

'I was only nine when she died. It was 1934, a little while before the war. I remember my mum saying that it was all going to be fine, and that I would see her again someday.' She stopped, dropping her head; her eyes glistened in the bright sunlit room, with more emerging tears.

The room fell silent, the Christmas carols had finished, and no one said a word for a moment or two.

Then April gathered the breakfast plates and quickly bustled around the table, taking a pile of balanced plates and cutlery to the dining room door. Julia swiftly followed her with the cold teapot.

April stood at the kitchen sink, staring into the garden, whilst silent tears trickled, down her flushed cheeks and dropped from her chin into the running water. The view from the window was bright, and glared into April's aching eyes. Julia scraped the remains of breakfast into the kitchen bin, placing the plates on the work surface, ready for washing.

'It will be OK, darling. We all have to go at some time, and it's just the way it is. We all lose people we love, but they are never really gone, you know. When your grandfather died, I felt as if my heart had been ripped out. Although I was in my twenties, and a grown woman, it didn't seem to matter; I just felt like a little girl and I had lost my Daddy. I locked myself in my room for days, and then something happened.' Tears formed puddles in her eyes, as she stood with her daughter, staring at the cold, frosty landscape.

'Mum,' April turned to face her. 'Mum, what happened?'

'The strangest thing, I know this is going to sound ridiculous, but…well he was there with me.' She looked at April with wet eyes. 'It was late in the evening, and I lay on my bed, just looking out of the window. The room filled with a smell, his smell, the smell of pipe tobacco. He always smoked a pipe. I knew it was him. I closed my eyes and inhaled, and then I felt the bed move, just slightly, as if someone had sat down beside me. I lay there for what seemed an hour or so with the smell filling my nose, and my dad sitting next to me.' Tears gently traced down her cheeks as she smiled at April. 'I must have fallen asleep, because the next thing I knew, it was morning. I felt better that day, somehow. I knew he was with me, just as he always had. I may not be able to see or touch him, but he is here, nevertheless. People never really leave us, darling. Your nan is going to go, she is ill and… she's old and there's nothing we can do to change it, but she will always be with you. When you need her, she will be there, just as she is now.'

April had never seen this side of her mother before. Never before had she revealed these thoughts and feelings. A spiritual side to her, in deep contrast to her usual organised practical attributes. The possibility of being able to tell her about Annabelle, along with everything else that had been happening, now seemed an easier task. Perhaps she would believe her and not think she was losing her mind. April pondered on her mother's words as they finished the washing and drying. She knew her mother was right, that if it were possible, her grandmother would always be with her just as she always had.

'It's half nine, I think I shall make a start on dinner. Why don't you see if your Nan is up to a walk, just as she did with her grandmother? I think it will do you both the world of good to spend some time together before dinner. You know, just to reassure yourself.' She hugged April, holding her close. 'I shall miss her too, but I know she will still be here in this house.'

'Mum, have you known for a while? Is that why we moved closer?' April had guessed that was the case now, although at the time, she had never even imagined such a reason.

'Well, we are here with her now. Darling, is there something on your mind, you know, other than your Nan? I am aware that you have had something bothering you for a while. Your Nan said you would talk about it, in your own time. Whatever it is, you can tell me.' She hugged April again, tighter still. 'I understand more than you think. I love you, and I am here for you when you are ready.'

'Maybe later, it doesn't really seem that important at the moment. I love you too. Merry Christmas, Mum.' April eased herself from her mother's embrace. 'I shall see how Nan is; I think a walk is a great idea, if she's up to it.'

The morning air was fresh and clean, and the snow gave the scenery such an amazing, enchanted feel of traditional festivities. The two of them slowly trudged along the untouched snow-covered footpath, beside the aged graveyard, both their boots covered in newly fallen snow, soft and powdery. They left footprints in the direction of a wooden bench. April held her grandmother's arm tightly, giving her support, as well as satisfying April's deep felt need to be close to her. No words were exchanged for many minutes.

'Nan, shall we sit here for a while?' April gently squeezed her arm with love as they approached the seat.

'That's a wonderful idea, just like I did with my grandmother.'

They sat beneath the canopy of trees, which were naked of their leaves, bare and forlorn that lined the footpath. Old gravestones worn by time sat with their frosty covering.

'Nan, I love you.' April sat, her hand tightly wrapped round her grandmother's glove covered fingers.

'I love you too. Everything is going to be fine now. I know that it is nearly my time to go. I shall be with your grandfather again; I have missed him so these past years. But I shall be with you, whenever you need me.'

'But Nan, I will always need you; I don't want to think about life without you.'

'Just as we spoke about last night, I will never really be gone.' She smiled at April; her words were true, she did understand. However, this was her Nan! April's selfish want and need was always to have her there beside her, to be able to touch and hold her, in flesh and blood, not spirit.

'But Nan, what am I going to do without you here?' April shivered, as the cold frosty air penetrated through her coat, numbing her aching heart.

'Here I am, sitting on this bench on Christmas morning, with my favourite granddaughter, just as I used to each Christmas morning with my grandmother, over seventy years ago. I know how awful it is to lose someone you love. I lost *my* grandmother, and at the time, I was devastated. Annabelle was not gone for long, was she?'

The harsh Christmas sunshine glared reflectively, on the snow-covered scenery around them. Her Grandmother's words circled April's mind, over and over, the words repeating.

'What about you Nan? Do you think you shall come back again? Emily didn't, did she? She never left. I still don't know why she is here, or if she has always been here and we didn't know?' April paused gazing into her grandmother's face, before she continued. 'I dreamt about her again last night. Nan, was that her bedroom I slept in?'

'That has always been a spare room for as long as I can remember, why?' replied Sarah, rubbing her cold hands together, as she watched her feet. She moved her brown leather boot back and forth in the snow beneath the bench, until she had carved a channel in the frosty new laid snow.

'I dreamt about her last night. Well, everyone actually, the whole family. I think it was Emily's room. It hasn't changed since then, the same curtains, the same floral bedspread, and the same bedroom chair. I feel really comfy in there.'

April shuffled along the bench, closer to her grandmother, putting her thickly padded arm around her. Her shoulders seems smaller than normal, her body thin and fragile. 'Nan, I think we should head back now. It's so cold, you look freezing.' April hugged her grandmother, rubbing her arm to warm her up.

'I'm fine. After dinner, don't forget, I promised to get the old photo albums out for you. We can sit by the fire, like we did when you were small.' Sarah turned to April, with her frail features cold and shivery in the wintry chill. 'Yes, I think we should head back, see how your Mum's getting on with the turkey.'

They headed on the short journey back, passing through the deserted graveyard. The cathedral glistened in the low sunshine; a mantle of crystal snow graced its roof and tower with a truly festive appeal; the stained glass windows, colourful and brightly lit in anticipation of the congregation's arrival for the day's service. Slowly, with careful tread, they retraced their footprints home.

April turned the key in the brass lock and guided her grandmother down into the warm and welcoming room. Music travelled through the ground floor of the town house, filtering into every room and space, with festive cheer.

'Ah, this is my favourite. *Chestnuts roasting on an open fire, Jack Frost nipping at your nose...*' Julia had simultaneously entered, carrying a sizeable tray of warm mince pies, whilst singing at the top of her voice. '*Yuletide carols being sung by a choir, and folks dressed up like Eskimos,*' she continued, as she rested the silver tray onto the low polished table. 'Talking of Eskimos, you two look frozen solid! Come on, get those coats off and warm up by the fire. I've just put some more logs on, so it's lovely and toasty.'

April swiftly unbuttoned her full-length coat; taking her grandmother's, she laid them both over the arm of the red velvet settee. She sat and watched as Sarah rested in her favourite chair. The close vicinity of the blazing fire bought life back to her pale cheeks, whilst warming the hands that unzipped her long boots.

'Ah, that's better. I'm starting to defrost now; I don't remember it being so cold when I was a girl.' Her tired eyes stared into the open fire; bright red sparks spat from the logs, a firework display of darting and dancing flashes. The loud hissing and crackling of the fresh logs was barely audible over the mellow tone of The Christmas Song.

April reached forward, and took a warm mince pie, the sugary pastry top crumbling as she took a bite. Sarah rested her weary head back, and closed her eyes, cocooned by her deep-buttoned winged chair. The heat from the fire, and the warming music eased and soothed her body. Her defrosted toes nestled inside her beige suede moccasin slippers. Her elbows rested on the wooden arms of the chair, her fingers gently cupped round the curved ends. April finished the last of her festive treat, and snuggled back on the settee, the gold cushion hugged to her chest, as she sat watching her grandmother. Memories of the past two days crowded her head.

The volume of the music drifted from her ears as her eyes skimmed the room. Curious warmth spread through her body, her mood lifted and her spirits soared as she fixed her sights on the area behind the winged chair. April concentrated hard, staring in amazement with un-blinking eyes. A form gradually appeared - a figure - which stood behind Sarah, a tall, dignified gentleman, garbed in a dark grey suit. He stood proudly, his large hands resting on the back on the winged chair. His thick silver hair framed his handsome face, and a large silver moustache neatly graced his middle-aged features. On a sudden impulse, April closed her eyes and inhaled, filling her lungs, and the distinctive aroma of pipe tobacco consumed her senses. She opened her eyes, immobile, as the large dominating gentleman beamed, placing his left hand on her grandmother's shoulder. Sarah sweetly smiled as she slowly placed her hand on his, her eyes still closed. April gasped, in both delight and astonishment, at her grandfather, and he disappeared as quickly as he had arrived.

The dining table was dressed with its traditional yuletide theme of red and gold; large gold chargers, paired with white china and gold plated cutlery. An heirloom white linen tablecloth covered the polished mahogany, ornate with embroidered corners, which cloaked the carved table legs. Matching linen napkins, with identical embellishments of Christmas garlands, sat neatly folded at each setting.

Michael passed over the threshold, carrying a large box of kitchen matches. He reached across the cloth, striking a match over the five tall gold candles, which stood regally, nestling amongst glorious red poinsettia blooms and an abundance of dark green foliage.

'There, all ready, that looks lovely, really festive!' He rapidly shook the matchstick to extinguish it, putting it in the end of the box with the other used matches; he then slid the matchbox shut and placed it on the sideboard. April eased a dining chair out from under the table for her grandmother, who gently sat on its pink damask upholstery.

'You sit next to me,' requested Sarah, as she shuffled her chair, closer to the tablecloth. April took up residence on her usual chair, next to her, with the view of the garden. Glass doors slightly steamed with the heat from the cooking, revealed large snowflakes falling from the icy white sky. April sat transfixed, as she pondered on the Christmas morning's events; it was not the present she had expected to wake up to, after such a bizarre Christmas Eve, this was turning out to be a festive holiday of yuletide sorrow, rather than cheer.

Julia entered the dining room, carrying an enormous china platter, with a hot steaming turkey. 'Oh, we are such a gloomy bunch today, it's Christmas!' The aroma filled the room, generating smiles on all faces.

The family tucked into their Christmas dinner with renewed enthusiasm. Periodically, Sarah glanced at her granddaughter throughout the meal. April's endeavour to uphold an optimistic outlook continued successfully, her mind reliving her grandmother's words of reassurance that she would never really leave, and her mother's recollection of her dad's visit. All this reinstated by the unexpected, breathtaking apparition of her late grandfather.

April knew the truth; her grandmother would indeed be there for her, just as she was now. However, her heart was still a little heavy and tired from its journey through these past few days. April was beginning to appreciate how simple, how straightforward and normal things had been. Nevertheless, all that had changed, and in a way that she could never have imagined. Here was her new life, filled with memories and feelings, from an old, long ago life. Another century, another era, had been brought back to life. Her visions and dreams had captured a forgotten part of history, her own family history, like the photographs themselves. What had happened to Emily, and why did no-one know anything about her? Her mind puzzled upon the lives of the two sisters, Emily and Annabelle. As April sat and pondered on this, she realised just how odd, how strange this would seem to an outsider. But she had yet to tell and explain all this to her parents. Would they see things as straightforward and as truthful, as her grandmother had?

BECKY BYFORD

After the family had consumed every last Brussels sprout and honey roasted parsnip, they each sat back on their mahogany dining chairs in contentment.

'I think it's time to open the presents, don't you?' announced April with newly found jollity.

'I shall clear the dinner table, while you go sit in the front room,' declared Julia, as she started gathering the plates. 'Michael, can you put another log on the fire? Why don't you and your Nan go and sit down? I shall be there in a minute,' Julia continued, as she whizzed round clearing the table.

'I shall be back to help you, then.' Michael left, as April rose from her chair. She placed her hand on her grandmother's shoulder.

'Merry Christmas Nan, I love you.'

'I love you too; I always have and always will. No matter who we are in life, we shall always be together.' Sarah smiled up at her granddaughter, and held out her hand. 'Here, give me a hand, I'm not as young as I once was.'

They both settled down in the front room, as the freshly placed log hissed and squealed loudly in the grate. April glided across the carpet in the direction of the Christmas tree. The afternoon sunlight was dimming, and the twinkle of the tree lights filled the room with their enchanting glimmer. She knelt down on the carpet to collect the neatly wrapped gifts, each with a pretty bow or metallic ribbon. Julia and Michael soon entered the room, and each snuggled onto a red settee. April carefully piled the wrapped gifts and, with them barely balanced; she rose and wandered over, placing them on the polished table. Meticulously she distributed the presents to their rightful owners, and took her seat next to her mother on the red velvet settee under the window. The family members sat, each with their own collection of gifts.

'You open yours first, Julia.' Sarah leant over and gestured to April. Julia slid her forefinger under the thin gold ribbon and eased it off, gently pulling on the sticky tape; she revealed a small leather box.

Remember to love me

'Ooh, April what can this be?' squealed Julia, with childlike exuberance.

'Well, open it and you can see. Oh Mum, you are such a big kid,' she teased, as her mother jumped in her seat with excitement.

'They're so beautiful, they're gorgeous.' Julia stared in admiration at her amethyst earrings as they twinkled in the afternoon light in truly glamorous fashion.

'I am glad you like them. Nan said you would as soon as she spotted them!'

Julia continued with the same enthusiasm to find a purple velvet scarf with a beaded tassel fringe, and a matching beaded evening bag from Michael, which complemented the amethyst earrings perfectly. Then she ripped open the paper on a long box. The long smooth box opened with ease under her fingers. The lid revealed a splendid white gold watch, its delicate Celtic style links extended from a heart shaped face, inlaid with an iridescent pink mother of pearl dial, and a diamond at each hourly station.

'Mum, it's lovely. But you shouldn't have, it must have cost a fortune!' Julia sat admiring her new watch.

'Take it out and have a good look,' Sarah requested, as her daughter released the bright shiny links from the interior. Julia lifted the watch to the light of the window behind her, reading the ornate inscription. On the back of the dial, engraved in tiny but perfectly formed letters read, '*My darling daughter, till we meet again, you will always hold my heart*'.

Julia sat motionless, simply staring at the inscription on the polished gold casing. The room fell silent. Sarah's departure tugged at their aching hearts. The crackling of the logs rose to a deafening pitch, along with the loud ticking of the gilt mantle clock, in perfect rhythm with all heartbeats. Sarah gracefully lifted herself from her velvety chair, and wandered over to the far corner.

'Well...I don't know about you, but I think I could do with some Frank.' She reached down and released the door latch, revealing her hidden stereo, and with a push of

BECKY BYFORD

a button, the front room filled with favourite Christmas carols, sung by the crooning talents of Sinatra. Sarah returned to her fireside chair.

'I think I need to say something to you all.' Sarah sat, neatly perched on her chair with authority, as she addressed her family. 'I do not wish to spend my last days with everyone tip-toeing around me. We all know I am going soon, and it isn't worrying me. I want to spend my last days in the company of my family, at my most favourite time of year. I am old and I have had a wonderful life. I am now ready to go...I miss Edward so much.' Sarah paused, and with a deep sigh, she continued. 'I can't believe he has been gone for over thirty years. He is waiting for me; he will take me with him when it's time... Now, everyone open their presents with joy and happiness, not with miserable faces.' Sarah concluded with a jolly smile, almost her old youthful self.

Michael began to tackle his pile of presents. With no regard for the beauty of the paper, he ripped open a large package. Beneath some white tissue laid a silk paisley waistcoat in wonderful shades of green, along with a complementary cravat. April leant forward to capture her father's thoughts on his new attire: his reaction was clear.

'How fantastic, it's the one in the shop window I admired last week. How did you know?' Michael stared in wonder at his daughter.

'I have my sources,' laughed April as she encouraged him to open the rest.

Michael progressed through his pile of gifts. A very large heavy gift called to him. He tore the paper from it, and hiding under the festive wrapping sat a large book *Art Deco Ceramics*.

'Julia, it's just what I wanted, I love it.' Michael flicked through the pages, pausing to study the chapter on Clarice Cliff's Bizarre Range.

April pottered around the room, gathering the ripped wrapping paper from the opened gifts, and handing her father his remaining present from the polished table as she passed. Michael settled his book and waistcoat onto the upholstery behind him. The gift before him was carefully

Remember to love me

presented in gold paper. He un-wrapped it, to find a square box. Inside, beneath folds of black tissue paper was a wonderful vintage, silver and tan crocodile skin card case; an original from the thirties.

'Of course, glamorous gentlemen in the twenties and thirties would have left their calling cards with every exotic woman they met,' he sighed, continuing, 'I shall have to use it for my business cards.'

Michael opened the card case, finding an immaculate sterling silver interior displaying its top London maker's mark.

'Sarah, that is the most fantastic card case I have ever seen. It's an antique piece, and in immaculate condition, you must have spent a fortune. I don't know how to thank you enough. I love it!' Michael's ecstatic face was all the thanks she needed.

'I am so glad you love it,' Sarah replied with a beaming smile.

'Nan, I think you should open yours now.'

'Yes, your turn next, Mum,' Julia announced in excitement, as she shuffled herself to the very edge of the red upholstery.

'Very well.' Sarah lifted the first gift from her pile on the polished table. She placed it carefully on her frail knees as she began to unwrap it. Sarah pulled back the paper to expose a large antique gilt frame.

'Ah, that was such a fantastic day. Julia, Michael, this is perfect.' Sarah lay back in her chair to admire her gift. Within the confines of the gilt frame, a memento of a treasured moment, a glorious summer's day the year before, the warm summer breeze, and the salty sea air. Sarah had spent some time with her family at their Norfolk home. The house had overlooked the beach; from the long grassy garden, you could hear the lap of the sea as it met the sandy shores. The photograph captured a family picnic, as the evening sun lowered on the lazy afternoon. Sarah closed her eyes in deep reflection, her heart full of cherished memories.

Becky Byford

April silently wandered over to her grandmother, picking up the remaining gift from the table, placing it in her lap, as she gently knelt down beside her chair. Sarah opened her eyes.

'April,' she smiled. 'Shall I open yours now?' Sarah handed her the beautiful frame, as she started to open her final package. The gold paper fell away as she pulled on the metallic ribbon.

'How did you know? How did you find it? How did you get it?' Sarah relished the sight of her most favourite French fragrance. 'I thought they stopped making it; I haven't been able to find any for years. I only had a tiny drop left.' Sarah stared in astonishment, as she lifted the lid on the satin lined box. The rosy fabric shimmered against the cut glass bottle; the perfume took on a blushed hue from the coloured satin, the long proportion of the atomiser bottle lay elegantly adorned with the large pink tasselled atomiser.

'Mum said you couldn't get it anymore, but you will be amazed what you can find over the Internet, if you know where to look!' April sat on the floor beside the roaring fire, her heart warm with satisfaction at her achievement, and her grandmother's appreciation.

'Oh, this is perfectly lovely.' Sarah once again beamed with delight at her truly treasured gifts. 'But now it's your turn. We all want to see you open yours, come on.' Sarah nudged April as she insisted.

April got up from the floor and headed back to the settee next to her mother. She looked down at the pile of gifts by her feet, then reached down and clasped the nearest. *To our daughter,* April read the words on the gift tag. The present was quite heavy and neatly wrapped in bright green metallic paper. April pushed her finger under the gold ribbon and pulled it free, and the thick green paper fell away, revealing a large leather book. April lifted the weighty item to inspect the workmanship. The white pages were edged with silver leaf; the cover was bound with fine grain leather - slightly padded - in emerald green. A long, green satin ribbon bookmark lay beneath the front cover where April read the inscription in black ink, *"for your thoughts and dreams"*. As she closed the cover, she noticed something shine from within the wrapping paper on her lap. April placed the leather book on the settee beside her and retrieved the silver object from the paper. It was a beautiful ornate pen, with silver scrollwork of leafy foliage and wispy tendrils, inlaid with glorious shimmering green enamel. April removed the lid of the fountain pen, to reveal a hallmarked silver nib embellished with engraved scrolls and swirls.

'Mum! Dad! I don't know what to say, they are so beautiful.' April was stunned by the present. Did her parents know about the events of the last few weeks? The poignancy of the message, *"for your thoughts and dreams"*, seemed too coincidental!

'We are glad you love them; we thought they might be of some help. We all know the move has been a bit of an upheaval for you, and maybe keeping a diary may help you find your true path in life.' Julia smiled. 'Maybe now would be the perfect time to start it?'

April pondered for a second. 'Hmm, I think I'll give it a while; I think I should finish my original one first.' Her grandmother understood her sentiment.

'My gift next. Come along.' Sarah shifted closer to the edge of her seat, to get a better view. April placed the pen on top of the book beside her. She reached down to the last gift by her feet.

'Whatever is it Nan? I got the most amazing present last night. I could not imagine anything as wonderful as Annabelle's bracelet.' April just gazed at her grandmother; it was almost as if she didn't want to open this one. What could be as perfect as her bracelet? On an impulse, she looked at her wrist as she twiddled with the silver charms; they twinkled hypnotically within the fast diminishing light of the afternoon.

April took the small wrapped item and hesitantly removed the paper. A very small black velvet box sat in her hands. She lifted the lid to see a sparkling charm. It glistened against the backdrop of dark velvet. The small sterling silver charm, fashioned into a letter A, glittered with a continuous flow of tiny white diamonds; the letter A was suspended from a polished silver ring.

'Nan, it's lovely.' April stared at the gem set charm, as the lights from the Christmas tree and roaring fire caught in the reflection of the diamonds.

'You can either put it on a ribbon or chain, or maybe put it on your charm bracelet. It is an original Victorian piece, so it will fit your bracelet perfectly. Your mum found it for me especially.'

April took the charm from the box and held it up in the fading light. It was certainly a perfect addition to her bracelet, whether the A was for April or Annabelle.

'Here, would you like me to put it on your bracelet for you?' Michael rose from the settee, holding out his hand.

'Yes please, Dad.' April removed the bracelet from around her wrist. She laid it on the polished table to find the perfect location for her new charm. She scanned her eyes along the multitude of charms. Julia moved in closer, to assist in the task.

'There, Dad, in the middle between the tiny church and old fashioned pram.' April pointed to the spare link, as Michael leant over to view the spot.

'No problem.' Michael lifted the silver from the table and headed for the kitchen. Julia followed to supervise the work.

'Nan, it's lovely. It is beautiful.' April walked over, and sat once again at Sarah's feet.

'This now makes it your bracelet, not just Annabelle's.' Sarah placed her aged hand on her granddaughter's cheek. 'Merry Christmas.'

'Nan, can I stay here with you again tonight? I feel at home here. More at home than I have ever felt. I really do belong here don't I?' April rested her head upon her grandmother's knees, as she gazed into the glowing fire. 'Nan, I saw Granddad earlier, he was here in the front room after we got back from our walk this morning.' She remained unmoved, just simply staring into the red embers. Her statement seemed ordinary, not alarming, as it once would have been.

'I know. I know. He is waiting for me… but I'm not going quite yet,' Sarah gently stroked her pale hand over her granddaughter's young cheek. 'Not quite yet.'

'That's better, isn't it?' Sarah switched on the light as she wandered through the door into the hallway. The late afternoon light had diminished fast, leaving only the luminosity of the freshly fallen snow. Twinkling tree lights cast a multi coloured enchantment to the greenery of the tree. The festive evening brought a cosy comfort, with the warmth from the crackling logs, the hot mince pies, and an iced Christmas cake that sat on the polished table.
    April twiddled with her new charm as it hung perfectly in place, the heavy silver links draping her delicate wrist. She inspected every decorative drop of her bracelet, as they sat brightly illuminated by the chandelier above her head. With the sheer shock and emotion of receiving such a glorious gift, April had not inspected the charms with such scrutiny before. Over fifteen sterling silver adornments hung from separate links, a delicate fan with ornate sections that opened out hung from the first link, next to the heavy lock and safety chain. A selection of charms connected periodically; a filigree opal set charm fashioned into a heart, and a rather plain polished cross with a black onyx centre. Next, April came to a delicate oval charm inset with beautiful mother of pearl, which was intricately carved with a rose. April unfastened the piece of jewellery to take a closer look. She held the charm between her fingers and gently tugged, releasing what was in fact a locket.
    A silence rang through April's ears, as she studied the image of the photograph that lay nestled inside. Her whole body tingled with excitement, as before her lay the unmistakable image of Richard Hardwick. His strongly dark elegant countenance was distinctive within the sepia caption. The now familiar tingles travelled her body, her heart warmed, her cheeks flushed as she stared deep into the photograph.

Becky Byford

'Here we go, I had nearly forgotten.' Sarah returned carrying a pile of large leather bound photograph albums.

'Ah, the photos, Nan.' April quickly rose from the settee as she grabbed the leather albums from her grandmother's arms, the charm bracelet still clutched between her fingers.

'Careful, they are really quite heavy.' She helped put the albums on the settee next to the open fire.

'I always remember them being so huge when I was small. They used to look like the size of the table top,' April remarked with a giggle, as she sat with three albums that fitted comfortably on her lap.

'Here we go, a nice pot of tea.' Julia entered the cosy space holding the silver tray.

'How does the bracelet fit, April? I made sure your dad was extremely careful putting the charm on for you.'

'Perfect.' April quickly retrieved the bracelet from under the albums. Swiftly closing the locket, she refastened the bracelet around her wrist.

'Ooh yes, Mum, your photo albums, I haven't seen them for years. What a lovely treat.' Julia sat down with enthusiasm, reaching out to take one from her mother; Michael entered and sat down beside his wife.

It had been many years since the family had enjoyed the photographs. Five very full, leather bound albums in deep shades of red and green, each accommodating several dozen old pages with gold leaf edging; black and white memories held in place by thick card corners. Between the pages, sheets of translucent tissue paper protected the treasures.

April sat close to the fire, the warmth heating her cheeks. The dark red album sat warm on her lap, as she carefully turned the bound cover to reveal its secrets. So many years had passed since it had sat before her. Her heart leapt with excitement, as though it where the first time she had held it, the supple leather moulding under the shape of her fingers.

'Oh,' she gasped.

An old and aged wedding photograph; April scanned her eyes across the congregation, gentlemen dressed in smart suits, women wearing elegantly softly draping dresses, skimming their hips and ankles - but none that she recognised, until she came to one beautiful lady wearing a heavily beaded gown. The woman was in her forties, her hair fair and worn neatly up. She stood close to the bride and groom, along with an elegantly tall gentleman with fair hair and beard.

'It's Annabelle isn't it, Nan, it's Annabelle!' April's excitement shone on her face. 'I can't believe all the times I've looked at this photograph…'

'But, it's never meant as much to you as it does now, has it?'

April lifted her head in the direction of the voice, only to find her mother gazing back at her, not her grandmother, as she had assumed.

'Mum?'

'Annabelle, she's very important isn't she? As I said, when we go, we never really leave. And if we do, we're not gone for long.'

'I suppose not.'

Julia turned back to the album she was flicking through, a smile gently gracing her face. April studied her mum as she carefully turned each stiff page, her eyes scanning each memory. Did she know? How could she? But why say such a peculiar thing? April looked back at the photo, her heart pounding in her chest. Once again, her thoughts were on Annabelle, her dress, her hair, her bracelet. April's bracelet, there fastened around her wrist, right where it always belonged. The bride, pretty, petite and with short, dark bobbed hair, stood elegantly in the centre, her new husband proudly beside her, young and fine looking.

'Nan, who's wedding, is this?'

'Well, that's my mum and dad, and that, of course, is my grandmother. And there's that lovely ruby and diamond bracelet she wore; you know, the one in my jewellery case.'

For many minutes, April scrutinised the photo, carefully studying each member of the wedding party, their clothes, their hair, and their smiles. Annabelle's face beamed back at her, an expression of happiness and pride.

Hours passed, April cast her eyes over the albums, photo upon photo, but none of Emily or the young Annabelle, and none of the dashing Richard Hardwick.

'Nan, I'm just going to pop home and get some things. It is OK if I stay again tonight, isn't it?'

'Of course, you know this is where I like to have you, close to me, where you belong.' April glanced at her mother, who nodded and smiled.

The evening sky was bright with snow clouds; the lamp posts lighting the short but cold walk home. Her bedroom was as she had left it the evening before. April grabbed a large holdall from her wardrobe and began to gather her essentials. After a few short moments, she perched on the edge of her bed, clutching the silver and mother of pearl frame.

'Emily, why can't I find you? And where's your brooch?' Her softly whispered words lingered in the cool air, her eyes scanning the photos yet again, searching for a hidden clue. Abruptly, she turned. There was the box, the locked box; her thoughts fell upon its hidden contents. The box was lightly placed on top of her clothes, and the holdall zipped shut. April closed the front door behind her and headed back.

The rest of the evening passed with the usual festive activities, Christmas cake, warm mulled wine, and a singsong of the family's favourite carols. When it came to bedtime, April kissed her parents goodnight at the front door, Julia giving her a nod, and a *look after your Nan,* kind of look.

'What a lovely day we've had, apart from everyone's gloomy faces to start with, I must say it has been one of the best Christmases we've ever had.'

'Yes, Nan, I suppose it has. Nan, can I ask you something? I know this is not the normal sort of thing I should ask, but I need to know.' April sat on the edge of the settee facing her grandmother, the last few red embers casting a flush over Sarah's cheeks.

'You can ask me anything you want and, if I have the answer, I shall give it to you.' Sarah shuffled back in her chair, laying her old head on the soft velvet.

'Nan, yesterday, when we got back from shopping, I saw Annabelle. Do you know what I mean by saw? I mean, I felt I was her, I felt her emotions and thoughts.'

'Yes, I know you did, and I do understand.'

'Annabelle lost a baby, she had a miscarriage. I felt the pain deep inside me, her pain, not just the physical pain, but also the hurt and torment inside my head.' Her face contorted at the remembrance, her body slumped forward. Slowly she raised her head and continued. 'Nan, did you ever lose a baby?'

Sarah watched the expression on her face; April's eyes were full of truth and trust. Sarah turned to the fire; slowly she raised herself, and wandered over to the coal scuttle. Gently, she shovelled some coal on the slowly diminishing fire.

'That's better, that'll keep us warm for the night.' She sat herself back in her chair and relaxed her hand over the carved wooden ends.

'Once, a long, long time ago, when I was a very young woman, something very awful happened. It was devastating for everyone. I lost two babies, two very beautiful little girls.'

'Nan, I am so sorry. I really am so very sorry. I should never have asked, please forgive me.'

'Well, my darling, if you never ask things in life, you'll never know. And sometimes we forget to say what's important; you must never forget that, always to say what's in your heart. The truth is always in your heart. And now, I think it's time for bed, I think you need some sleep.'

'I really do love you, Nan.'

'I know you do; I know what's in your heart.'

The bedroom was as beautiful as ever, the warm pink glow softening the harsh cold night outside. April, in her white cotton nightgown sat up in her bed, her pillow puffed behind her, the marquetry box in her lap. The tiny silver lock, sat empty waiting for its key.

'Where is the key? How can we have a box with no key?'

'You hold the key. You hold the key.'

'I hold the key? I don't understand. I hold the key?' April answered without much thought, the voice repeated in her head. *'You hold the key, Annabelle.'*

'Annabelle? Annabelle, she held the key?' April looked about the room for a clue, for a sudden spark of inspiration. 'I hold the key?' Idly, she fiddled with the silver charms around her wrist, 'of course...the key!'

Smoothly, April unfastened the silver charm bracelet, and laid it on the white sheet. The bright silver metal shone in the pink light, the gems twinkled and glistened. She eliminated each charm in turn, until she reached a key, a small ornate key, with fine scroll and filigree work. April clasped the key firmly between her thumb and forefinger, and eased it into the lock. With a careful twist, the lock clicked and the lid released.

A fine linen handkerchief, much like the one that wrapped the silver dressing table set, and embroidered with the same three initials, covered the contents. Underneath, a bundle of letters, tied with a pale blue ribbon. April flicked her thumb along the edges, examining the pile, each hand written envelope in elegant black ink. However, all the letters remained sealed. April placed them to one side, as she continued to explore the box. She lifted out a black leather item; it was bound in the softest hide, with gold embossed scrolls at the corners. Turning the leather object over, she found it was an album, an antique Victorian photo album. The front had an oval, gold-rimmed frame, complete with photograph.

April stared in disbelief and amazement at her find, the one thing she had been searching for, had been there, at her fingertips, and the key to it, she'd been wearing. She leant towards the bedside lamp, holding the album beneath its light.

Before April's sleepy eyes, lay Emily and James' wedding photograph, its superior sepia quality flawless and unaltered by the passing of time.

Remember to love me

Telegram

'Poor Annabelle.'
The morning sun bathed the dining room with liquid sunshine as its bright golden rays gradually seeped into every corner.

Emily stood at the glass doors watching the birds on the lawn pecking at the moist dewy grass, eager to grab an unsuspecting worm.

'Poor, poor Annabelle,' she sighed, 'It's what she desires, more than anything.'

'I know.'

'Richard, I'm so sorry...please, forgive me...I know it's just as hard for you. It's just that...well, I know she felt so thrilled when she told me about the baby.'

'It's all right, Emily, I do understand. I know exactly what it means to her, and what this means to us.' He paused. 'She hardly spoke a word.'

'I am sure it is just the terrible shock of it all. You know what the doctor said; it affects the mind, not just the body.'

'Yes, maybe you're right; I know you are, everything will be fine when she gets home,' Richard sighed. 'It will all be fine...I just need to have her in my arms.'

'How long do you think she will stay at Aunt Anna's? Did she say at all? I must say...I thought you were going to stay with her for a few weeks?'

Richard paused. He too watched the early morning birds devour their breakfast. The long case clock chimed the hour, eight o'clock.

'No. I thought it was better if I came back.'

'Well, I am very glad to see you, and of course she's in safe hands. There is no one better than Aunt Anna, to look after her.'

'Mmm, I'm sure you're right, Emily. I'm sure you are.'

'Richard, Annabelle will be back before we know it, much more her happy self.'

* * *

'This just came for young Emily; I think you should give it to her. I would like for the Captain to, but since he's not here, I think you should.'

'Whatever is the matter, Mary?'

'Look, I think you should give it to her.' She laid her open hand out in front of her. 'Oh...Richard, I do so wish Annabelle were here. I think...' Mary couldn't finish the sentence and found there was no need; the words were in Richard's eyes; the anxiety and apprehension.

'Yes, we all do, Mary, we all do.' Richard spoke quietly, his words almost silently mouthed. He took the piece of paper from Mary's fingers, carefully inspecting its source.

'Where is she, Mary?'

'In the garden...she's been there since breakfast, the dear girl.'

'Mary, let's not jump to any conclusions,' Richard whispered with a sharp pain of dread in his throat. He looked out of the glass doors. Emily sat, peaceful and calm, her face shining like porcelain beneath the shade of lush leaves.

Richard very slowly stepped outside, standing steady on the top step, his feet motionless, anxiously fixed to the spot. The lavender was too sweet, the scent of roses toxic to his nostrils, the sunrays burning his face, the paper sharp in his hand, the words poisoning his fingers.

'Ah, Richard, what do you say to a game of chess? Let's see if I can beat you again.'

Emily watched, as Richard very cautiously descended the garden steps, one by one, pausing each time, almost to gain his bearings, reluctant to take another step, wanting to retreat. The tree's leafy boughs shielded the sun from her eyes, but Richard, Richard squinted, almost squirming at the intense glare as it stung with burning intensity. He walked towards her without a word of reply. He moved the small wooden stool, placing it in front of her, and sat, his eyes level with hers.

'Emily...' he swallowed hard. 'Emily, this came for you.' Richard held the piece of paper close to his chest, tightly in his strong grip.

'Oh, for me, is it from James...oh, Richard, a letter from James?' Emily grasped at the corner, the most part still clutched in Richard's hand. Reluctant to release his hold he gripped without thought or conscious mind, his heart unwilling to read the words. Richard stared deep into Emily's hazel eyes, as she increasingly tugged at the corner.

'Richard?'

Then releasing it, he closed his eyes tight.

'Oh, it's not from James…it's a telegram…'

A cold silence fell upon the garden, as time in its cruelness, refused to pass.

The warm air lingered, thick and suffocating, fingers of fear clawed at the flora, tainting the atmosphere with the stench of dread. The birds refrained from singing, the breeze stopped in its tracks, the tree's emerald leaves ceased from rustling. However, the sun's unrelenting rays continued to scorch and blister.

'Emily?' Richard's new found word floated, suspended in the air, his eyes boring into his hands. 'Emily, dear Emily,' pleaded Richard as he lifted his gaze to her ashen face.

No words found their way to Emily's lips. Her hands shook, uncontrollably. She rose from her seat, swaying, dizzy and nauseous.

'Emily, sit down. Sit down, before you fall down.'

'No. No. No.' Her words were weak and broken, her feet began to trudge the silent garden, navigating their own way to the house, her mind swirling, spinning somewhere in her head, somewhere in her cheated, harsh reality.

* * *

Her bedroom grew darker, with the unnoticed passing of hours; her heart lay heavy and lifeless, her body immersed in this sudden emptiness, engulfed by grief.

A gentle knock echoed through the door, the brass knob twisted.

'Emily, Emily...I'm worried about you. It's been hours. Do you want to talk about it? Please Emily, I am here for you, I promised your sister that I'd take care of you while she was away.' With the door ajar, Richard remained behind it, his voice seeping through the crack. 'Emily...can I get you anything?'

'No, but you can come in, if you wish.' Her voice was lifeless and devoid of emotion.

Richard gently pushed on the wood of the door; it eased open into the dusky space. A few steps into the room, he could see her outline, her motionless silhouette lying like death itself on the bed. He lit the gas lamp beside her, and the soft light spread through the darkened room. He sat on the velvet chair, inside the bay window; the wispy curtains softly undulated in the evening's breeze.

'Richard? When's my sister coming home?'

'I don't know Emily, I don't know, she didn't say,' he paused for a moment. 'She didn't say anything.'

'I don't think I can carry on without her,' she announced. 'Do you think me selfish and cruel?'

'Cruel?'

'I must be cruel. Cruel, otherwise why would this be happening? I don't understand. I don't understand, Richard. Do you?'

'You are not cruel in any way, Emily. Life, it can be cruel and evil, but this is war. It is nothing that you have done. It's not your fault. I wish I could take away this pain.'

'I need Annabelle, Richard. That is what makes me selfish; I need her. After all, she has also just lost someone.' Her childlike words crept towards him, soft and fragrant.

'No Emily, you could never be selfish. She will understand and want to be home with you. I sent a telegram to her this afternoon, letting her know.'

'Richard, my poor sister will worry so. She's not well enough to come home just yet.'

'She loves you. Have you ever known her to put you anywhere but first?'

'But she's not here now, is she?' Her slow words floated on the humid evening air. The pink blush of the room cast false colour to her pasty cheeks.

'Oh Richard, my heart has died, I shall never be able to live again. My life has been snatched from my fingers. I had everything once, and now I have nothing. It has cheated me.'

Richard sat silently, simply listening to her shattered thoughts. Emily's words were his wife's, unspoken by her lips, but still heard by his ears. He arose from the soft chair and looked out onto the peaceful night.

'Is there anything I can get you, a cup of tea or glass of water?'

'No.'

'Then I should leave you. It's very late and you should sleep.'

'Richard?'

'Yes.'

'Come, sit next to me?' Her voice trembled. 'I'm so cold, can you hold me like my sister would?'

For several long, agonising moments, he continued to stare out into the night, the fine drapes lapping at his face.

'Richard?'

Gradually, he turned and paced the rug over to the bed. Emily lay unmoved; her lace dress pale like her skin, her red hair tousled across her pillow. Carefully, and without a sound, Richard lay next to her, their bodies still and silent as the house.

'Hold me, I'm so cold.'

He eased his arm under her neck, cradling her head on his shoulder. Her face lay close to his, her breath warm and sweet on the skin of his neck. The dense darkness veiled the room; only the soft hue illuminated their bodies. She raised her hand to his face; her forefinger tenderly traced the outline of his features, his defined cheekbones, and his masculine jaw line down to his soft full lips. She set her palm on his cheek, and turned his face towards her, their eyes met.

His lips quivered with the hesitance of unspeakable words.

He laid his large hand on hers, moving his fingers between hers, entwining, and clasping them together. He led their hands down the cotton of his open shirt collar, pushing their fingers between the buttons. As her fingers touched the flesh of his chest, Richard pressed her hand on his skin, over his heart.

'She's in here,' he spoke softly, his breath on her face.

'I know.'

The drapes billowed under direction of the evening breeze, the room silent, but for the beating of their broken hearts and shattered dreams.

Remember to love me

Dear Diary

Sudden anxiety, in the hollow of her stomach, wrenched her body forwards and she sat up. The room was still, dark and silent. Her eyes were open; however, the dark was so dense they could have still been closed. For a moment, she couldn't quite tell.

April reached for the bedside lamp. For several seconds, she lay immobilised by her vivid recollection, her dream, her memory, with her rapid heartbeat still thumping beneath her nightgown, her body tingling with uneasiness. Her rational mind kicked in and she sat up, her thoughts switched to the box and the key.

It turned smoothly, the tiny silver key. April sat with the box in her lap, as the doorknob twisted and opened.

'Hey, you awake already?'

'Hi Nan, sorry. Did I wake you? What time is it?'

'I was already awake; I haven't been sleeping much lately.' Sarah walked into the bedroom, closing the door behind her. 'It's about half seven.' She wandered over to the bed and perched on the side next to the lamp. 'Ah, I see you found the key, then.'

'Yes, last night, it was so late and I didn't want to wake you.' April pointed to the bracelet on the bedside table. 'You'll never guess where it was!'

BECKY BYFORD

'Ah...Annabelle's bracelet.'

'Nan, you don't look very shocked. This means I've been wearing it all the time, and you'll never guess what I found inside!'

'Well, move over and you can show me.'

April shifted herself to the other side of the mattress, the large bed ample for the pair of them. Sarah lifted the sheets and climbed in beside her.

'Are you ready for this?' April placed the beautiful marquetry box between them and then very gently lifted the lid. Inside, nestling within the protection of the box, was the leather album. April lifted it and handed it to her.

'Ah, Emily, and I presume this is her husband.'

'That's Lance Corporal James Wright, he was in the Suffolk Regiment.'

'James?'

'Yes, they got married at Christmas, I think it was at the turn of the century, he went off to fight in the Boer War, but...' April stopped herself from continuing, the remembrance of her dream, and the desperation in the depths of her stomach. April had no words to add, they had vanished; no words she could muster would do her feelings justice, the sheer panic that still lingered inside her head.

'She was very beautiful, and James was very handsome, don't you think?'

'Yes, I suppose so.' April studied the wedding photograph. He was indeed a handsome young man, tall and fair.

'But not quite as handsome as our Richard, is he? Although I myself only have stories of him to go by, my grandmother would tell me how handsome her husband had been, but there are no photos of him.' Sarah leant towards her granddaughter, nudging her slightly with her elbow.

'Yes, Nan, he was by far the most gorgeous man I've ever seen. I know you think I'm nuts. But I can't stop...' The dream crept its way back into her thoughts once again, bombarding her mind with its cruelty. April sat with her face in her hands, desperately trying to drive her nightmare from her brain.

'Do you want to talk about it? I know there's something bothering you this morning. What is it?'

'Nan, I had the most awful night, full of nightmares, but the difference with these are that I know they are real. Well, they were real, once.' She pondered on where to begin, re-tracing her thoughts back to the start.
'Annabelle, she lost the baby. So she went to stay with her Aunt Anna.'

'Aunt Anna?'

'She lived on the coast, somewhere in Norfolk. I hadn't thought of it before, but that's where I've lived all my life; I could have lived in the same town, walked along the same beach.' April smiled, an awkward smile, not so much of a happy thought, but a sudden realisation that everything seemed to be linked in one way or another, history in full circle.

'I'm not sure if I've heard of Aunt Anna, but carry on.'

'Richard took her up there, but he came home again, I think, after a couple of days. I think he wanted to stay there with her, but for some reason… well, when he got home…' April laid her head back on the headboard, her spine nestling into the soft feather pillow. 'Emily was at home and she missed Annabelle so much. She was in the garden and Richard brought her a letter, or something, but it wasn't from James, it was to say he…Oh, Nan, he died, he was killed in the war, all that way out in South Africa, away from everyone, away from Emily.' Tears trickled down her face, as she laid her head on her grandmother's shoulder. 'She spent the day in her bedroom…' April sat up and her eyes wandered the dimly lit room. 'This room...her bedroom. Oh Nan, it was horrible. She sobbed and sobbed, her heart was broken, I can still feel her broken heart, inside me.'

'My darling, you feel all this because you are so sensitive and perceptive. I think you are having these thoughts and memories for a reason. Maybe, Emily herself is giving you these for a purpose; we just have to find out what it is. But you have to remember these are things that have been, you can't change them, no matter how terrible they were, and how sad they make you feel. Do you understand?' April nodded, wiping her tears with the corner of her bed sheet. 'Now, let's have a good look through this box, shall we?'

Sarah held the soft leather album in her palms, and gently opened the gilt clasp. Within the cover were several pages of framed photographs, an abundance of glorious family portraits, holidays and celebrations.

'My goodness, look what we have here, it's another wedding photo.'

'Nan, it's Annabelle and Richard.'

'I see what you mean, he was very handsome, no wonder my grandmother married him.'

Sarah watched the expression on April's face; it was filled with joy, but there was some anxiety and sadness deep inside her eyes. April quickly closed the album, putting it down beside her, tucked away like a treasured possession.

'Well, what do we have here? Letters, and nothing else, somehow I'd imagined a whole menagerie of treasures and jewellery.'

Sarah picked up the box, inspecting it further. 'I could be wrong, but I know that sometimes, these types of boxes have...yes here, do you see?' She tipped the box back; inside the lid was a very small pin. With a quick flick from her fingernail, the lid opened into another compartment, with just enough depth to hide some very special possessions. April held out her hand with anticipation; into it fell a dark green leather bound book.

'Well, all these very important treasures, all in this one box, and to think, you have been wearing the key around your wrist.'

The leather book sat tightly within April's fingers, her grip very reluctant to release it. She closed her weary eyes tightly; the book nestled flat against her breast.

'I know what this is. It's my diary.' The words were Annabelle's and not Aprils. 'I'm writing in it, not the words, but I'm holding a pen and there's the inkwell, I'm sitting by a window, the sun's bright on the white page, it makes my eyes sore. They are so sore, they ache, my body aches, my heart aches. I miss Richard.'

'You can read it when you are ready.' Sarah pressed her hand against April's, still gripping her diary. 'Would you like me to leave you?'

'No.' April eased her eyes open, 'No, it's OK, I shall have a look later.' She carefully tucked the diary under her pillow.

'Well, it's getting light outside, I think I'm going to get up now anyway. I'll go put the kettle on for a cuppa. You want one?' April merely nodded. Putting the letters back into the box, she replaced the key, her bracelet dangling from the charm. With a twist, it was locked once more, its secrets carefully guarded.

The day drifted, long hours mingled together. With no comprehension of time, April wandered the house, unaware of the day. The family left her to it. Neither asking, nor questioning the cause of her state of mind. Sarah, from time to time, would nod and smile, Julia and Michael simply organised the festive activities, lunch, music, and games.

With the customary ritual of board games on Boxing Day afternoon, the polished coffee table was cleared of its refreshments and laid with Monopoly. The board was tatty and worn at the corners, some of the counters replaced many years before with festive cake decorations and the like; a plastic robin, and an angel with net wings, aged and frayed.

'It's your turn, sweetheart? Here, April, here's the dice.'
'Hmm?'
'The game? It's your turn.'
'Hah, sorry.' April tossed the dice across the table; they landed in Julia's lap.
'I think that's a three, yeah, definitely a three.'
April idly moved her counter, a silver coloured plastic hand mirror, which had once belonged to her Sindy doll, long since forgotten.

'It's no good, why don't you have a hot bath, tuck up in your nightie, and have a nice early night? I know it was an early morning. You didn't get much sleep last night did you?' Sarah took the counter from April's fingers and gave her a nod.

'That's a good idea darling, you don't look yourself today. I'm not surprised you're exhausted, you've been through a lot lately.'

April gawped at her mother, the first expression of consciousness that had occupied her face the whole day. However, her curiosity soon faded, with the thought of the diary tucked away in its safe place.

Hot, soapy bubbles soothed her weary body; it ached with anxiety from the previous night, which had lingered with her the whole day.

As the cool cotton of her nightgown and the smoothness of the sheets touched her cleansed skin, she was transported, mind and soul to the place she longed to be.

The few hours since she had sat with her diary had seemed an eternity, a lifetime. At last, it lay within her palms; the green leather was supple and creased along the spine, and its leaves were full and brimming with feelings and recollections that she could no longer leave to the custody of its pages. Her fingers flicked the edges of the old paper, as it fell open at a particular date, and a photograph.

The eyes smiled back at April, the dark lustrous hair, the smart tailored suit, and the strong, handsome features. Her fingers traced the outline of his face, as she could feel someone had done so before.

* * *

June 16th 1900

Oh diary, how can I continue with this pain, this pain that is in my heart and my soul?

My body is mending, although the doctor says it's too soon to know if I will ever be able to conceive again. Inside I feel broken, ripped apart, and unable to heal. I have lost someone very dear to me, someone who will go forever unknown, but still existed. My longing is so strong that I cannot see my life without it. I have no place, no purpose in this world, if not as a mother.

    Darling Richard is sweet. He tries so hard, I know he does. Why can he not see what this means? If there is no child, there is no us. What can I give him? If not an heir, then there is nothing. He continues to pretend this does not matter, but I know that it does. I want him to talk to me as a woman, his wife and not a goddess. He placed me high upon a pedestal, but he seems oblivious that I have slipped and fallen.

    I cannot find the words to tell him what is here, in my heart. I do not want him to think me weak, he pretends to be strong and to cope enough for the both of us. However, I know he longs to tell me, but I fear he will never bare his true soul to me. After all, he is a man, a modern man, yes, but still a man, a wonderful, loved gentle man. I love him with every beat of my heart.

    I long for his touch, the softness of his skin, the tenderness of his lips. However, I no longer deserve him, if I cannot give him what he needs.

June 19th 1900

    The journey passed me by. I was unaware of the scenery and other passengers. I know dear Richard held my weary hand for the whole journey; his was warm, soft, and full of love, while mine was cold and lifeless.

    Why can I not find the way to reply to his devotion? I am afraid of the words that would seep from my lips. Words to make him afraid of me, afraid that I have changed and am no longer the young woman he fell so instantly in love with.

    When I look back to those days, when motherhood was a thing of the future, I feel that it was another woman, another female, wearing my skin, walking my path. I cannot remember how my mind felt, when it was not filled with this soul wrenching pain, which now consumes my whole body.

BECKY BYFORD

June 22nd 1900
   Richard left today. He went back home. I am here, without him. I could not find the words to tell him to stay. I so longed to put my hands on his face, kiss his waiting lips, but they left untouched by mine, his arms left without my embrace. I am here, cold and torn. The summer sun drenches my body, but never warms my heart.
   I am now filled with a tremendous guilt.
   I am pushing my Richard away. But what can I say to him?

June 26th 1900
   Oh, my poor darling Emily, my poor, poor Emily. I am leaving for home in the morning. I received the worst news today; James has gone, missing in action, presumed dead. I received the news from Richard, and I must return to look after my sister.
   I have let myself be devoured by my self-pity, and wallow in my sorrow. I cannot, I will not let my dearest sister go through this alone. I have always, I shall always be there to look after her, and if not now, when she is at her most vulnerable, then when should I be there to take care of her.

April closed the diary, the green leather guarding her heart's secrets. She could take no more, the words buried deep inside her mind, recalling past, long ago recollections, conjuring the deepest feelings of her soul.

Remember to love me

Confrontations

Annabelle stepped through the front door and down into the room; and as she did the sun behind her, illuminated a halo around her golden hair. Richard stood in the hall doorway, gazing, waiting, wanting to say something, but not knowing what.

She placed her bag on the carpeted floor, her hand still clutching its leather handle, unwilling to release it, and acknowledge his presence.

'I had no idea when you would arrive home. If I had known...I would have received you at the station,' he announced.

Richard's manner was polite and unfamiliar; he held the wood of the doorframe, his hands clutching it with white fingertips as he gripped.

'Richard, I am fine. I could not stay at the coast when I heard your news.' Annabelle unbuttoned and removed her kid gloves and laid them on her luggage. 'Where is Emily, how is she?'

'Emily? She is in her room. She has been there since...since the telegram, she will not leave it. I...I could not...I could not...help. She needs you.'

'And I am here now. I am home, Richard.'

BECKY BYFORD

'So it would seem,' he snapped, then quickly regained his composure. 'She will be relieved, she has missed you.'

Annabelle tentatively stepped towards her husband, her arms nervously by her side but eager to touch his skin. Richard moved aside letting her pass, seemingly oblivious to her needs; the want that she felt sure shone on her face?

'I shall go and see her...let her know I am home.' Making her way to the staircase, she turned on her heel to face him once again. The warmth of his body was palpable to hers as her lungs consumed his musky scent. 'I am home, Richard, I am here, where I belong.'

Her lips were tormented by the evident softness of his and her heart was screaming to be heard. Annabelle eased up the hemline of her dress as she climbed the stairs, and gently knocked at her sister's door, leaving her husband alone at the bottom.

Richard stood, waiting, wanting to say, and not knowing what to say. Finally, soft whispered words left his lips, 'I love you, my Belle,' but his lonely words plummeted too late, unheard by her heart.

Alone in her mind, Emily lounged on the pink bedroom chair. She blindly gazed through the windowpane at the garden below, but it was unwilling to partake in her sorrow. Instead, it was bursting with joyous bird song, aglow with hazy sunshine and bountiful with sweet fragrant roses.

'Darling, Emily?' Annabelle entered the room, and knelt on the floor beside her sister, unaware of her hand on hers, the softness of her voice. 'Emily, I'm home, darling, I'm home now, and everything is going to be fine.'

'James? James?'

'Darling, it's me, Annabelle.'

Annabelle gripped her sister's hand. It was cold and clammy, and lay heavy and lifeless in hers. The blackness of her dress, made her skin paler than its natural fairness, her hair lay lank and dull about her shoulders, her eyes stared blankly at her sister.

'Emily, please, it's me. I'm home to look after you. Please, Emily, it's Annabelle.'

A spark of life glimmered in the deep depths of her dull hazel eyes; somewhere behind their gaze, a flicker of acknowledgment.

'Annabelle? Is that you? Is it really you?' her strained voice was low and hushed. 'Oh...my James, he has left me, and...oh Annabelle, oh, poor Annabelle, I am so sorry.' Tears seeped from her tormented eyes, as she covered her face; her hands shook in spasms with her gasps of breath.

'Darling, please don't be sorry for me. Not now, everything will be fine,' Annabelle gritted her teeth with the pain of her statement, took a deep breath and continued. 'I am mending and we can try for another baby soon, I'm sure of it. It is you that needs love and care now, and I am home to look after you, as I always have and always will.'

'James, my James, he's gone, he's left me. Left me, Annabelle...he promised he would come home. He said that no man was strong enough to take him from me. Only God, only God could take him from me.' Her head dropped, her lifeless hair limp and matted over her face, then she began to shake; but there were no tears. Her body moved with spasms as she lost control. 'Why has God taken him from me? Why, what terrible deed have I done, to deserve this?' she wavered and sobbed. 'Oh...oh Annabelle, oh no, Annabelle...' Then a gush of tears began to flood. 'Oh Annabelle, why? How did this happen to us?'

'Why don't you have a lie down? You need some rest.' She guided her sister to the bed, removed her silk slippers, and neatened the sheets over her legs. 'There, you have a sleep. You look like you have been awake for days.'

'I cannot sleep; I am tormented, tormented and tortured by the nightmares.'

'Hush darling, I shall call for Dr Hickson - only to give you something to help you sleep.'

Annabelle pulled the floral drapes too, softening the brightness of the midday sun. She eased the brass knob round, and with a gentle click, closed the door behind her.

Becky Byford

'I have given Emily a mild sleeping draught, just to help her rest; she needs sleep and plenty of it. The poor girl looks as though she hasn't slept in days. It is a terrible thing, this war. My sister lost her youngest son last month,' he sighed with the weight of a thousand worries on his shoulders. 'I'm afraid, when you get to my age, you encounter death so frequently, in so many ways...but to lose young men in their prime, and see their young wives left behind, well it breaks your heart.' Dr Hickson turned to leave. 'I shall return tomorrow; other than that, I'm afraid there isn't anything more I can do for her. She shall need to grieve in her own way, I'm afraid. Sleep is the most important thing at the minute, the body can cope a lot better when it's rested.' He saw himself to the front door. Annabelle and Richard sat quietly in the dining room; the air was thick and choking between them.

'Poor Emily, she is suffering so, she hardly knew I was there, and when she did, it was so awful...She seems to be punishing herself for what happened, as if she could have helped it, the poor darling. Whatever can we do?'

Richard rose from his chair, pacing across the room, from the door to the clock and back. His long strides, uneasy and out of character, his hands wringing behind his back, his lips longing to say what was on his mind and in his tormented heart. After several long moments, he found his voice, although unsteady and low.

'I was always there for you, Annabelle; I always have been.' Richards's voice was low and husky.

'There for me? This isn't about me, Richard. We are not important. This is not about us. Our thoughts should be on Emily, and what a terrible ordeal she has had to endure.' She stood, stunned by his proclamation.

'But this *is* about us. There has been far too much loss in this family.'

Richard continued to pace, his eyes tracing the line in which his feet led.

'I've been here alone waiting for you, even though your heart shut me out, mine was still open. You only needed to, had to say one word, and I would have done anything,

anything for you.' This time his words were harsh and loud.

Annabelle was stunned by his confrontation and emotional outburst. 'I could find no words to say, Richard...no words worth saying.' She retorted, attempting to defend herself.

'Not worth saying?' Richard stopped, mid step. 'Not worth saying? You could have said, "I love you".' He sat back down on his chair, his eyes still on the carpet.

'That has never changed, never! I have always loved you and will always. I was grieving; I am still grieving. My body may be healed but my heart is not.'

'So, you think mine is? Did you stop to think...think of anyone but yourself...of me...that I had also lost someone dear to me? Grief is not something you own, Annabelle, it was not...*is* not only you who is grieving, who feels the pain of loss. While you were lying in your silent misery, did you not think of me? Did you not think of how I was to cope with the grief of losing our baby, of losing my wife?' He abandoned his chair, pacing the floor once more.

'Losing your wife? You have not lost me...' she paused to gain her composure; desperate not to let her tears flow. 'I am here for you.'

'You are here now, but what about the time you were not...You came back to be with Emily, you didn't come home to…for my benefit, for us.'

'I was sent to the coast, to Anna's, remember, you sent me there, Richard. You sent me away, and left me there, alone. I needed you. I did not go to escape you. You came home without me?' She could feel his eyes boring a hole inside her heart.

'Annabelle, you had left me, long before I came home. You shut me out, without a word. Not one word to me passed your dear, sweet lips. Not one of love, or future, or of grief did you utter; just silence, cold and harsh.'

Realisation of the situation drenched Annabelle with a downpour of agony.

BECKY BYFORD

Richard's feet came to rest at her chair; he bent down, one knee resting on the floor. He lifted his hand to her face, raising her chin, so their faces were so close, his skin felt the warmth of her skin; he had longed to be this close to her for so long.

'I do love you, I always have. I am so sorry, Richard.' Annabelle closed her eyes tight; she could not bear to look into his face.

For a few ticks of the clock, Richard's eyes absorbed his wife's face. Every detail of her delicate but uncharacteristically pained features.

'It is not you who needs to be sorry. I am so sorry for what I have done to you,' he reassured as his heart sank.

She lifted her eyelids, and her weary eyes met his.

'I am so sorry for losing your baby, for failing at my purpose.' Annabelle's eyes dropped to her lap.

'Your purpose?'

'My role as a wife, I am meant to give you an heir and I have failed.'

'I think the pain is the loss of what you feel you need to be, but in truth Belle, you are my wife, and if you never become a mother, so be it. I could have lost you, Belle, and then I would have had no one.'

'We shall never know, but the truth is that I may never have a child, I may never give you an heir...if not for that, then what purpose does my life hold.'

'I don't need an heir as much as I need a wife, as much as I need you, Belle.'

June 27th 1900

I arrived home this morning to Richard's surprise; I had not told him of my arrival, there was no time. I needed to get back to my dear sister. My poor dearest Emily, she is overwhelmed, I feel helpless, what can I do? I cannot bring James back, and I fear that that is the only thing that would soothe her soul. She is inconsolable.

We fetched Dr Hickson. He gave her a sleeping draught, but we all know there is nothing he can do for her. There is no cure for a broken heart. She wanders her room, aimlessly searching, but what is she to find, there is

Remember to love me

nothing that will take away this pain. If I ask, she cannot answer me. Her words are so full of sorrow. They make no sense, just a jumble of muddled nonsense.

Today was the first time Richard and I have spoken about what happened. I feel guiltier now than ever before. I know that in punishing myself, I have punished him. My darling Richard, I do love him so. I am hoping that our life will return to what it once was, but in reality, I know that with the tragic loss of James, none of our lives will ever be the same.

August 7th 1900

Oh, diary, regardless of the time that has passed, my life is as it was, still the devastated mess of turmoil. There are no words of joy and happiness. The house has become a place of mourning, a deep sorrowful state of blackness.

Father returned from a business matter the day following my return; Richard had sent him a telegram. Father tries his best to keep some normality in the house, but I feel he fails.

Richard is distant with me, he tells me he loves me, but he does not show it as he once did. He no longer holds me as he did, his touch is not as calm and pure as it once was; there is something that keeps him from it, some invisible restraint. I have watched him, when he thinks I do not, he is plagued by misery.

I so long for Richard to hold me in his arms, to kiss my lips and to touch my skin. The pain of the past few months has become tangible; its wound scars us all.

I observe Emily sometimes, whilst she is not looking. She will search every corner of the house, opening every drawer and cupboard. In her bedroom, she will open her marquetry box, over and over again, each time removing its contents, counting them and placing them back in the box in the exact same order as before. But, each time she is never satisfied, she will wander her room searching for her missing belongings, and I cannot help but think, that she has not lost anything but James, and the pain of it, the emptiness inside, keeps her searching.

BECKY BYFORD

I understand that emptiness. My heart remains as it was, with a missing piece. I have seen Dr Hickson, he is optimistic that we shall be able to conceive another child. We would be able to try again, if only Richard would let me near him. Things just aren't the same. I feel he is trying, he looks at me with longing in his eyes. However, there is a force greater than his desire, and he cannot stand to touch me in the way he once did. Dr Hickson has said that grief affects each person in many different ways. This family has lost greatly.

I did go home for a few weeks, but our marital bed feels tainted by the loss, the loss of our relationship as well as our baby. I remain here. Richard spends his week, while he is working, at our home.

My place now is with Emily, I know she needs me more than she needs anyone.

Emily's hand silently slid the length of the polished rail, as she carefully descended the staircase, her heavy bag clutched in her steadfast hand. She reached the bottom step, placed the bag on the rug, and fastened the buttons of her long black travelling gloves, as her foot finally stepped onto the hard surface of the hall floor. Securing her hat with a jet hatpin, her fingers teased any stray hairs neatly beneath it. With her eyes wide, she stared almost wildly at the mirror, with its gilt frame that hung reflecting her unnatural guise.

Annabelle stood in the parlour doorway, her eyes dazed with bewilderment and disbelief at the unexpected sight of Emily's attire. It was not so much her travelling clothes of sombre black or her veiled mourning hat that distorted her pale face, but the solemnity of the expression she wore, the dark cold that her eyes glared, masking the depression inside her soul.

'Emily?'

'I am going to stay at Aunt Anna's,' she retorted with not so much as a look in her sister's direction. Instead, her eyes numbly stared at her hands; inspecting her gloves with her finger, meticulously smoothing the kid leather between each of her fingers.

'What do you mean?'

'Aunt Anna's by train.'

'Emily, I don't understand. Why are you leaving?' Annabelle felt her voice begin to plead, as panic formed a lump in her throat.

'I think the sea air will do me good.' She turned to look at her sister.

'Well...maybe I should come with you. Let us talk about it...we can go together, a holiday, together, just you and I.' Annabelle swayed on the spot, her legs starting to buckle beneath her. 'Please Emily.'

Emily stood opposite her sister, her expression as blank and distant, cold and indifferent as a passing stranger. 'I shall be going alone.'

'But you can't, Emily, you cannot go alone. I agree that a holiday, a change of scene will be good for you, but you are leaving now, does Father know?'

'Yes, he knows. Now is the best time for me to leave.'

'He knows, and he is letting you go? You are not fit for travelling.'

'Not fit? I am not ill, Annabelle.'

Her mind full of thoughts, confusion, abandonment, the incomprehension that her father knew and yet he felt fit to let her leave, leave at such a time of need. What on earth, what possible good could be achieved by leaving the comfort of her family?

'Let me look after you. What will you do, alone?' she pleaded.

'I will have Anna there, I will not be alone, will I?' She adjusted her veil, her eyes closed. 'Annabelle...I know that I have lost James, he will never return to me. Everywhere I look, I am reminded of him...every chair in which I sit, every door I open, every breath I take in this house is suffocating me, covering me in the memory of James.'

'I understand that, really I do. It's just that...I shall miss you.' Annabelle took her sister's hand in hers; the softness of the kid leather was cool, the touch of an impostor. Emily eased her hand from Annabelle's grasp; her guarded and concealed fingers pulling away; her eyes twitched, almost with pain at her sister's touch. Annabelle's body shivered and her hand lay open and empty. This stranger, cruel, and cold looked upon her with a form of distaste.

'Are you well enough to be travelling?'

'I am well enough, my body is not ill; it is my heart that is broken. The scenery will be a nice change.'

Emily's words were distant and almost rehearsed, but from somewhere deep inside came a small flicker of sentiment. Annabelle gripped her sister's hand, reluctant to release it; however, Emily pulled away, eager to fasten the buttons of her coat.

'I made you come home...before you were well enough. You needed more time to heal, both of you,' she announced, her eyes still blank but her voice quaking with an emotion; not love but a kind of compassion. 'It's my fault.'

'Darling, of course it is not your fault,' beseeched Annabelle, in a hopeful tone.

'If I had not needed you home here, you would never have left Aunt Anna's so early, before you had properly recovered.'

'I am perfectly recovered now. It was not only for you that I came home.'

'Precisely,' she snapped. 'You came home to be with Richard. You should be alone.'

'Richard? I'm not sure I understand. Emily, please?'

'I have written to Aunt Anna, telling her of my arrival. My train leaves this afternoon.' Emily occupied her hands as she smoothed down her jacket over her hips.

'Emily, you need to explain this to me. I am so confused. I don't understand. What is this all about? Why Emily? Please explain to me why you are leaving,' Annabelle ordered as the questions exploded from her mouth, demanding answers, demanding enlightenment for her sister's actions.

'You need to be here, you need to be looked after...'

'No. Annabelle, I don't need to stay for my benefit...'

Annabelle stared, her brain trying to comprehend the words and their meaning.

'You need me, *you* need *me* here...you need to look after me.'

'I need to look after you? Well...of course...for you, you are grieving. Emily, you are still grieving, you don't know what you are saying.'

With a calm glide, Emily passed her and entered the parlour. Standing with her back to the room, she watched the outside pass; gathered clouds daubed in tones of grey moved in a funeral procession with the harsh wind. She took a silent breath, inhaling, filling her tightly restricted chest. Slowly, she turned her eyes, slightly softer and calmer.

'You cannot put off your relationship any longer.'

Annabelle stood in the doorway; with her hand gripping the frame as her sister's words entered her brain.

'Richard needs your full attention, but instead I have it. You are his wife, first and foremost.'

'Of course I am his wife. Emily, you make no sense.'

'Annabelle, I am your sister, I shall always be your sister, but some things are more important. I no longer wish to be the wedge between you.'

'But...you are not a wedge between us.'

Emily's eyes bored into her sister's panic-stricken features. 'Annabelle, I shall never know what it is to be a wife. My married life was so short. I do not wish to deprive you of yours; you would not wish my fate... I have to go, my carriage is waiting.' She took a step towards the front door.

'No, Emily. You can't leave, you need to stay.'

'You need me here for you, for your benefit, not for mine. Annabelle...' Emily left her sentence unfinished.

'What? You know that is not true. You know how much I love you, how much I always love to look after you, and now, now of all times...you need...you are grieving.'

'I am not your child...I do not need to be looked after...it is you who needs, Annabelle. Needs to have someone to look after...but I am not the one who needs your attention.'

The sound of hooves and wheels echoed from outside.

'My carriage is here, I have to go,' Emily added quickly, as she placed her hand on the doorknob. Her fingers clutched it hard, until she could feel the pain from her grip and tears stung her eyes, but she still looked directly at the painted door, refusing to look at her sister.

'Emily…' wept Annabelle. 'I love you.'

'I cannot bear my eyes to look at yours. The pain is too much to take,' she responded. 'I love you,' and she closed the door behind her.

The heavy door clicked shut with a deafening clang to Annabelle's ears, her head felt fit to split in two with the pain of the parting. For many moments, she stared at the door, waiting for it to open; she would be standing there having changed her mind, second thoughts of what a ridiculous notion it was to leave. However, the door remained closed. After what seemed a lifetime, she turned and left the room, with her stomach in her throat, the bitter taste of nausea in her mouth.

'I cannot believe that you let her go.'

Annabelle sat her tired body on the dining chair, her face in her hands as her mind continued to spin with the deep, sickly sensation.

'Did you try to prevent her; did it make the slightest difference?' Charles softly replied as Annabelle lifted her face to look at his. She saw the same expression, a look of misery. 'I tried, just as you did. Emily had made up her mind, there was no changing it.'

'But, she…she needs…' she couldn't bring herself to say it.

'She needs you, is that what you feel, that she needs to be looked after?'

'Yes.'

'Darling, she is a woman now. She is not the child she once was; she's a married woman. Grief has gripped this family with both hands. I know and understand, I remember far too vividly the pain of loss.'

'We are all feeling that loss. However, I do not see that hiding away by the sea will help, and how she can need that more than…'

'More than being here with you? Perhaps, Annabelle, it is you that needs her. Leave her to grieve and mend, while you do the same. Maybe then this family can return to a state of peace.' Charles stood, carefully placed his chair under the table, and with silent steps left the room.

* * *

Tears pierced their eyes with the might of daggers as they sat in the confines of their grief. The rain clouds began to bleed, weeping their bitter tears, crying puddles, then bleak rivers of hopelessness. Annabelle and Emily, devoted sisters, both consumed by the misery of death.

* * *

The monotonous view of field upon field dazed her eyes. With the soft motion of the train and warm sun that streamed through the window, it was easy to doze. In and out of consciousness, she drifted, dreaming…

…hidden beneath the leafy boughs of the vast tree, she could taste the cool lemonade on her tongue; hear the sweet morning song of the birds. His hand on her skin, tenderly it touched her cheek. Her eyes closed, she could sense the brightness of the sun through her eyelids. Her mouth open, her lips eager to speak his name.

'Hush, my darling, we need no words.'

Her cheeks blushed; her skin tingled, as his tender fingers, long and masculine, traced the line of her chin, her neck, and her breast. Her dainty hand moved up his back; through the cotton of his shirt, she could feel his burly physique, and clarity of each defined muscle. Over his shoulder, she reached his bare skin, his neck; warm, fragrant and soft. Her forefinger came to rest on his lower lip, his mouth open, and the warmth of his rapid breaths, moist on her fingertip.

The closeness of his face cast a shadow over her eyelids, and she heard his heartbeat, its pounding rhythm, fast and in time with hers. Slowly and tentatively, she opened her eyes, his wondrous face, so close, his striking eyes penetrating hers through to her very soul. Gently, he slid himself closer, pressing his aroused body hard and heavy on hers. Just the fine layers of fabric between them, hindering them, preventing them. Every inch of her was over-laid by his strongly defined body, his blood pumping fast through his veins, pulsating with hers.

He laid his hands on her face, easing her tousled hair from her flushed cheeks, smoothing it away to see her features, glowing and radiant. His face lowered to hers, his moist lips touched hers. Warmth spread through their flesh, their breath mingled, becoming one.

With a bumping motion and a loud whistle, the train came to a stop.

Emily opened her eyes, her cheeks flushed, and her hands hot and clammy within her kid leather mourning gloves.

August 10th 1900
Oh Diary. Emily left for the coast today. It was such a shock, I'm sure I have not recovered from it. Still, it was not my sister who stood before me, I'm sure it was an impostor. There was no sign of love in her eyes, only some distant light of grief. She had not spoken before of going to Anna's, but I understand that the sea air and change of scenery will be a welcome holiday to the familiar, daily grieving that continues relentlessly in this house.

I cannot believe or understand her words. I love her; she is my sister, my life.

Maybe, this is a sign that I should go home to Richard. There is nothing to keep me here now. Emily has gone.

Why does my poor grieving sister feel that she is the cause of our marital strife? The loss of James has hit us all very hard, harder that anyone could have imagined. However, her mourning and need of care cannot have hindered my relationship with Richard. I am her sister; Richard would never question my loyalty or need to care for her. My poor dear Emily, the loss she feels has taken away her ability to see things as they really are. She is blaming herself for everything. Maybe this is her way of dealing with her loss, the loss of James.

I would like to write that my loss is easing, slowly. I would like to be able to write this, and mean it. Perhaps, going home to Richard, we can ease over this void and maybe try for another baby. I know I belong with him. I do miss him so. I still yearn for his tender touch, the warmth of his skin, touching mine. I love him.

BECKY BYFORD

Remember to love me

Partings & Reunions

With cool tiles underfoot welcome in the humid evening air, the muggy heat journeyed through the hallway. The atmosphere was thick with unease and expectancy, awaiting the anticipated thunderstorm. Behind her, intense, dazzling rays of light from the setting sun projected in multi tones through the coloured glass of the front door. Richard went in ahead and turned on the gaslights and the space exploded with an optimistic radiance.

Annabelle felt at home.

For the first time, she belonged in this house, it was hers; she was no longer a visitor within its walls, a stranger in her own marital home. Instead, she delighted in the modern decoration, its newly papered walls of bold leaves and birds. The detail of the beautifully painted edging floor tiles, the polish on the recently turned stair banister. Home; this was their home.

Annabelle began to unbutton her gloves. 'I think I shall retire to bed.'

Richard smiled in reply. 'I think that's a good idea. You look tired.'

For the first time in weeks, his expression was truly calm, without the undertone of sadness or apprehension.

He stepped towards her, taking her bag, his eyes fixed to hers.

'I shall take this up for you.'

Annabelle followed a few steps behind. Her eyes were on his body as he walked, the line of his back, the strength evident in his shoulders, the taut roundness of his buttocks, the shape of his forearm, as he ran his hand along the smooth wooden rail. As Richard reached the landing, he turned. Annabelle's eyes followed the length of his body, reaching his face as his foot left the last step.

'It is good to have you home, I've missed you,' he spoke shakily, almost with embarrassment at his confession.

'It feels good to be here,' she replied and smiled. Soothed by her tone, his expression of unease faded.

'Annabelle?'

'Yes, Richard? What is it?'

Richard paused for a moment; his eyes traced her tender features. 'It is good to have you here.'

Richard placed his hand on the cold brass handle, turned hard and pushed on the door. He stepped aside to let her through. Annabelle walked into the bedroom and switched on the gas lamp; the coloured glass filled the area with blues and violets from the dragonflies and flowers formed within the leading of the large glass shade. Richard rested the bag on the stool at her dressing table. He stood for a moment, gazing at her reflection in the mirror as she wandered about the bedroom, oblivious to his stare. Her hair was worn high in an ornate butterfly clip. Richard watched as she moved, the fit of her dress, the slimness of her waist, the fairness of her skin, but it was the bareness of her neck that teased and tempted till his body ached.

'The room looks lovely, it really is lovely.' There was almost surprise in her tone, 'I feel really at home in here,' she turned to Richard, their faces met within the reflection of the mirror.

'It is your room, just how you wanted it.'

'I know, I've actually realised, for the first time, just how much I love it,' she smiled into the mirror.

'I shall leave you to unpack.'

Remember to love me

'Richard?' There was desperation in her tone. He turned to face her directly, her reflection inadequate for his eyes, he needed the true clarity to gaze upon. She took a step towards him within touching distance, their hands awkwardly at their sides.

'What is it, Annabelle?' Richard spread his fingers as they stretched. He placed his warm palms on his trouser legs, the heat burning through to his skin.

'Richard, it is good to be home.'

He smiled, a spark from his eyes caught hers, and he left through the open door.

With long sweeping strokes, she brushed her fair hair; it hung down her slender back, as she sat on the stool. She swept it over one shoulder, and the familiar ivory teeth smoothed through the ends. Meticulously, she continued until it shone, with the likeness of silk. Her nightgown was white, with a small ribbon tie at the low scooping neckline; the paleness of her fragrant skin glistened against the cotton.

With a low knock, the handle twisted and Richard stood in the doorway.

'Richard?'

'I'm sorry to disturb you. I was wondering if I could get you anything. Maybe a nightcap?' He hesitated on the threshold, his eagerness to enter was apparent; however, his politeness held him back.

'Richard, darling, do come in. I am fine, no nightcap for me, but please, if you wish one…maybe…' she paused. Unable to finish her line, she took a deep inhale. 'Will you come in?'

His entrance was slow; his feet gently stepped across the threshold, deliberating his move and the position of his feet.

'Do shut the door, there seems to be a draught. Maybe we shall have that thunderstorm. There is still humidity in the air, do you feel it?' Her eyes met his, as she finished her last words.

'I feel it in the air, the lull before the storm, isn't it?'

'Yes, I think so.'

Richard glided across the carpet to where she sat. Her hair still lay over her shoulder; he placed his hand about it, sweeping it away. His touch made her jump with the tingle of his skin to hers. Richard's green eyes glowed in the coloured lamplight.

'I have missed…' Annabelle watched the reflection of his hand as he stroked her hair, 'I have missed this.'

He stood behind her, his knee resting on the stool, his tense thigh touching her side. He laid his soft hands on her shoulders, the bareness of her skin on his palms. She rested her head back against his body, and it exposed the contours of her throat and neck. Tender hands skimmed her skin, his fingertips sensing each flutter of her heartbeat. His forefinger ran around the edge of her neckline, his flesh hot against hers as the tips of his fingers teased open the ribbon ties. The gentle mound of her breasts lay exposed as the cotton fell aside. Raising her hands to her shoulders, she pulled the gown from her skin; it lay about her arms, and rested on the curve of her breast. The pounding of his heart thumped against her head, she could sense the beating increase as his breaths became faster. With her eyes closed, she lay absorbed in the effects of his touch. He felt her breath, hot as it touched his arm in waves, as his fingertip teased her nipples.

Richard removed his knee and stood back a pace. Annabelle opened her eyes, which met his smile, his strongly defined cheeks flushed in the dim light. In one silent movement, he slid his strong arm under the curve of her knees, sweeping her up into his arms. She flung her arm around his shoulder. He remained standing in front of the mirror, and for a few moments, the rapid beat of his heart echoed through the room, the deepness of her breath heating the air between them. Annabelle lay vulnerable in Richard's arms; he stood mesmerised by the fragrance of her hair, the lucidity of her skin, the deepness of her eyes.

Without a sound, Richard strode to the bed and laid her upon the pristine bed linen. Annabelle watched as he removed his shirt, the powerful movement of his muscular structure in his arms and shoulders; she could almost trace each muscle fibre through his perfect skin. Richard stood beside the bed, as she lay transfixed at the sight of his body, his tall physical form, the broadness of his chest, his slim hips and followed to his well defined thighs.

'Belle, I…'

'No, Richard, please don't say anything.'

She held up her hand and traced her finger over the subtle line of hair that travelled down to his naval. Richard clasped his fingers around hers and stopped them as they reached the waistband of his dark trousers. He rested his knee on the bed and reached down to kiss her, her sweetness intoxicating to his mind. She clasped her fingers around his waist and pulled him beside her. She manipulated the buttons of his trousers, pressing herself against his body, as she felt the true passion of the moment as he pressed it hard against her. His heart began to quicken and the tenderness of her touch had recaptured his soul. Their bodies so close and intertwined; overcome by the neediness of her body, he ran his hand up her thigh, and at last entered her, softly at first. A glorious feeling, which it seemed they had felt for an eternity.

Thunder rattled the windowpanes, spasms of lightning lit the bedroom with blinding flashes, and throughout the night, the rain beat hard in a hypnotic, musical rhythm.

* * *

Sarah laid her head back against her pillow.

'Nan, the doctor said that you aren't well enough to be at home now. Maybe you should just spend a day or so in the hospital?'

'April, you know as well as I do. If I go into hospital, I will never leave it. Well, not how I'd like to, anyway.'

'Oh, Nan.'

'We all know my time is nearly here, I want to spend it in my own bed, with my belongings around me.'

'I know. I know you're right, I'd want the same thing.'

April took her grandmother's hand and placed it very gently within hers, the smallness and frailness of it made her heart miss. The lively, vivacious lady she once knew now lay vulnerable as a child, her bed, huge and dominating around her.

'Grandfather's here isn't he?' April laid herself next to Sarah, her head resting on the pillow, her hand still clutching her grandmother's.

'Yes, he's waiting, very patiently, until the time is right.' Sarah took a deep sigh and closed her eyes. 'I miss him so much, it's been such a long time that I've had to live without him at my side.'

'It must be so awful, to lose someone you love so much. Someone you planned to spend the rest of your life with.'

'We had many wonderful years together, lots of wonderful memories. The memories always stay, you never lose them.'

'I can't imagine feeling that way...' April left her line unfinished.

'You'll find someone, someday. And, when you do, you'll know straight away that he's the one. The one you are meant to be with, it is the most wonderful feeling.' Sarah smiled a long smile from her heart.

'I do know; I do know how it feels.'

'Oh, Little One.'

'I don't want anyone else,' April was adamant in her statement. She closed her eyes with stubborn defiance, 'No one else.'

'I know, I know.' Sarah squeezed her April's hand.

'Nan, when it comes to Richard, my thoughts and memories as Annabelle are so strong and real, as if they are my own. Do you understand that, do you really know what I mean?'

'Yes darling, I do. But Richard, he belonged to Annabelle.'

There was a silent pause. The clock that sat upon the dresser ticked, creating waves of rhythm across the room, towards the bed.

'Yes he did, but I feel Annabelle's love for him, as though it was my own. Do you see? I love him, Nan. I love him with all my heart, as April. My heart loves him, and I know that. I will never be able to love any other man, only Richard.'

April opened her eyes and cast them towards the window. Although it was midday, it was dreary; the snow had begun to melt, and rain through the night had left slushy puddles amongst the dirty white mounds of old snow. Gently, so as not to disturb her dozing grandmother, she manoeuvred herself off the bed, and advanced to the window.

The magnificent tree stood naked and vulnerable at the bottom of the garden. Its boughs no longer wore sleeves of white, but wept with the last droplets of melted snow. April longed to see it, abundant with its emerald leaves, rustling in the summer breeze. It had seen so much life, that tree, standing its ground for generations, unspoken scenes of life, love, and loss.

'Poor Emily,' she sighed; the glass pane warmed with her breath, misting her view, absorbed her whispered words, 'Poor Dearest Emily.'

'Annabelle...oh, Annabelle.'

Swinging round, April searched for the words, searching for Emily.

'Emily, Emily. Are you here?'

Only the short, rapid breaths of her grandmother, penetrated the atmosphere, no other sound found her ears. She paced the floor, eagerly listening, and all her senses alive. Her feet led her to the dressing table. Its large oval mirror, the softly upholstered stool, was familiar to her touch. She gently eased the stool out, and sat down. Her reflection was central in the mirror, the room timeless around her. April closed her eyes, her ears listening, her body waiting, and her heart wishing.

Her grandmother's rhythmic breathing melted into the back of April's consciousness. Her ears fell prey to a beat, it became stronger, her eyes still tightly shut; she let her body relax into its pulse. Her own heart was rapid and in harmony. Her breathing heavy, her skin tingled with a sensation of touch, a gentle, exhilarating touch. The softly upholstered stool moved, and she felt a touch by her side and a heat to her back. Softly, she sensed warm soothing hands on her skin, touching, gliding, and loving.

Becky Byford

'Oh!' In an impulsive reaction, April opened her eyes, her cheeks flushed and hot. The familiar sound of her grandmother's breathing returned to her ears.

'Oh Richard,' she whispered, 'Oh Richard, how can I live without you?' April watched her reflection in the mirror; the pinkness of her flushed cheeks, the swift rise and fall of her breast.

'Annabelle' again the voice, the soft, whispered words, touched her ears. 'Annabelle'

'Emily? Where are you?' she whispered in return.

'Find it Annabelle, find it for me.'

'Emily, find what? I don't understand.'

With a sudden thud, April's senses fell back into reality. She turned on the stool and watched her grandmother as she stirred.

'April, are you still here?'

'I'm here, Nan. I'm still here, it's OK.'

'Ah, there you are.'

'I was just...um; I was just sitting at your dressing table. It's lovely, I think I recognise it.'

'Of course you do. It was my grandmother's; it came out of her house in Northgate Street, hers and Richard's house.'

April lay back next to her on the bed, their heads touching.

'I remember when you were very small. I would sit at that dressing table and you would sit on the end of the bed, and I'd let you brush my hair for what seemed like hours. You would love to brush my hair, oh so very gently until you said it shone like glass.'

'Nan, I don't...'

'Yes, many hours. I would sit and my Little One would brush my hair.'

'It's OK, Nan, you go back to sleep.'

'It's all right, I remember.'

September 17th 1900

Diary, I have had no word from Emily. Each week I write to her and with each passing week, I have no reply. I cannot help but think that her melancholy has changed

Remember to love me

her; she no longer wishes to see me. I have had some letters from Anna; though she writes regularly, they seem oddly vague. However, she is quite adamant that Emily shall return home soon, when she is ready.

I feel so helpless in this matter. No words I write can change her mind, what can I do?

I am back home with Richard, my sweet Richard. I love him so; I feel that we are almost as we once were. His touch is gentle and tender; his love is strong like his touch. When his hands glide over my skin, I tremble, as when we first met; his kisses are as if they were our first.

It is very early, too soon to be certain, but I am hopeful that we may be expecting another baby. I have not mentioned this to Richard. I know that I am eager, but my heart hopes, and skips with happiness at the very prospect.

I wish dear Emily were here. I should be telling her my thoughts and secrets. Instead, I must continue to confide in the pages of this diary.

* * *

'Will you get that please, Lizzy?' Annabelle sat in the front parlour. The soft afternoon light was fading fast; she positioned herself next to the large lamp, its elaborate shade bright over her book.

The heavy glazed front door opened, and she could hear faint whispered words, hurried and breathless. With curiosity, Annabelle rose from her settee and walked into the hallway.

'It's Mr Hardwick Senior, Madam.'

'Well, I can see that, Lizzy. Let him in,' she walked towards the door. 'Father, an unexpected visit, to what do I owe this pleasure?' Annabelle gestured towards the parlour door. 'Please come in and sit down.'

'Annabelle...my dear.'

'Yes, please come through.'

Mr Hardwick was a very tall gentleman, his hair thinning and grey, a large moustache covering his top lip.

He was handsome, mild tempered and accommodating, generally an older model of Richard himself.

'Annabelle, my dear, I think you should sit down.' Mr Hardwick sat opposite her, on Richard's green leather armchair. 'Annabelle, it is Richard.'

'Richard? What's the matter, what is it?' She fidgeted to the front of her seat. 'Please, you are concerning me. Whatever is the matter?'

'Please, my dear. You must not panic. However, there has been an accident.'

'Richard!' At the words panic and accident, the worst possible scenarios flooded into her mind. 'Please, tell me, please!'

'My dear, Richard is all right. However, he has suffered some injuries.'

'Injuries? Richard? I need to see him, now! Please take me to him, this instant.' Annabelle stood by the door, twiddling with the charm bracelet around her wrist.

'Yes, yes, of course, my dear. My carriage is waiting outside.'

Richard lay in the metal bed, the starched sheets unfamiliar about his physique. His face, his perfect beautiful face, was bruised, with a mass of swollen skin and congealed blood above his right eyebrow. He laid, his eyes closed, the nurse fussing over his hand; it lay in her lap as she re-fastened his bandage tight around his wrist.

Annabelle stood in the doorway to the hospital room, her father-in-law beside her, his hand upon her shoulder.

'Don't worry so, my dear. The doctor has assured me he shall be fine, and well enough to come home in a few days.'

Annabelle remained silent; she could find no words for this, any words that her thoughts would string together, an inconceivable situation. Her heart was as weary as any heart could be; it had suffered about as much as it could take. The only thoughts that travelled her mind, as it swirled like an uncontrollable whirlwind, were the ones Emily had spoken before she left. The cool, unloved words: *I will never know what it is to be a wife; I do not wish you my fate.* These words flew in somersaults about her brain. Over and over, they repeated.

'He won't die, will he? The doctors, they will make him better, he won't die will he?' Erratic, uncontrollable questions flew towards her father-in-law.

'No, my dear...no... My dear Annabelle.' He softly spoke as he placed his strong arm about her shoulder and guided her towards a hard wooden chair. 'The doctors have assured me; just a broken wrist and a few cuts and bruised ribs, nothing more. He shall, as I said, be home again in a few days.'

Annabelle sat, dazed by the situation. The atmosphere was strange, the room foreign. How could this be happening?

Mr Hardwick sat on the cold chair beside her. 'We were out riding. Richard was helping me on the estate. We were checking the fencing along the far side, near the river. Something startled the horses. I'm not sure what it was. Well, mine was a little uneasy, but Richard's bolted and threw him off. He landed hard against the wooden fence.' He took her hand, gently rubbing the top of it with his fingers. 'It was just an accident. Richard has ridden that horse many times, and that track many, many times, as you know. It was simply a riding accident. Nevertheless, as the doctors have said, he will be home in a few days; just a broken wrist, bruised ribs and the odd cut.'

Richard stirred and, opening his eyes, he saw his wife.

'I shall leave you two alone. I shall be outside if you need me.' Mr Hardwick left the room, closing the door behind him.

'Oh Richard, my darling Richard.' Annabelle sat beside him, perched on the side of the bed. Tenderly, she placed her hand upon his.

'Belle, my beautiful Belle. What a day I have had.'

'Richard, I cannot believe this has happened.'

'You know how it is; just one of those things, I suppose. It was no one's fault, just an accident.' He flinched at the stabbing pain as he spoke, his breathing short and sharp.

'How are you this afternoon, my darling? You seemed pre-occupied this morning. I watched you in the mirror.'

'Richard, I am fine, perfectly fine and wonderful.'

His green eyes were slightly duller and weaker than usual, looking straight at her; he moved his head to aid his view of her beautiful face.

'I know, I have seen it before, remember.' Richard gulped and coughed. 'I have seen that look; that look in those eyes before.'

The pain of his ribs; harsh and sharp with each inhalation of his hoarse breath. 'Say you are, please. Is it true?'

'Oh, Richard,' Annabelle gripped his hand at the pleasurable thought. 'Maybe, it is too soon to be certain, but I hope so. I really do hope so.'

'Belle, you look so very beautiful. The most exquisite I have ever seen you. I am sure you are. How wonderful!' Richard uneasily edged himself across the bed. 'Here, let me hold you. Lay with me?'

'But Richard, what about your ribs and bruises?'

'They are fine, you are far more important.'

Annabelle lay next to her husband, his arm around her shoulder. She laid her head against his upper chest. He kissed her silky hair. Small and vulnerable, she lay within his strong frame. Annabelle closed her eyes, wishing they were at home.

Richard laid still, his eyes open, full of pain. Sharp, stabbing, throbbing sensations in his chest, they quickened with each new breath. His large chest pulsated in spasm as he coughed. Deep, harsh coughs. His rib cage so badly bruised, the pain was confining. His shortness of breath grew more rapid.

'Richard?' Annabelle sat up with a look of panic.

Richard's eyes were dull, his skin ashen. The pain intensified. Blood filled his mouth as unrelenting rasps of sharp, short, gargling coughs, left his chest.

'Doctor...quick, a doctor!' Annabelle ran from the room, out into the corridor. 'Please, it's Richard, help him!'

A doctor, closely followed by a nurse dashed past Annabelle. Richard's coughing became constant, with no time for air to fill his collapsing lungs. Dark blood quickly filled his mouth and with each desperate exhalation, splattered the clinical white sheets. His face paling with each rasping, heart wrenching cough and breath that left his body.

'Richard! Richard!'

'Please, my dear, let the doctor do his job.' Mr Hardwick held her strongly by her shoulders; she desperately writhed within his grasp, tormented at her distance from her husband. His own hands shook at the sight of his son, losing his fatal battle.

'No! No! Richard!'

The hospital room was dense with terror and panic; soul tugging, hopeless gasps for air, white sheets splattered and sodden with blood. The pandemonium continued relentlessly for what seemed millennia. Until all fell silent and still.

Annabelle observed as the room froze, all movement and sound ceased. Paralysed to the spot, her feet unable to shift, her limbs numb, her body cold, her voice mute. Her eyes transfixed to the sight of her husband. The moment passed in slow motion before her, as a scene from someone else's life. Her legs buckled beneath her weight, she lay crumpled on the floor, her knees on the coarse tiles. Long silently mouthed cries left her body, until at last; her words broke free of their barrier.

'Richard! Richard! Richard!' Her long screams echoed off the cold medical walls, filling the space with the desperate cries of torment.

Annabelle sat, cold, desperate, and lonely on the hard floor. Richard lay, still, distant and splattered with his own blood. No one existed for that second, no doctor, no nurse, none except them. In staggering steps, her numb feet barely able to hold her weight, her dress tangled about her legs, she stumbled her way to the iron bed. Before her, lay her husband. The last few sparks of intense emerald green radiated from his eyes. Her hands grasped at the soaked sheets as she reached his side, his hand open to meet hers.

BECKY BYFORD

'Richard?' Annabelle's despairing syllables reached him in a surge of harsh realisation. Richard's mouth moved in faint motions, eager to talk, but his body unable to comply with his need.
'Don't say anything. Richard, I love you.'
'Look...look...after my ba...by.' The words left his lips in a hush of whisper. His last rasping breath left his broken body and touched her face. She watched as the emerald light left his eyes. Annabelle took Richard's hand and eased herself under his arm. Her heart plunged into the depths of her despair, shattered and crushed, as she lay in Richard's limp and lifeless embrace.

* * *

The door ajar, she could see the bed. The room was full of dusky light and had been all day, only wisps of sunlight had peeped passed the drawn curtains. The silence was deafening to her ears. Aching fingers gripped the doorframe, unable to resist, she pressed hard, the pain of pressure to the tips, white and numbing. Pain, that's all she felt; agonising, ripping, tearing pain.

Softly, a hand touched her shoulder, then a whisper.
'The doctor will be finished in a moment. Then why don't you go in?'

A lump, a choking mass in her throat, her reply was muffled, a mumbling gabble of nonsense. 'Can't do it, not meant to... Why? Not now...too much to say! This isn't happening.' She wiped her face on her sleeve; her cuff was damp with the wetness of her tears.

The doctor turned and headed to the bedroom door. 'You can go in now, she's comfortable,' he nodded, and walked down the stairs.

She slipped through the gap in the door; it creaked with the breeze of her movement; Sarah lifted her head, her eyes on April's wet face.

'Please don't look so sad. You know this is what I want. It's my time to go, and I will be so happy to see your grandfather. I've missed him so much.'

'I know you have, Nan,' she replied with a gentle sigh and the tiniest hint of a smile.

'You know what that feels like, don't you?' Sarah nodded with a knowing smile. 'It's time I was with him; it's finally here, I've waited so long.'

'I know Nan, I know. You'll be with him soon.' April forced a smile to her mouth. She sat on the bed next to her grandmother. Her very small hand was pale and fragile. April held it inside hers; she examined the soft transparency of her delicate skin, memorising each blemish, every crease and wrinkle.

'So, my Little One, what have you been up to the past couple of days? I'm sorry, I haven't been very good company, have I?'

April responded in the same vein. 'Oh, not much', she lied. She was desperate to tell her, to confide in her, about her memories and her feelings.

'I think you must have been up to something. What about the box?' Sarah asked, with her usual perception and understanding.

'I've been reading the diary…and…oh, so many dreams, too awful to…well, just too awful.' April's face dropped, her stomach churning with the intense emotions.

'It's OK, I know,' Sarah sighed.

'You know?'

'Yes. Richard?'

'Hmm…it was so awful, no worse than that. He's…' April couldn't bring herself to say the words, the pain of it so intense.

'I know he is, darling. I know he is.' Sarah patted her granddaughter's hand. April almost squirmed at the sight of her movement, the sheer frailness of her limbs, and the thinness of her frame; only paper-like skin sheathed her delicate bones.

How quickly she had deteriorated.

'The accident?' whispered Sarah.

'You know? You knew?'

'Yes, not in detail. But yes, I knew about the accident.'

'But Nan, you never said. All this time, and you never once said.'

'My darling, how could I have told you? You love him so, don't you? You really love him. I know you do. So how could I have told you that? It was something you had to find out, to remember for yourself, just like everything else. I knew that when the time was right, you would find out. It just had to be like that.' Sarah flinched, at her distant anaesthetised pain.

'Nan, shall I get the doctor?' April tenderly gazed down at her grandmother's delicate hand.

'No, no,' once again she looked back at her granddaughter, her life fading, eyes moist with tears.

'I know how you must feel.' April's voice was soft, as the light that filled the room.

'Little One?'

'The longing to be with Grandfather, longing to be with him after all these years, to have him hold you in his arms, to have him tell you he loves you, just to hear those words again, softly whispered in your ear.' Slow, gentle, silent tears trickled down April's cheeks and along her chin, and dropped in sequence onto the cotton sheet.

'You will meet him again, one day,' Sarah replied, through her own tears.

'When I'm dead!' April's quick response was of deep emotion, not of conscious choice, 'Oh Nan, I'm sorry, so sorry. I didn't mean…' April sobbed.

'Hey, hey come on. Come on now. I know I'm dying, and I'm not scared or sad about it. I'm eighty; I've had eighty full years here. There have been some hard and sad times. Nevertheless, I've also had some wonderful times; especially with you, lots of lovely memories.' Sarah gripped April's hand with an astonishing strength, despite the brittleness of her fingers. 'You have to remember, all the lovely, special times we've spent together, we've had twenty beautiful years, haven't we, and my goodness, to think that you are now almost twenty-one.'

A long rasping breath took hold of her chest. With a deep inhalation, she rested for a moment, her head back against the suppleness of her pillow, and she waited to let it pass.

'I feel blessed to have seen you grow up into a fantastic woman, strong and determined, but gentle and compassionate. I didn't miss it, I saw you grow up this time.' Another long rasping, choking breath and she lay still, her eyes closed, waiting for it to ease.

'Nan, you should rest now.'

'No, not yet, I have the rest of time.' She opened her eyes, and reached up under her pillow. 'This is for you.'

'What is it?'

'For you after I'm gone. It's something that belonged to you. It used to be mine, but it truly belongs to you now.' She handed the small envelope to her granddaughter. 'No, don't open it yet. Sometime soon, you'll know when. When you open it, you'll understand.'

'Nan, what is it?'

'You're not ready yet. One thing at a time, there's no need to hurry, we have all the time in the world, and you must always remember that. Time is nothing but a tick of a clock; it continues to pass, regardless, just as we do.' April placed the envelope on the bed and examined it, just a regular white envelope addressed with the words, Little One.

'Nan, it's all going to be all right…in the end? Isn't it?'

'Darling.' Sarah lifted her arm. 'Come here, come lay by me, just like when you were so small.' April lay there; her grandmother's fingers patting her upper arm. 'Of course it will all be all right. Everything will sort itself out, it always does.'

'But, Emily? I still don't understand?'

'I know darling, I know. But, you are strong and clever and I know everything will resolve itself when it's time. And when it is, you'll meet a nice young man and settle down.'

'No. No man, no-one will ever be Richard.' April's voice aired her adamant opinion of the situation.

'Yes, I know, only Richard. Just promise me one thing?'

April turned her head on the pillow next to her grandmother's. 'What is it, Nan? I'll promise you anything, you know that.'

'Just promise not to push every man aside. One day you will find one who you will be able to love. Don't lose him because you are too blinkered to see.'

April hesitated, how could she promise to love another man, when in her heart, the memory of Richard was so vivid, so strong, so painful?

'Promise me!'

'I promise, Nan; I promise not to let myself be blinkered. I'm not sure I can promise to be able to love anyone but my Richard.'

'Well, that's all I can ask of you. That is all you can ever ask of yourself.' Sarah heaved her body forward with the repressed pain that finally shot through her chest.

'Nan, I think you should rest now. Can I get you anything? Drink of water?'

'No, I don't need anything,' she paused as she closed her eyes. 'I think I'm going to go soon, Edward's very close, I can feel him.'

'Yes, Nan. I know he is.'

April lifted herself from the warm pillow. Sarah lay still and silent; her slow breathing now short and shallow, in the evening air. With her eyes constantly on her grandmother's face, April stood up. The room was full of peaceful, calming light. Facing the bed, April could sense a presence behind her. She glanced at the door; it was as she'd left it, slightly ajar. Gently, creeping through the atmosphere, a very distinctive aroma of pipe tobacco caught her nose. A serene smile graced Sarah's face, as April watched in tormented delight.

Her grandfather placed his large hand tenderly on his wife's forehead. An ethereal light illuminated Sarah's tranquil face.

April stepped backwards to the door. She left the room, leaving her grandparents to their long awaited reunion.

Remember to love me

Grief

Northgate Street, Bury St Edmunds
December 2nd 1900

Dear Aunt Anna,

    I have no words to express what is in my heart. Richard is gone. An accident, they keep telling me, just a tragic accident. Nevertheless, how can this be? How can it be just a tragic accident, to take my Richard? What is just about it?

    I need Emily. It has been so many months since I have seen her, and even more since we have spoken as sisters. Each week I write to her and never, have I had a reply. Surely now, if not before, she can find some place in her heart for me.

    I feel I must have pushed her away, pushed her aside with my own grief. I feel so cruel, how could I have done such a thing, when she, herself was grieving for James. Fate has cruelly dealt me this same hand. I am so alone in this world, only having Emily.

    Please, please try to make her see how much she means to me, and how much I need her. The funeral is soon and I fear it so. I cannot say goodbye to him.

                        Yours truly,
                          Annabelle

Becky Byford

Northgate Street, Bury St Edmunds
December 2nd 1900
My dearest Emily,
    My heart is hollow and empty as I write these words. I have lost my darling Richard. A tragic riding accident, just an accident, they keep telling me. It happened so suddenly, that I still pour his nightcap and call his name. How can I continue without him? I feel I have nothing left in this world.
    We had hoped for a very short time, that we might be blessed with the chance of another baby. Sadly, my hopes were dashed too soon, as it was a premature thought and was not meant to be.
    I do hope you read this letter. We have drifted so far apart, that I'm no longer sure of our relationship.
    Grief has captured this family firmly in its grasp and is reluctant to let go. I feel we are all that is left. Please say that you will see me. It has been so long since we have spoken; my heart is desperate for your love and compassion. I remember our parting words. You said that you would never know what it is to be a wife, and hoped that I should never suffer your fate. Well, fate has a cruel way, as I am here suffering with every breath of my lungs and every thud of my heart.
    I beg of you, Emily, my dearest sister. Please read this letter, please reply. There is so much for us to say, I need you more than I ever have.
                          Always,
                          Your Sister

Beach Cottage, Winterton-on-Sea
December 7th 1900
Darling Annabelle
    My heart is with you, my darling girl. You are strong, my darling girl. Strong and true, and although fate has indeed dealt you a cruel hand, you will overcome it and continue. I know you will, you must, for Richard's sake and for that, of your own.

Remember to love me

I urge Emily each week with the arrival of your letters, that she must reply, she must see you. I am afraid, that my words are ignored.

She speaks very little.

She has spent most of these months gazing into nothingness. You must see her. You have many words to say to each other. I am afraid that I have let it continue for far too long, and now with the tragic loss of Richard, maybe too long, for some resolve. Nevertheless, you must be strong, as so must she. For if nothing else, Emily is your sister, she is your flesh and blood; you shall always have each other, if nothing or no one else. I fear that I cannot leave her at this time, I have no choice, and my heart will be with you on that day. Please say you'll come and see us afterwards. Let me know as soon as you can.

I have written to your father expressing my sympathies, my brother may appear reserved but remember that he has suffered as you do now. You must take his words as consolation, they're from his heart.

All my love, my darling,
Anna

* * *

December 8th 1900

Diary, he is gone. No longer my husband in flesh and blood, no longer will he walk up to our bedroom, no longer will he hold my hands in his. He is dead and so is my heart. The carriage arrived, the horses with their sombre black feathers, the pomp of the ceremony. I sat, as a dutiful wife should, beneath the mask of my veil. My face, my numb face, sheathed in black. Father sat beside me, with the pain of a familiar loss. Words of peace left his well-meaning lips, but not enough to soothe. I am sure that there are no words, which can soothe this throbbing; the aching that consumes me beyond all hope.

The journey was endless. Endless to its destination. My body was frozen and numb, we sat cold to the core as my heart, the heat that thrived was the love we shared, without that love I am but a shell, empty and broken.

Continually, our carriage followed in the wake of Richard's hearse, his empty body, encased in a wooden casket. My thoughts wandered to his poor body, cold in the winter's chill and alone, so alone. I wanted to break it open, break it with my bare hands, scratch at the wood that covered him like a shell, hold him in my arms until I too died. Still, I sat and watched and I gazed upon it, a continued reminder of my fate, the callousness that has been bestowed upon me.

An eternity! I had to bear the service, the tears, the silence. Tears from the mourners, mourning a man that many hardly knew; how dare they cry my tears, tears that I cannot? How dare they miss his smile, a smile that was meant for me? How dare they speak of his qualities and love? Only I, only I as his wife knew his love. Only I knew the tenderness of his touch, the softness of his kiss, the strength of his body. I watched with scornful eyes their faces, awash with salty tears and sorrow. The words that were spoken, went unheard by my ears, sentiments of Richard's abilities and triumphs, his loyalties and loves, all these he shared with me and now I have nothing. I have no ability to continue and nothing to triumph; my loyalty was to my love, my Richard.

Today, I put my husband in the ground, beneath the cold hard earth. His empty body will lie there, alone and dark. My body lays here, in our bed alone and I will forever be in the dark. Therefore diary, I have no words of consolation; I have received none to console my dead heart.

Remember to love me

Patchwork quilt

'Annabelle...darling girl, did you get my letter? I am so sorry about Richard. I wanted to come, really I did, but just couldn't leave your sister. There was just no way in the world that I could have left.'

'Hello, Anna, where is she?'

'Emily...she's in the garden. Would you like a cup of tea?'

'No. Thank you, I just want to see my sister.'

'It's so cold out there; see if you can persuade her to come in? She says she likes the sound of the sea. Even if she sat closer to the cottage with some protection from the wind, but no...'

Annabelle paced the floor to the backdoor, down two stone steps and into the garden. The white painted wooden fence around the garden was low, purposely so as not to distract from the most incredible view. The cottage sat high upon a hill, the garden backing on to the dunes and then the sea. At this time of year, the beach was deserted, private, and peaceful, only an occasional local walking a dog. Only the strong sound of crashing waves and lapping shoreline filled the salty sea air.

'Emily? Emily it's me, Annabelle.'

The garden was empty, the bench vacant.

BECKY BYFORD

Again, she called her name, with no reply. Blustery wind thrashed the long grass, whipping the sand in a storm, as her feet trudged the first dune. From the brow of the hill, she saw the strands of Emily's hair. High above the sea, the colourless sky wrapped the vista, touching the violent waves. From here, the world appeared abandoned but for a lone figure standing against the wind.

'Emily?' Annabelle struggled to be heard over the wind; it blasted at her face, numbing her lips and choking her. Carefully, pushing against the blustery weather, her shoulders forward, her head down, she staggered over the dunes.

Emily remained frozen and unmoved, even by the wind, as if she were planted within the earth, a natural beauty amongst the wild heather and long grasses.

'Emily, I have so missed you. My goodness, it is freezing out here.'

Her eyes fixed upon the wild, rolling waves, her once wonderful auburn hair lay long and now equally as wild as the North Sea; in a tangled knotted mass down her back, it blew in whipping motions with the easterly wind.

She stood wrapped in a large patchwork quilt made from oddments of material squares, floral cottons, pretty brocades and luxurious silks. Annabelle recognised this quilt, a favourite of Aunt Anna's, meticulously made, crafted over many of her younger years. This was always placed upon your bed if you were poorly or needed some extra special comfort.

Annabelle instantly thought of James. How Emily must be suffering, devastated and eaten by her grief and loss, to be swathed in the special patchwork quilt. Then, her own terrible loss came bombarding at Annabelle's mind, the all too raw bereavement of the love of her life and the unfulfilled yearning for motherhood.

No matter how the time drifted, it was no healer; it devoured her ability to function.

How she longed to be wrapped in love as she once was, to feel secure and safe. Just to taste once again the contentment and happiness she once held in her hand, before it slipped away from her like water through her fingers. As a child, she had lost herself in the warmth of the patchwork and soothed her soul with its reassuring comfort and its miraculous ability to absorb pain.

The cold wind came crashing over the waves, lashing at her face. Icy, bitter and cruel, her feet came to rest behind her sister. Still, Emily remained motionless and silent.

'Emily, I really need to talk to you.' Annabelle stood beside her; her long travelling coat and gloves, no match for the protection her sister had.

'Annabelle?'

'Yes, it's me. I'm here, I am so sorry I haven't been here before now. Oh, it is so awful of me to have waited so long.'

The overwhelming sense of guilt churned in Annabelle's stomach and acid bile crept into her throat. The choking lump made it nigh on impossible for her to speak.

'I am so sorry, Annabelle, I am so sorry.' The suddenly spoken words startled Annabelle, as she stood hypnotised by the view; she turned to look at her sister. Emily's eyes never left the sight of the waves and their devastation on the shore.

'I know darling, I know. I am so sorry too...I am so sorry for James and I'm so sorry I have not seen you until now.' Annabelle leant towards her, wanting to find her sister's hand. However, Emily remained closed tight, no limbs visible, only the large wrapped folds of the patchwork, from her neck to her feet.

'Emily, please say you forgive me, I so tried to be a good sister, but I feel I must have pushed you away, to force you here to escape me. Forgive me?' Annabelle pleaded; her voice vulnerable and needing forgiveness.

The silence battled with the deafening wind for capture of their ears. Emily did not answer. Annabelle stood lost. Lost for words, lost in life.

'Richard. I am so sorry,' Emily whispered. 'I am so sorry for Richard.'

Emily's sentiments carried in the cruel air. Annabelle, desperate to answer, remained silent, unable to unearth the words at the sound of his name; they were buried somewhere beneath the hard frozen earth. His wonderful name brought memories, memories of his touch, of his aroma, of his emerald green eyes. Then came the remembrance of the last light from his eyes, as it went out, snuffed like a spent candle.

'We need to head back, we can't stay out here.' Annabelle, trying to find Emily's arm, simply grasped the quilt and guided her away from the sea.

Turning around, Annabelle cast her eyes over the dunes, scanning the beach below. A sharp intake of cold air stung her lungs. Shaken, she gasped at how close to the edge they stood, how Emily had remained static, against the thrashing elements, mere feet from the sheer plummet to the shore. Emily's feet trekked the dune, but her mind was oblivious to her direction, and Annabelle eagerly clasped the quilt to keep her close.

'Girls, come on in now. I've made some soup. It's far too cold to be out there, you must come in at once.' Aunt Anna stood on the back door step. Her ample figure, dressed in a dark blue dress, her greying hair, worn high, wispy at the sides due to the strength of the coastal wind. The girls entered the garden. Emily dropped to the bench as her legs almost collapsed beneath her.

'Come on Emily, we must go in. You know what Anna's like. God forbid you don't do as she asks.' Annabelle placed her cold, gloved hand on her sister's shoulder. 'Emily please, please come on inside. It is far too cold and harsh to be out here. It's not good for you.'

'I don't deserve to be warm.' Emily's words held no emotion; monotone, with no expression or feeling.

'You don't deserve? What on Earth are you talking about? It's too cold!'

'I don't deserve to be anything but cold. I am cold.'

'Darling, of course, you are cold. It is freezing out here; you must be frozen to the bone by now. How long have you been out here?'

'I deserve it. I deserve to be cold. I don't deserve to be warm and restful. I am so sorry, Annabelle, I am so sorry for Richard.'

'Oh darling, I know you are. However, Richard's death has nothing for you to be sorry about. It was awful...' She paused, desperate to remain composed for Emily's sake. 'It was terrible, but it was an accident, a tragic accident. It was no one's fault. You were not even there. Please come in, the coldness has confused you. You need to warm up, before it makes you ill.'

'Richard. It wasn't his fault. It was mine. He loves you so much and I love James. I miss him. I don't deserve to miss him; it was my fault.' There was a silent pause, only the sound of the sea. 'He will never forgive me; I shall never... I can never forgive myself.'

'Richard? James? Emily, you are confused, so very, very confused. It is so very cold out here. You are talking nonsense; the cold has over taken your mind and senses.

'Come along darling, come inside with me, and we shall have some nice warm soup, you can cosy up by the fire.' Annabelle placed her hands on Emily's shoulders. Emily's eyes were dull. Dull and lifeless, her body stiff with the freezing air. Annabelle tried to lift her sister, to entice her to stand. 'Come on Emily. Please darling, you are worrying me so...Emily!'

Annabelle shook her sister, gently at first, then harder and more forcefully, to bring her to her senses, to make her look at her face.

Emily made no eye contact, like a rag doll, her head rolled back and forth on her shoulders, with her sister's motion. Her body sat lifeless and cold with a complete lack of response. Her head lay bowed, facing the hard ground, matted strands of her untamed hair strayed across her face, in a webbed veil.

'Emily? Emily please, please I cannot bear to see you like this. Oh, this is my fault. It's entirely my fault. I should have been there for you. I have always been there to look after you, the one time you needed me more than ever, and I let you down. Emily, Emily, please look at me.' Annabelle knelt in front of her, her hands hunting for her arms amongst the vastness of the patchwork quilt. 'Please look at me, I am so sorry. You have to believe me. I vow I will never fail you again,' wept Annabelle, her voice filled with panic.

Very slowly, Emily raised her head. Her eyes were sunken with dark shadows from sleep deprivation and her denial to rest. She looked through her sister, with no acknowledgement of her desperate pleading.

'Please, Emily?' Annabelle wiped the wild hair from her face as she whispered her plea. 'Please!'

Finally, Emily stood; the large patchwork quilt fell from her grip. It tumbled onto the bench and draped the icy, hard grass. Emily's eyes met Annabelle's astonished dumb expression, but she remained motionless; with no emotion displayed on her face.

The brutal northerly wind persisted as her long tangled locks lashed her pale skin. Annabelle stood with her back to the violent waves, her hair whipping at her face in reflection.

Annabelle's eyes left her sister's…

Annabelle found it impossible to think as her mind cleared of every thought, of every belief she held in her heart to be true and pure.

No longer was Emily as she had been when she left, no longer petite and slim. She stood before her sister, expectant, carrying a child, clearly close to being born.

Annabelle raised her hand to her face, covering her mouth, with a choking lump in her throat, as the feeling of nausea rose to her lips.

At that moment, here and now, their world crumbled, as simply and surely as the castles of sand they once built.

* * *

'Please Annabelle, please darling girl! Don't leave like this, you must sort this out,' Aunt Anna pleaded with her. 'This must be resolved; you must stay. Don't leave, you will regret it.'

'Resolve?' she snapped. 'What on God's Earth do you expect me to do?'

'The baby, think of the baby…Emily cannot.'

'Oh, I see...it is down to me to think of the baby. Of course Emily cannot...she just sits there...look at her...not even thinking of herself. How long has she been out there?'

'Annabelle, please darling, the baby.'

'Baby, how dare you even use that word to me, as if it will make a difference?' she yelled.

Annabelle sat down hard upon the wooden chair, looking out of the back door. Emily remained seated on the cold garden bench. The seconds progressed to minutes; no words, no sound but the harsh beat of her heart echoing in her ears. Finally, she spoke, but softer this time.

'So many happy times, Anna...so many wonderful times we've spent in that garden, playing as children...' She strode to the window. 'But now...now, all I can see is cold and dread, death and pain.'

'You will have happier times again.'

'What happened to us, how did this happen? My own sister and my husband! My husband!'

'Annabelle, I can imagine how this makes you feel, especially now, with Richard...gone.'

'Do you know, Anna? Do you really? How can you possibly imagine how this makes me feel? It was a sacred vow, exchanged in the presence of the Lord, and now...well, what is left? How am I supposed to feel?'

'I am sorry, but the truth of the matter is, I do understand how devastating it is, but the baby will be here in a matter of weeks. Then, there will be no time to grieve what is passed, what is done: you will need to think about the baby.'

'BABY! How can I think about the baby? That baby... of how it was conceived?' she spat, as she walked back to the table, and sat down heavily.

Aunt Anna sat beside her and clasped her hand.

'You must be the one to think of this baby. Emily can't! Emily won't! I have tried to reason with her, to convince her of, well...that she must stop thinking of herself and start thinking of this new life.'

BECKY BYFORD

Aunt Anna's voice was tender, but to the point. 'Think about it, Annabelle, think about this baby. Emily wants to give it away. She says she can't bring this baby up. But she will regret it, you both will.'

'What can I do about it?'

'You just need to make her listen! Listen to reason. Listen to you. I know how angry and hurt this makes you feel, but you both need to listen…listen to each other. Find a way through this, Belle.' Anna walked to the back door, watching Emily.

'Please, Anna, don't! Don't call me that, no one but Richard can call me that.'

'He's gone, Annabelle.' The words had left her lips before the comprehension of it entered her brain. 'I am sorry…I didn't mean…'

'Don't Anna…just don't. I am sick to death with those words. My mind has been saturated with words the past few weeks and now…well, they mean nothing. Nothing has changed, my ears have absorbed the word sorry so many times, and it has made no difference to how my heart feels. It no longer has any meaning to me.'

'Look at her. Look at Emily, Annabelle; she is a child, innocent of nature. This didn't happen out of malice or deceit, this happened through grief and her need to be loved. She has only ever needed to be loved, you know that.'

'Now, the task lies with you. You are the only one left to love her. If she doesn't have you, she'll have no one. Who else do you have? Either of you? Other than each other, you only have the baby, don't let this baby go.'

'Grief, there was grief everywhere.'

Annabelle stood and grabbed her bag from the tiled floor and walked out of the kitchen.

'Annabelle?' Anna quickly followed her to the door, she watched as her niece stopped in the hallway. 'Annabelle?'

'Richard is gone, he was my husband, mine.' With her back to Anna, she spoke to the tiled floor, cold underfoot; her eyes examined the old terracotta.

'I know, I know. But Emily is your sister.'

'My sister, yes; my sister, my sister and my husband.' She took another couple of steps towards the front door then turned to face her aunt; she reached out and gripped the banister of the staircase. 'My husband!'

'Annabelle, don't walk away.'

'My husband...what I do, will not change that. Do you understand? He was mine, in the eyes of God, he was mine.'

'Annabelle?'

'I shall go and unpack.' Annabelle stepped round to the foot of the staircase, placing her leather boot on the bottom stair with apprehension.

'Good girl.'

'I'm not doing this for thanks! I'm not doing this for you! And I am certainly not doing it for Emily. Nor myself...as I know this can only give me more pain,' she sighed. 'I'm doing this for that baby, that baby who has been brought into this world with no choice of what is to happen and neither...neither does it seem, have I.'

Her weary legs trudged up the staircase.

Annabelle unpacked. Meticulously, unfolding and refolding each item in turn, as the task absorbed all her energies and thoughts.

The last of the afternoon light diminished, leaving her room dark and cool. Her energies spent, she wilted onto the bed; her head lay heavy upon the pillow, her blood barely pumping through her veins. She could bear no more, her eyelids slowly drooped and the darkness covered them...

...Lightly a hand glided up her arm, the tingling sensation travelled her spine as his hand reached her breast. Tenderly, smoothly it caressed and teased the silky skin of her bosom, the long fingers tantalising her aroused nipple.

The neckline of her dress, cut low in the summer heat, enticing his eyes. His longing was evident, his breath hot and moist on her skin, with each glide of his fingertips her body ached with desire.

BECKY BYFORD

She turned her face to his, the midday sun dazzling behind his dark hair, his face glowing with the intensity of the moment. She could see her reflection, deep inside the green pools of his eyes...

...She sat upon the edge of the bed, his hand reached out, touched her back.
'Lay with me, lay here beside me, let me feel you close.'
She turned and laid back, her legs barely on the mattress. He grasped her around the waist, pulling her close, closer to his body.
His body lay bare and glistening with life. The sheet about his waist allowed her eyes to trace every line and curve, each defined shape of his tense muscles, the soft sheen on his skin.
His long fingers clutched hers, encased them tight in his strong grip. With one swift but gentle movement he pulled and heaved her delicate body upon his; she lay pressed against his hot skin, only the cool cotton of the gown between them.
The strength of his passion pressed against her body, longing for hers. He could bear it no longer, as her heart thumped against his chest; he plundered her mouth with his lips. His warm breath mixed with hers, caressing, taking her mouth with hunger.
Within moments, the heat was so intense; her nightgown became hot and moist. With his long arms, he reached down and clasped the hem, dragging it up her body, exposing every inch of her. Her skin tingled at his touch. With one last manoeuvre, he pulled the gown up over her arms and head, their bodies naked...

'Richard, Richard...where are you...why can I not find you? I am so alone...so alone without you.'
'I am here, Belle, my love... I shall always be here.'
'Richard, I don't understand. Why Richard? Why did you leave me...I need you here with me.'
'Belle, you only need to look for me, I'm here with you, just look. I'm inside your heart.'

'I'm so alone...so alone. I am so sorry, Richard, for what I have done.'
'I love you Belle.'

* * *

Aunt Anna removed the hot bread from the oven.
'There you go. Come on both of you, I won't have this any longer. Let's eat breakfast. Annabelle, can you please pass the jam pot?' Anna sat herself at the table, Emily between them. 'How did you both sleep?' Annabelle remained silent, although the question had been aimed at her.
'Annabelle?' Still she said nothing; her eyes met her Aunt's and said it all. 'Well, it's a cold windy day. No sitting outside today, Emily. You need to be by the fire. Annabelle will sit with you, won't you, Annabelle? I need to go into the village, to the butcher's, so I shall leave you two.'
Annabelle shot her a look of panic.
'I shan't take no for an answer. You are not children. You are sisters, the same flesh and blood. Best you both start remembering that. There are some hard times ahead and you'll need each other more than you realise.'
Aunt Anna got to her feet, and went to the kitchen door.
'Emily?' Anna looked directly at her, but Emily remained unmoved. 'Emily, my dear girl, you need to talk to your sister. You'd best make a start while I'm out.'

Annabelle put another log on the fire; it crackled and hissed as the heat warmed the damp wood. Emily sat on the large tapestry settee, her legs outstretched and covered by the patchwork quilt.
'I remember one Christmas you were poorly. Aunt Anna tucked you up in that quilt and you slept so soundly that night, as if it had absorbed the illness out of your body,' Annabelle spoke softly.

She sat on the chair opposite her sister. The pain she felt, just looking at Emily's face was so immense it hurt her eyes and made her head pound; stung her heart.

'It's nearly Christmas, isn't it?' Emily whispered.

'Yes, very nearly.'

'I don't want it this year. Nothing is the same. I have no James.'

'It will come, nevertheless…if you wish it or not.'

'I don't deserve any happiness.'

'No Emily…No, you have no James and I have no Richard. Richard who was my husband, he was mine, and now he has gone!'

Her words hit, cruel and harsh, in the space between them, but her heart ached too much to care.

'You have no husband! I have no husband!' She spat in bouts of unleashed callousness.

'We are both alone.' Emily's words were untouched by her sister's heartlessness. 'We have nothing left, you and I, no one and nothing.'

'My God, Emily, what has happened to you, if only you would open your eyes and look, look at me. You have me. Despite how I feel inside, in the depth of my heart, you have me. I am your sister. You have to stop this, stop this wallowing, and let us live our lives. We are all we have, we have lost everything else.'

'I don't deserve anything, or anyone. I am guilty. It's my fault.'

'Emily, no matter how this happened or who was to blame, it did happen and we have to deal with it. Despite it all, I am still here for you. I am your sister and you are mine.' The pain of her own words stung her lips, but her head overruled her heart's emotions.

Emily's voice lowered. Her whispered words at last had a conscious thought behind them, her eyes finally showed an emotion. She looked at her sister for the first time in months; she looked at Annabelle with feeling.

'I don't deserve you, Annabelle. What kind of mother will I be, to this poor bastard child…?

Annabelle could not take her eyes from Emily, despite the suffering it caused them.

Emily continued, with misery consuming each word that left her lips.

'I was to be a mother some day, and a wife. James and I were to have a baby, which is the baby I should be carrying. That is the baby I want, not this one. It's not James' baby.'

'No, Emily. That is my baby, mine, the baby that I was meant to have, the baby that I could not have, mine and Richard's baby!'

Annabelle stood up sharply. She quickly paced to the fire, and reached for the long iron poker. She plunged the cold metal point into the depths of the hot smouldering logs. Repeatedly she stabbed and thrust with the poker. Red burning sparks spat and leapt with each jab. She stood, facing the chimney-breast; the large oval mirror reflected her tormented image. With the angle of the mirror, she could see her sister, her face buried in her hands.

'That is my baby, Emily! I will not let you part with it…it is not yours to give away…it is mine and it's all I have of Richard.'

Emily sat on the chair beside the fire, the quilt over her body, her large pregnant bump rising like a mountain beneath the coloured fabric squares. A sturdy wooden box rested upon a small table in front of her. With pale fingers, she rummaged through, removing selected items, placing them regimentally in order of size and colour, in her lap.

'How about this red one next, right there at the top near the star?' She picked up the fragile glass bauble, holding it out in front of her.

Annabelle took it from her fingers. 'About here?' she replied as she reached up to the top of the Christmas tree, the bauble dangling in her fingers, and displayed the red ornament in position.

'A little to your left…yes...that's it.' Emily leant slightly over the arm of the chair to get a better view around her sister.

Becky Byford

Annabelle hung the bauble from a spiky branch, the gold coloured thread lying between the needles. It twinkled with the reflection of the blazing fire.

'Can I have a blue one now? I'll put it just here.' Annabelle gestured to a branch just below the red one.

'Oh no, we will need a green one there; you have a blue bauble behind your arm, they will be too close.' Emily sat in her chair, supervising.

'Where?' Annabelle moved her arm, and stepped back from the tree, to get a better overall view. She tutted and sighed.

Annabelle smiled, taking a green decoration from Emily's fingers, hanging it on the branch. 'Well, yes, that looks better.'

'I know, I have a better eye for these things,' Emily stated, in her most eloquent voice.

Annabelle paced backwards across the room, studying the impressive tree. It stood in the corner of the room, as tall as the ceiling and wide enough to touch the far wall and the wood of the nearby fire surround. Its branches were thick with needles, arching upwards, and graduated to a single lone branch that stood tall, poking the ceiling, upon it a silver star.

Annabelle stood behind the fireside chair. She leant over the back, placing her arms about her sister's shoulders. Annabelle laid her head to one side, and rested it on hers. Their hair mingled, strands of golden ribbon-like tresses and wisps of auburn hair that was lacking its youthful lustre and red glow. Emily ran her frail hands across Annabelle's sleeved arm.

'It will all be just perfect, you'll see,' Annabelle kissed her sister's hair. 'Just perfect.'

'Yes, perfect.' Emily laid her weary head on her sister's arm. 'Maybe I'll have a little rest.'

'Do you want me to help you upstairs?'

'No, I think I'll stay here beside the fire, and just look at the tree...you know, just to inspect your work,' she giggled.

'I'll be in the kitchen if you need me. I think I will start supper.'

Remember to love me

'When will they be back?' Emily asked.

'Soon, darling, soon. They only went into the village to collect the goose.'

'I do love Christmas. It will just be a little different this year, Annabelle?'

'Yes.'

'Do you believe James will be waiting for me?' Emily's voice had become childlike and innocent.

'Waiting for you...?'

'Waiting for me when I go?

Annabelle remained behind the chair, unwilling to observe her sister's face, to see the look in her tired eyes.

'Annabelle, please, I need you to promise me something. It is very important,' Emily pleaded.

Annabelle walked around the chair to see her sister's face, pale and lined with worry. She removed the wooden box, putting it on the floor and sat on the small table in front of Emily.

'Now darling, what's all this about...?' Annabelle's voice quivered with unease.

'I know that things are not what they should be...I'm so frightened...I feel so weak...'

Annabelle lowered her head, not wanting to hear.

'Emily...everything is going to be just perfect...you wait and see. You will have a beautiful baby and...' Her words drifted off into silence.

Emily took her sister's hand and held it tightly in hers. 'I need you to be there for the baby...you're always so strong.'

Emily laid her head back on the chair's soft upholstery. 'Remember how you looked after me when I was small? You were always there for me. Just as you are now.' Emily shut her eyes and a silent tear trickled down the cheek. She sat motionless for a moment, before looking at her sister once more.

'You need to promise me that you will be there for this baby, your baby. This has always been your baby. It is yours and Richard's.'

Annabelle closed her eyes at the sound of his name; it had not been spoken for weeks, yet had resounded in her thoughts day and night.

Emily took a deep breath and gazed into the crackling fire. 'Do you believe James will be waiting for me, or will I be alone…after all, I betrayed him, didn't I? Do I deserve to be happy in death?' She paused a moment and pondered on her sister's expression. 'I love you…and I am sorrier than I could ever find the words to express.'

Annabelle patted her sister's hand. 'I know you love me, and I love you too. Now, you must stop worrying about all this; it will make you ill.'

'But do you promise me?'

'I promise to help you look after the baby…I will stay here with you both for a while. When you are fitter, then I shall return home.'

'I shall never return home. I belong here; there is nothing for me back there.' She gripped Annabelle's hand. 'If I stay here, then you can take the baby back with you as your own; it is your baby after all,' she sighed and paused… 'I like it here. I like the sea…watching the waves and feeling the wind blow my hair, the sun warming my skin.'

'You want me to take the baby back home with me?'

'Yes, of course. You will make a wonderful mother; I know you will. It's there in your heart; it is your purpose in life, remember? You told me that you wanted nothing more in the world than to be a mother.' Emily rested a moment, before she continued.

Annabelle simply stared at her sister.

'After all I have done, this is the only thing I have left to give you. The only thing within my power to make amends. I know I can never bring Richard back to you, but I can give you the one thing that is part of him. I am so sorry, Annabelle, I never meant for any of this to happen. I loved James.'

'I know, I know.'

'Do you believe he will be waiting for me, Annabelle?'

Annabelle reached over and kissed Emily's cheek.

'Of course he will be waiting for you. James loved you very much; he is waiting for you right now. But you are not ready to go…he will just have to wait. We can all stay here by the sea if you wish. The sea air will be wonderful for all of us. In the summertime, we can sit on the sand, build castles, and paddle our feet in the water. Remember how we used to be when we were children, our hems would be drenched with the salty sea water, and how Aunt Anna used to chase us around the bedroom so she could wash our dresses?'

Annabelle's voice grew soft, almost a whisper, as Emily closed her eyes and drifted off to sleep.

Becky Byford

Remember to love me

Rose

February 11th 1901
Diary, Christmas passed quickly. Father spent the days here with us. It is so hard for him; he is a very proud man. I watched him over Christmas lunch; he could barely bring himself to look at her, our dear Emily.

Nevertheless, she is his daughter, and he cannot cast her aside.

As a family, we have no choice but to continue as best we can. It has been difficult, the most difficult decision I have ever had to make, but there was only one answer. I am to bring this baby up as my own. We shall remain here for a while. Emily, however, is unsure if she shall return home. She feels better here by the sea. Something about it seems to soothe her soul. She always did prefer the sea air to that of the town. She is grieving so terribly, more so than anyone had expected.

Today brings an added reminder of her loneliness, as today is the anniversary of James' departure to South Africa. Emily stayed in her bedroom for the whole day. I took up her meals and stayed with her while she picked at her food. She ate very little and said nothing. I'm not sure if she cried or not, her face was so numb with grief.

BECKY BYFORD

Oh, my poor dear Emily, I am lost for answers. The weeks are ticking past and the baby is due in a matter of days. Our concern is growing for Emily; she is so tiny and frail these days. I am sure that she will be fine, and we can start being a family again, rather than two lost lonely souls.

My love and concern for my dear grieving sister has erased any hurt that I may have felt. I know, in my heart, that it was not only Emily who was grieving so, but that Richard also felt the loss of our baby and indeed the loss of me. I pushed him away so that he had nowhere to turn. Through my neglect, I pushed him into the arms of my sister. The fact still agonises my heart, but it is an agony of my own doing. I am to blame for this turmoil.

* * *

'You will love it, like your own, won't you?'

'Of course I shall darling. I love you so much. How could I not love this baby?'

'I am so very sorry, Annabelle. I really am so sorry.'

'Emily, look at me. What is done is done, and no amount of wishing and sorrow can alter it. You only have one thing to concentrate your efforts on, and that is keeping your strength for later. Rest now, you must rest while you can.'

Emily dropped her head back against the pile of pillows. Only a few moments slipped by before another contraction.

Annabelle rinsed and wrung out the cloth and put it to Emily's head, soothing her brow as the pain subsided and she lay still once more.

'Oh Annabelle, I don't know if I can do this. I am so frightened, so very, very frightened.'

'You are doing just fine; it will all be over soon, my darling. I shall go and get some clean water, and another drink; you need your strength.'

Emily lay; her eyes uneasily closed as her anxiety twitched her eyelids and tortured her face. Annabelle quickly left the room.

'Anna, is the doctor on his way?'

'Yes, my dear, he's on his way.'
'I'm so scared,' her voice broke and shook with tears. 'She's so weak...'
'I know what's going through your mind. Your mother had always been weak and frail. She was of a sickly disposition, not like Emily. She will be fine.'

Anna opened the front door. The doctor entered the hallway; small beads of moisture sat on the shoulders of his long grey overcoat, his brown bag hung from his hand.

'Well, let's see her. How's she been doing then, Anna? Last time I saw her, she hadn't had much sleep. How's she been doing these past few days?'

'She hasn't slept and she's still so frail.' Annabelle quickly answered, before her aunt had the chance to respond. 'I am so scared...'

'Ah, Annabelle my dear, why don't you go and boil some water?'

Annabelle headed to the kitchen, as Dr Williamson led Aunt Anna to the foot of the staircase. 'So Anna, how's she been doing?'

'She is very weak, and they are quite far apart. We have a few hours yet, which worries me somewhat.'

'Well, let me go and see her.' Dr Williamson quickly ascended the stairs. He gently opened the bedroom door. Emily lay still in the large bed, covered by the patchwork quilt, her hands gripping its edge for comfort. He placed his bag on the floor and took out his stethoscope and a large glass thermometer.

'Emily, my dear girl...well, how are we today? Let me pop this under your tongue, that's a girl. Now I'm just going to check yours and the baby's hearts.'

Emily lay perfectly still. She could feel the onset of another ripping contraction, but she tried with all her might not to flinch.

'That's a good girl, now you rest up. I'll send your sister in.'

The daylight hours dwindled into the dim dusky eve, and a soft pink hue flowed through the cottage.

BECKY BYFORD

Aunt Anna brought the brass carriage clock from downstairs, and placed it on Emily's dressing table. The minutes ticked by. The contractions grew closer and stronger.
Hour after hour, the hands of the clock swept its painted face.

As Aunt Anna and the doctor stood on the landing, Annabelle flung open the bedroom door.
'Quickly, Dr Williamson, I think she needs you. Quickly!'
'You wait out here, Annabelle, and let the doctor have a look at her.'
'Oh Anna, I'm so afraid, I'm not sure she's strong enough, she's just Emily, just tiny Emily.'
'Well, it's just as well she has you for a sister, isn't it? My darling girl, she is going to be fine, and so is the baby.'
Annabelle leant against the dark wood of the balustrade. The only light was that of a lamp on a table in the front hall, low and soft, gently illuminating the landing. However, from the bedroom, the light shone in bright rays through the cracks in the door.
She could hear Emily inside the bedroom, her muffled cries of pain. The air was thick and dense with an awful anxious concern, a deep rooted fear, and dread.
Annabelle gripped the banister hard, her knuckles white under the pressure.
Aunt Anna stepped towards the door, placing her ear to its darkly polished wood. For several minutes, cries and sobs came from within, then a loud piercing scream.
'No! I must go in. She can't do this without me. Not by herself, Aunt Anna, not by herself.' Annabelle opened the bedroom door, quickly rushing to her sister's side. Dr Williamson looked at Annabelle as their eyes met. Silently he shook his head.
'Emily darling, I'm here. It will soon be over.'
Emily was barely conscious as the next contraction wrenched at her insides. Aunt Anna came rushing to her bedside. The doctor spoke softly to them both, his back to

Emily, as she lay with the unbearable pain, ripping her apart.

'I'm afraid it isn't good. Emily is very weak… the baby is in some distress.'

The doctor paused for a second, to regain his composure. Annabelle looked at him.

'How long before the birth…is it very close?'

'Soon, I think. Her heart is very weak; it's almost as if she has given up on life. We will have to hope for the best and pray for them both. Leave me in here; I shall call you when…well, when you can come in.'

Annabelle simply nodded; there were no words.

Annabelle's heart sank to the floor, her body paralysed by the shock. Her head began to spin.

'NO! NO! We can't lose either of them. They are all I have left in the world!'

'Annabelle, darling, come, let the doctor do his job.'

Annabelle sat on the carpet, her back pressed hard against the spindles, her elbows on her knees, and her head in her hands.

'Please God, please don't let me lose them, they are all I have. All that I have in this world. You cannot take them from me; you have taken everything else. Oh God, please God.' Her soft muffled words repeated as the deathly silence from the bedroom permeated her ears.

The deathly silence seemed to grow louder and louder; it deafened her.

'No God…NO…don't take them from me.'

Annabelle took a deep intake of breath, a cool breath that filled her lungs. She heard a sound that penetrated the deathly silence. It was a cry, a baby's cry. Her heart leapt, but she sat paralysed, as she waited.

She waited and waited.

She could hear the baby; its soft sound caressed her ears. The seconds increased to minutes, the intense ticking of time as it ticked loudly from behind the closed door.

The brass handle lowered and the door creaked open. Aunt Anna stood in the door; in her arms, a cocooned bundle.

BECKY BYFORD

'It's a girl.' The words should have been sung from the top of her lungs with joy and laughter, but they came in a tearful sigh.

'Emily?'

'I think you should come and sit with her.'

Annabelle fell mute. She raised herself to her feet and entered the bedroom. Emily lay, perfectly still, her auburn hair smooth against her pillow, her skin pale against its colour.

'Annabelle, is the baby...?'

'It's a girl, darling, a beautiful girl, as beautiful as you.' Streams of tears fell from Annabelle's eyes. One by one, they dripped into a puddle on the quilt. She looked up at the doctor.

'I shall leave you two alone.' His face was pallid against his cotton shirt.

'Annabelle ...' Emily took a deep breath, 'I'm so sorry, so very sorry.'

'My darling, you have nothing to be sorry about.'

'But I have to leave you, just like everyone else...' Emily closed her eyes as she drifted in and out of consciousness.

'No darling, it's all going to be perfect, you just need to sleep. It's been a hard day.' Annabelle took the wet cloth and wiped it over Emily's forehead. 'You have a sleep, darling, and when you feel better you can see your baby.'

Emily opened her eyes, 'She doesn't belong to me.' Emily closed her eyes once more, and her head relaxed to one side. 'I think I'm going to sleep now,' her dull eyes gently closed. 'I can't see him, Annabelle, I can't see James. Will he will come...come and take me with him?'

'James will always be waiting for you, darling...not now because you are not going to leave me, are you?'

'James, he's not here. I can't see him, Annabelle. He's not waiting for me...I betrayed him, didn't I...'

'Don't be ridiculous. James will always love you, you were grieving, I know that now.'

Annabelle laid herself on the bed beside her sister; she cradled Emily in her arms, rocking her like a baby.

'No, Emily you are not going to leave me, my dear sister...whatever will I do without you here? I need you...No Emily! Don't you dare leave me, NO!'

Emily's cheek sunk onto her sister's damp sleeves, her eyelids fluttered open.

'Remember to love me....' her last warm breath escaped into the night air.

* * *

September 2nd 1901
I cannot believe that she is no longer here.

Time has passed but the pain is still strong, it eats away at my already broken heart. She was my sister, my family, my flesh and blood, and she has gone, like everyone that I care for. They all leave me. All I have now is Rose.

Oh, beautiful Rose; she has Emily's hair and fair skin. As the months have gone by and she has grown, I have watched her; sometimes I cannot take my eyes from her.

Her bright blue eyes are changing, over the past weeks I have seen them alter in colour; they shall be bright green, like her father's.

I see Richard.

She lays in my arms, warm and content. It is when she looks at me, her expression mirrors Emily's. It unnerves me sometimes, as it rips at my heart. I have to look away, I can only see my sister, and I miss her too much for words.

I stand on the beach and hear Emily's voice echoing through the waves as they crash at my feet; I feel the touch of her soft hand as the wild wind brushes my cheeks. I see her every time I close my eyes. I am haunted by the thought of my lost sister. I cannot stay here. I know she is in her heavenly place with James, but I cannot help but think she stands beside me.

September 4th 1901
We are leaving for home tomorrow. Part of me wishes we were not, and were able to stay here forever, but I know where I belong. My home is with Father and that

will be Rose's home. The town will be the perfect place for her; she will attend Miss Amelia's School for Girls, just as Emily and I did and our mother before us. She will become a wonderful, educated woman. Oh, the future seems so far off, but Father has already begun to make plans.

Poor, poor Father. He spent most of the summer here with us. For hours I watched him, he gazed upon Rose, as a fine jewel. He even played with her on the beach. However, his poor heart is still aching. He cannot talk about Emily. The mere mention of her name sends darts of agony through his eyes. I am very worried for him. He will not talk of his sorrow.

Her birthday was the worst day. Father spent many hours by her graveside, talking, listening, and wishing. He misses her so much, and to lose the precious child that you lost your dear wife to… but of course, I know all these emotions, this pain. To lose my baby, then Richard.

All we have is Rose. She is now our life and my reason for living. I am so very lucky to have her. We could have so easily lost her too.

The pain of the circumstances has eased. I know and understand now how very ill Emily had become, and she missed James so very much. I cannot blame her for what happened. After I lost the baby, I closed myself off to everyone; everyone who loved me and was there for me. My Richard, my dearest darling Richard, I shut him out of my heart.

However, time passes, and with each new day comes a new memory. A memory of my sweet Rose. I add these memories to my cherished thoughts of Richard and of Emily.

Therefore, Diary, this will be my last entry. I shall lock this diary away with so many other things, so I shall not be reminded of the past, and can always look to our future. Rose and I have a completely new life ahead of us. The past will remain in the deepest corners of my mind and pockets of my heart.

* * *

Remember to love me

'Will you look after Rose, just for a while? I need to do something.'

Annabelle walked to the front door, and wandered down through the village. The air was warm and close. She reached her destination, her feet sinking into the lush late summer grass, the birds chirping high in the treetops.

She stood in silence, her slender figure casting its long afternoon shadow. The early September heat penetrated the fine silk of her dress, as the rays of the intense sun emblazoned the words before her. Wearily, her head sank into her palms.

'It was not meant to be like this. How can I go on?' Her despairing words shattered the afternoon calm, but of course, there was no reply.

She slid her fingers down her salty tear-stained cheeks and her arms wilted beside her. A hand gently slipped into hers; it was soft, tender and it bore familiar warmth. She closed her eyes, savouring the silent moment, though she made no movement - how could she respond?

Her heavy heart lay spellbound, as slowly, time played out the ethereal experience.

'I shall always remember to love you' she whispered.

* * *

Bitter chilled air nipped at the early Christmas Eve crowd. The market square was filled with its usual festive traders. The hot aroma of the roast chestnuts surrounded Annabelle as she strolled past.

She pushed the large baby carriage through the market, relishing the sight of Rose in her knitted bonnet and coat, snug amongst the many folds of the patchwork quilt, gnawing on the ivory of her teething rattle.

'Mr Sedgwick.'

Annabelle stopped as she gazed upon an ageing gentleman, a short man of slight stature. His kind eyes were deep set in his thin frail wrinkled face. He stood on the footpath outside his premises, Sedgwick & Sons Fresh Green Grocery and Produce. Behind him, a large display

of fine Christmas trees and holly wreathes obscured the windows that displayed fruit and vegetables.
'I'm looking for a Christmas tree, Mr Sedgwick.'
'Of course Mrs Hardwick, I have just the one for you. I put it aside especially...I had hoped to see you.' Mr Sedgwick wandered around the side of his shop, nearing the alleyway. He returned heaving a huge tree; its needle-laden branches poked and prodded at his jacket sleeve. 'It's nice and full, as you always like them.'
Annabelle studied the tree's branches, her gloved fingers teasing at a pine needle.
'Thank you Mr Sedgwick, it looks just perfect, as usual.'
'It's been quite some time since you last visited us, Mrs Hardwick.' He paused a moment, switching his gaze to the carriage. 'We were very saddened when we heard the terrible news of Mr Hardwick, such a young man, very kind and honourable.'
There was an awkward silence. The sudden apparent din of the rambling crowds crashed at Annabelle's cold ears, as the shopkeeper's words repeated in her mind, over and over, such a kind, and honourable man.
Once again, Mr Sedgwick looked at the baby. 'She has her father's eyes.'
Annabelle battled to regain her composure; she looked down at the carriage. Rose bounced with the rhythm of the tinkling silver charms, as she frantically waved her rattle in the frosty air. Her beautiful large eyes glowed with contentment.
'Yes.' Annabelle smiled at her daughter, 'Yes, yes, she does.'
'It must be nice to be home, Mrs Hardwick, especially at Christmas. It's a time for the children, don't you think?'
'Yes, Mr Sedgwick.' Annabelle couldn't remove her eyes from Rose. The cold air nipped at the infant's delicate cheeks, giving them flushes of pink.
'And of course, your dear sister. Mrs Sedgwick was quite taken aback when she heard the terrible, terrible news. A sudden fever was it?'
'The Christmas tree, Mr Sedgwick?'

Remember to love me

'Of course, Mrs Hardwick, please forgive me. You have our condolences. Yes, the Christmas tree: shall I have it delivered for you?'

'Yes, please. And that wreath, the one full of holly berries.'

'Of course Mrs Hardwick. It will be just after noon, if that's convenient?'

'That's perfect. Thank you and Merry Christmas to you and your family.'

'Thank you, Mrs Hardwick and Merry Christmas to you.' His words fell in the icy air, as Annabelle with eagerness disappeared into the bustling hordes.

Annabelle headed home, through the market and down towards the Abbey Gate. Carol singers stood on the hill outside the gateway, their lanterns, light and bright in the dull winter dim. She rested for a few moments, listening, remembering. Her eyes fell upon sweet Rose, who delighted in the singing and waved her rattle in front of her, then handed it to her mother. Two small bottom teeth graced her perfect beam.

'For Mama? Thank you, Rose.' Annabelle took the ivory rattle and shook the small silver trinkets. She then handed it back to her daughter, with an equally delightful smile. Rose continued to shake the jingling charms to the sweet, festive music.

The town heaved with joyful charm; familiar faces shopped for gifts and wandered the streets. The hill gathered with dozens of local townsfolk as the carollers sung. Annabelle watched and sung, as her gaze travelled the crowd. Something caught her eye. Something unexpected, but before her mind had time to register, it was gone, and within a blink, the moment had passed. She eagerly scanned the crowd, her eyes dodging from face or face, but there was no sign.

'Just a dream Rose...just a sweet dream.' She gazed at her daughter, her flushed cheeks and red nose. 'It's time to go home Rose, time to go home my darling, sweet Rose.'

BECKY BYFORD

'You look cold to the bone, are you quite all right? My dear girl, your face is as white as my apron.' Mary took Annabelle's gloves and hat and placed them on the hall table.

'I'm fine Mary, just cold.'

'It must be the cold. I told you not to be out so long, I think we'll have snow later. Did you get a Christmas tree?'

'Yes, Mr Sedgwick will have it delivered just after midday.'

'That's perfect. We can decorate it this afternoon. Rose will love that. You and Emily always loved it when the tree was delivered.'

'I know, her favourite time of year. This time last year we...' Annabelle swiftly turned towards the fireplace, removing her face from Mary's sight.

'Has my father arrived home yet?'

'Early afternoon, my dear.'

'It will be good to spend the season as a family...'

'I understand, my dear. Rose will bring some young life back into this house; bring joy back into our lives.'

'Yes, but it will never be the same, we have lost so many...'

'Well, you sit by the fire for a while; I've just made it up, so you sit and relax. I'll take care of Rose.' She turned her attentions to the jingling of the silver rattle. 'There you are, Rosie Posy: are you Mary's little Christmas angel?'

The infant waved her arms in anticipation, as Mary lifted her out of the carriage.

Annabelle relaxed in the winged, fireside chair, her fingers numb with the stiffness of icicles, her nose frozen and pink against her pale cheeks. She rested her elbows on her knees as she leant closer to the fire.

Vivid red and amber flames danced along with the crackles and hisses from the damp logs in the grate. Annabelle stretched her fingers within the heat of the fire; her slender fingers slowly regained their mobility as she stretched them each in turn.

The thin band of gold glistened with the reflection of the flames. Mindlessly, with her thumb and forefinger, she spun the ring against her cold taut skin. Lost in her dreams of what had once been, she gazed upon the gold band, remembering the moment it was placed on her finger. Annabelle lay back, nestled to one side, her weary head against the plush velvet. Her awareness lifted from her melancholy reality to the warmer depths of the subconscious mind, drifting...

'Emily? Where are you?'
'I'm here, darling, my beautiful sister.'
'Emily, but I can't find you, where are you?'
'Open your heart, darling.'
'Is that really you...are you here?'
'Annabelle, I shall always be here with you.'
'Oh Emily, I don't think I have the strength to go on. This was not how life was meant to be...yours or mine.'
'My darling sister, you are far stronger than I could ever have been. You will go on, you have to for Rose.'
'Sweet Rose, sweet, darling Rose. But Emily, you should be here with us.'
'You need to be strong for her, you are her mother; Rose is your baby. She was never meant to be mine. She is my gift to you.'
'I love you, Emily.'
'I love you, my beautiful sister.'

Her body jerked suddenly, she awoke with a start.
'It's all right, don't worry, I'm on my way.' Mary's voice grew louder as she entered the room. 'I should think that's the Christmas tree.'
'Christmas tree?' Annabelle sat perfectly still upon the chair, her back to Mary, startled, trying to gain her bearings.
'Yes, the front door. Did you not hear the knocking?'
'Oh, the door, the knocking...yes.'
Annabelle leant forward, as she studied the crackling fire; the logs now burning fully; it spat bolts of crimson sparks.
Mary stepped up to the front door; she unbolted the lock, easing the large door open.

Becky Byford

'My goodness!' Mary stepped backwards, her plump hand to her mouth. 'Oh my goodness…'

'Mary, whatever is it? It's the same size we normally have, I'm sure it is. I know the branches are quite full, but I'm sure it will fit…'

'Annabelle, my dear… It's not…the Christmas tree…'

'Not? Then what is it?'

'I think you should come here…'

Annabelle lifted herself from her chair. She straightened and smoothed the taffeta of her dress and turned round to face Mary. She continued to adjust the cuffs of her sleeves. 'Oh Mary, what's the problem?'

'There's no problem. There's someone here to see you.'

Annabelle turned on her heels and gazed toward the open door. With small precise steps, her feet slowly carried her to the doorway.

'Hello, Annabelle, may I come in?'

He paused with a smile; a soft beautiful smile that shone through his eyes, but he was different, worn and distressed. This young face now wore a mask of age, far too old for his years.

'I think it's about to snow,' he continued.

Annabelle stood transfixed, her body rigid, her head spinning. She stepped closer to the door as her mouth, very slowly found the word that her mind kept repeating.

'James?'

Remember to love me

Teddy bears' picnic

Crisp fresh snow lay thick and dense. Pale and icy blue, the sky was the perfect backdrop to the bright morning sun; it hung low in the winter blue sky and the scenery dazzled with winter brightness. Never had there been so much snow. For weeks, it had melted away into slushy puddles only to be re-covered by a newly fallen layer, brighter and whiter than the last.

April stood inside the bay window; her left knee rested on the bedroom chair. The view beyond was her favourite: the pathway and grass, camouflaged beneath the new white blanket, the old gravestones wearing snowy jackets. Tall, skeletal trees stood in regimental lines, their brittle branches weighted with snow. The frosty air penetrated the windowpanes, chilling her face. She leant closer, so her warm breath could form misty patches on the glass; she watched them vanish between each exhalation.

For several minutes, she mindlessly played her game.

A movement caught her eye. Beyond the stony graves, between the bare trees, sat a wooden bench. A woman brushed the powdery snow from the seat with her leather-gloved hand; she then turned and carefully sat down. The lady's green coat was bright and lush against the white setting, her long silver hair was smoothly tied back; her face was pale and peaceful, emanating calmness.

She sat elegantly upon the bench as April watched with her body paralysed. She urged her legs to budge from their spot, but they did not respond. She begged her hands to let go of the back of the chair, but she gripped harder. Then, the elderly lady looked at April. Though her eyes were so far away, April could see the expression in them. Peace, love, and contentment. She smiled and April responded with a nod. The lady then rose from her seat, brushed down her emerald coat, and smoothed her silver hair, then she slowly strode along the footpath, under the tall canopy of trees, bare and spindly.

Within a second, she had evaporated, disappeared into the frosty setting.

April lost grip of the chair, her knee slipped from the seat and she collapsed onto the pink upholstery. Laying her head back, she dreamily watched the icy sky grow lightly grey and dull with snow clouds. The impression of the lady danced in her mind's eye.

'It was,' she thought. 'I know it was.' There was no point in trying to put a rational reasoning on what she had seen, she knew by now that this was the logical perspective. She was twenty-one soon and her adult life had taken on a new outlook, a new viewpoint on what was normal and believable. There was certainly more to life than what was just tangible.

Her eyes, oblivious, stared into the grey sky. Slowly, fluffy snowflakes drifted from the clouds, gently resting on the frosty glass. Her eyes gradually focused on the snowfall, tracing each new flake as it rested and then melted on the windowpane.

'More snow,' she whispered softly. 'More snow, Nan.'

April steadily stepped to the bed; the day's outfit laid out ready, the dark, depressing black trouser suit, and long black wool coat. She ran her fingertips over the soft fabric of the trousers, smart, elegant, and perfectly tailored.

'You'd like these Nan; really smart, but I hate the colour,' she whispered. 'Dad said it was appropriate, but I can't help thinking you'd have liked something a bit brighter.'

'Mum, do you think Nan would mind if I borrowed her amethyst brooch and earrings for today?' April sat at the kitchen table watching her mother finish washing the breakfast plates.
'Of course not. In fact, I think that's a wonderful idea.'
'Mum, I don't think I want to go home.'
'Home?'
'I mean I feel happier here…in this house, Nan's house.' She paused, watching her mother, anticipating her reaction. 'She's here, you know? Nan's here with us, I know she is.' April sat back in the chair.
'Do you think so…hmm…what makes you say that?' Julia turned and sat down opposite her daughter.
'Mum…this morning, I saw her this morning. She was outside; she sat on the bench in the snow, just as we did on Christmas morning. I could see the peace in her eyes; she was letting me know it was going to be all right.'
'I know, darling; she was with me this morning as well. I awoke to smell her perfume all around me. It reminded me of when I was a child…when she would wake me. This morning, before I even opened my eyes, I knew it was her. I knew she was standing there because I could smell her.' Julia reached for April's hand.
'But it's just that…you know,' sighed April. She clutched her mum's hand and rested her cheek on it, trying to ease her anxiety.
'Today will be OK, you wait and see. You know she's here with us all, it won't be her we put in the ground, just an old shell she doesn't need any more. Her young and vibrant soul will be with us.' Julia smiled, with her mother's same reassuring smile. 'You don't have to come home yet, if you don't want. Your dad and I will be going home tonight. But if you feel you want to be here, that's OK with us, as long as you'll be all right by yourself?' She kissed April's hair, resting her lips there as the moment lingered.

'I'll be OK, Mum; you're only across the road if I need you,' she replied, lifting her head. 'I think I need to be here, you know; I just feel I can get my head round things if I'm here.' April grimaced, her expression somewhere between a smile and a frown.

'Things will get better, you know. I do understand. You know you can talk to me; I really don't want you to think you have to do this all by yourself. You really don't.'

'Mum, there is something.' The hesitation was simply shrugged off by her mother, as Julia smiled knowingly.

'Emily.'

April could feel her stomach turn as her head expanded with confused thoughts. How could she know? April had no understanding, no comprehension.

'Emily?' enquired Julia again.

'Emily, she was Annabelle's sister. She was Nan's great aunt.'

'The two young women in the photo frame? You don't need to say any more.' Julia squeezed her hand. 'I think I need to tell you a little story.'

'Mum?'

'One day, when I was about seven years old, I was playing in the garden,' Julia began, 'right at the end, under the tree. That was where I always played, the sun always seemed brighter...you know, warmer, at the bottom of the garden. It was a beautiful summer day, and the sun was the brightest I'd ever seen it and it was so warm; the sort of heat that warmed you right to the heart.' Julia sat back on her chair and closed her eyes for a moment, recalling the heat on her cheeks. On opening her eyes she looked at April, who returned her smile.

'Well, I had laid out a checked picnic blanket and had sat all morning playing with my teddies. I had loads; I loved them, and everyone knew it. Most birthdays I got a new one, but I still had my favourite.' She nodded. 'I remember, I had a lovely porcelain tea set; it was white with tiny pink roses tied with swirly ribbons painted on the front of the cups. It was the most wonderful set, really delicate now I'm thinking about it, but I was so careful with it. I felt like my mum, with her best china.' She paused again; a nostalgic sensation travelled over her; cosy and warm.

'We had a teddy bears' picnic, my furry friends and I. I'd read them stories of fairies and princesses and unicorns; I had a whole library of books, full of tales of fantasy and adventures. That was my favourite game in the summer, and I so loved being in the garden. I felt so safe and protected, right there under that tree, guarded by the high walls, closing out the rest of civilisation. It was as if that tree held some sort of magic, something enchanting, do you know what I mean?' She gazed at April, not really expecting an answer.

'Mum, I think I know exactly what you mean,' she replied, as a smooth grin grew on her face.

'The garden was silent, well as silent as it could be with the sound of the birds and grasshoppers, even the odd bee around the flower borders. Not that they really worried me, you know; I felt protected under my tree, peaceful, no other noise than nature itself.'

Julia rose from the chair, and headed to the kitchen cupboard, removing two large coffee mugs from the top shelf. April noticed a new softness in her step – a sort of peace resonated from her movement, even emanated from her skin; she watched in wonder, absorbing the calm.

'Fancy a cuppa?' she nodded in question. 'Tea or coffee?'

'Coffee sounds good,' replied April. 'Thanks, Mum.' April didn't pursue the story; she knew it would continue in its own good time. The kettle seemed to boil at quick speed as if time was in fast forward, with urgency for the tale to continue. Julia finished with a swirl of the coffee spoon, then sat herself back down. Both hugged their huge mugs.

'Where was I...yeah, Mum stood just inside the French doors, calling me for tea; I'd been out the whole day, only leaving the picnic through the day to use the loo. "Come on, Julia, your tea is ready," she called. I said I'd be there in a minute; I just needed to make sure the teddies had their tea first, before I had mine. I continued to fuss with the tea set. I remember I was holding the china teapot and was pretending to pour into Fred's cup; he was the oldest bear and my favourite, I'd had him since I was born. A present - not that I know who from; well, I certainly can't remember. Anyway, Fred always had his tea first. Then I heard her. I didn't take much notice at first, and then she called me again. "Come on, Julia, we can play again tomorrow." The voice was beautiful and sweet and as it filled my ears, a soft flowery fragrance filled my nose. I will always remember how I felt; I felt loved.

'Now, I know there was no one else in the garden with me that day; well, no one I could see. But I heard her with these very ears, and I will never forget the sound of her voice. I knew I was never alone in that garden.'

'Did you ever tell Nan?'

'No, I was only a child, it was great! I thought, this is my friend; I didn't want to share her with anyone else. There was no thought on whether or not Mum and Dad would believe me. I didn't think that she was a ghost or anything like that; I was a child, only seven. Why should I question my own senses? We only do, when we become adults.'

Julia took a breath and smiled at April, her head to one side, almost examining her daughter's thoughts on her words.

'Mum, was that the only time you...'

'Oh no,' Julia quickly interrupted. 'That was our favourite game; teddy bears' picnic. I'd set her a place for tea next to Fred. I called her Princess, she always smelt so lovely, I thought that was how a princess would smell; like sweet flowers.'

'Did you ever see her, Mum?' April was curious; it was such an unexpected revelation.

'Not when we played, I knew she was there; there was never any doubt about that, I could sense and feel her. Odd, now I really consider it, but then it was simple: she was my Princess.' She took a gulp of coffee.

'Somehow, I didn't need to see her...I knew she was there, I felt her so strongly that I could almost see her in my mind's eye, although not with my physical eyes. Does that make sense?'

April nodded, 'That makes perfect sense.'

'That winter, about November I think, I was really poorly. I had glandular fever, and I was ill. Now, looking back, I understand just how sick I was. My whole body ached and I couldn't get out of bed for days and days; it felt like weeks. I longed to play but I just didn't have the energy. I slept by day but lay awake at night. One afternoon, I lay in bed, cuddled up to Fred; he was lovely; he was light brown mohair and had the most adorable expression and glass stud eyes. He was a Steiff, not that I would have appreciated that then, even if I'd known,' she smiled the warmest April had ever seen.

'Anyway...it was just getting dark outside and Mum said I needed to see if I could eat something, so she went to make me some tomato soup. I lay snuggled up to Fred and then I smelt it. I smelt her; her beautiful perfume. I didn't open my eyes at first; I just lay there cosy and warm. I can remember smiling, and feeling so peaceful, as I felt a soft hand on my forehead. It stroked my hair off my face. Her skin felt like silk, not like any hand I had ever felt before. Then, I heard her voice as she sang; I can't remember what the words were; only that it was beautiful and sweet. A soft serene voice, almost angelic.

'After a few moments, she moved her hand and sat beside me on the bed, I felt the bed clothes pull tighter over my body with her movement. Slowly, I opened my eyes and saw her. She sat next to me. Her dress was pale and lacy although I don't think I could see the actual colour of it; a pastel shade, I think. Her hair was red and very long; her face was pretty, much prettier than anyone I had ever seen before. She really was my Princess.'

'Mum...that was Emily.'

'I know, darling, I know.'

'She was so stunning, probably more beautiful than you could imagine,' sighed April, closing her eyes.

'She was my Princess. I never saw her again, that was the only time. I started to get better the next day, and within a week I was back to school.'

'I know you said you never saw her again, but did you…'

'Did I ever sense her again? Yes, when I played in the garden, I think she must have liked it in the garden. Then, as I grew older, it became less often; then gradually, and probably without really noticing it, I stopped playing with my teddies and started going out with my friends, and before I knew it I was grown up.'

'Mum, she's still here in this house. I don't think she has ever really left it.'

'I wonder what happened to Emily, you know in life.'

'I know exactly what happened to her.' April looked at the kitchen wall clock. 'But I think we should have this conversation another time. Nan will be waiting for us.'

'I have a good feeling about things. I know it's going to get a little harder before it gets better, but better it will get! You do have me, you know?' Julia stood up and wandered round behind April's chair; she leant down and hugged her daughter's shoulders, kissing her hair.

Remember to love me

Where there's a will...

'The cars are here. Are you ready?' Michael held out his hands.

'Yes, let's get this over with. It's so cold.' Julia buttoned her long black coat and adjusted her silk scarf high about her neck. A neat black hat sat perched upon her head, 'Ready, sweetheart?'

April nodded from beneath her cosy felt cloche hat. She pulled on her leather gloves and followed her parents to the front door.

Outside, parked on the snowy road were two long limousines. The leading car was laden with flowers, Sarah's dark wood coffin almost hidden by the wintry floral spray. A very tall gentleman dressed in a fine black suit held open the door of the second car. The limousines were the shiniest black, almost like glass.

'Nan would like that, very swish,' April thought, as a slight smile graced her face.

Inside, the seats were upholstered in fine beige leather, smooth and luxurious. The journey only took a few minutes but seemed never ending, with the monotonous views of white field after white field, edged with sparse trees. Not many words were spoken on the way, a few odd polite comments regarding the weather and such. The limousine followed Sarah's as they headed east out of the town.

'Almost there,' Michael repeated periodically as the car turned left or right.

Finally, they pulled round a corner to see the village church. The stone building stood historical and stark against the white backdrop, its tall round flint stone tower, and stained glass windows, ominously touching the icy sky. Thin, twig-like trees barely lined its boundaries, and a freshly laid white carpet led the way to the church door.

'I think it looks more appealing in the summer,' announced Michael.

'I think Nan would approve, even in the snow. She loved the snow.'

The tall, darkly dressed gentleman opened the car door, his face very sombre and mournful.

'Don't look so serious, young man.' Julia spoke, as her boots crunched on the gravelly surface.

'At least they swept the drive ready,' said Michael as he followed out of the car.

April stood at the church gateway, waiting. 'Was this the worst moment of the day?' she thought. 'Or will it be worse in the church, or maybe when we go back home?' Her mind drifted like the windblown snow as she stood still, waiting. 'Nan, are you here, with me? I hope you like the flowers; I thought you would have preferred a tree. Mind you, I think that will be a nice idea, planting a tree somewhere in the summer. Or maybe a bench in the Abbey Gardens, a bench with your name on it, what do you think?' April, lost in her thoughts, came too with her mother's hand on her shoulder.

'Ready?'

April nodded. It was time.

In procession, they followed along the forlorn pathway, the fresh snow crunching beneath their feet. They trailed in Sarah's wake as she was carried into the church. Once inside, the dark wood coffin with polished brass handles and fittings was sat central on a stand. April traced her mother and father's steps into the front pew near where Sarah lay.

Remember to love me

The congregation began to fill in behind them. April dared not turn round to see who was there, who had come to grieve. If she did, she felt sure she wouldn't be able to hold it together. Her tears were barely held back; one false move and she'd lose control. Fix your eyes on a spot! Any spot!

'Concentrate on something,' she thought. 'Anything, just something in front of you, April.'

Her eyes wandered until she saw a carved marble plaque on the sidewall; it was fashioned into a scroll with fancy gold inlay words. As to what it said, she couldn't see, but her eyes travelled the outline of its profile, each rolling curve of the carved scroll.

Stifled sniffles and muffled weeping echoed through the heights of the ancient church, bouncing off the stonewalls and wooden beams. Sobs, sympathies and the rustling of tissues, made their way to April's ears. All were grieving the passing of her grandmother.

The service progressed, not fast enough for April. 'Nan, where are you Nan? This is awful. I need you here, to get me through. You were always with me, when things were hard, where are you now?' Her thoughts grew stronger as she repeated them in her head. 'Where are you?'

A soft warm hand slipped into her gloved one. She did not look at the empty spot beside her, but she knew, she knew whose hand it was, and her heart eased.

'I'm here, Little One, never fear, I'm always here when you need me.' The soft whisper found its way to April's lone ears.

Julia leant towards her daughter, the strangest expression on her pale face. 'Can you smell that, April?'

'Yes Mum, I can smell it.'

'She's here isn't she? She's here now.'

April could hear the singing coming from behind her, but her mouth did not move. The whole service passed in a blur, a muddled hour of bewilderment and emptiness. Julia nudged April.

'Time to get up, sweetheart.' Julia nodded to the centre of the church.

Becky Byford

April left her seat and waited beside the pew to follow her mother and father. Sarah's coffin was carried out into the snowy coldness. Wind blew the falling snow in great flurries of white blindness. Four sturdy men carried her with ease, along the pathway to the side of the church.

They stopped. April saw it; the hole, the hole in the ground.

How dare they put her grandmother, such an extraordinary woman, in a cold, dank hole in the ground? April studied the graveyard; she noticed how dingy and gloomy it was. How the winter had hung a bleak cloud over the churchyard. No light, no colour, no solace.

'No!' she cried.

'Hey, come on.' Michael took April in his arms, cradling her as she wept.

'Not in that cold hole. That's my Nan.'

'April, April, you listen to me. You are strong, much stronger than you realise. You must see this through. Do you hear me?'

April raised her head from her father's arm.

'Do you understand me? It's just a hole; some dirt, that's all. No big fuss. Now come on. Come on, Little One. I'll stand here with you.'

April looked at her father's face as he stood at the graveside. She turned to her mother, who wiped a tear from her face with a fine cotton handkerchief, but neither had heard it, neither had noticed anything. April pulled away from her father's embrace and stood beside her grandmother. Her emerald brooch glistened in the bright whiteness of the scenery; her coat seemed untouched by the falling snow. Her bright face was more youthful than April remembered it; her smile sweeter, and her eyes full of life.

'Nan, I miss you.'

'I know. But I haven't left you.'

The vicar spoke his last few words of prayer and comfort. Gradually, the subdued voices of the mourners silenced and the crowd began to disperse.

Slowly, each car pulled away on the crunchy gravel drive. The coffin lay deep within the hole; thick snow now lay on its polished wood, gradually covering it altogether.

'Come on, April, we must get going, the car is waiting.'

'Can I have one minute, Dad? Please, I promise, just a minute,' April pleaded. 'There's something I need to do.'

April rambled through the maze of old head stones. Something was pulling her from deep inside her stomach.

'I think this will help.' Sarah stood by a large stone tomb, she pointed to the far side, beckoning April to follow her.

'Here, Little One. Here it is.'

April traced her grandmother's invisible steps and looked to where she was pointing.

Before her was a great expanse of grey stonework; the top was covered in deep snow. Each side of the rectangular tomb was engraved with the names of the Hardwick family. April wiped her leather fingers over the stone surface, dusting away the fresh snow. Carefully, her forefinger traced the carved letters that still sat deep inside the stone slab. Her lips silently mouthed the words before her. Bowled over by what she saw, her tongue became numb and useless. A nauseous lump began to build in her throat, her pulse thumped against her temples, her hands hot and clammy within the fleecy inside of her gloves. Woozy and off guard, she freed her hands from the leather and tugged at the buttons on her coat. Inexplicably warm, April looked at her grandmother.

'You needed to see this April; you need to lay these things to rest, to ease the pain.'

Once again, April let her eyes fall to the carved writing...

Here lies the body of Annabelle Jane Hardwick
Devoted Wife, Mother, and Grandmother
b. 27th March 1876, d. 8th September 1934

There it was, her last resting place. Stunned by the view of Annabelle's name, there was her life engraved in stone,

BECKY BYFORD

not her life, another's. She stood back a pace. Strangely, it felt peaceful, not at all morbid, or creepy. After all, it was not her name, but, Annabelle's body, a past body, an old body.

Then, after a moment or two, she thought of what lay in front of her: this was a tomb, a family crypt, the Hardwick family tomb. With quick, hurried motions, she brushed her hands over the stonework, her arms flying in large sweeps to clear away the snow, a sudden spurt of energy thrust through her body.

Until, she found it...

Here lies the body of Richard John Henry Hardwick
Beloved Son and Husband
b. July 10th 1873, d. December 1st 1900

Underlining both their names were carved the words; *where immortal spirits reign, there we shall meet again.*

The reality and enormity of the harshness was just too much, too much for today, for her heavy heart to take, today of all days.

'No.' April's cry carried across the empty graveyard. Her legs buckled beneath her, her limbs were frozen and numb. She knelt huddled against the rough bitter tomb, her face resting over his name. 'Richard,' she sobbed as tears fell from her closed eyes, stinging her cheeks. Realisation crushing her bruised heart, she whispered between inhaled spasms. 'Richard. Why do I lose everyone, why are they taken from me?'

Gently, she opened her eyes, and re-read the engraving.

'Where immortal spirits reign, there we shall meet again.'

Her anaesthetized fingertips traced his name over and over.

'Is he there waiting for me, why didn't I stay here with him? Why did I come back, only to lose him again? Is he waiting for me, Nan, where the immortal spirits reign?'

A vast torrent of tears fell from her eyes, her face sodden, glistening, and sore in the snowy air.

Her grandmother stepped towards her, placing her hand on her forehead. April could feel a spark of sensation but no longer her grandmother's warm flesh.

'You must realise, you were once reunited, but you chose to return; only your soul knows why. But you must go home now. Richard is not here; he is in your heart. Look at that name, it says, Annabelle. Those bones lay in the depth of this earth, but Annabelle's soul, your soul is inside you. Do you see? Only Richard's bones lay here in this tomb, just as mine lie there in that grave.

'Our souls, the love, the warmth, the compassion, the peace: we take that with us, that is what's with you. Richard will always be in your heart, because he has always been in Annabelle's. But you must move on, you must try to let go. That body lies here, you cannot bring it back.'

Gradually, her tears faded, leaving only red eyes and smeared make-up. She lifted her face from the stone, and looked hard at the writing.

'I loved you, Richard John Henry Hardwick.' April stood up on shaking legs, brushing the icy snow from her coat and trousers. She turned to where her grandmother had stood, but now the spot was empty, leaving only the sight of the snow covered gravestones and bare-naked trees.

April walked through the maze of headstones back to the church pathway. Her black boots carefully trudged through the fresh snow that crunched beneath her soles. Slowly, one step followed the next in her quiet contemplation.

The tall, sombre gentleman stood beside the black limousine, an enormous black umbrella above his head. The new snowflakes drifted onto the fabric, dusting the dense black like icing sugar. As she carefully approached, he opened the car door.

April stopped and stood under the umbrella, and looked deep inside the man's brown eyes. 'Thank you for waiting for me.'

His voice was smooth and low; as he leant down to speak to April. 'My pleasure, young lady. Did the elderly lady get a lift back in one of the other cars, or shall we wait for her?'

For a second April stood startled, and then she took a deep breath and replied. 'No that's fine; I think she's made her own way home.'

* * *

'Are you ready sweetheart? It's nearly half past; we need to be there at quarter to.' Julia quietly knocked at the bedroom door. With her ear very close to the wood, she waited for a reply.

'I'm coming.' April emerged around a small chink in the door. Her face was pink and flushed, her eyes were red, and tear stained. 'Mum, I don't think I can do this today.'

'I know, but we have no choice, we have to go. Mr Walters will be expecting all of us.' Julia took her daughter's arm and guided her down the staircase.

The wind blew in strong gusts, lashing their faces with icy whips. They took the short journey along the footpath, turning right into the next street to the solicitor's office.

The large Queen Ann building stood exceedingly regal, and Michael twisted the doorknob on the dominating front door. Inside was a large panelled reception area, housing generous leather Chesterfield sofas for waiting visitors. The taut upholstery was a deep red ox blood, with colour variations in the worn leather as it darkened around the sunken studded buttons. The low back was hard and rigid.

April perched herself on the edge of the sofa; her eyes travelled the original features of light oak woodwork.

An elaborate gilt clock resided upon the mantelpiece, supervising the daily activities with its regimental ticking. It ticked away the moments as Julia and Michael sat either side of April, waiting.

'Mr Walters will be with you in a few minutes. Can I get you some tea while you wait?' The routine words were spoken by a calm husky voice that came from the reception desk. The young woman sat with rectangular framed glasses in a mock tortoiseshell finish, balanced at the end of her slender nose. Her hair was tightly pulled into a long blonde, poker straight ponytail that swished across her shoulder blades as she moved. She was not so much pretty, as striking. Her build was slight and bony, and her rather sharp collarbone protruded through her slim fitting top.

'Maybe some coffee?'

'Thank you, coffee would be lovely. April?' Michael stood up and wandered over to the receptionist, turning to look at April on his way, 'April...coffee?'

She simply shook her head, with a wrinkle of her nose and slight turn up of her top lip to suggest the idea that coffee revolted her. Then she turned back to the sight of the mantle clock. Hypnotised by its sound, she stood up and approached the fireplace.

For several minutes, April watched as the hands crept round the clock face. Suspended in her thoughts, she recalled her grandmother's words.

'Time is nothing, but just a tick of a clock; it continues to pass, regardless, just as we do,' April repeated softly to herself.

'Quite true and very apt for today,' Julia's statement startled April; she spun round to find her mother standing close beside her. 'I know you miss her, I miss her too. I have now lost both my parents.'

'Sorry, Mum.'

'What for, sweetheart? It continues to pass, regardless, just as we do, remember. We all pass away at some time; it's the way of things.' Julia placed her arm around April's shoulder, pulling her close. She hugged her daughter. Tears seeped from April's eyes, creating a wet patch on the collar of Julia's black silk blouse. 'Hey, hey, it's fine; you still have your Dad and I. Look, I know that you both had a very special relationship, a special bond; something that no matter how I tried, I could never compete with. She loved you very much, but so do we. I'm not your Nan but I am your Mum, and no matter what, I love you more than life itself.'

'I love you too. It's just that…' April wasn't sure how to put it, how could she sum up these feelings?

'I know you have had a lot to deal with over the past couple of months, but I promise things will get easier. Come on; let's sit down, my coffee's getting cold. Besides, I think I should rescue that poor girl from your father.' They both turned to see Michael, with his hand casually leant on the corner of the reception desk. Michael was explaining about the interior woodwork, animatedly pointing and gesturing around the room. The somewhat befuddled receptionist simply smiled and nodded when it seemed appropriate.

Julia guided April back to the Chesterfield, then took hold of her husband by the elbow and led him away, saying, 'Thank you very much for the coffee, it's very kind of you.' Then, casting a knowing smile to the girl, they sat down.

The large oak door opened, and there stood Mr Walters.

'Julia, Michael, April, how nice to see you again. I just wish it were under happier circumstances.'

Michael stood up and held out his hand. The two shook hands with genuine friendship. 'Yes, quite so, quite so, John, it's been a couple of years. How are you keeping? And the family, how are they? We didn't really get a chance to chat on Monday, did we?'

'Fine Michael, all fine. And you're both back in town, I see, and making quite an impact, very impressive.' Mr Walters patted Michael on the back in a chum like manner; he then turned to the receptionist. 'Thank you, Naomi; I have no more appointments until after lunch.'

They all followed him through the door, across the hallway and into another room. It was much the same size as the reception area, the same original oak panelling, and high ceilings and another beautiful fireplace. At one end stood a huge mahogany table. Richly covered matching chairs surrounded it, about twelve in total.

Some people must have very large families to leave their money to, not like us; the rest of my family are in another century, April thought.

It only took a few seconds for her to realise what an astonishing statement that was too. Indeed, she did have her parents, but now with the loss of her grandmother, everyone else she held dear to her heart had been lost many, many years before, however real and present they seemed to her now.

Mr John Walters sat at one end of the large table, and gestured to some chairs either side of him. He was a tall man, in his sixties. He was bald, all but for some very wispy grey hair, still evident above his ears. He wore half-moon, thin gold wire glasses, that he kept on a black woven cord around his neck, for quick access when reading.

April remembered him and his wife Annette; they had attended quite a number of parties and celebrations at their country house. She couldn't recall where they lived exactly, only that it was somewhere in the depths of the countryside, and somewhere near a large church and a field of sheep.

Strange, some of the memories that you hold on to, she thought. Her mind was wandering once more; her ability to concentrate these past days had almost diminished completely.

'Now,' stated Mr Walters. 'Let's get down to business.' He placed a large file upon the polished surface of the table; reached down to his glasses, and slipped them over his ears. The framed lenses nestled familiarly on the middle of his large nose, the cord lying on the collar of his navy blue pinstriped jacket.

'As you all know, Sarah, and indeed Edward, had been very good friends of mine over the years, and I have always looked after their financial affairs.' He looked straight at Julia, and with a very honest smile, he continued. 'I do hope that you will continue this tradition in the future with your own financial affairs.'

Julia simply smiled very coyly as she fidgeted on her chair. Mr Walters opened the file and removed a few sheets of thick white paper.

'So,' he began. 'This is the last will and testament of Sarah Parkinson.'

April's mind began to wander once more, the mere sound of her grandmother's name brought harsh stabbing pains to her chest. She sat back on her chair with her head resting on the polished wood as she closed her eyes; they didn't need her for this. She had been dreading this moment for days. Somehow, the reading of the will made it all so much more real and definite; an ending, an underlining of this chapter in her life.

But where was she to go from here?

Nothing in her life seemed to have any stability; this she always had from her grandmother. What was her path in life? Who was she to turn to, who could make sense of it all? Her mother was grieving enough, without having April adding to it.

'To my daughter Julia, I leave the sum of £5.8 million.'

The room was drenched in silence, as the family sat speechless. April lifted her head, and her eyes opened in bafflement.

'Sorry, I thought you said…5…'

'Yes, Julia, £5.8 million,' Mr Walters cleared his throat and continued, not even batting an eyelid. 'To my son-in-law Michael, I leave my husband's collection of vintage cars, which are currently held on show at Beaulieu Car Museum.'

'Cars…what cars?' queried Michael as he sat up with his hand over his mouth, his eyes wide and astonished. 'Did I hear you correctly; did you say collection of vintage cars?'

'Yes, currently in a car museum.' Mr Walters placed the papers on top of the file and removed his glasses, letting them dangle from the cord. 'Am I to assume that you were not quite aware of the extent of the assets?' He turned to look directly at Julia.

'Extent? To be quite honest, John, I thought it would be a matter of the house deeds and the balance in her current account.' She shrugged in bemusement.

'Ah, the house deeds; well, we haven't quite got that far,' he replaced his reading glasses, peering down at the papers. 'To my only granddaughter April, I leave my house in Crown Street. This is for her to live in, where I know she belongs.' He paused, raising his head and glancing at April.

'The house, Nan left me her house?'

'Your house, April.' Julia looked across the vast table at her daughter.

'Yes: To my granddaughter April I also leave...' he coughed. 'Please excuse me; I also leave my three-storey town house in Northgate Street. A plot of land on the Norfolk coast...'

'Hang on, I'm very sorry but...but I just don't understand all this.' April sat with her head on her arms, her forehead almost touching the cold surface of the table. She shut her eyes tightly, blocking out this strange and obscure situation. After a few moments, she quickly sat up. 'Did you say something about the Norfolk coast?'

'Yes, a plot of land on the Norfolk coast,' he repeated the sentence.

'That's Aunt Anna's place, I just know it,' she announced with conviction.

'April? Aunt Anna? I don't understand,' Michael asked with a mystified expression.

'She was Nan's great...' April looked past her father as she counted the generations, 'hang on, her great-great aunt, I think. Anyway, I don't think Nan knew about her; she obviously knew about the land, but well, that's where Anna lived, so it must be hers, although of course now the house isn't there anymore, well sand erosion or something isn't it? I remember doing about it in school, and how the sea was wearing away our Norfolk coast line and...' April continued, with all eyes on her, very taken aback by her sudden impulsive outburst. Then she stopped mid sentence, her mouth still gaping, her eyes wide, her face draining of all colour.

'Sweetheart, whatever is it?' Julia gazed at her daughter with a very worried frown.

'Nothing, no nothing, it's fine, absolutely fine.' She smiled at her mother and turned to the solicitor. 'Thank you, Mr Walters, I just can't believe Nan left me all that,' she nodded.

'Oh April,' he replied, 'we haven't finished by any means.' He cast her a very warm knowing smile. 'Now where was I? Ah: To my granddaughter I leave...north Norfolk coast, and my Art Deco villa, in Juan Le Pinn in the south of France. The rental profits from both the Northgate Street property and the French villa are to be deposited quarterly into a bank account for her. I also leave the sum of £4 million in trust until her 21st birthday. All my other belongings, such as jewellery and items in the house are to be divided between my daughter and granddaughter as they see fit.'

He quickly glanced around the table to find dumbstruck faces staring back. Mr Walters sat back in his chair.

'I understand that it is a great deal for you all to take in, especially at this time. It is a great shock to accept the loss of a loved one. On a personal note, I know how close you all are, as a family.'

He looked directly at April, his face calm and reassuring. 'In light of the shock Sarah knew it would be, she prepared a letter for each of you.' He reopened the file and removed three creamy coloured vellum envelopes. He handed one to each of them.

April tentatively took hers. The vellum envelope felt thick and stiff between her fingertips.

Mr Walters leant forward, his elbows resting on the polished surface; as he repeatedly pressed his fingertips together, in a contemplating motion.

'You do know that I am here to help. Please don't hesitate to call me, if you need anything. Of course, I will need to see you again to sign some paperwork, but I think we should leave that a couple of days, just to let things sink in a bit. You all seem rather stunned, if I may say so. Sarah was a very special lady.'

His ageing features expressed the true loss of a friend, his vulnerable depths apparent beneath his professional manner.

Mr Walters stood up, straightened his jacket, and adjusted his crisp white shirt cuffs. 'She will be greatly missed. She made a great impact on everyone she met.'

'Thank you, John. Thank you for being so understanding.' Julia slid her chair out, ready to leave.

Mr Walters led the way back through the hallway to the front door. He shook Michael's hand. 'I shall be in touch, look after them.'

'Thank you John. Thank you for your compassion.' Michael closed the door behind them, as the frosty air hit their pale faces with its icy fingers.

* * *

April drew the curtain too, switching on her bedside lamp. The space instantly glimmered with a warm and cosy ambience.

A slightly bizarre excitement had choked her during the afternoon. This persisted to battle with the emptiness she felt, the hollow hole left by her grandmother's departure.

The cool cotton sheets quickly warmed to the heat of her body. Her feather pillows propped up behind her head, April sat with her knees under her chin, and her arms wrapped round her legs.

'Well Nan, it's now or never.'

She took the thick vellum envelope in her hand, flipping it repeatedly in her fingers. Hesitation kept her hands fidgeting and fumbling. After a few minutes, April sighed, slipped her long fingernail under the corner of the flap, and ran it along the seal, gently lifting it open.

April unfolded the sheets of buttermilk paper. They lay on her knees, as her eyes began to scan and digest the smooth, blue ink…

My Little One

Please don't be sad, it was my time to go; time to be reunited with your grandfather. I belong with him and always have. I have had eighty wonderful years on Earth with all my loved ones. I have watched so many leave me; now it's my time to leave and join them.

I know the way that you are feeling. I know the emptiness that sits in the pit of your stomach and the loneliness that lives in the depths of your heart. However, remember it will pass; each day things will get a little easier to deal with.

Soon you will feel lighter, and when the weather warms, everything will be easier to bear.

When I lost my grandmother, I knew I had lost a dear friend. I was so very young that our friendship was short lived, but when she died, it left a large gaping hole in my world.

When you were born, at the very first moment I held you in my arms I knew. I just knew. I really don't know how, only that my heart recognised you at once.

I know you very well; you are now sitting asking me how and why. How I kept it a secret, why I hadn't told you before? Well, the truth is, I knew one day you would know, that you needed to go on this journey. One day you would return home to where you belonged. I only ever tried to guide you, to help you.

My darling, I'm not sure if you realise how special you are. What an amazing special gift you have. You have the ability to remember your past life, to relive another time and another life with your thoughts. There are people who would give anything to have that ability, to live with that knowledge every day.

However, with the gift comes a burden. I know and understand the sorrow and terrible traumatic memories that are being re-lived by your soul.

Nevertheless, you must remember, these are only memories that have already happened long ago; there is nothing you can do to change them. All you can do is learn from them and maybe the wounds will begin heal. I know you have lost those who were important to you, but you have so much life ahead of you, so many new loves to find along the way.

Remember to love me

There is something I must confess; I haven't been totally honest with you. I must say, that when we saw Emily on Christmas Eve it did really knock me for six!

Well, I had had an encounter with her before; many, many years ago. I know that perhaps I should have told you, but you would have wanted answers that I didn't have.

When I was a small girl, my grandmother would take me into the park; we spent many, many lovely times in the grounds of the Abbey gardens. When the weather was warm, she would take a picnic and we'd sit by the river. I loved those days, just lying there in the sun. She would tell me stories of how she had brought my mother there when she was young.

It was funny, as a child of only about seven; it was hard to imagine my own mother as a child herself: I could only see her as a grown up.

Well, one particular afternoon, we laid the checked blanket out on the ground; I remember how the long grass was warm and soft beneath the blanket and how it was as inviting as my own bed. I lay outstretched on my back, with the bright sun warming every inch of me.

Through my closed eyelids, I could see the bright pink sunrays.

We would play games; my favourite was closing my eyes and concentrating very hard on the sounds around me, to see if I could pick out each sound, one by one. My grandmother would say; maybe if you listen ever so carefully, you may hear the fairies flying on the wind and dancing in the grass. I loved the thought of that; my imagination was full of magical worlds, with dragons, unicorns, but most of all fairies.

I can see now how she fed those fantasies, how she loved my childhood daydreams.

This particular occasion we lay on the blanket together, I can remember every tiny little detail about that day, as if it was yesterday. I wore my best summer dress; it was the palest blue with a lacy collar and a large bow that tied at the back; my hair was dark then. My mother always kept *it very long. She would tie it in a ribbon to match my outfit. My grandmother always said how much like my mother I was, right down to the auburn curls that hung down my back. My grandmother wore a beautiful dress with a large white collar and large buttons on the front. It was the loveliest pale green and she always wore gloves; they were white and fitted just to her wrist. She was so elegant, I suppose that is the most memorable detail about her, how immaculate and refined she was.*

She never raised her voice; I loved her so much and relished our playtimes so much that I never gave her cause to. My goodness, I'm reminiscing again.

That day, as I lay listening, describing the sound of the birds and the trickling of the river, I heard something new. I opened my eyes and looked about me.

My grandmother was lying beside me and her eyes were tightly shut. She asked me what I could hear, but for a second or two I couldn't answer. I lay back again and strained my ears to home in on the new sound. It was hard; the more I tried the more the usual sounds bombarded my ears.

Then it got louder and clearer.

I can remember that it was the most beautiful thing I had ever heard. Despite the warmth of the sun, I had goose bumps all over my arms and I could feel each and every hair standing on end. Don't get me wrong though, I wasn't afraid, I was just amazed. I was so young; I didn't understand what was so strange about it.

My grandmother sat up, shook my shoulder, and asked me if I could hear that. I just nodded, I didn't open my eyes; I just wanted to get soaked up by the sweetness.

After a few moments, I opened my eyes to see her looking straight at me with the most terrifying look of astonishment on her face. I asked her what the matter was. She didn't answer me at first. I asked who it was. I could see her mind trying to work out what to say, then she simply answered; it was an angel, a sweet angel who was looking after me.

Remember to love me

I realised many years later that I could hear singing, sweet singing; it was Emily. My grandmother of course heard it and she knew straight away that it was Emily.

I never saw her, but every so often, if things were tough I would hear her singing. I don't think I am the only person who has heard her either.

Now, I suppose, I should get to the will. I know exactly what's going through your mind. You must be confused and bewildered, full of questions, like where did it all come from? Well, my darling, Little One, that's quite a story. Some things you'll already have the answers to, having to untangle the knot of family confusion.

Well, as you will know I have left you the house, your house. It belonged to you long before I was born, so I am returning it to you and therefore returning you to where you belong. This includes everything in the house for you and your mum to do with as you wish.

I can hear your voice right now, 'I don't want to change a thing!' Just don't hold onto unnecessary bits and pieces that you don't need or don't even like.

This is your home now, yours for you to live in.

As for the town house in Northgate Street, a lovely family has rented the house for the past twenty years. I don't think they have any thoughts of moving, so the income from that is enough for the upkeep and running of your house, and of course plenty for you to live on.

Mr Walters will look after the boring money side of things for you. You can trust John; he has been a dear friend for many years. I have made all the arrangements for him to continue on your behalf. If you have any questions, about any of it, please ask him; he will always do his utmost to help. As you've guessed, this was my grandparent's home, so it is yours anyway.

Or should I say it was Annabelle and Richard's home?

Well, that's all the obvious things out the way. I know you must be bursting to know about France, but that will have to wait a while.

The land in Norfolk is a lovely seaside plot, it's a good size, so enough for a lovely cottage and garden, overlooking the sea. Perhaps in the future, it may be nice to spend time there in the summer months. I can imagine you in a lovely quaint cottage with pink roses and children playing in the garden. I know I'm letting my imagination carry me away. My mother inherited this plot of land.

You must feel like your world is in turmoil. I am sorry darling, I really am so sorry; I know that leaving you now was bad timing on my part. Unfortunately, we don't seem to get a say in when we go, do we? I suppose no time would be a good time. The cancer took hold last summer. The doctors hoped I had at least a year left, but, well, never mind. Please don't be angry at your parents, I made them promise not to tell you. I hoped to be able to tell you myself, but then you had so much to deal with; it got to the point there was never the right time.

You are far stronger than you realise, your soul is strong and true.

I have faith in you.

I know how terrible the feelings were when you found out about Richard's accident: these are things that cannot be changed; you cannot alter the past, no matter how painful. However, you will find someone you can love. You will, I promise.

Richard was an only child, therefore the sole son and heir of his family's fortune. They owned a large estate in the village where you just buried me. The church graveyard contains the Hardwick family tomb. I am almost hesitant to mention it.

But did you see it?

I hope I managed to make it there on time. I was so ill, that by the time you fully understood Richard's fate, I was already bound to my bed.

After Richard's death, of course, Annabelle was left their Northgate Street house and a rather substantial sum of money on a yearly basis.

Only two years after his death, Richard's father, Richard Hardwick Senior fell ill and passed away that winter. After that, his mother soon followed. My mother said she mourned herself to death of a broken heart.

Remember to love me

Then the manor house, the stables, and all the land were sold off. The sole beneficiary was my mother; Rose. It was in trust until she turned twenty-one.

Annabelle's money was more than enough to keep them both very comfortably. So, that is where it all came from, I suppose you have probably worked most of that out for yourself, apart from maybe one more thing, the villa in France?

The villa is a stunning Art Deco masterpiece in the most picturesque Juan Le Pinn, on the French Riviera. It was quite the place to be in the 1920s, very avant-guard, and full of the rich and famous. At that time, the small fishing village was just being built as an exclusive holiday destination for the wealthy.

It is very close to the beach and overlooks the sea. It has been rented for as many years as I can remember.

Your grandfather and I did visit and stay there in the early 1950s just before I had your mother; it's the most glamorous and elegant place I have ever visited. I know you will absolutely love it!

I suppose there is one more thing you should know, and I think probably the most important detail of all; that the villa was mysteriously left before. Annabelle was left it a while after it was built. Unfortunately, that is all that is known; I know no more than that.

April, my Little One, you must remember, money is to be respected, appreciated and to be used well. That is why I never told you that you were to be so wealthy.

You were never to be lavishly spoilt; I knew you would have it one day. Love is far more important than anything that money can buy.

I have full faith in you. I love you more than you will ever know; it can never be put into words.

We shall be together again one day, on this side or the other.

Your loving grandmother,
Sarah

BECKY BYFORD

April re-folded the letter and placed it back in the envelope. The bedroom, her sanctuary, had dimmed as the night pulled the light out of the sky. She pushed her pillows back down under her head, as she lay curled up in her bed. Her arms tightly wrapped around her body, she sobbed. Great drops of salty tears made mascara-muddy puddles on her pillow. Her body shook in spasms as the sorrow seeped, bleeding into every bone of her body.

Remember to love me

Ploughmen's & Wisdom

She sat in the back of the car as it passed the sign; Winterton-on-Sea 1 mile.

She was going back to her childhood hometown, the place where she had grown up, where she'd played, and laughed. The place that gave her security, solace and assurance. The home of pale, sandy beaches and magnificent crashing waves. The summer months were always full of multi-hued floral rainbows, dripping from the hanging baskets, window boxes, and flowerbeds. The birthplace of her heart and soul; where her young spirit felt untroubled and calm, that after protest she had reluctantly abandoned.

The place she had always called home.

'This is where the land is?' April's question was far more a statement, bursting with astonishment and disbelief. 'You mean we lived in the very village and never knew it.'

Her exhausted but enthralled brain mused over the possibilities. How many times had she walked passed that piece of land; the very land where her very soul had once walked in another life.

From that very piece of land, that small piece of hell tainted heaven; you could see the view of the sea and the sandy dunes. The great pull of the waves and salty air dragged at her stomach, as her soul soared with the exhilaration of being back, coming home.

Home: she mulled the thought over in her head. Home, well that is what it had seemed, but was it now? Nan had said she had arrived home, where she belonged, where she had always belonged. So, if that was the case, why? The longing to be back here, by the sea, where the closeness to the elements, no matter how harsh they could be, soothed her soul and eased her mind.

Michael slowed the car, pulling into the pub car park.

'How about we stop here for some lunch first? Maybe someone knows where it is.' He turned off the engine and opened the car door. 'Do you know it's been at least a year since we've eaten in here! I wonder if they still do that fisherman's omelette. It's the best thing I've ever tasted.'

Inside was welcoming; April couldn't imagine it any other way.

The wood panelled interior was dark but glowed with the dusky pink walls. Its warm and cosy feel projected a soft red glimmer to the interior, an appreciated contrast to the cold February day. Finger marked walls were scattered with a collection of paintings, photos and fishing memorabilia. The bar was covered with souvenir trinkets, tankards, china curios and postcards. The pub bar was speckled with half a dozen or so weathered locals wearing their winter woollies and boots; men and women alike.

'Hello there, what can I get you?' A middle-aged lady, of well-built proportions rested her palms on the wooden bar; the words rolled off her tongue with the familiar slow Norfolk drawl.

'Hello, there, how are you?'

'Ah, it's Michael, hey, how you all doing? It's been quite a time, thought you'd moved away? Didn't think I'd see that lovely old smile again in 'ere!' The bar maid moved closer to the bar and, folding her arms, she rested her elbows on the wood. Her large fleshy bosom oozed over the tight knit of her shocking pink, scoop neck sweater, waves of natural blonde hair were clipped up at the back, with hints of sparkling silver framing her features. Her wispy fringe mingled with her eyebrows, her lashes fluttered.

Michael's handsome face blushed as she winked. He unbuttoned the collar of his overcoat and loosened the paisley scarf from around his neck, as his face warmed with the attention.

Julia appeared a few steps behind him. 'Ah, hello Sandy how is everything?'

'Julia! Well, not much differs 'bout 'ere.'

Sandy's permanently tanned face bared resemblance to an old weathered wax jacket, although her pretty smile and honest nature made it glow under the log firelight, which was complemented by the sparkle of her long crystal earrings. She wandered along the length of the bar, gesturing to Julia with a flick of her head. Sandy leant further over, as far as her ample proportions would allow.

'How's your dear mum? Will we be having the pleasure of her company this summer? I was really shocked when I heard she was poorly.' Her voice lowered with genuine concern. Sandy's long drawn out sentences made Julia squirm with the choking lump of her looming reply.

'Well, I'm afraid we lost her a few weeks ago, just after the New Year.' Julia wanted to add more to her answer, to cushion the news for them both, but there were no more words left in her mouth. She could almost taste the emptiness.

Sandy reached out her hand and rubbed Julia's arm. The thick knit of her brown mohair cardigan brushed against her skin.

'Oh, I'm so sorry, Julia, really sorry. Well, you know how much I thought of her...how much we all thought of her. Lovely lady, Sarah, lovely.' She kept blinking sympathetically as she pursed her pink lips and nodded to enhance her sentiments.

'Thank you, Sandy,' Julia responded. She felt uplifted by the genuine condolence.

'Now, how about some lunch; you must be cold to the core. Something to warm you all up: we've got winter vegetable soup on the specials, with warm crusty bread?' Her smooth Norfolk accent at its full height boomed over the bar.

April gawped at the specials menu. The blackboard was sprawled with coloured chalk; the words gently slanted as the list of choices progressed down the board; numerous locally caught fishy dishes and warm stodgy, comforting puddings. After a while of musing over some of the hearty stew-like concoctions, she decided for the fail safe.

'Can I just have the cod and chips and a coke please?' she called over her request.

April took a seat at a small round table by the window, and removed her denim jacket, pulling down the sleeves of her jumper, holding the cuffs in her fingers and folding her arms, her elbows resting on the polished table and her chin on her forearm.

April could smell the fresh furniture polish on the wood; it reminded her of her grandmother's house - her house. How long was it going to take her to come to terms with that? It had always been Nan's house, and no matter how many times her mind went over the fact, it would always remain that way.

She inhaled the furniture polish again. Everything she smelt or heard conjured up those memories. She closed her eyes and tried to put it from her mind.

Slowly, her ears began to isolate the sounds around her; the wind blew past the cold glass panes, rushing in and out of the bare branches of the winter-worn shrubs outside the window. Lonely, thin branches whipping against the glass, like fingers tapping a familiar tune; a single seagull screeching as it flew overhead to the sea; crunchy rustling of crisp and peanut packets and the scraping of chair legs on the old wood floor. Clear, sharp clinking of beer glasses and the smooth gush of golden liquid from the beer pump made her mouth water.

Then a deep voice with a distinctive local accent drifted over it all.

'You alright there, young'n?' The slow mellow tone came from the corner of the room. April opened her eyes and lifted her head. Two tables away, an elderly gentleman sat on a red leather chair behind a coat stand. The abundant mountain of waxed jackets and old wool coats topped with tweed caps and fishing hats hid him from view of the bar. His cosy nook was decked with a single table and a matching chair; its low sweeping back coming round to form the arms. It was studded with tarnished brass tacks that edged the old leather.

The man rested his right arm on the table and his left hand on his knee, as his leg juddered with the similar rhythmic tapping of his fingers on his trousers. A large empty glass tankard, stained with the dregs of his pint of best, sat in front of him. He nodded at April's bewildered expression.

'You feel all right, young'n? Mighty cold by that window, better move further in along the room, if I were you. The coldest year in decades, so they say. Haven't had this much snow in over a hundred years.'

With no deliberation to her actions, and with a smile April lifted her coat and moved to the table beside the cosy nook. A framed collection of fishing hooks and a large painting of a fishing boat hung over the man's head. The crashing waves and dark stormy sky was lightened by the shine of the lighthouse beam. It seemed to replicate the storm in her stomach, the ever-churning waves of emotion rumbling through her soul, with only the dim shine of the memories of her grandmother to light the future.

'Got the world on your young shoulders, have you? I can see it in those youthful eyes, but they don't seem that young to me.' He smiled and tilted his head to one side, examining April's face.

The elderly man was thin and quite small; his frame seemed wiry beneath this thick winter attire. Very thin white hair sparsely covered his weather-beaten head and stray strands stood on end from the wild northerly wind. Gentle eyes of watery blue, like the sea itself, protruded from their sockets; his face was battered and beaten by decades of exposure to the elements. However, something about this man was pure and welcoming, even fascinating.

BECKY BYFORD

His stare remained on her face; but she did not move her eyes from his. Something intrigued April, obviously as much as something regarding her, occupied his curiosity.

'You've trouble and unrest in you; I think you're hoping you'll find it here. Maybe you will.'

The obscurity of his profound observation jolted her into consciousness.

'Sorry, find what?'

'Well, the answer or what's missing, I presume.'

'What makes you think I'm looking for something?'

'I know your look, the expression in those young eyes.'

April was utterly mystified by this man, simply an elderly gentleman that she would normally never have even noticed in his cosy nook. Now, no one else seemed to exist. This captivating character had possession of her attention; the strangeness of his inner knowledge of her thoughts compelled April to continue their exchange.

'I don't think we've ever met before. Have we?' April leant across the table as though to disappear from the view of the bar.

'I don't think we've ever met, no. Nevertheless, I know, I know,' he responded with a smile.

'Do you?'

'I know I know your face.'

'Well, I grew up here in the village.'

'I know, I recognise those eyes of yours. Just like hers. You have no idea just how alike you are. They don't know. No one knows. I know, only me.' The man continued, never moving his bright blue eyes from April's.

His words were odd and her stomach leapt in somersaults in reaction to his strangeness. She felt a peculiar inquisitiveness brewing as she did not answer or react to him, but purely listened. His local Norfolk droll was pleasing to her ears; she had forgotten how much she missed the place and its characters. The smell of the sea air, the sound of the gulls and the sight of the pastel painted houses. Even in the coldest winter months, this place held a special beauty, a peace that she loved.

'Know what? Who doesn't know what?' she asked after a while.

'You are searching for something, something that will help, will help you and help her. Although…' he paused. The man removed his arm from the table and scratched his chin with his fingers. The loose skin around his jawbone was thick with bristles of pure white whiskers. The tips of his fingers massaged them in small circular motions, as he crumpled his lipless mouth. 'Although,' he continued. 'Although, I don't think you have any idea what it is you're searching for. Do you?' He looked directly into April's eyes.

April straightened in surprise at the question, and it was a moment before she opened her mouth to speak. 'No,' she replied as directly as the question was asked.

Neither spoke again for a while. Finally, April's eyes wandered about the pub. Her parents seemed to be musing over old times with the barmaid; sighs and quiet tittering laughter were faint beneath the continued din of the other occupants. The noise now seemed to be overwhelming. She covered her ears with her hands and rested her elbows on the table.

The old man began to jerk his knee again, and his fingers started up in their tapping motion on his kneecap, in silent rhythm.

April sat bolt upright. 'Do you know what I'm looking for?'

'I don't have the answers, young'n. All I can do is see what's in your eyes. They're the windows of the soul. Yours is good but troubled. I think you have been troubled for many years, but you can change it. I think you have a way. I think you know the way. I think…' He pressed his hand down on his knee, stopping it from its jig. 'I think you have waited a long time for this. But, you know that much, don't you?'

She shrugged her shoulders. 'I'm not sure…'

'Of course you do. You know more than you're willing to tell me, and that is, of course, how it should be. But you know!' He exclaimed, as he sat back in his chair and smiled at April, this time with a final smile, to symbolise the end of their conversation.

A voice called from the bar. 'Hey, Bertie, have you ever heard of a plot of land around here, that's been neglected or maybe…' Sandy's mellow voice carried through the bar room. 'D'you reckon that could be the land past…'

'Past the round cottages,' interrupted Bertie, smiling at April. 'Yes, the old Warner cottage stood there, a long time ago, mind. It overlooks the beach. It's about time someone did something to that place; it needs to be brought back to life and a few things laid to rest.' His eyes never removed their intense look from April's astonished face.

'You knew didn't you, you knew, how did you know?'

'It's in your eyes, young'n. They reflect your soul.' Bertie grinned, his whole face beaming with sheer delight. 'It's what you've been looking for.'

'But I know that we came to look for the land. I inherited it.' She sat back in the hard wooden chair, her face almost disappointed.

'Ah, yes, you inherited it. But I wasn't talking about the plot of land, young'n.'

'Just down the road, turn left past Rosebud Cottage and carry on up the road…' Sandy explained with animated points and movements of her arms. Michael couldn't help but watch as her bust undulated under the motions. 'Continue up the road just past the turning for the round holiday cottages. Be careful not to miss it, it's just a field of overgrown grass really.'

Julia put down her soupspoon and folded her burgundy napkin. 'I never knew it was there. I mean, I know that bit of land, but had no idea that Mum owned it,' Julia shook her head in stunned realisation. 'My god, Mum owned that bit of land and we lived not more than twenty minutes' walk away for all those years! I don't understand.'

'I know, I never realised it belonged to your family. Sarah never mentioned it. She was a sly old thing, weren't she? Well, maybe she forgot or didn't realise until recently or maybe just thought it'd be a nice surprise,' Sandy laughed, as she cleared away Julia's bowl.

'A surprise, all right! There's been quite a few of those lately, I can tell you.' Michael finished the last of his fisherman's omelette and gulped the remains of his bitter lemon.

'Well, April, what you got planned for the land then, girl? A nice fancy beach hut for all your friends to hang around in? Great for summer parties! No neighbours really, not to speak of, not unless you count the seagulls, of course,' laughed Sandy.

April sat at her table, next to Bertie. He tucked into a plate of ploughman's as she poked about at the crispy batter that covered her piece of cod and lined up the chips in regimental rows, the white fleshy fish lay in flakes across the plate.

'Cod not good?' Sandy called again from the bar. 'I don't know Julia, these young girls nowadays; they don't eat enough, do they? Never had that problem, I didn't.' She gestured to her ample, womanly figure, smoothing her ring-laden hands over her hips, with a voluptuous wiggle.

'Hah, sorry, no the cod's lovely, thank you. And no, no beach hut. No summer parties… maybe a cottage, with some rose bushes.' April looked at Bertie. 'Thank you.'

'What for, young'n?' enquired Bertie, as he stabbed a chunk of mature cheddar, 'I ain't done anything.'

'You understand. You seem to understand without even knowing anything; how?' April dropped her fork, giving up the cod as a lost cause. 'How d'you know so much?'

Bertie took a long gulp of his fresh pint of beer, and then wiped his mouth on his dark cuff. 'When I was a boy, a long, long time ago, mind...' he grinned, 'I saw things others didn't...I think that maybe some saw them, but most were too busy going about their own business to even worry about looking. When I was a boy, I used to play on the beach just in front of that cottage. The best bit of beach I thought, full of rock pools, and great for crabbing.

Sometimes, when it was wild, when the wind would blow, sometimes it was so strong I'd be blown clean off my feet. My poor little legs were so skinny the wind would up…and down I'd come,' Bertie chuckled in a reminiscent manner. 'Nevertheless, young'n, it was on days like that I loved the beach the most. It was days like that when she'd be there, watching, just gazing into the sea air; watching the sea crashing down and churning the sand up into the foamy waves.' His story-telling tone continued as he leant further towards April.

'I'd sit and watch her...couldn't help me self, so lovely she was, so very lovely...a vision of loveliness, you might say.' Chuckling again, Bertie paused a moment, taking another bite of his cheddar and deep swig of beer.

'She'd sit on that bench for hours, never moving, never even flinching with the easterly wind; well, why should she...but...my goodness, she was lovely...as true as I sit here, she was the loveliest thing I'd ever set my eyes on, and...well...I can see those eyes right now. I can see those eyes; they're yours. They are the same hazel eyes. I knew it the moment you walked in. I've seen you grow up over the years, I remember you playing in the village as a kid, but now you've grown up. Now I can see her in you.'

Bertie leant forward again, almost touching April with his nose. 'Yeah, that's 'em; you've got her eyes, young'n...there's no mistaking that.'

'You saw Emily? Have you seen her... you know, since?' April asked.

'Ah, no, not for many a year, well...come to think of it, not for a few decades. I stopped going down the beach, too many people, especially in the summer. But, well...I don't think she's there much anymore.' He beckoned to April, as if she could get any closer, his old nose twitched an inch from hers. 'My old granddad, long gone now - he passed when I was as young as you - he used to tell me stories about her, how she would sit there, with her sister. They would never talk...he'd say. Just sit; her sister would hold her in her arms and she would watch the sea. So many times, he'd tell me the story, of when she went, the sadness it brought upon the family...not, mind you, that he had much to do with the family. But sometimes he'd take her sister into the village in his cart...lovely old horse - Dolly, her name was - a lovely grey dapple...' He beamed, 'not that I remember her, but those stories... never the same after she'd gone and her sister left, but he knew it was no place for her here, not after all that'.

April edged to one side, her cheek in her hand and her elbow on the worn polished table. 'Bertie, you're saying your granddad knew them?' enquired April.

'Oh yeah, young'n, course, well...everyone knew each other in the village in those days, not like nowadays, all those city couples coming in, buying holiday homes. Granddad did errands for the Warners, good sort they were...good stock, the Warners...well...just look at you young'n. You've got a good soul in you...an old soul, mind...but a true one.'

'You ready, April?' Julia rose from her bar stool, straightened her long skirt, and wrapped round her long cardigan. 'Ready?'

April stood up at the table. 'I think it's time we were off. Thank you, Bertie, thank you.'

'You take care of yourself, young'n. I knew Sarah, you know.'

'You knew my grandmother?'

'Fine lady, Sarah, fine lady. Good man Edward, very good man. Looked after Sarah well, he did. The best man won, you know. Well, that's how it goes, ain't it?' Bertie picked up his fork and pierced a large pickled onion.

April left the pub, a little dismayed and in shock at Bertie's last comment. They left the car in the car park and strolled up the hill. The air was frosty but the sun was bright and low, lifting the spirit in the village. Seagulls whooshed overhead, diving down towards the sea and back to the land.

'Rosebud Cottage, that's Mrs Carter's place isn't it? D'you remember, April? She used to run the Brownies at the village hall. Not that you lasted there very long, did you?' Julia pointed to the charming cottage. Thick thatching and two chimneys weighted the roof down to the candy pink plaster.

'Not long, a week I think. Too many kids, I just couldn't deal with the kids, I hated being told what to do, and they were all so...I don't know, silly and childish.' April shook her head and crinkled her top lip.

Becky Byford

'You were only nine, you were a kid, you were one of the kids,' laughed Michael.

'No, I don't think you were ever a kid, April.' Julia clasped her hand in April's arm and they proceeded past the cottage.

A couple of hundred yards later they stopped, just short of a site of sandy earth overrun with weeds and wild grass. Remains of an old rotten fence sparingly marked its boundary.

'Well, sweetheart, this is it. This is yours. What are you going to do with it?' Julia stood with her hands on her daughter's shoulders and her head resting on hers. 'I just can't believe your Nan kept this a secret all these years.'

'I don't think she kept it a secret, so much as didn't bother to mention it. She knew I'd have it one day; why mention it before, I suppose.' she announced.

April looked at the expanse of land in front of her. Gradually, she moved her feet, one step at a time, as if she'd just learned to walk, taking those first vital steps. An old wooden gate hung from its rusty hinges, and the remains of some ancient white paint flaked into her hands as April wedged it open on the thick grass. She wandered along the crumbling pathway into the garden. The old remains of the cottage stood in the midst of the rambling weeds and brambles. Julia and Michael slowly followed. Julia carefully lifted her feet high above the grass between each step, watching meticulously where she stepped, the stiletto heels of her boots barely keeping themselves level upon the dirt, every so often threatening to sink.

Ornate wrought ironwork, scrolling with organic tendrils and leaves, adorned the neglected garden bench. April stared at the reality of her memories. Tentatively she sat upon its cold seat; the view was incredible as the cold February wind thrashed and flogged the surface of the wild North Sea.

The sheer magnificence of the natural energy that surged through each drop made April's body fill with immense emotion. It started in the depths of her toes and began to travel the length of her legs until it reached the pit of her empty stomach. Its churning whipped up a frenzy of sensation that bubbled up into her chest and lurched into the cold atmosphere. With a loud outbreak of tears, she sobbed and wailed.

Michael approached the bench and sat beside his daughter. Not uttering a word, he merely placed his hand on hers and watched the sea. Julia sat the other side, clasping her fingers about April's. For many long minutes, the tempestuous North Sea rolled in white waves, lashing and beating the defenceless sand into submission as it tossed it over and over.

April wept until there were no tears left, no strength in her body, and her mind lay drained and empty.

Julia retrieved a tissue from her handbag. 'Here, sweetheart.'

April held the cool tissue to her eyes; for several seconds it remained there to absorb the tears. She wiped her cheeks to remove any mascara smudges.

'I think I'd like to go. Can we go to the church? I think I need to go to the church, please?' April's voice pleaded in a strong, child-like manner.

'Of course, if you want to go to the church, then to the church we shall go.' Michael took April's hand and they all left the garden bench behind and walked through the gate.

No one spoke as they trod the quiet village roads. Grey streams of smoke flowed in frayed ribbons from the chimney pots above the thatched roofs. Thick curtains were drawn, protecting the residents from the wintry elements, as the fingers of the February wind flogged the windows.

Still, charm continued to emanate through the village.

'I always did like it here,' April's words were sudden. 'I think I shall have a cottage here, rebuild the cottage, sit in the garden, and watch the sea. I think a part of me still belongs here.'

'I agree, sweetheart, I agree.' Julia smiled to herself and they walked down to the church.

The parish church was only a few hundred yards down the road. The enormous tower was visible from across the

BECKY BYFORD

village; its magnificent square structure had always been valued by the locals as being 'a herring-and-a-half higher' than the church tower of the nearby fishing town.

As they reached the flint wall, April stopped. 'There's something I need to find.'

'We'll wait here for you, if you want. You go do what you need to; we'll be here if you want us.' Julia perched on the edge of the wall and wrapped her arms around her body, snuggling in the cosy folds of her sumptuous mohair cardigan. Michael stood beside her and placed his arm about her shoulders, briskly rubbing his hand up her arm.

April rambled through the myriad of grey head stones; the causal rows spread across the flat grass, dozens of lopsided and leaning stones filled the churchyard from boundary to boundary.

Stopping dead in her tracks, she closed her eyes tight and listened; for what, she had no idea. Nevertheless, listen she did. The sound of the gulls overhead and the crashing of the waves that travelled on the bitter wind became more and more distant. Soon, her ears fell silent as she waited. Which way? Which way? Delicately, it found her ears, that soft sound, that light tuneful voice.

'Annabelle, Annabelle.'

'Emily,' she replied, and followed the direction of the words.

Her feet pursued without consideration, her mind unconscious to everything but her sister's voice. It led to the far end of the church grounds. The top of the flint stonewall of roughly four feet was laden with ivy that twisted and entwined along it, gripping onto the crumbling mortar between the ancient flints, dripping in evergreen tendrils onto the frosty grass below.

Along the old stone perimeter stood a small row of gravestones. April's heart guided her eyes to an arched stone, deeply carved with a large rose, severed, and broken, scrolling coils surrounding it.

She quickly fell to the knees, took the damp hanky out of her pocket, and frantically rubbed the stone to eradicate the moss that obscured the carved words. Slowly they became visible. April wrapped the tissue around her

Remember to love me

forefinger and traced the tip over the engraving, clearing the letters of a century's worth of dirt...

*In memory of
Emily Rose Wright,
beloved Wife, Daughter & Sister
Passed away February 25th 1901 aged twenty years.
This lovely bud, so young,
so fair, called hence by early doom,
just came to show how sweet a flower
in paradise would bloom.*

April's eyes read the words repeatedly, until she felt a smile grace her cold face. 'I found you, I've lived here with you all my life, I've played on the same sand, walked on the same paths, and now I have sat and watched the sea on the same bench. And I know I felt your pain and sadness. I understand why you loved it here; I know how the sound of the sea soothes your thoughts and helps wipe away your worries. But it's time I went home; I belong there now.'

Becky Byford

Remember to love me

Love Lost & Found

Longer days, brighter nights, lighter hearts.

'My goodness, April, I had no idea your Nan had so many handbags. Look at all these…I think…'

Julia opened a small black crepe evening bag; the front was meticulously pleated and adorned with a crystal encrusted clasp, '…yeah… it's an original 1920s. Can you imagine…how sophisticated…in some fabulous casino in Monte Carlo,' she mused.

Julia hung the bag over her forearm and sauntered across the carpet, in pretence of a glamorous flapper.

For many hours, they organised, cleaned and tidied the house.

Room after room, April discovered treasures that Sarah had inherited, collected and hoarded over the decades: cupboards brimming with boxes of an unused china tea set; canteens of cutlery that had never seen the light of day; drawers wedged full of damask table clothes, fine linen napkins, mountainous heaps of crocheted doilies and embroidered dressing table runners.

'Shall we make a start on the spare room?'

'My room?'

'Well, yes. I've always known it as the spare room.'

'Actually, Mum, it was Emily's room.'

'I know. Sorry, I can't get used to that, having a great-great-aunt whom we knew nothing about.

They both entered Emily's room. The open curtains let in the dusky light of the spring evening. April sat down on the pink chair, inside the bay window. It had become her favourite spot, one for thinking and contemplating.

So much had happened over the past months, filled with life's complications; that April relished the peace and solitude of the quiet nook in the bedroom.

'Hmm, I suppose it has put a whole new look on the family history, hasn't it?' She paused for a second as Julia sat on the bed. 'Mum, she isn't your great-great-aunt, though. She was your great-grandmother.'

Julia lounged on the bed, her hand supporting her head and the other resting on her hip. 'Great-grandmother?'

'I know how odd this all sounds, but really, really, I know. Annabelle couldn't have children, the baby that she bought up, Rose, she was Emily's baby.'

'Rose, my Nan, your Nan's Mum? She was Emily's baby?'

'Yeah, Emily died giving birth and Annabelle bought Rose up as her own. No one in town knew, and even if they did suspect, well, I don't think they said, so over the years it was just assumed, I suppose, that Rose was Annabelle's baby.' April laid her head back on the soft pink chair and lifted her knees up under her chin.

'Hang on a minute. Rose inherited everything, all the Hardwick estate, the lot!'

'Yes, Mum, Rose inherited everything.'

'But...oh...you mean Rose was Richard's baby.' Julia sat, opened mouth. 'Well...' Julia began, 'I think it's time you put those photos around this house. They shouldn't be locked up in this box.' Julia sat up on the end of the bed, the pretty floral bedspread rumpled underneath. The marquetry box was in sight on the dressing table. 'Not any more, they mean so much. They mean so much to you.' She wandered over to the box, picked it up and took it to April. 'Come on, let's have another look.'

'Mum, we only had the photos out this morning.' April took the box, quite content at the prospect of seeing

Richard once more. April unfastened her silver charm bracelet, resting it and the box in her lap. She inserted the small key and with a gentle but firm twist the lid clicked, revealing its contents.

Julia delighted in the photo album, each time remarking on how beautiful Emily was and how handsome James had been.

'Oh, she was so very lovely, wasn't she?' Julia gently turned the heavy pages, fingering the intricate gold embossing around each photo. 'My goodness, it all makes sense now, doesn't it? Look at Emily, look at her wonderful long hair and her smile, and look at her smile. Tell me what you see?' Julia pushed the photo in front of April's eyes, 'Look.'

'I see it,' April smiled.

'Yes, so do I, look at her: she's beautiful April. She's beautiful, like you. She is where your beauty comes from. She was your great-great-grandmother.' Julia smoothly kissed her daughter's cheek. 'James, he was…' she stopped the words from rolling off her tongue, 'oh…what about James?'

'Emily lost him at war. Missing presumed dead, the telegram said. She completely mourned herself to death. I know she died in childbirth, but…she died of a broken heart.'

'I'm getting the picture. Poor Annabelle.'

'Poor Emily, Mum.'

'But, her own husband!'

'Everyone was grieving, I don't blame Emily or Richard; it was Annabelle's fault really, shutting them out.' April lost herself in the concoction of self-loathing and sorrow for Annabelle's loss. Julia sat and stared; her face baffled her mouth mute. After a moment, she looked back at the photo. 'James, he really was a dishy young soldier, wasn't he, lovely fair hair and very strapping? Mind you,' she turned the page to another wedding portrait, 'Richard was fabulous don't you think?'

April sat, her eyes in her lap, occupied with the numerous silver charms of her bracelet. 'Yes he was. He was the most amazing man you could ever meet. No one will ever come close. I know they won't.'

'You really love him, don't you?' Julia and April stared at each other, at the enormity of the question. 'I know I am not your Nan, but I do understand. I really do. I understand more than you think. Your Nan said you'd tell me when you were ready.'

April smiled, an easy smile, one of the first, truly happy smiles that had adorned her face for many months. 'I know you do Mum, I know you do.'

'Well, anyway. Just thought I'd let you know. So, shall we make a start on that wardrobe? God only knows what your Nan's got tucked away in there!'

Julia wandered over to the far end of the room. A large mahogany wardrobe with lavish scrollwork and arched top stood along the end wall, dominating the area with its rich red hues. She ran her fingers over the elaborate carving. A smooth polish, glass-like finish, adorned the door. Her fingertips led to the ornate brass lock. 'Oh!'

'What is it? Oh, there's no key in that one. I have looked, but Nan never knew where it was either.'

'Ah, let's see.' Julia dashed through the doorway and disappeared into another bedroom. April remained seated at the window. Her thoughts still occupied by Richard, again, for the thousandth time that day.

'Here we are, let's try this one,' Julia returned with a small brass key in hand. 'It's the one from your Nan's. I think it'll fit, they all look the same.' The key was inserted, turned, and the lock made a loud click and the door swung open on its creaking hinges.

'Well I never...what have we got here?' Julia ran her hands over the assortment of clothes that hung before her. 'Look April...just look at all these, I've never seen any of them. Have you?'

April strode across the room, until she reached the wardrobe. It was packed with coats and evening gowns. There was a mink stole, draped over a padded hanger, from which also hung a wonderful beaded dress. A multitude of tiny gold iridescent beads and sequins adorned it, from neck to hemline. April lifted the hanger from the rail. She attempted to give it a little shake, to release any dust and cobwebs.

'My God, feel the weight of this! There must be a million beads on it. Mum, just look!' April laid the dress on the bed, the detail of the workmanship was truly intricate, the hemline, a fringe of long beaded tassels of painstaking craft. 'Mum, I've seen this dress before.'

Julia stood beside her daughter, both gazing at the incredible, museum quality garment.

'Yes, I think you have. It's the one your great-great grandmother wore to her daughter's wedding, or well...your great-great-great-aunt anyway...is that right...?'

April gasped at the sight of the dress, and the revelation. 'It's Annabelle's! It's Annabelle's dress.' April took a deep breath and steadied her mind and her feet. 'Mum, I think I should tell you. I'm not sure how really, really, odd this is going to sound to you, or whether you'll even believe me...to be quite honest, it will sound as if I need locking up...'

'April, you just need to say it. Just say what's in your heart; remember to always say what's in your heart, the truth lies there.'

April looked at her Mother, with newfound eyes. They were almost the words of her grandmother that had just left her Mother's lips: the words, the phrasing, the sentiment, even the expression that seeped from her features. For the first time, April could see the distinct resemblance between them.

'Mum, I think you should sit down.' April took her arm and guided her to the bed, seating her on the end of it, 'Mum, I can feel all the emotions of Annabelle, your great-great-aunt. I'm not sure how it happened, or why, but I can. I know I can. Do you understand what I'm saying?' April sat beside her. Julia took her hand and held it tightly in her lap, her eyes concentrating on April's. 'Do you understand, Mum? 'Cos, to be quite honest, when the words come out of my mouth, I think I sound completely nuts...but there you have it! I have Annabelle's soul, reincarnated, come back again, I see and feel her life, as her great-great-great-niece.'

'I am so glad you finally said it. Do you feel better?'

'Mum?' Puzzlement muddled her thoughts, 'Hang on...Mum...are you saying, that you already knew? I don't understand, this is...well...'

'Sweetheart, listen. I know I'm not your Nan, but I am your Mum. I have always known, well not that you...well...*something*. I've always known, since you were very small that there was a connection between you and your Nan.'

'When you were born, she was with me in the hospital. I lay there in the bed, absolutely knackered as you can imagine, and your Nan sat in the chair next to me. I still remember the look on her face, I can't put my finger on what was different, but she looked at you, well, in a way that I've never seen. It was as if she'd been waiting for you, waiting to hold you in her arms. I know this sounds really odd, but I don't want you to misunderstand what I'm about to say.'

Julia took April's hands, holding them tightly. 'It was as if you belonged to her, and that there was no way I could ever compete with that kind of love, no matter how much I loved you. I loved you so much; you completely changed my life, everything that had ever seemed important before faded into absolute insignificance. You were the only thing that mattered, and still that never seemed to come close to the intensity your Nan felt. Do you see?'

Julia sighed. 'I think it's wonderful, absolutely wonderful. And above all, have you realised what this really means?'

April sat dumbfounded by their conversation, or rather her mother's reaction.

'This means, we never really leave, do we? We always come back again, time and time again, back to the ones we love and places that mean so much to us.' Julia smiled an enormous smile. 'Well, shall we have a good look through that wardrobe? See what other antique clothes your Nan has had tucked away, all these years. Do you know, I grew up in this house, but because this was always the spare room, I wasn't allowed in here. I never had a clue what treasures hung inside that wardrobe.'

Julia jumped to her feet in sheer delight. April sat gazing at her mother. She seemed a new woman, a new mother. Perhaps April had never looked at her like this before. She could now see that she was not so much her mother, as she was indeed Sarah's daughter.

They rifled through the many antique gowns, furs and stoles that filled the huge expanse of the Victorian wardrobe.

'Look at this, how wonderful is this fur coat? Real, I know but, as it's antique and not new...what do you think?' Julia had found deep inside, tucked toward the back, a thick full-length fur coat.

'What is it Mum, mink?'

'No, don't think so, wrong colour, that stole is mink. I think it's fox!'

'Fox...Uhrr.

'No, I think you're right.' Julia shoved it aside. Behind the coats, in the dark depths of the wardrobe, was something, something else. Julia took hold of the hanger and eased it out; it was a tight squeeze between the fur coats and the door. The old padded hanger was covered with a long linen sheet. She hung it over the top of the wardrobe door, covering the large inside mirror.

'What's that?' April stood close to the linen cover, and ran her hands down the length of it. 'What's underneath, shall we have a look?' She gently raised the covering up and over the top of the hanger.

'Goodness,' Julia ran her fingers over the pale blue lace.

April stunned, dazed, stepped back until her calves met the footboard of the bed, and sat on the soft mattress. Her eyes fixed, unable to move, her voice struck dumb, her ears deaf to her mother's words. She had never imagined this; it had never occurred to her, never a possibility that she should find anything like this. The thoughts continued to swirl around her mind, over and over, and the words 'Oh, my God! Oh, my God!' went through her head. She had slept in that room for months and it had never occurred to her. Well, why would it? She had no idea. Just as when she found the key, there it was under her nose, all the time.

'Darling, whatever's the matter? This wasn't yours, I mean Annabelle's...I mean...well...you know what I mean.'

Slowly, her voice along with her reasoning returned to her conscious mind.

'Mum...this was Emily's. This is Emily's dress and...' April desperate to keep her footing, walked to the dress where it hung, so beautiful, and so like new, over the wardrobe door. 'This is Emily's cameo brooch, her blue Jasperware Wedgwood cameo brooch.' April, in a slow steady motion lifted her hand to the high neckline of the dress. Her fingers, just the tips, tentatively touched the brooch. Her heart leapt, with sheer excitement and exhilaration inside her ribcage.

'Oh Mum, we found it, we found it. Do you understand? The brooch, it was here all the time. And we found it, at last we found it.' April jumped and squealed with exhilaration.

'Yes, darling, we found it. I'm not sure what that means, but I understand that it's very important.'

April ran over to her bedside table, quickly grabbing the mother of pearl photo frame. 'Here see, Annabelle and Emily. Annabelle, she's wearing her charm bracelet. My charm bracelet, see?' April jingled her wrist in front of her face, 'Emily, here is Emily, and there it is, the cameo brooch, on the neck of her dress.' April sat, right where she stood. She sat upon the patterned rug that covered the majority of the bedroom floor, her body weary, her head spinning, and her heart jubilant. 'It's what she's been looking for, I just know it. She wanted me to find it for her. She asked me to find it, and it's here. It's right here on her dress, her lovely dress. It was her favourite! Mum, she was so beautiful.' Tears filled April's eyes as emotion charged through every cell of her body.

Julia dropped to the floor, next to her daughter. There they both sat, gazing up at the most beautiful pale blue lacy dress, complete with the Wedgwood cameo brooch, right where Emily had left it.

'Hang on.' Julia, her voice perplexed, as her fingers delicately teased the hemline of the dress. 'You said she asked you to find it for her. Do you mean, she asked Annabelle to find it for her, or do you mean, Emily asked April to find it for her?'

'Emily, Mum. She's here, in this house. And I have seen her. For some reason she never passed over or, whatever it's called. You know, she was never able to rest in peace. I think it has something to do with the brooch. I think she lost it, or forgot where she'd put it and she's been asking Annabelle's spirit to find it. Does that make any sense? I'm not sure it does, but that's basically what's been going on.'

'Ah, I see. So you are the reincarnation of Annabelle's spirit, and the ghost of her dead sister has asked you to find her lost brooch so she can rest in peace?'

'Well, yeah, that's basically it.'

The pair of them lay back on the patterned rug, their heads swirling with the thoughts of the afternoon's discoveries.

* * *

The evening air was warmer than it had been; April went to the window. The soft wispy curtains swayed in the breeze. The garden had begun to resemble its summer glory. The grass was lush and the tree boughs were wearing their leafy coat.

She sat upon the pink bedroom chair, watching the evening from the bay window. Beyond the garden was the path lined with its abundant trees and perfectly stationed benches.

Oh, how different it looked from when she had sat with her grandmother, with the snow about their feet. The memory brought a smile to her face, a thought of her grandmother.

She laid back on the chair, her legs up, and her head resting on her arm, almost hypnotised by the beautiful view and the peacefulness that now occupied her heart.

A soft fragrance disturbed her reminiscing and travelled her face. She inhaled the wonderful aroma. Gently, April sat up and gazed around the room.

'Emily?' she whispered, 'Emily.'

April watched with delighted eyes. At the far end of the bedroom, the blue lacy dress complete with Wedgwood cameo hung on the wardrobe door. Emily, beautiful Emily, stood, admiring it.

'I found it. I found it for you.'

'Annabelle, thank you. I thought it was lost. I just could not remember where I had put it.'

April rose from the chair and walked to the edge of the bed, her hand resting on the mattress. She felt eager to approach, but remained.

'I know everything. I remembered it.'

Emily turned to face her, 'Everything?'

'I remembered to love you.'

'I know you did, my darling. I know you did.'

'You know?'

Emily's translucent, lustrous face, smiled. 'I watched; I watched you, so close, but so far away.' She turned her attention to the dress once more.

'You have been here in this house all the time, for all these years, haven't you?'

'Time is nothing to me, it is endless, but it means nothing, and it passes regardless of us all.'

April sat on the bed, her legs no longer capable of holding her weight. She watched as Emily studied her dress, the fineness of the lace, the detail of the collar. Her hand reached out to touch its fabric; then she withdrew it, curling her fingers, resting her clenched hand at her mouth.

'I watched, I watched you and I watched Rose. Dear, sweet Rose. I was so near to her, I would sit and watch her play, watch her sleep and grow. Grow into a young woman, a beautiful woman.'

'Emily?' April hesitated; the words just couldn't make their way to her lips.

'Yes…I saw him.'

April's heart sank; she knew exactly what was in her thoughts. 'James? He didn't...'

'No Annabelle, he didn't. My James. He didn't die, and I watched him. I would lie down with him at night. I would kiss his lips, but he could never kiss me in return. I was invisible, invisible to his eyes and ears. I was just a memory.'

'Oh, Emily.'

'I have spent so many lifetimes waiting, watching everyone living their lives, whilst I merely existed in mine, my new life, my afterlife. Invisible, then they have left, but I am still here.'

'Emily, I'm so sorry.'

'I have been with you every day of your life. I knew you were true to your heart and Annabelle's soul and James to his,' the words were oddly whispered as her eyes admired the dress.

'Emily.' This was the only word April could utter; Emily's tone shook her.

'I am sorry for Rose.' Discarding the dress, she turned her attentions to April.

'Rose? What are you sorry for?' April asked.

'For leaving you, every moment of every day, I have been here. Thank you for raising her to be such a wonderful woman. I took everything from you, didn't I?'

April sat, as Emily tortured herself, just as she had done so for decade upon decade. 'You were grieving. You were both grieving. I couldn't see it at the time. It was my fault. But, darling, you gave me something.'

'I took what was yours. It was never your fault, you were never to blame. Grief takes us all.' Emily whispered.

'You gave me Rose. She was your gift. She was all I had left of Richard; she was all I had left of you.'

'Richard...I only ever loved James. However, we both loved you. I still love you; my heart is still full of love for you.'

They both gazed back at the blue lace dress.

'I cannot touch it. Can you read it to me?'

'Read it to you?' April was so perplexed she rose from the bed.

'My letter!' Emily's finger pointed to the Wedgwood brooch, 'My letter from James.'

April walked over to the wardrobe. Emily stood within inches of her, and her sweet, floral aroma filled April's lungs; she took deep breaths, inhaling it, filling herself with Emily.

Gently, April unfastened the cameo. It lay in her hand, the shiny silver cold to the touch; she held it in front of Emily.

'Where's the letter?'

'Turn it over.'

April turned the brooch over on her palm. Behind the Jasperware plaque, lay a piece of paper, tucked securely within the silver mount. Meticulously, she prised it free with her fingernail. The paper was neatly folded, as thin as a single sheet.

Carefully she unravelled it.

Before her, with its clean folds, lay a letter; the paper was fragile and flimsy, almost transparent at the creases. Black ink lay embedded in the fibres of the untouched paper...

My dearest Emily,

If you are reading this letter, then I have gone. I shall no longer be able to touch you or hold you with my flesh and blood. Please remember that I did everything for you, for us. My death is no fault of others, but a cruel truth of this terrible war.

My heart and my soul will always be there, with you. Each day I shall sit with you and hold your hand. Each night I shall lie by your side and tenderly kiss your lips. I shall listen to you sing and hear you laugh.

As each day passes, it will be a day closer, closer to the day we shall be reunited.

Yours forever and beyond
James

April refolded the fine paper and placed it back into the brooch.

'Emily, I am so sorry.'

'I have waited so very long to hear those words.'

'I know. If only...' April dared not finish her sentence. How cruel life and indeed death had been.

'If only I had read it?' Emily sighed, 'Yes, if only...Instead, I am the one that watched, I am the one that lay by his side, I have kissed his lips, and I waited. I waited and waited.'

April dropped her eyes to the cameo. She could not bring herself to look upon Emily's tearful features.

'I have watched everyone that I love grow old and leave. Leave me. I have waited for them, but they have gone and I am still here.' Emily stood once again staring at her lace dress.

'Emily. Come Emily, my darling wife.'

Emily turned as April looked up from the cameo. A bright light, a golden glow flooded the dusky room.

'Emily, it's time.' James stood there, tall and proud in his military uniform. His brass buttons gleamed and his face, his wonderful face, beamed. 'It's time.'

'Oh James, I have waited so long.'

'It's time to rest now. There's nothing more to do.'

James stretched his hand towards her, and he stepped closer, his tall stature towered above her petiteness.

'Thank you, my darling April. Remember?'

'I shall always remember.' April watched as they faded and were gone. The room was shaded, cool, but at last, there was peace.

BECKY BYFORD

Remember to love me

Introductions

April hurled the last few crusts of her sandwich upon the grass, and an influx of ducks and geese gathered at her feet, flapping their wings, eagerly scrapping over the pieces of brown bread.

Her back rested against the warm, sun drenched wood of the bench. She watched the birds feeding, the small children playing, the couples walking, their hands clutched together.

The park was filled with an abundance of life.

A duck flew up past her head, over the fence and landed on the cool surface of the river. It swam down towards the old Abbots Bridge; the bridge where she had once sat, lazed, eaten, laughed and dreamed of her future; a future that she had already lived.

April opened the supple leather flap of her handbag, reached in, and retrieved the photo album. It lay in her hands with the warm midday sun brightening, heating and softening its leather bounds. Out fell a small white envelope, on the front, the words; Little One.

'Oh Nan,' she sighed. 'I think it's time.'

April slipped her finger under the seal, gently gliding it along. With the very tips of her fingers, she eased out its contents. A small photograph sat in her grasp: a beautiful woman, and a small child; a girl with long fair hair. Their dresses were both pale and had an air of formal beauty. The exquisite woman sat on a large velvet settee, April's red settee. The young Annabelle sat perched upon her mother's lap; the two looked peaceful and content. April turned the photo over, written in black ink were the words, Rose and Annabelle 1879.

April was amazed; a photo of Annabelle so small, before Emily's birth. As she went to put the envelope down, she noticed something still inside. Her fingers pulled out a folded piece of paper. As she opened it, she instantly recognised her grandmother's writing, and smiled. Warmth filled her body, more than the summer sun could ever do. April read the words...

Dearest Little One

I never got a chance to say sorry. Annabelle passed away before I knew our connection. However, her soul was not gone for very long was it? Now it is my turn to leave, but not before I tell you what I have waited so very many years to say.

I am so sorry, my Little One, so sorry for leaving Annabelle and her father. Emily grew up into a wonderful young woman, and my soul, as Rose, missed it.

I know that in your soul, you still ache at your loss. Your soul has lost so many of those who have loved you so dearly. Nevertheless, you were always strong and true to your heart. I am so very proud of you. Annabelle was so very small, but her soul remembered, remembered to love.

Annabelle, you will always be my Little One.

April's heart sank into the pit of her stomach. 'Nan, I didn't know! How could I not see, it was there in front of me all that time.' April leant her head back and gazed up into the warm sun-filled sky, her eyes closed; it warmed her face. For many moments she remained, basking in the heat of her revelation. She carefully folded the letter and enclosed the photo within its folds, placing them back in the envelope.

April reached back in her bag and removed her new green leather diary and pen. The pages were untouched and pure white. 'Maybe it's time Nan; time to start a new chapter, hopefully with some peaceful memories and thoughts for my descendants to read…maybe for you, when you return.' She closed the diary and hid it back in her bag. 'Later…it can wait.'

April opened the leather photo album at the wedding photograph of Rose and Charles.

'That's a very nice antique piece you have there.' The voice came from beside her. 'High Victorian, circa 1870s, good condition, very sought after.'

'I beg your pardon.' It was more a statement of shock than a question.

'Your photo album, it's an antique Victorian piece, and very beautiful.'

'I'm sorry?'

'Your album.'

'I'm aware of what you said.'

She couldn't understand what it was about this man that disturbed her so. April kept her eyes down; she couldn't bring herself to look up. Somehow, it frightened her. How she could fear this stranger; he seemed harmless enough, although it wasn't that she feared, perhaps more the exchange of words with someone from her own century. She tried to ignore the gentleman stranger beside her. For a moment, she closed her eyes, maybe hoping when they opened he would be gone, however, there he was. His feet uncomfortably close to hers. She noticed the shine on his shoes, the leather a rich tan tone, the toes highly polished. Do men still buff their shoes like that, *a good spit and polish*, she could hear her dad's voice. The laces were neat, as were his trousers, expensive, she thought.

Unperturbed, he continued, 'I'm sorry; I didn't mean to startle you. It's just I have rather a passion for old photographs: they intrigue me; a history of someone's life captured, suspended in time. You can tell so much about life from them, don't you think?'

'Do you think so?' Why was she still talking to him, why didn't she just walk away, but he seemed generally polite, just a little odd. 'I'm not so sure you're right.'

'I must say, I know it's said there isn't much a woman doesn't carry in her handbag, but do you make a habit of carrying old photo albums around with you?'

'You really have a cheek don't you?' April barked, the retort leaping from her lips quicker than she intended. However, behind her snarl, she felt a smile appear.

'I didn't mean to offend you,' he quickly added. 'Let me assure you, I don't normally go round harassing young women.' His voice had an honest tone.

'No, I'm sorry, I didn't mean to snap. You didn't offend me.' April turned her attention back to the photograph, turning the next page and stated. 'I just don't think you can tell as much about someone's life as you think. Life looks so perfect and idyllic in a pose for a camera.' April sat bewildered by her conversation with this stranger, but she remained there, compelled to continue.

'Well, they look perfect to me. Look at the way he holds her hand and the love in his eyes. Sometimes, life is just there to see in someone's eyes. They say that the eyes are the windows to the soul. Look at the woman, for instance... her fair hair, almost angelic.'

'Angelic?'

'If you look deep into her eyes, you can see how pure her soul is. A true beauty; I don't mean just because she's attractive, but she has beauty from within.'

April kept her eyes on the photograph, tracing the outline of Richard's hand, the look on Richard's face; how his eyes twinkled back from the photo as she stared. 'Maybe you're right.' April closed the album on Richard and Annabelle's photo. She packed it away in her bag and stood up.

'I'm sorry. I really didn't mean to offend you, really. Sorry, where are my manners, I'm…' the man's voice was soft, and strangely alluring, with mellow, slightly husky tones.

'I'm leaving anyway, I'd better get back to work,' she interrupted quickly, walking away past the ducks. Still she kept her eyes front, desperate to separate herself as far from the stranger as possible. Across the lush grass, she headed up to the long pathway; and followed the wide avenue through the flourishing flowerbeds and huddles of tourists with snapping cameras. She reached the Abbey Gate, pausing beneath the ancient stone gateway.

April turned to look, dozens of locals with shopping bags, smart suits with newspapers and take-away sandwiches. The tourists were now heading her way, but no stranger with shiny shoes, as far as she could tell.

* * *

'Nice lunch, sweetheart?' Julia stood behind the shop counter.

'Hmm,' she responded with a mused tone.

'Hmm... What does "hmm" mean?'

'Nothing, Mum...nothing, really,' she paused, putting her lunchtime episode to the back of her mind. 'I've decided: what do you think about putting all the family photos in frames and hanging them around the house?'

'Sweetheart, I think it's about time. You know I think that's where they should be. Not locked away in that album, as lovely as it is. Your dad did a house clearance last week; he's sorted a lot of it out, but before the auctioneer comes to look at the furniture, why don't you go and see if any of the photo frames are to your liking?' They're out the back. Your dad's going through the last of it all now.'

April wandered behind the mahogany counter and out the back to where Michael stood, amongst pieces of furniture, tea chests, and paintings.

'Dad, Mum said I could have a look for some photo frames.'

'Ah, yes, they're here...well they're here somewhere. Don't suppose you fancy giving me a hand with these tea chests? We've got a guy coming from the local auction house to value the furniture in a while.'

'Yeah, Mum said.'

Becky Byford

'Ah, there they are, they're in that box, along with some other silver bits.'

April pushed the large box across the floor with her foot. She sat upon a small wooden stool and began to rummage.

'Michael, Mr Taylor is here,' Julia called from the shop.

'Send him through, dear, send him through.'

Mr Taylor followed the direction of the voice to the room at the back of the shop. Michael stepped over a wooden crate and held out his hand.

'Nice to meet you Mr Taylor, I'm Michael. Please come through. Sorry about the mess - as you can see, we haven't got much room out the back.' Michael guided him towards the large antique wardrobe and matching drawers. 'These are the pieces of furniture. Oh, and those paintings,' he stated, pointing to the large framed oils that stood beside April's stool. She remained silent, too preoccupied by her task in hand; her head hung low over the box as she leaned forward.

'So, Mr Taylor, please don't think me rude, but you're quite young to be interested in old objects,' enquired Michael, intrigued by his youth.

'Oh, I'm not sure that age has any relevance to the passions you acquire. I've always had it...my mother was always on at me to go and play with my mates, but I'd rather sit and read. I'd spend my time in the library on a Saturday researching antiques, and hunting through junk shops. I know, before you say it, a bit strange, I know.' Mr Taylor smiled at Michael, with openhearted truthfulness.

'Well...do you know, I think we shall get on very well, you and I. So, getting down to business...what do you think?' Michael stood casually, his arm resting on a heap of leather albums.'

'Well, Michael, we would be extremely interested in the furniture as they are wonderful examples. And, of course, the paintings, not a particularly well known artist, but very fine pieces of work all the same.' Mr Taylor glanced again over at the paintings, very close to April. She continued to rummage in the depths of the box, her long hair tousled over the contents. She had already made her judgement on those paintings; not worth the wall space of the shop, but quite sweet in their own right.

'But, I was wondering if you were interested in selling those leather albums? Could I have a look?' Mr Taylor pointed to Michael's elbow.

'Of course,' Michael removed his arm from the heap and placed them on top of the chest of drawers.

'I have rather a passion for old photographs you see, and just can't help myself. I had boxes of them as a kid; you know under my bed, probably where normal boys may hide something else, if you know what I mean,' he grinned.

April placed her hand inside the box, but it dangled there, paralysed at the words that he spoke. She slowly looked up. Mr Taylor stood with his back to her, he was extremely tall, and wore dark perfectly tailored trousers and a cool crisp shirt. The strongly defined muscles of his back and broadness of his shoulders were evident beneath the white cotton. April's eyes continued to travel to his hair; dark and lustrous, with just enough length to sit upon the collar in polished waves.

'Ah, your passion for old photographs and the like is much like my daughter's.' Michael pointed in the direction of the wooden stool. April had already risen to her feet; her heart obscurely pounding in her ribcage as she recalled her lunchtime encounter.

Mr Taylor turned to face her. 'Ah, hello again,' his smile lightening his face to a point of glowing.

'You two have met before?'

'Lunchtime, in the park. We didn't get the chance to be introduced; your daughter was so eager to get back to work.' He stepped forward. The light from the shop reflected off the cotton of his shirt; it glowed like an angelic symbol of hope.

'Well, this is my very conscientious daughter, April.'

'Nice to meet you April, I'm...'

'You're Mr Taylor, an auctioneer with a very annoying lunchtime habit.'

Becky Byford

'Well, April...as someone who seems to know me so well, perhaps then, we shouldn't be so formal. The name's Richard, but my friends call me Ritchie.'

She moved closer into the beam of sunlight. Her eyes constantly on his hand as it lay open waiting for hers. In a peculiar sensation of slow motion, April placed her hand in his open palm; her fingers looking very small and pale as his strong and masculine hand enclosed hers. Tingling started in her hand, smoothly flowed through her arm and whooshed through her body, sending flushed redness to her cheeks. She looked up into his face. It was handsome and defined, his cheekbones strong and his jaw line square, but most notably about his alluring features was his eyes: deep, glassy emeralds.

'Ritchie?' April's voice quaked at the sound of his name as it left her mouth. 'Richard. Of course you are.'

Rose de Mai

The second novel in
The Legacy Trilogy
coming soon

BECKY BYFORD

CHAMPAGNE

Champagne; millions of tiny bubbles soared; chasing their way to the sparkling surface, erupting in a cascade of golden foam over the glass. Reaching out to the drinks trolley, she gently grasped the stem of her champagne flute; the sweet liquid amber dripping over her impeccably manicured nails. She sipped, letting it linger in her mouth, savouring each subtle nuance; the floral ambience of luxury brought a smile to her lips as the bubbles tingled, finally, the warmth of the rich opulence and sheer decadence of the Pinot Noir grape.

Pink silk, cut on the bias, embraced her svelte figure, elegantly hugging her young womanly curves. Rose paced the polished marble of the terrace. The view was breathtaking. Such a contrast to her rural English upbringing.

Bury St Edmunds, with its historical charm had delighted her appetite for knowledge as a child. She had studied and explored. Miss Amelia Hitchins' Selected Establishment for Young Ladies had equipped her with all the necessities a young woman would need: posture, etiquette and the correct protocol for elegant occasions, evenings at the theatre and afternoon soirées with the town's elite. However, this was not her world; it never would be, and she mused why her mother had so eagerly intended it to be so.

No, Rose had felt starved, so hungry for life and for excitement, not the staid and sober conventions of the narrow-minded aristocracy; the self-elected hierarchy of society, the rich landowners born with their fortunes and affluent houses, whose limited conversations reflected their pampered positions and status. The narrow mindedness of her Suffolk upbringing had held limitations compared to the vast open space and fresh new thoughts of the French Riviera.

Afternoon, as always, had succumbed to the allure of nightfall, and as the cobalt blue sky deepened, filling the scene with intense regal purple, it reached down to caress the stardust-scattered ocean, where it shimmered with the haze from the still humid temperature.

Rose sighed. Beyond the street and the beach promenade, the sea gently rippled beneath the lavish yachts. The sumptuous lifestyle of the nouveau riche, their money gained by effort, determination and even deceit.

Extravagant money, yes, but in the hands of the inspired, those enthused with a lust for life. Glittering diamonds of candlelight flickered on the stretched decks, women in silk gowns and fur stoles alluring virile tuxedo clad gentlemen.

Surveying this new society, the villa sat nestled in the mountainside, amongst the tall sculptured trees.

Rose leant across the carved stone balustrade, and it gradually warmed to her hand. The view was so different from home, the heat, the humid temperature, everything was inviting; enticing her into it's midst. She turned and strode over to a soft lounger. Her drink still fizzed; the sound brought a tingle to her ears in the otherwise silent evening.

Champagne; it seemed to sum up the beauty of this kingdom. The glory of the landscape, the sensual aroma of the plants, she could somehow even smell the heat as it seeped from the warm earth into the hazy atmosphere.

Rose realised at that very second, exactly how numb she had felt. Would she ever go home - at this precise moment in time, the notion of returning was as far from her thoughts as it could be? This place, Juan le Pins, with its avant-garde charm, enlivened her. Reviving a part of her soul that had lay dormant, maybe not ever existing, until now.

She had been colour-blind; surely, she now saw the magnificence created by the lush green and azure blue, each brushstroke of nature's palette. Home had never had such an array of vibrancy and vitality. Her mother's eye for colour; an artist's appreciation she had never inherited.

Her love was the written word, poetic arrangement of phrase and verse. For Rose, France had opened her eyes to art in its vast spectrum. Her entire life here was artistic; the buildings, new and angular, with sweeping arcs and curves, white and glowing, a new world for the creative. She belonged here.

Here, she would thrive.

She lay upon the lounger, her legs outstretched beneath the silk of her evening gown, her smooth young skin glowed, the hot Riviera sun had brushed gold over her shoulders and arms. Her hair was cropped short, dark and lustrously glossy, bobbed neatly into the nape of her slender neck.

Her mother stood at the balcony, her hands resting on the cool stone as Rose had done.

Moon glow softly touched her hair. She turned to Rose as she glided her way to the other lounger, her blue dress sculpturing her petite body. As she lay, she gazed in wonderment at her daughter. How naïve she had been, how this world had changed. This century had bought new ideals, another war, yes, and far greater and devastating than the one that had initiated the beginning of the end, for her.

However, despite the Great War, life had become more lavish and abundant than she could ever have imagined. The world had retaliated against the suffering of loss, leading itself into a creation of new and expressive beliefs and principles.

Becky Byford

She had watched Rose's childhood and realised how cosseted her own had been. She had simply existed; tutored and groomed for the moment that love would befall her; bringing with it marriage and motherhood.

Now, as her daughter turned twenty-one, this strong young woman beside her had a fresh world at her feet; a world that Rose was craving.

A world she wouldn't find in England.

'You love it here, don't you?' She asked Rose, 'You needn't answer; I can see it in your eyes. They glow with passion and longing for something new, there is so much here, darling.' She felt herself sigh. 'New and exciting things to taste and encounter.'

Mesmerized. Rose didn't answer but continued to gaze across the view of the sea, the stars dancing upon the glassy surface of the Mediterranean Sea.

'It is beautiful here; you deserve it all and of course, to be happy.'

Rose closed her eyes as she laid her head back against the cushion. She could sense the stillness of the evening, as if the air had held its breath. Her heart almost stopping, pausing with the serenity that hung in the atmosphere.

'I can see your soul through your eyes; I know how stifled you've been there, at home. I've watched and could do nothing; everything has been so out of my control, with life in England being so stilted compared to…well here.'

Once more, she gazed upon the miracles of nature, the sheer magnificence of creation. As she stood up, Rose opened her eyes, staring into the night as if the air had once again remembered to breath.

Rose remained lounging, as her mother strode the terrace, watching her feet, counting each step, allowing the mood of the evening to imprint every second into her memory. She could never recall a moment when she hadn't longed to see her daughter brimming with life, with passion for the future. This emotion had been suppressed in England. Stamped upon with the heavy foot of respectability, of modest behaviour and decorum. Rose had wished to throw open her arms to her surroundings, to chant at the top of her lungs, enthuse everyone with her hunger for existence.

She had watched Rose, alone with only her thoughts.

Never having a sibling, as she herself had done, and not having a father either. This had been the hardest thing for her heart to bear. Watching her child grow without the guidance and comfort of her father.

As she had reached the far end of the terrace, the mountainside was in almost touching distance, almost, but not for her hands. She leant back against the balustrade and faced her daughter. Rose sat on the edge of the lounger, the champagne flute in her hands, her elbows resting on her thighs, her slender neck and throat open to the evening air as she gazed into the sky. She could almost sense her counting each star as it hung in the dark sky. A darkness that echoed so strong in her own heart.

'Rose, your father was a good man; you have missed him without even knowing it, I feel.'

Her words went un-remarked, she knew her daughter had felt the void left by Richard's passing; it had been almost condescending to state it.

'That void is in your eyes; they are his, the same depth of emerald green.'

Eyes that she had never seen so intense and impossible to ignore, until she had met Richard. Now his daughter, his only heir, who had inherited his family's fortune, had his eyes. It had haunted her each time she looked at Rose. As a small child, the innocence of those green eyes had stunned her, the total purity of them, but still they had pierced her heart with a great sword of guilt.

The Hardwick family fortune. It seemed so ironic, with Rose's ideals and judgment of the rural rich, that she was one herself. They had seen her as an equal, with her status and upbringing that had been forced upon her. This in itself had made her wanted, desired and hunted. Hunted by suitors, sober young gentlemen with all the intellect, Rose thought, of superior bred stallions. Every man, no matter how handsome and appealing he appeared at the moment of encounter, had lost all his charm, leaving only the regal splendour of a thoroughbred. Her money and wealth had given her the position of those she so detested.

As she looked at her daughter, she knew that it had been almost an element of guilt that had brought Rose to embrace the ideas of a new world, a world of opportunity.

Perhaps this is where James had been the most significant. Bringing Rose here, away from her old life, his old life.

'I'm so grateful. So many times over the years, I have wondered why he has never found another to replace… well…to fill the void, maybe. He always deserved happiness, he's been lonely for so long. To lose a love…while love itself is so young and new, it's devastating. I know, of course I do…of course a part of my soul, would have wept, for his loss was mine too.'

'But, my darling, there was you, and nothing else mattered. You were tiny. He saw unconditional love in your eyes, and as it grew, he loved you in return. It was that paternal instinct…something…I knew he always had. He would have so loved a child of his own, but…he had you and…well, it was never meant to be.'

'I understand that now, so much time has passed, that is so evident, just by looking at you now, a beautiful young woman, to see how years have flown, just blown on the wind.'

The violet sky had deepened to an inky black velvet against the satin of the sea; both scattered with diamond dust. Rose took another sip of her drink.

She had felt stifled, here, she knew she could grow, as a woman with passions, her longing to write, to create.

This emotion existed here; she could feel it in the air. Maybe this was where her heart had finally learnt to fly; she felt her soul soar with the birds. When she closed her eyes, she could sense that feeling of freedom, of spreading her wings, taking flight…

'Rose…there you are.' James spoke softly.

He sat down on the lounger next to her, his arm gently around her shoulder.

'We thought you were coming in…'

'I love it here, Uncle James…I really do.'
'I know you do.'
Rose sensed the love in the warmth of his smile. She rested her head on his shoulder.
'What are you doing out here by yourself? Most of the quests have gone.'
'Oh…sorry. I needed to be alone…it's so peaceful here.'
'I know it was hard, when I moved. But this is your home too…you have a home with me, wherever that is.' James squeezed her, rubbing his hand over her arm. 'Your mother was just telling Mademoiselle Delphine, how much you seemed to have settled. Which is why I'm here…' he gestured to the villa doorway, the large white stone arch. 'She would like to know if you will come in and join us? Delphine has an interest in poetry…'

James kissed her forehead and left Rose sitting alone on the terrace. Her champagne glass in hand, she watched him return inside. However, as he reached the doorway, James turned his face pallid, listening…

'Rose…?'
'Hmm…what is it Uncle James?'
'Did you say…did you call…? I could have sworn you called my name…'

Rose shook her head and smiled, James shrugged his shoulders as he went inside.

A soft warm breeze drifted across the terrace. Rose knew; she felt she always had.

'James is such a good father figure for you Rose, my dear sweet Rose. Annabelle is so lucky to have had him near all these years…'

Emily's lips touched her daughter's cheek in a kiss. Rose gently closed her eyes.

'You should go inside, live and be alive. I am always with you.'

"the advantage of a helping hand"

"Through life, we have to endure challenging episodes. Times when you may feel, you have nowhere to turn, that the world is against you. However, in most cases, if you just look a little harder you may find what you're looking for inside yourself, and with a helping hand, your dreams may become reality."

One such organisation that lends a helping hand is Advantage Foundation. Their aim is to help disadvantaged people in the community, by empowering them to change their circumstances through education, training and work experience, including starting their own businesses.

Advantage Foundation achieves these aims by offering financial, advisory and mentoring services to the people that need its help.

This is why I have chosen to support them for the coming year. If you would like future information, please visit www.advantagefoundation.co.uk"

Best wishes and much love.
Becky.